THE
BEWILDERED
PROPHET

BY

SUSAN DAVIS SANDBERG

ISBN-13: 978-0-9849923-7-9
ISBN-10: 0984992375

To
My son Paul
For his wholehearted
support of me
and my dream

Chapter 1

Bertha Carlson pulled alongside the road in front of the field on the far side of which was a seemingly modest house.

No one hires an accused murderer to be a domestic, she thought. No one. What the hell am I doing here? What am I getting into?

She turned off the car motor and sat as the icy November wind cooled the car rapidly. She couldn't be early. She was told to be prompt and ready to go to work if she was hired.

She'd purchased a beige dress similar to the ones she'd seen at Judge Davis' house the day before when she waited in the drawing room of an elaborate two story colonial for her turn to be interviewed. The others sitting in various chairs around the room were all younger and professional in appearance. Her brown coat was old, her shoes, while shined, well worn, her dress simple and her graying hair pinned up in a neat bun.

Her interview had been short and she'd been sent to a second room for a second interview. Both women had told her that her interview with Aleta would be unique.

What had surprised her the most was the caliber of the two women doing the interviewing. One was a Superior Court judge, the other she'd been told had just retired from her position as vice president of a California bank.

The second interviewer was older than the first by twenty years but her manner was equally authoritative. She skipped past the details of Bertha's experience as had the judge, an omission which had told Bertha that both women were interviewing her as a favor to their friend Martha Cook who sent her. Both had simply asked friendly questions.

Probably the only query that truly surprised her was the last one. She was asked if she'd be willing to work for a Negro couple or a homosexual couple. When she replied in the affirmative the interview had ended and she'd been given an appointment for a final interview the next morning.

She couldn't believe she made the cut. Were these women picking the worst candidate on purpose? Or did they know that this young woman was so difficult that they were sending her several bad candidates first so she'd appreciate the better ones coming later?

She stared at the long concrete drive leading past the orchard to a one story frame house. Except for those three anomalies the set-up was typical of a Northern Illinois farm.

At three minutes to eight, she left her car, gathered her coat close to her body and trudged up the long driveway at the end of which sat a new bronze Lexus. She wondered where the garage was. How could there not be a garage?

She spotted an RV parked behind the orchard on a concrete slab. Next to it, sitting on the hard packed dirt leading to the barn, sat a new jeep.

She'd been told the house was unfinished inside and she wondered why a couple even needed a permanent housekeeper. While the young woman had recently had a stroke, she'd been told it had been a mild one. Why was she here?

"Martha, this is for you," she murmured as she knocked on the handsome oak door.

She heard voices inside. She stomped her feet wondering if the crepe soled shoes which she wore at the nursing home before she was fired were appropriate. It was, after all, an interview.

While she was waiting, she opened her purse and pulled out the envelope with her resume. Just as she clicked her purse shut, the door opened.

Bertha, who'd been prepared to smile her greeting, forgot to smile when she saw the barefoot man in a white terrycloth robe. Instead she glanced at her watch and began to apologize.

"Come in," he said his voice pleasant although his annoyance colored the tone of his words. He pointed at the coat rack, and Bertha took off her coat and entered a huge room with a massive stone fireplace practically separating the living area from the kitchen. The first half of the kitchen was fully exposed and Bertha noticed at once that not only were there two ovens but the stove had six burners.

She quickly moved across the room and sat on the love seat opposite the man who had seated himself in the wing chair and was busy adjusting his robe. As she sat down next to the massive stone fireplace, she noticed dog hair imbedded in the tapestry of the cushion. She didn't see a dog.

The man seated opposite her seemed uncomfortable. She assessed him as she clutched the envelope containing her resume. He was not a tall man and not particularly handsome. His nose was large and dominated his face, his eyes close set and his ears lacking the fold that keeps ears close to the head. His chin, however, was strong and his voice pleasant.

"My mother interviewed you?" he asked.

"It was a short interview, Sir," she replied.

A voice came from the other room.

"Stanley, you aren't interviewing my housekeeper, are you?"

"I was giving my wife a bath when you arrived," he explained.

"I can do that, Sir," Bertha replied. "I'm a practical nurse."

"No thank you," he replied, a bit stiffly.

He went on to explain that Aleta, his wife, didn't shop for herself. Others did that for her.

"It doesn't matter what—groceries, clothes, household help—she doesn't shop," he began. "As a matter of fact there are a lot of things she doesn't do."

Bertha was getting an image of her perspective employer as someone she didn't want to work for. While she was willing to help old people no matter how querulous, she didn't want to spend the rest of her life catering to a petulant, spoiled, rich woman.

"I'm sorry, Sir," she said politely. "I'm afraid this isn't going to work out."

"Why?" he asked, surprised.

A voice from the other room called, "Stanley, are you interviewing my new housekeeper? You better not lose her."

"I don't work well with spoiled, rich women," Bertha said. Being honest wasn't going to cost her this job. She wasn't really in the running as it was.

Stanley called back, "She's turning you down."

"You didn't offer her enough money," Aleta shouted.

"We didn't even get to that part."

"She's not donating her services."

"She thinks you're rich and spoiled."

"And whose fault is that?" Aleta rejoined. "Up your offer."

"It's not about money," Stanley said.

"It's about respect, Stanley," the voice said. "And a good salary shows respect. So give it to her."

Stanley rose. "Please make some coffee. My wife will be out in a minute. It's her decision."

He left the room, "Aleta, you set me up!"

Bertha heard the light laughter. "Of course, I did. In your bathrobe I was sure you'd not scare her off with your questions. She's not a witness on the stand, you know."

"I don't scare witnesses," Bertha heard Stanley Praetzel say.

There was something about the banter that was fun. There wasn't a hint of animosity, no biting sarcasm, no jibes disguised as jokes, just witty verbal exchanges.

Bertha put the envelope with her resume on the counter and found the coffee exactly where she would have put it. She heard the two talking, and after plugging in the coffee pot, she went through the open doorway off the kitchen and surveyed the laundry room. It was completely furnished which surprised her a little as the family room was without furniture. The back door was off the laundry room. There was a blocked opening further down the hallway, and she figured it would lead to more bedrooms and bathrooms, the construction of which she saw from the road.

Bertha returned to the kitchen as Aleta emerged from the bedroom, dressed in a pair of jeans and a sweat shirt. The left arm was in a sling.

Aleta was a slender, attractive woman with auburn hair, lovely brown eyes and a nice smile.

"Hurry," she said. "Scramble some eggs. We need to have his breakfast ready before he leaves."

Bertha hurried to comply.

When Stanley emerged from the bedroom, Aleta was standing in front of the door and Bertha was standing to one side holding a tray with orange juice, scrambled eggs between two slices of buttered toast and coffee in a thermos mug. Stanley protested that he didn't have time. Aleta told him he wasn't leaving without breakfast.

"But I just brushed my teeth," he argued.

"You always brush them again when you get to the office. "This time they'll need it."

"I'm already late."

"It'll take three minutes. The longer you argue the later you'll be."

"Aleta, you're taking advantage," he said.

"You bet I am. So eat."

He drank the orange juice.

"It's fresh," he remarked.

Aleta giggled. "I don't serve stale juice."

He took a bite of the egg sandwich.

"My favorite," he said.

"I know," she replied. "We aim to please."

When he finished, she looked at her watch. "Two minutes, fifty seconds. You've got time for a ten second kiss."

"You timed me?" he said.

"All talk at this juncture comes off your time. I still get my ten second kiss."

To Bertha's surprise, Stanley Praetzel set down his briefcase, took his wife's head in his hands, whispered, "I love you," and then kissed her for much longer than ten seconds.

He grabbed his thermos from the tray and breezed out the door saying, "See you two tonight."

That's when Bertha knew there was no interview. She had been hired.

Aleta closed the front door as soon as Stanley left and smiled at her new housekeeper.

Bertha stood breakfast tray in hand. "Ma'am, is this how Mr. Praetzel will take his breakfast each morning?" she asked.

"Depends on how long it takes me to retrain him," Aleta grinned.

"We are training him?"

"Isn't that what one does with husbands?"

"Yes, Ma'am," Bertha said.

She had only been hired seconds ago and she wasn't sure whether Aleta was serious or not.

"Now we eat," Aleta announced.

"I'd like pancakes. Make enough for three."

"We are having company?" Bertha asked, looking through the open bedroom door at the unmade bed and clothes scattered everywhere.

Bertha took the tray to the kitchen. Aleta punched in a single number.

"Grams, come over for breakfast. Bring the dogs."

"Your grandmother lives close?" Bertha asked trying to get a handle on what she should do first.

"She lives in the RV parked by the orchard," Aleta answered. "She's having a house built. This is her furniture. Her dogs are allowed on it."

Bertha breathed a sigh of relief. It would have taken a couple hours to clean the upholstery.

"Ma'am, should I do the bedroom first or the breakfast?"

"The breakfast. Grams and I need to talk afterward."

"And the third place setting is for whom?"

"For you, of course," Aleta said.

"Ma'am, I don't take breakfast with my employers," Bertha said politely. If Aleta's grandmother found her being that familiar, it might mean immediate dismissal. It would in Judge Davis' house.

The door opened and in walked a slim, lithe woman the spitting image of Aleta except for the gray hair and the wrinkles that forty years bestows upon a woman. Age had not destroyed her handsomeness. Her granddaughter, however, while looking like her, had a more feminine jaw and softer dark eyes. Crowding in beside the older woman were three large Chesapeake Bay Retrievers. All three ran to Aleta and greeted her exuberantly but not one jumped up on her.

"Stoney, go lay on the couch," Aleta said. When the big dog was settled Aleta sat beside him. The dog put his head in her lap and she stroked it gently.

"You know I don't allow him on the couch," her grandmother scolded.

"Neither do I unless I tell him to do it," Aleta returned.

"It isn't a command I wanted to teach him. And where's the sheet?"

"Somewhere," Aleta said casually. "I figured if I got the couch hairy enough you'd let me have it."

"I like my furniture," Harriet protested.

"I love it. It reminds me of home and you. And Stanley likes it. He said he'd find a furniture maker who'd duplicate it."

"Well, then, consider it my wedding present," Harriet said, her eyes alight at giving her granddaughter something she couldn't buy for herself.

"Then get me a sheet," Aleta said.

Harriet scurried off to the bedroom. Bertha followed apologizing.

"How come Stanley left such a mess?" Harriet asked Aleta when she returned with several sheets.

"He overslept."

"He never oversleeps," Harriet said, handing the sheets to Bertha.

"I reset the clock because he needed the sleep. He was up every two hours checking on me."

Harriet's eyes swept around the kitchen. "Tell me you didn't cook."

"Bertha did," Aleta said.

"Did you even interview her?" her grandmother asked.

"Lydia did that, didn't she, Bertha?"

"Not for very long, Ma'am," Bertha said. "Would you like to see my references now?"

"We'll take our coffee now," Aleta said getting up. Stoney rose with her.

Bertha quickly threw the sheet over the couch and hurried into the kitchen.

Bertha was there before Aleta and pulled out a chair for her.

"Did you know that Martha Cook and Grams here arranged for Stanley and me to meet?" Aleta asked.

"No, Ma'am."

"She picked out one terrific husband, wouldn't you agree?"

"It appears you are well-matched," Bertha said warmly. "I like Mr. Praetzel, and he does care about you."

"Oh, he more than cares for me, but if ever he gives you an order contrary to mine, you are to obey him."

"Yes, Ma'am."

"You thought I was in charge, didn't you?"

"Yes, Ma'am. Considering what happened, yes Ma'am. I'm sorry, Ma'am."

Harriet eyed her granddaughter and raised one brow.

"I had Bertha come early. Stanley was in the middle of giving me my bath and I made him answer the door in his robe."

"Just his robe?"

"You know Stanley would never get his pajamas wet." Aleta giggled. "He was so upset, but he did exactly what I thought he would. He began to ask questions. He couldn't help himself. He'd have interviewed her thoroughly, but since he'd left me in the tub, he couldn't. By the time he was done dressing me, he was late."

"And he stopped for breakfast?" Harriet inquired nodding toward the tray with the empty plate and glass.

"Egg sandwich and orange juice," Aleta said. "And he ate every bite. We wouldn't let him leave until he did. We let him take his coffee in that thermos cup of his though. One step at a time."

"And he didn't argue?"

"With me home less than a day from the hospital?"

While they were talking, Bertha managed to find the ingredients for the pancakes.

Aleta rose to show her where she kept the cooking oil and Harriet snapped at her, "What are you doing?"

"Just opening a cabinet to…"

"Aleta, sit down and stay put!" Harriet said with an authority which bordered on harsh. "You are to do nothing for at least two weeks Dr. Cook said. No bending, lifting, twisting, reaching, carrying, driving or even putting on your own coat. Bertha, this is one of the reasons you're here."

"I thought it was a stroke she was recovering from," Bertha said pulling various items from the refrigerator.

"We aren't entirely sure that reinjuring the arm didn't send a blood clot floating around her body," Harriet said listening to the beaters whir while Bertha was whipping the pancake batter by hand.

"They threw me around a lot," Aleta clarified. "I didn't just bend over to get a pan."

"I don't understand," Bertha said, not pausing for a second from the task at hand. "How did you injure your arm?"

"I was shot," Aleta replied sitting back in her chair.

"And the shoulder was operated on. It hadn't healed when we were kidnapped and the men were pretty rough and my wound opened up and I needed another surgery. Then Sunday, I had a small stroke."

"We aren't sure the two are connected," Harriet said, "but we don't want a repeat."

"Yes, Ma'am," Bertha said as she put butter and syrup on the table.

"I have a special cell phone for you, Bertha," Harriet said putting a phone on the table. "It's preprogrammed with four numbers: Stanley's, mine, Dr. Cook's and Lauren's. Lauren is Aleta's best friend. If Aleta gets dizzy, call one of us. Aleta doesn't ordinarily get dizzy, so if she does, it's an emergency."

"It's not going to happen," Aleta said confidently.

Bertha put the pancakes on two warmed plates and poured more batter on the griddle. She set the plates on the table and set a bowl of freshly whipped cream in the center along with a bowl of sliced strawberries.

"Where'd the strawberries come from?" Aleta asked.

"Same place as all the rest. Beatrice and Evelyn heard you had hired a real cook and…"

"I hadn't hired her yesterday."

"They knew you'd never question anyone Mrs. Cook sent over, which is why I told you to sit still," Harriet said. "They stocked your shelves yesterday and you won't know where anything is. The reason Bertha can find everything is because two cooks stocked your cupboards. You do know, Bertha, that Aleta doesn't cook much. She needs you. I just thought I'd mention it."

"Yes, Ma'am," Bertha said putting a second pancake on each plate.

"So what are you going to do today?" Harriet asked.

"Borrow law books from Lyle and plan my party."

"Stanley has a full set at the office," Harriet pointed out.

"I can't take those home to study," Aleta explained. "And Lyle has a terrific up-to-date library. And he doesn't use his every day."

"Neither does Stanley."

"Going to the Wests' means I get to see Lauren every day," Aleta confessed.

Harriet switched to the second item on Aleta's agenda. "What party?"

"My thank-you-everyone party," Aleta said. "A buffet Saturday evening. Bertha, what dish do you do best? These pancakes are terrific, by the way."

"Duck, Ma'am. My late husband was a hunter."

"Duck it is then," Aleta said. "Grams can you shoot me enough for my party?"

"You want me to go duck hunting alone?"

"Take Lyle. Lauren says he's dying to go and she won't sit in a cold duck blind almost five months pregnant."

"It's the middle of his work week."

"Grams, he's the chief of police. His work week is whatever he says it is."

"Aleta, what are you doing?"

"Checking out Bertha's phone," Aleta laughed. "Hi, Lyle. I need ducks for my party Saturday night. How about you and Grams shooting me some... Yes, enough for twenty... She did...? Well, move it here. I've got this great new cook and I want to share her... Tomorrow is fine... Goodbye."

Aleta hung up laughing. "Now I have to go to Lauren's. She has my party half-planned. Lyle says he'll pick you up at four AM."

"Lauren was planning a party?"

"We think a lot alike," Aleta observed. "It's time to celebrate. We've all been through a rough patch."

"Won't Lauren be upset?"

"No. She can still be hostess. We'll just do it here. My place is bigger. And Lyle is delighted he doesn't have to do the list of chores she'd set out for him. He's much happier with his one chore on my list."

"I'll need to get my heavy rain gear out of storage. It's going to be freezing out on the water," Harriet mused aloud. "And I need to clean my guns."

Harriet shook her head and focused on her auburn-haired granddaughter whose head was bent slightly as she forked in a bit of pancake. The width of the scar on her scalp was still absent any covering of hair.

"I don't think you're ever going to get hair on that scar," she observed. "You do know Stanley saved your hair clippings when Julie cut it. I know you couldn't stand anything on your head then, but is it still sensitive?"

"He's offered to have a piece made," Aleta said. "But you know how I've always hated to wear anything on my head."

"It could be made so it's very light."

"Maybe someday," Aleta hedged.

"Ma'am," Bertha said. "Do you want another pancake?"

"No, thank you, Bertha," Aleta said. "Tell me, how did you become acquainted with Mrs. Cook?"

"She used to visit some of the patients in the nursing home my husband was in. Ralph was so weak at the end and he was suffering so. I felt so helpless, but, at least he knew I was there. That was a blessing."

"He was murdered, wasn't he?" Harriet asked as if hers was a normal query.

"Yes, Ma'am," Bertha said, her brows drawn together in a questioning frown. "The person who did it hasn't been found."

"You were accused?"

"Yes, Ma'am. Mrs. Cook got me a good lawyer, a Mr. West. She told him I was innocent. Chief Ramage didn't believe Mrs. Cook when she warned him about Ralph's murder before it happened. Later he said that Mrs. Cook had heard me say my poor Ralph would be better off dead which is true, and he said that lots of relatives of sick people say that but they don't do anything. After Ralph died, he assumed I was an exception and killed him. Smothered him with his pillow. I would never do that. Never!"

Bertha's last few words were uttered in a tremulous tone as tears gushed forth. She turned away and murmured an apology. She then removed her apron and began folding it.

The phone rang.

Bertha reached for it, swallowed hard and managed, "Praetzel residence… Whom may I say is calling…?"

"He refuses to give his name, Ma'am," Bertha reported, her voice back under her control. "Do you want to take the call?"

Aleta reached for the phone, "This time I will."

The voice on the other end was masculine.

Harriet looked at the housekeeper standing in the kitchen holding her folded apron, "I'll have another pancake, Bertha."

"Yes, Ma'am," Bertha said, setting her apron on the counter. "Sorry, Ma'am."

"Don't apologize," Harriet said. "I believe I shook my head, but I've changed my mind."

"Yes, Ma'am," Bertha said, flipping the pancake. She wished she could stay. This would be a good place to work.

"Better put your apron back on, Bertha or you'll splatter grease on that dress," Harriet said. "I like the color. It matches your shoes and it's nicer than black which is so funereal."

Bertha quickly tied her apron back on and took Harriet's plate and put a fresh hot pancake on it.

Aleta hung up the phone and sat back down. "That was someone telling me why I shouldn't hire Bertha."

Bertha's face fell. "Not again," she murmured despondently.

"It's happened before?" Aleta asked.

"Yes, Ma'am," Bertha said. "I'm sorry I spoke up. This is not your problem. It's mine."

"Why would anyone want to keep you from working?"

"I don't know, Ma'am," Bertha said. "And I will understand if you've changed your mind."

"He didn't say anything new, Bertha," Aleta said as Bertha freshened her cup of coffee.

Harriet looked up and smiled. "You were thoroughly vetted before you set a foot inside this house. The president wouldn't have passed as cleanly as you did."

"But I was indicted."

"Martha said the hand that held the pillow over your husband's face was large and hairy."

"Chief Ramage didn't believe Mrs. Cook," Bertha informed them.

Aleta burst out, "That scullion, that pompous fat-assed jerk! He's the worst excuse for a police chief that ever existed."

"Scullion?" Harriet asked.

"That's Shakespeare. The Bible doesn't provide a lot of good insults," Aleta responded.

"I wish I could see things like Mrs. Cook," Bertha said abruptly.

Both her listeners chorused, "No, you don't!"

Bertha looked into the faces of the two women at the table. "Wouldn't you?"

"No!" they chorused again and then both laughed.

"Are we going to tell her?" Aleta said.

"If she's going to be your housekeeper," Harriet said, "she'll need to know that there's one time she needs to obey you without question."

"I'll do that, Ma'am," Bertha said. "You mean you really aren't going to fire me?"

Harriet put a hand on Bertha's arm. "No, we really aren't. You are exactly the kind of person Aleta needs."

"Oakwood Nursing Home fired me because even though they had no proof, they said their patrons would feel uncomfortable with me working there."

"We know," Aleta said. "It's my good fortune you decided to look for another type of work."

The worry lines faded from Bertha's face. She began to clear the table.

Harriet saw her look at the scar across the top of Aleta's head.

"You want to know where that came from, don't you?"

"It is none of my business, Ma'am."

"I was shot," Aleta said. "The bullet missed."

"Do you get shot a lot?" Bertha asked casually.

Harriet hastened to explain.

"Those were unusual circumstances. The cases involved criminal activity. Aleta is a corporation lawyer, so she won't get shot again."

"Stanley is going to monitor my caseload," Aleta said with a modicum of dismay. "I can tell. I think he'd have been easier to live with if he hadn't gotten shot and almost blown up too. A man doesn't forget those things."

"But that's all in the past," Harriet stated with assurance. "And now I…"

Aleta interrupted. "Grams what time is it?"

"Around nine."

"Don't guess. Check!"

Harriet looked at her watch.

"Nine sixteen."

"There's still time," Aleta said getting up and grabbing the phone book before anyone could stop her.

"Aleta, what is it?" Harriet asked as Aleta flipped open the book to the emergency numbers.

"Who's chief at Oakwood now?" Aleta said picking up the cell.

"Peets."

She punched in the number.

"Does he know about us?"

"I don't know. He was Milani's right-hand man."

"Chief Peets, please. It's Aleta Praetzel calling. It's an emergency." Aleta turned to the two women at the table. "Let's hope he believes me enough to investigate."

Harriet pulled out her cell and made a call.

Bertha heard both women talking at once. It appeared that each were talking with police chiefs. She decided to stand motionless. Both were agitated.

"Chief Peets," Aleta said, "This is unusual but at nine twenty-seven a woman with a ruby ring on her finger is going to put a pillow over the face of a resident in the Oakwood retirement home. All I can see is the hand and the digital clock on the nightstand."

"See? How can you see that? What room?"

"Hurry! Turn your siren on at exactly nine twenty-seven. Just do it!" Aleta said.

"Who is this?"

"Aleta Praetzel. You can arrest me for turning in a false report later, but please investigate now!"

"Okay, Miss. I'll check it out," Peets said.

"Now what?" Bertha ventured when both women hung up.

"Either they save the man or they don't," Harriet said.

"Who'd you call?" Aleta asked.

"I told Milani to tell Peets to listen to you."

"So the man has a chance." Aleta breathed.

"You sure it was a man?"

"Actually, no, I'm not," Aleta said. "Did I say man or person?"

"Man," Harriet said.

"I meant person. What a terrible time for my brain to play a trick on me! Suppose it was a woman. Now what do I do?"

"I'll handle it," Harriet said pressing the redial button.

"Tom, you remember that Aleta had a stroke. Well, she said a man was being killed. She meant to say person. It could have been a women."

Harriet turned to Aleta, "How do you know it's the Oakwood Nursing Home?"

"I don't know how," Aleta said. "I just know."

"She affirms that it is," Harriet said. "Let us know what happens."

Harriet closed her phone. Aleta rose and began pacing, wringing her hands.

"Sit down, Aleta. Tell me what's troubling you."

"Grams, it was so vague and so fast. And I reacted without thinking. I don't even really know if it was the

Oakwood Nursing Home. Suppose I said that because I was moved by Bertha's story. Suppose it was somewhere else?"

"God wouldn't misdirect you."

"But I wasn't paying attention."

"To what? A momentary glimpse of someone's future?"

"A person I don't even know," Aleta said. "Always before it's been someone close to me. And that I could live with. I don't want to be responsible for the whole world."

"There must have been a reason why you didn't need to know more," Harriet said. "You can't let this stress you out. You are only responsible to act on what you are given. The rest is in God's hands."

Bertha went to Aleta and gently guided her back to her seat.

"Let me get you another cup of coffee, Ma'am. Mrs. Locke is right. It's in God's hands. Just like my Ralph's life was. If Mrs. Cook hadn't seen what she did, I'd be in jail right now. And I wouldn't be here. Poor Ralph was suffering so. He weren't hurt by the man who killed him. It was me hurt the most. Maybe this is another time like that."

Abruptly, Aleta got up. "I need to go to the bathroom."

Harriet spoke up.

"Bertha, go with her. She can't handle her jeans."

When they reached the bathroom, Aleta reached for her zipper, but Bertha was quick. "Let me do it all. I've done this for a long time. Don't feel uncomfortable."

After the jeans were loose, Bertha helped Aleta sit down, despite her protests that she could handle that part.

"Let me do this with you until we both know you aren't going to have another dizzy spell. You are going through a stressful time right now," Bertha said.

Aleta gave in. The woman was making sense. She'd used the wrong word. How could she have made such a mistake? She had no idea if it was a man or woman. Every word was important in a prediction. Why didn't she say she didn't know? Why did she declare herself so strongly?"

"So you and your grandmother have the power, Ma'am?" Bertha asked.

Aleta was startled. She almost giggled. What a place for such a question.

It told her, however, that Bertha took her employer's sitting on the pot as a normal activity. Somehow it comforted her.

"Yes, we do," Aleta said.

"It is a gift, you know," Bertha said as she helped her to her feet and redressed her.

"I guess it is," Aleta agreed. "We complain a lot because it's scary."

Bertha reached behind her and flushed the toilet. As she left the bathroom, Aleta said, "You can pick up in here. Grams will make sure I behave myself."

"Yes, Ma'am," Bertha murmured as she picked up the discarded towels.

"Call me if you need me."

"And change the sheets. I'm sure Stanley didn't do it while I was gone," Aleta added. "I'll show you where the washer and dryer are."

"I believe I know where they are," Bertha said.

"Let me know if you have a question."

"Yes Ma'am."

When she got back into the kitchen, Harriet asked, "When are you going to have her drop the Ma'am'?"

"I'm not," Aleta said. "Grams, I need her to call me that. She had to help me go to the toilet. No one's done that, well, except for Stanley of course, since I was a little girl, and I can only handle it if... if... well, you understand."

"Especially after what you've been through," Harriet said.

"Oh, Grams, you don't suppose she read about that!" Aleta wailed.

"I'm sure she did. So what? It was just a word in the newspaper. There were no pictures."

"I'm sure there are some out there," Aleta said.

"Maybe not. My guess is that your picking up the ransom money in the nude was not something anyone was prepared for."

"Neither was I."

"That I do know," Harriet said. "I was there you remember. You carried yourself with such dignity, I was proud of you."

"Proud?" Aleta gasped. "How could you be proud?"

"Because you showed a grit uncommon under such circumstances. I know how embarrassing it was for you to walk across that field, knowing the bushes were loaded with police officers watching your every move," Harriet recounted. "And I know how embarrassed needing to be waited on hand and foot makes you."

"Did you ever call Dad about the stroke?"

"Of course, I did," her grandmother said. "I'm not sure if he told your mother. She's pretty involved with your sister's wedding and since you recovered so quickly, I think he's going to forget to mention it."

"So, you've kept him informed."

"I call him every day."

"Tell him about Bertha. He'll be pleased."

"He wants to come out," Harriet said. "How about Saturday morning? He's already told your mother he's going on a business trip."

"Absolutely not! Tell him I don't want him lying in order to visit me."

"Well, it is business. Daughter-business," her grandmother responded. "Aleta, let him make his own decisions. He doesn't have the same relationship with Marian that you have with Stanley. Your mother would have trouble with as honest a relationship as you have."

"The answer is no," Aleta declared. "Absolutely!"

The sound of the washer surprised Aleta. "When did Bertha pass by?"

"About five minutes ago."

"Where was I?"

"Right there, talking," Harriet said.

"She heard me?"

"Probably."

"And you didn't caution me."

"When you have a full-time servant, you can't keep secrets." Harriet said matter-of-factly. "So, don't try. Remember they clean up after you. Besides you have nothing to hide."

"No phone call," Aleta worried, her mind still on whether or not her prophecy was real or imaginary.

"Actually, that's nothing to worry about," Harriet assured her. "They don't know we worry."

"I guess I should be glad it's just a small prophecy. What's the worst that could happen—besides the man dying, that is."

"That they won't listen the next time," Harriet suggested.

"And I'll be arrested for filing a false police report."

"And that'll be the end of you as a prophet," Harriet said. "You know we could have been called on to predict something much larger in a place where we are virtually unknown."

"I think He's trying to see if I can handle things now."

Harriet drew in her breath sharply. "Aleta, He knows! Besides I'm here. He purposely chose to give you the vision, not me!"

"Oh, my God!" Aleta burst out.

"Exactly!" Harriet exclaimed. "God chose you for a reason. We'll just have to wait and see why. Meanwhile let's take the dogs for a walk."

Harriet called toward the bedroom. "I'm taking Mrs. Praetzel for a walk, Bertha. When we get back, she'll need you to drive places."

"Yes, Ma'am," Bertha called. "Do you need me to help Mrs. Praetzel into her coat?"

"I have a cloak," Aleta said. "Stanley's mother had it made for me."

"I can help her," Harriet said. "We'll be gone about twenty minutes."

The cloak was a heavy all wool garment dark gray in color, with a hood. It dropped to below her knees and had slits for her hands.

Harriet helped Aleta with her gloves and opened the door. The three Chessies rushed out and ran past the RV toward the restored barn at the far end of the orchard. They were over a hundred yards away when Aleta stopped.

"I have to go to the Home," she said.

"Right now?"

"There's still danger. The man needs me."

"So it is a man?"

"I believe so."

Harriet pulled out the whistle draped around her neck by a thin leather lanyard and blew a triple trill. Upon hearing it, all three dogs spun around and raced toward her. Harriet opened the RV door and the three dogs barreled in. Harriet followed them. Both females had already put themselves inside their crates. Harriet latched the crate doors and told Stoney to guard the place. He was left free.

Aleta was already walking toward the house.

"I'll drive you," Harriet called.

Aleta opened the door and told Bertha that her grandmother was driving her to the Oakwood Home.

"Do you want me to watch the dogs?"

"The dogs are in the RV. You can clean the couch and chairs and then cover them. We want them nice for the party."

"Yes, Ma'am," Bertha said. "Will you be here for lunch?"

"I don't know," Aleta replied hesitantly. She wasn't ready to explain what was happening. In fact, she didn't know herself. She just had this urge to go to the Home.

"I can fix it when you get here, Ma'am," Bertha said politely. "That's no problem."

On the way to the Home, Aleta said, "Bertha was a good choice. I hope nothing happens to scare her away."

"We're going to visit one sick old man in a nursing home," Harriet said. "We're not diving into a huge criminal conspiracy. You need to relax and let God take care of things."

"Why does He want me there?"

Harriet laughed. "He didn't tell me."

Aleta blustered. "You know what I mean!"

"The answer's the same. He didn't tell me."

"He didn't tell me either. I don't like this. I have a bad feeling."

"Describe bad feeling."

"As if we're going to get into something we don't want to."

Chapter 2

Chief Alan Peets stood pensively outside the entrance to the Oakwood Nursing Home. He was wearing his old Willow Glen uniform which had been especially tailored for his tall frame. His wife had painstakingly removed the patches from the former Oakwood chief's uniform and sewn them on her husband's old uniform. Ramage had several brass badges in his desk drawer. Peets found one that merely said 'Chief of Police' and attached and fastened it to his new uniform. Ramage's hat fit. He was a short fat man with a big head. Peets' head size was the same only his head matched his muscular frame.

Beside the tall, black man stood his former chief, Tom Milani, who headed the Willow Glen force. The two towns were like two slices of bread with Arborville sandwiched between them. Until the recent scandal that affected half the Oakwood town council and the heads of both the police and fire departments, Oakwood had been a city unto itself. The only thing they agreed to share with their two neighbors to the north was the building of a huge new hospital outside Arborville that serviced all three towns. While little monetary support had come from Oakwood, their mayor had insisted that all three towns have an equal voice in the hospital administration.

The new Oakwood mayor, appointed by the court after most of the Town Council was arrested on conspiracy charges in connection with the perpetration of a fraud, had looked to Willow Glen's Police Chief for a suggestion as to whom she could hire to fill in Ramage's spot temporarily.

Milani knew that Peets had little chance of making it as permanent chief, but he wanted him to know that he personally considered him the best man for the job.

Peets who's emigrated from New Jersey on a racketeering case that involved both states proved to be a sharp investigator and, when Milani discovered that Peets couldn't return to his corrupt police force after taking down one of their men, saw to it that Captain Terrell hired him. Milani took over Terrell's job shortly afterward and West, Terrell's other lieutenant, went to Arborville as its new chief.

Milani and West remained close friends and Peets watched them work as a team for years. So when Aleta's call came, he turned to his old chief to check her out.

Milani wasn't a tall man. He wasn't lean either. He was a stocky dark-haired man of Italian descent who'd spent his first five years as a Chicago patrolman. He was well-grounded in the fundamentals of police work and rose quickly on the Willow Glen force.

West, a later arrival, straight from law school, rose just as quickly. West came from a privileged background and his father didn't give up trying to persuade him to be the lawyer he'd studied to become, but Lyle West wanted to do police work and, when Lyle made chief, his father finally acknowledged that his son probably knew best.

"Now when they get here," Milani warned, "just remember that these are two of the richest women in Willow Glen."

"I know that," Peets returned, blowing on his hands and stomping his feet. "Why are you warning me?"

"Because they are different and it takes a lot of blind faith to believe them," Milani replied.

"My faith I save for church."

"Just hold a little out, in case God has wondered into our world," Milani said. "Where's your coat. It's November, Man."

"Don't have one that fits yet," Peets said. "Anyway I believe the director of the Home. That old man somehow got his pillow over his own face."

"And Aleta saw it from ten miles away?"

"Okay, so she got some sort of feeling that someone was in trouble," Peets said. "I'll 'Yes, ma'am' her real nice."

"You're reading me wrong here," Tom retorted. "You don't need to kowtow to these ladies, just hold back prejudging them because they're rich and white, okay?"

"Why is she coming over?"

"Your guess is as good as mine. There's no pattern that either West or I have been able to figure out."

"We had one psychic for years. Now suddenly we have three?" Peets scoffed. "Can we discuss this inside?"

"Too many ears inside," Milani said stuffing his hands deep into his coat pocket. From what West has told me, Martha Cook's visions only deal with people dying in various nursing homes. West always figured she picked up some sort of vibe when she visited."

"I like that theory," Peets remarked. "That makes sense."

"But these two ladies seem to specialize in murder."

"Well, they're dead wrong here," Peets said clapping the sides of his body with his arms. "We didn't find a single staff member with a ruby ring. Can we go in now?"

"You're the chief of police here," Milani grinned. "You can do anything you want."

Peets straightened up, then he saw a minivan turn into the lot in front of the Home.

"No need. They're here."

To Chief Peets' surprise, the younger of the two was helped out of the car by the elder. She was wearing a long dark gray cape with a hood, only the hood wasn't on her head and he saw the deep scar down the middle of her scalp parting her auburn hair.

No wonder Milani wants me to be nice, he thought. She's had some sort of accident and isn't right in the head. And why the cape? Does she see herself as some caped avenger? Well, he could be as polite as the next man.

Harriet Locke extended her hand to the tall black man first, a gesture of real respect. "Chief Peets, it is a pleasure. Congratulations on your promotion. I hope it's permanent."

"Ma'am," Peets said, shaking her hand and kicking himself because this woman had earned his respect in ten seconds flat.

The younger woman followed suit, acknowledging Peets before Chief Milani. "Thank you so much, Chief, for listening to me. I know I must have sounded like a crazy woman."

Peets smiled as he shook her hand. At least she had that part right; however, she seemed self-assured and sensible, cape and all.

"Did Chief Milani make you wait out in the cold to greet us?" Aleta went on. "Does he think youth can handle cold better than age? I see the city hasn't supplied you with a full uniform yet. I hope it's in the works."

"It is, Ma'am," Peets said, wondering how she knew. His wife had done a beautiful job he thought.

"I'd like to meet your wife. She is obviously an expert seamstress," Aleta said as they entered the building.

"It's Mr. Hoskinson in room 112," Peets said. "He's had a stroke and his speech is garbled. We can't understand a word he's saying."

"So he can't identify the attacker?" Aleta queried. She stopped once inside the door and her grandmother removed her cape. Peets then saw the arm in the sling and her cloak made sense.

"No, Ma'am," Peets replied.

The foursome proceeded to the room. Peets told the police officer to wait outside and see that they weren't disturbed.

"Mr. Hoskinson," Aleta said as soon as their eyes met. "I understand you've had a stroke. I had one recently myself so I know how difficult it is to find words. I'm going to ask you some questions. Nod your head if I guess right. Shake if you want to say no. Do you understand?"

The man in the bed nodded and then proceeded to spiel out a long series of unintelligible sounds.

Aleta turned to the others in the room. "He seems to be expressing himself quite clearly. What's the problem?"

All three faces registered shock.

"You mean you understood him?" Harriet asked.

Now it was Aleta who was taken aback. "You mean you didn't?"

"Not a word," Harriet responded.

The two men were glad she was saying it because neither of them wanted to.

"He said someone tried to smother him with a pillow and stopped when the police siren started up," Aleta said. "You didn't hear him say that?"

"I heard him say something," Harriet said, "but I couldn't make out the words."

"Mr. Hoskinson, does everyone here have trouble understanding you?"

The tumble of mixed up sounds seemed to follow no recognizable pattern.

"Really?" Aleta gasped.

"What did he say?" Harriet prodded.

"I'm the first one." Aleta turned to her grandmother. "I don't understand. Tell me the truth. I am speaking English, aren't I?"

"I understand you perfectly," Harriet replied.

"So do I," Chief Milani said.

"I do too," Peets added after she looked to him for confirmation as well.

"Can you find out what happened?" Peets asked, deciding that he'd play along. If she was faking it, he'd soon know.

Aleta turned to the man in the bed. "Are you the Hoskinson of Hoskinson Lumber?"

The man nodded his head as he again uttered a series of nonsense syllables.

"I see. You have seven other lumber yards besides the one in Oakwood. Nod if I'm repeating what you tell me accurately."

Mr. Hoskinson nodded. He was an old man with a short white beard and neatly trimmed short white hair. Aleta could hear the pride in his voice as he listed the locations of his businesses.

"Three in Illinois, one in Indiana, two in Ohio and two in Iowa," she repeated.

The head nodded.

"Let's get to today's events," Aleta said.

Peets sighed audibly. Finally something she couldn't have read in a newspaper.

"Did you see your attacker?"

The head shook.

"So you don't know if it was a man or woman?"

A string of sounds burst forth.

"You're sure it was a woman because you heard her heels click on the floor. They were high heels."

The old man nodded vigorously and then spoke again.

"The staff wear soft soled shoes," Aleta repeated. "Besides you smelled perfume."

"How could you smell perfume? You said the pillow was over your head and that's why you couldn't see."

An explanation poured forth which Aleta repeated. "When you knocked the pillow askew, you smelled it."

"Any idea who would want to kill you?"

The head shook. Then there was a long string of sound.

When Hoskinson finished, Aleta turned to Chief Peets and said, "He is afraid whoever it is will try again."

Peets watched the old man's head nod.

"He wants to be moved to a safer location."

"This is the best convalescent home in the area," Peets said. "And since none of the staff is involved, he'll be as safe here as anywhere."

Another spiel followed Peets response.

Aleta repeated his question: "Will you post a guard?"

"I can post one for a few days while we're investigating," Peets said.

The man's head shook violently. Again he spoke.

"Not good enough," Aleta said. "He wants you to hire him a bodyguard."

Peets looked aghast. "I can't do that. He'll have to do that himself."

Aleta looked askance at the new Oakwood chief, "And how is he supposed to do that?"

"He can ask a relative to do it," Peets retorted.

Aleta, who was watching Hoskinson's face when Peets spoke, noticed he paled when the chief said the word 'relative.' "You suspect one of your relatives?" she asked.

Hoskinson shook his head vehemently.

"If you won't tell me the truth, I'm done," Aleta announced abruptly. She turned and walked out of the room.

Harriet followed her.

The old man cried aloud and held up his one good arm in supplication. Peets went to the door. The man's cry could be heard down the hall, but neither woman hesitated.

Peets called in his officer. "You're on until relieved. No one comes near Mr. Hoskinson that's not staff."

Then he and Milani raced after the two women. They caught up to them as Aleta was gingerly getting into the car.

"What was that all about?" Peets demanded.

"I like you," Aleta said. "Saturday I'm having a party at my house. Bring your wife. Tell her it's not formal, but dressy. There'll be people there you'll want to meet. Lauren is hostessing."

"We need you to help us interrogate him further," Peets insisted, brushing aside the party invitation.

Aleta smiled knowingly. "He suspects a relative but is afraid to say so. You're a cop. Investigate."

Peets watched open-mouthed as Harriet drove away.

Milani clapped him on the shoulder. "Looks like you're in, Chief. Lauren West throws great parties."

"Chief West's wife?"

"One and the same."

"Am I the token black?"

"You're the new Oakwood Police Chief. Race isn't an issue here," Milani said. "And you'll know some of the people so you won't be among total strangers. Come on, loosen up a bit. You'll have fun."

Peets' cell phone rang and he answered it. When he hung up, he was smiling.

"Who was that?"

"Aleta Praetzel."

"What did she want?"

"To give me a reason for accepting her invitation."

"And did she?"

"Yes."

"Well, what is it?"

"It's private," Peets said, grinning.

"From me?" Tom jibed. "After all I've done for you you're not sharing?"

"Nope!"

"How'd she get your number?"

"Harriet Locke asked me and I reeled it off. Who knew she'd remember?"

"Harriet used to be a bank VP and was the financial guru for the biggest trust they had. You'd better believe she's good with numbers."

"She just asked as if it was her due and I responded without thinking."

"She's good, isn't she?" Milani added.

"Good?"

"Conned you out of a number I think only three people have, right?" Milani queried smiling.

"Four, now five, or six if I count Aleta Praetzel." Peets sighed. "Great! Now two psychics have my cell number."

"They won't misuse it," Milani said trying to keep his smile controlled.

"You're enjoying this aren't you?" Peets asked.

"West enjoyed my first encounter," Milani said. "And I was upset too. Welcome to the club. It's exclusive, you know."

Peets smiled. "There is that."

As they drove away, Harriet said, "I guess that's that."

"Not quite," Aleta said. "Hoskinson asked me to send him a lawyer."

"What good would that do?"

"He asked for Stanley."

"And he expects you to come along and translate, right?"

"That's my guess."

"Did he tell you why he wants a lawyer?"

"He wants to execute a power of attorney."

"That makes sense," Harriet said. "You can't refuse that request."

"Stanley's not going to be happy."

"Listen, it's a simple request by a man who's lost his power of speech. Stanley won't mind," Harriet said. "Or is there more to it than that?"

"As a matter of fact, there is," Aleta said. "His exact words were 'I want your husband and that P.I. of his.'"

"To investigate what?"

"I couldn't ask," Aleta said. "He asked me not to."

"You have to go through Peets to get access."

"I know that."

"Is that why you invited him to the party?"

"No, I invited him because I like him. I want to be friends. It seemed like a good way to start."

"Why did you say what you did on the phone?"

"You know how your father's family has kept your secret all these years."

"It's something you can trust blacks to do."

"So, we can trust him, right?"

"Why hint that I'm passing?"

"Grams, I'm sorry. It just came out. I'm a bit surprised at what I said myself. I can't explain why it seemed right at the moment."

Harriet looked at her granddaughter thoughtfully. Finally she said, "It's okay. I'm not ashamed of my father. He was a scholar and a gentleman. Most of my friends already know. If God wants one more person to know, it's all right."

"I wonder what Mr. Hoskinson wants investigated?" Aleta said.

"The attempt on his life, of course."

"No, it was something else. The term he used was 'mold'."

"Mold? Did you get that right?"

"I just hope he doesn't want Stanley to do more than set up a power of attorney for him."

As soon as the two women drove away from the Oakwood Nursing Home, Dean Arnetti slipped out the side door and made a call. A regular attendant, Dean had no love for old or sick people but with his record, jobs were hard to come by, especially low-profile jobs that covered his more lucrative line of work.

Whoever thought sick people automatically kicked their habit didn't understand the nature of addiction. In addition, there were the visitors. Certain Alzheimer's patients had multiple visitors. Dean usually stopped in to chat for the few minutes they were there.

Thus it was he got to know Rosalie Hoskinson long before her father-in-law had his stroke. She was the supposed niece of one of the Alzheimer's patients whom Dean selected as a person without close family nearby.

When Bertha Carlson's husband was admitted and Bertha spent long hours at his side, Dean noticed that she was noticing the stream of visitors to certain patients. He worried about this. When Rosalie Hoskinson offered him five thousand dollars to put a pillow over Carlson's face and help him depart a little sooner than he would have done naturally, Dean took the money.

He asked no questions. After half the money was in his pocket, he befriended Bertha Carlson, bringing her coffee in the evening before he punched out. The coffee sent her to the bathroom each time she drank it he noticed. She used the bathroom in her husband's room. She always locked the door. She was in there only a few minutes. That's all it took.

He'd hidden in another patient's room until he could sneak into Carlson's room without being seen.

As expected Bertha was the prime suspect. No one else appeared to have a motive.

After Lars Hoskinson was admitted, Rosalie refused to visit him. Neil explained to his brother that sickness made Rosalie uncomfortable.

Rosalie added a hundred dollars to her regular purchases from Dean for an update on her father-in-law's condition, especially his power to communicate. Even though he hadn't regained any speech, the fact that he was making sounds at all made her nervous. So Dean snuck her into a comatose patient's room for a thousand. From there she snuck into her father-in-law's room when the halls were empty.

Rosalie barely escaped before the police arrived.

Dean promised to call her and tell her how the investigation was going. This was his first such report.

"He's still talking garbage. The director persuaded the police that he'd somehow got that pillow on top of his own face."

"Who the hell called the police?" Rosalie asked. "They rolled up with their siren blaring before I was done."

"Some psychic," Dean responded. "Not the same one as last time though. Last time it was some old broad. This time it was a young chick and then she showed up."

"Gimme her name?"

"Aleta Praetzel," Dean replied. "That isn't all. She can understand the old fart."

"Damn you! You said no one could."

"No one but her," Dean said. "Maybe it's some psychic shit or else she's running a con."

"So what'd he tell her?"

"She left in a huff and the two chiefs ran after her and tried to get her to come back and finish."

"Come on. Give. What did she tell them?"

"She said it weren't nobody on the staff."

"So you aren't under suspicion?" Rosalie asked.

Dean saw where she was heading. "And I'm keeping it that way."

"You damn well better keep me informed."

"Cost you two hundred a pop now."

"What a shithead you are! You think I'm gonna be blackmailed, you think again."

"You want the info. You pay."

Rosalie Hoskinson walked into the family room where Neil was watching TV. He'd taken the day off to give his wife an alibi.

"We could be in deep shit," she opened. "He's found an interpreter."

Neil sat up and switched off the TV. "Someone understands that garble of his?"

"Yeah. Name's Aleta Praetzel," Rosalie said. "Why does that name sound familiar?"

"She was that rich dame that was kidnapped with her husband about ten days ago. It was in the paper," Neil replied. "How'd she get mixed up in this?"

"Dean thinks she's a damn psychic."

"Ramage doesn't go for that junk."

"We got a new chief, remember?"

"Oh, yeah." Neil went over to the bar and poured himself a scotch. He turned. "Want one?"

"Don't drink that! We gotta think."

"About what?" Neil asked.

"We gotta get rid of her."

"Why not the old man?"

"He's got a police guard. Besides he didn't see me and if he can't talk to nobody else, we'll be okay."

"What about that Arnetti guy?"

"He's not going to say nothing with what I got on him."

"Will he do it?"

"Says it's too risky."

"So what are you going to do about the Praetzel dame?"

"Send her a present."

"A present?"

"Yeah, one that explodes when she opens it."

"A mail bomb?"

"You got a better idea?"

"I like it, and I know just the guy who can rig one."

"Can we trust him?"

"Money talks. Besides it'll be his neck on the line, not ours."

"We need to get rid of her right away," Rosalie said. "Send it overnight. From Chicago."

"I'll make sure she gets it."

Chapter 3

As Harriet was driving them home, Aleta called Lauren.

"Did Lyle tell you your party is going to be at my place?"

"Sounds good to me, especially since your new cook is going to do the ducks," Lauren said brightly. "We have to get together soon."

"I can be there in half an hour. Bertha will be with me. You can make plans with her while I select the law books I want to borrow."

"You'll stay for lunch," Lauren said. "Bertha too."

"She has shopping to do," Aleta said. "She says she doesn't eat with employers."

"Wow!" Lauren said. "You got yourself a pro."

"Seems so," Aleta said. "Oh, I added two more guests. Chief Peets and his wife."

When Aleta was back in her own car with Bertha in the driver's seat, she told her housekeeper that she was also invited for lunch.

"It wouldn't be appropriate, Ma'am," Bertha responded stiffly.

"I told Lauren you'd say that," Aleta said, "so after you and Lauren hammer out the menu for the party, you can shop while Lauren and I have lunch."

Aleta reached into her purse.

"I'm going to give you my charge card as well as cash. You can treat yourself to lunch and buy yourself another couple of uniforms like the one you're wearing. I like it."

"Yes, Ma'am."

"We have to prepare something special for Mr. Praetzel this evening."

"Will you want me to stay and clean up afterward?"

"What I want is for you to leave at six every night. I want Mr. Praetzel to need to come home from work. It's his habit to work late. We have to train him out of that habit."

"But I don't want to leave you alone."

"Stanley'll see that you don't. We're going to stop at his office and give his secretary a heads-up. She'll have the files he needs to go over in his briefcase by five thirty."

The rest of the trip dealt with what Stanley's favorite menu would be.

Stanley walked through his front door at exactly six o'clock.

"Where's Bertha?" he demanded.

"I sent her home," Aleta said sweetly.

"Why didn't you call your grandmother?" Stanley asked perturbed.

"She is going to bed early. Lyle is picking her up at four AM."

"They're going duck hunting," Stanley surmised. "I'm surprised Lyle took off mid-week."

"We need the ducks for our party on Saturday," Aleta explained, closing the law book on the table. "Serve our dinner and I'll tell you all about it."

"We can't have a party," Stanley protested, not moving.

"I can serve the meal if you'd like," Aleta offered rising from the chair.

In response, Stanley tore off his scarf muttering angrily. "Don't you move."

He shed his coat and hung it on the coat rack next to her cape and hurried into the kitchen still muttering, "This is not going to happen again."

"Salad's in the refrigerator," Aleta directed ignoring his ill-humor. "Steak is in the broiler. It should be just the way you like it. The plates are on top of the stove."

Stanley opened the oven door. The smell of toasted mushrooms and onions hit him. His favorite smell. When he scooted his steak onto his plate he noticed that it was medium-rare.

"Vegetables are in the pot on the right. They go in the small bowl. The larger one is the mashed potatoes," Aleta directed. "Now sit down. We pray and then eat."

"I'm too upset to pray," Stanley pouted.

"I'll do it then," Aleta said.

"Thank you for protecting me today," she prayed. "Thank you for Bertha. Thanks you for this wonderful feast. But, most of all, thank you for the love You've showered down upon us. Bless us this evening. Thy will, not mine, be done. Amen."

Stanley added his "amen" and then looked at his wife skeptically. His blue eyes searched her face for some telltale sign of what she was up to.

She scooted her plate toward him and he realized she couldn't cut her meat one-handed.

"I forgot the rolls," she exclaimed getting up.

"Sit!" Stanley shouted. "Where are they?"

"In the bun warmer. They're homemade. Bertha would be upset if I forgot them."

Stanley took out the rolls, dumped them in the napkin-lined basket and returned to the table and his task of cutting her meat.

"Half is fine," Aleta said. "I'm hungry."

Stanley broke open a roll and buttered both halves and gave Aleta one and bit into the other half.

"You eat and I'll tell you about everything," Aleta said, "starting with Grams and Lyle. They're both excited at the prospect of getting a chance to get at least one hunt in this season."

Stanley nodded. The two were avid hunters who'd been chaffing because their normal hunting partners were both pregnant. Lyle had discovered that Stanley could shoot and had tried to persuade him to go out, but Stanley couldn't bring himself to leave Aleta until he was sure Sunday's episode wouldn't be repeated.

He paused to pour the wine and urged Aleta to continue.

"Lauren is giving me a welcome home party only she's doing it here. Bertha is cooking the ducks."

"How many people?"

"Twenty-three."

"That's too many!" Stanley exclaimed. "Besides you don't know twenty-three people."

"I do now. I met another one today and invited him and his wife."

Stanley paused in his eating. "What's his name?"

"Alan Peets."

"The new Oakwood Police Chief? How did you meet him?"

"Grams drove me over to the Oakwood Nursing Home and he was there."

"He's sick?"

"He was there on a case," Aleta said. "A case I told him about."

This time Stanley put down his fork and knife. "Aleta, tell me the whole story."

"After both of us finish eating," she said. "This food is too good to let grow cold. And don't worry, I saved the man's life, and Chief Peets is investigating."

"So it's done with," Stanley said, picking up his fork.

"Eat!" Aleta ordered.

"You are not investigating an attempted murder!" Stanley charged.

"Absolutely not!" Aleta said.

Stanley relaxed back into eating. She knew eventually Stanley would remember her sidestepping his question as to whether she was done, so she selected a topic guaranteed to engage him.

"Today Grams mentioned that you had saved my hair and I could have a piece made," she purposely looked down at her plate so he'd see her scar clearly.

"Do you want one?" Stanley asked.

"Does the scar bother you?" Aleta countered.

"I'm sorry you were hurt, but the scar doesn't bother me otherwise. Does it bother you?"

"It would have bothered Conan," Aleta commented with deliberate casualness.

"How did your former boyfriend get into our dinner table conversation?" Stanley snapped.

"Because I was thinking that if he were sitting across from me right now, he'd take all this goodness as his due. Then he'd focus on my scar and say I'd be prettier if I did something about it."

"That wouldn't be a lie," Stanley said." And I'd be handsomer with a smaller nose and ears that didn't stick out, especially with the one so disfigured. So are you hinting that we both need cosmetic surgery?"

Aleta smiled impishly. "You take the bait every time. +When are you going to accept the fact that I love you, disfigured ear and all? Your ear matches my scar. We were wounded by the same sniper, remember?"

"Conan has no wounds," Stanley observed still miffed that his name had even come up.

"Ah, but he hasn't lived with me," Aleta laughed. "It seems that marrying me has proved to be a hazardous endeavor."

"So, you aren't hinting?"

"Stanley, I never hint," Aleta said. "Grams told me I shouldn't let Stoney on the couch today and I told her I wanted to keep her furniture and guess what?"

"She gave it to you," Stanley said knowing Aleta's grandmother would give her anything she asked for.

"It's her wedding gift to us. Isn't that grand?"

"I was wondering how I'd ever get used to any other furniture in our great room. It is a grand gift. I know how much her furniture meant to her."

"That's why it's covered. Bertha brushed out all the dog hair. We're keeping upholstery dog-hair-free for the party."

"This party," Stanley posed. "You aren't doing anything, are you?"

"I'm the guest of honor," Aleta said.

"Bertha will need help," Stanley said.

"Lauren is taking care of that."

"Speaking of Bertha, I want her to stay at night until I come home."

"I can't do that to her. Working a ten hour day is enough. That's how long you're gone, you know."

"I didn't realize," Stanley murmured. "Did I see lemon squares for dessert?"

"How's your day tomorrow?" Aleta asked as Stanley took the two small plates from the refrigerator.

"Court all morning. Appointments all afternoon," he said taking a bite.

"Can you squeeze in an emergency client?"

"I usually can. Who's the client?"

"Mr. Hoskinson," Aleta replied.

"Hoskinson Lumber?"

"The same."

"He's not a child," Stanley said. "You know what I said this morning about the area of law I intend to practice which is, I might add, just in case you didn't hear me this morning, the area in which I have a flourishing practice which I enjoy thoroughly."

"He asked for you specifically."

"You could have told him I wouldn't represent him."

"He asked me not to say anything. There were people in the room."

"And they didn't hear him ask you?"

"They didn't understand his words."

"You speak a foreign language now?"

"Mr. Hoskinson has had a massive stroke. His speech is garbled. For some reason I can understand him."

"And just what am I supposed to do for him—sue someone?"

"Help him execute a power of attorney."

"But if he's not intelligible, how am I supposed to do that?"

"I'll be his interpreter. He can understand and affirm or deny what I say with a head nod or shake."

"Well, I guess with witnesses I could do that. Let me check it out with Mother. She deals with estates and trusts all day long. She'll be able to tell me what she as a judge would require."

"He made one more request," Aleta said. "He wants you to bring Ed. He has a job for him."

"Now I can guess why this great dinner," Stanley said. "If I said no, was I going to have to do the dishes?"

"No," Aleta said. "I have more persuasive techniques planned."

"Do I get to enjoy the whole evening or did everything stop when I said yes?"

"I don't waste plans," Aleta smiled. "You get the whole package."

"And what does it include?"

"More wine. A bit of dancing. Some conversation about your day. And a bath together. Then bed."

"I'm sold," Stanley said. "Have Bertha bring you to my office at two. Either Ed or I will take you home."

Aleta rose and turned on the stereo. The strains of "Someone Like You" filled the room. Aleta nestled close to him and the two danced slowly like the young lovers they were.

"There's nothing you're not telling me, is there?" Stanley asked when the song was done.

"Hoskinson said something about a certain mold, but I didn't understand that too well."

"Mold, huh?" Stanley chuckled. "Nothing ominous about that, is there?"

Chapter 4

Ten o'clock the next morning, as Aleta sat at the table studying, Bertha answered the door and brought in two small packages.

"Do you want me to snip the cord so you can open these?"

"Who are they addressed to?"

"One's addressed to Mr. & Mrs.; the other, just to you."

"Probably both wedding presents. Put them on the hall table. Stanley and I will open them when he gets home."

"Yes, Ma'am," Bertha said. "If you don't have anything for me right now I thought I'd get in the rest of the shopping before your grandmother returns with the ducks. It'll take me all afternoon to dress them."

"I'll be fine until noon," Aleta said.

"I opened a bottle of water. It's on the counter. It's been in the refrigerator so it's cold."

"Thanks, Bertha. Don't worry. I'll be fine."

Thirty minutes after Bertha left, Aleta got up and stretched.

Too much silence, she thought. I need music.

She walked over to the CD player and pushed the play button. The remainder of the album they'd played last night came on.

Last night was wonderful, she mused. Stanley was so much fun to be with. They'd danced by firelight, their shoes sliding effortlessly over the smooth hardwood floor. Then they'd talked until the fire died out. They bathed by candlelight, a new experience for Stanley. Knowing that Aleta wasn't to engage in any sexual activity. Stanley was prepared to sleep as soon as he hit the bed. What happened next was new too. Aleta had prepared the evening well. When she finished, he knew he would have said yes to any request she made.

Aleta smiled at the memories. Her eye caught sight of the two unopened packages on the table. She picked up the one from Marshall Fields and guessed it was an additional silver place setting. It was long and heavy for so small a box. It was sealed with tape.

The other box was lighter. It was almost square, wrapped in brown paper and tied so securely with twine; she understood why Bertha offered to cut the twine. There was no slipping it off in any direction. She opened the drawer and reached inside for the scissors. They weren't here. Who'd moved them?

She studied the package. It was addressed to her. The return address said 4806 Rice Street. She hadn't ever even heard of the street. The name was smeared so it was unreadable. There was no postmark. Funny that it was delivered to the door. It was small enough to fit into the mailbox. Her curiosity was now fully aroused.

She carried the package into the kitchen. Maybe the scissors were in the utility drawer. She opened the drawer and rummaged around in it but found no scissors.

Her cell phone rang.

"What are you doing?" Stanley asked. It was an ordinary question and Aleta said, "I can't find the scissors."

"You can't cut pages out of Lyle's law books. He wouldn't like it."

"We got two packages in the mail, and I need to cut the twine."

"Where's Bertha?"

"Shopping. I told her it'd be okay."

"So the minute she leaves, you decided to do something."

"I was just going to cut a bit of twine."

"Aleta, with you one thing always leads to another. Put the package back. Go sit down and don't move until Bertha gets back."

Aleta walked over to the table and set the package down. "There, I put it back. Now why'd you call?"

"I wanted to tell you what's going to happen this afternoon. Mother is bringing her court recorder with her and she's going to pass judgment on the validity on the spot. She knows that Mr. Hoskinson's life is at risk."

"You can't represent him then."

"She says Hoskinson Lumber has a law firm on retainer, so at her suggestion I called Oscar Johanson and persuaded him that he'd better be there if he wants to save this account."

"Hoskinson won't like that," Aleta pointed out. "He asked for you."

"Johanson would only challenge any decision if he weren't a party to its making," Stanley explained. "I'll tell Mr. Hoskinson that when I withdraw from the case."

"You're still bringing Ed, aren't you?"

"That's a separate request. I won't even stay in the room when Mr. Hoskinson talks with Ed and you won't discuss it with me. You're there as an interpreter only."

"Suppose I can't understand him today," Aleta worried aloud. "Suppose yesterday was a fluke."

"We can get him to acknowledge that he asked you to do this," Stanley said. "Don't fret about it. I'll be there."

"Does Peets know we're coming?"

"Everything's been taken care of," Stanley said kindly. "Tell Bertha you must be ready to go at one forty. Until then, you stay put and study."

"Yessir!" Aleta responded lightly. The package could wait.

At two o'clock, Chief Alan Peets allowed a select group of people to assemble in Mr. Lars Hoskinson's room. Aleta was the first to enter the room and she answered Mr. Hoskinson's questions one at a time. Since no one else was speaking, Aleta wondered if the others could understand him. He seemed to be speaking so clearly. She glanced at Stanley and saw nothing but a puzzled expression.

"I guess I can still understand him," Aleta observed aloud.

Oscar Johanson, an older, light-complexioned Swede, his carefully tailored suit lessening the extent of his paunch, burst forth, "Well, I can't. And there is no way that I'm going to accept any decision when I can't understand what my client is saying."

"Mr. Johanson, court is now in session," Judge Lylia Davis said. "You may address your concern in an orderly fashion."

Johanson suddenly realized, whether he liked it or not, a judge was present. This was no time for a tantrum.

"Your Honor, I apologize for my outburst; however, how can we know that this woman truly understands what my client is saying?"

"I do believe yours is a valid concern," Judge Davis said. "We will address it as soon as everyone identifies himself for the record."

That done, Judge Davis added that Mr. Lars Hoskinson was also present.

"Aleta," the judge said gently, "will it bother you if we blindfold you for a short test. You may hold your husband's hand so you don't lose your balance."

Stanley positioned the scarf over Aleta's eyes.

"Just so everyone present is aware," Judge Davis explained, the reason for the blindfold is so when I point to a person and ask Mr. Hoskinson to identify him, Mrs. Praetzel will not be able to follow the direction of Mr. Hoskinson's gaze."

When Oscar Johanson was pointed out, Hoskinson spat out a mouthful of unintelligible sounds that made Aleta respond, "I can't say that."

"She failed!" Johanson chortled with glee.

Lars Hoskinson told Aleta to repeat his words exactly.

Aleta said, "Mr. Hoskinson identified you, as that fat Swedish windbag who hasn't had a creative thought in that bird brain of his for half a century and, while he tells everyone he is fifty-five, he is the same age as me, 67."

"She could have looked that up!" Johanson declared, then flushed. It was a preposterous allegation. What difference did his age make? Still he wasn't ready to concede.

"Ask him something that she wouldn't know," Johanson said.

"Mr. Hoskinson, was your last conversation with Mr. Johanson privileged?" Judge Davis inquired.

Aleta, still blindfolded, replied, "No, your honor."

"Repeat a small portion of it."

"It was about six. We were talking about a whore he liked. Should I go on?"

Oscar Johanson jumped in. "That's good enough for me." "Mr. Hoskinson, whom have you selected to have execute power of attorney on your behalf in medical matters?"

He replied. Aleta hesitated.

Stanley said, "You are here as interpreter only."

"Why is he here?" Johanson charged glaring at Stanley.

"As I stated earlier, I'm Mrs. Praetzel's attorney," Stanley returned. He then addressed his wife who was still blindfolded, "Repeat exactly what Mr. Hoskinson said."

Aleta cleared her throat and said, "Aleta Praetzel because she currently is the only one who can understand my speech."

Aleta turned and whispered into Stanley's ear. "I can't do this. Tomorrow I might not understand him."

"Mrs. Praetzel has a comment on her suitability," Stanley said aloud.

"The court will allow her to make a personal statement at this time," the judge ruled.

"I am willing to act as Mr. Hoskinson's interpreter for as long as he needs me; however, I do not understand this gift I suddenly possess nor can I guarantee its duration. I may not be able to understand him tomorrow. That must be weighed in."

"Mr. Hoskinson, you may select another person at this time," the judge said.

Again Mr. Hoskinson spoke. Aleta was glad the scarf still covered her face because she knew it was red. She swallowed hard and hesitated.

Stanley prompted her again. "Repeat what you heard."

"I would like Mrs. Praetzel because she will work hard to understand me even if she cannot figure out my words tomorrow or the next day. She has no personal agenda. She gains nothing if I live or die. She can be impartial. She is my best chance at completing several critical tasks I need to complete."

"Mr. Johanson, do you have any objection to Mrs. Praetzel being given power of attorney with respect to all medical decisions to be made for Mr. Lars Hoskinson?"

"She's not a doctor," Oscar Johanson put forth. "So I object."

"Mr. Hoskinson, please address that issue."

Aleta repeated his words, surprising herself at her ability to remember them all.

"I want her to help me fill out a living will first and then I want her to interpret for me so I can talk to my doctors. That's what I want her to do. If she has my power of attorney, they will listen to her. And I know she will listen to me, so with her having the power, I'm still in control."

Mr. Hoskinson nodded his head with each sentence. Still blindfolded Aleta was getting no feedback except that

Stanley squeezed her hand lightly on a regular basis. Eventually, she figured out the squeezes were signals telling her Mr. Hoskinson was approving what she was saying.

"So ordered," Judge Davis said.

Again Mr. Hoskinson spoke. Again Aleta hesitated. And again Stanley urged her to remember that she wasn't making decisions, merely giving a voice to a man who had lost his ability to communicate.

Aleta repeated the words as she heard them.

"I want to give temporary power of attorney over all other matters to Mr. Stanley Praetzel."

Simultaneously, Johanson exploded and Stanley objected. Both men talked at once and were close to a shouting match when Stanley felt Aleta tremble. Instantly, he led her to a chair and bade her sit down. He removed the blindfold and held her free hand in both of his.

"Aleta," he said softly, kneeling beside her, "I can take care of myself. You are merely speaking for Mr. Hoskinson. I'm not confusing you with him. I know what you want."

Aleta nodded numbly. Stanley could still feel a tremor in the hand he was holding.

He leaned over and whispered, "Pillow."

It was a word with a deep history, selected because at the time it made sense. It was used several times after the kidnapping to evoke absolute silence on Aleta's part. She obeyed his order to be silent during the kidnapping and discovered he'd used it to protect her from the horror of being raped. She was surprised the first time he used it after the kidnapping, but she'd obeyed without question. She saw it as a matter of honor—her honoring the only promise she'd made on her wedding day that she would obey him. Knowing

Aleta, Stanley had accepted it as an expression of her deep commitment to him.

That he would use it in court, especially with his mother as judge, took her aback. Everyone would think he was crazy.

"Your Honor," Stanley said, "my client is not able to continue at this time; however, I believe we can proceed without her."

"Mrs. Praetzel, do you need a recess?" Judge Davis asked.

Aleta didn't respond. Stanley spoke on her behalf.

"Not at this time, Your Honor. She simply needs to temporarily withdraw as an interpreter."

"Is Mr. Praetzel representing you legally?"

Stanley looked toward Aleta. "You may nod to affirm or shake your head to deny."

As expected, Judge Davis took exception. "She will answer verbally. You know the rules."

"I have forbidden her to speak," Stanley said.

"You realize I can hold you in contempt."

"As Your Honor wishes."

"I can also hold her in contempt."

"As Your Honor wishes," Stanley repeated. "However, that would not serve the purpose for which we are here which is to aid Mr. Hoskinson. Since Aleta has helped us establish Mr. Hoskinson's mental acuity, perhaps we can determine his wishes by questioning him."

Mr. Hoskinson let forth a gush of syllables which considering the spittle accompanying them, those present assumed were replete with cuss words.

"I'll allow it—temporarily," Judge Davis said, deciding not to press Aleta to speak. Perhaps her husband had a better handle on her physical state then she did. "Please, Mr. Johanson, save your objections for specifics."

Johanson swallowed his objection. As long as he could object during the proceeding, he was satisfied.

"Mr. Hoskinson," Stanley began, "you are not happy with this arrangement, correct?"

Hoskinson nodded and Judge Davis put the nod in as part of the record.

"You asked that I be given power of attorney over your financial affairs, true?"

Again a nod. Johanson tensed and stepped forward. He was standing on the left of the bed and his movement was obvious.

Stanley went on, "I am refusing such an assignment. Do you understand?"

The nod was reluctant. Johanson relaxed visibly and stepped back.

"This upsets you, doesn't it?"

The nod was vigorous. The nuances of emotion in the nods were lost when the recorder typed in the judge's words verbally verifying that the witness nodded.

"Are you willing to consider giving one of your sons power of attorney over your financial matters?"

Hoskinson shook his head and uttered a long verbal answer as he looked at Aleta.

"Your Honor, please ask Mr. Hoskinson to refrain from addressing my client directly."

"Mr. Hoskinson, answer Mr. Praetzel's questions. Do not attempt to invoke Mrs. Praetzel's help at this time."

"Thank you, Your Honor," Stanley said continuing.

"What about Mr. Johanson?"

Again a head shake.

"Are you willing to allow the court to act as your trustee in financial matters?"

Again a head shake.

Johanson smiled. Old man Hoskinson was going to stone wall them.

"Is this refusal because you want to have the option to approve of whomever the court appoints to oversee your affairs?"

The head nod was vigorous.

Stanley turned toward his mother. "Your Honor, if it please the court I believe I have a candidate that Mr. Hoskinson will find acceptable."

"Present your candidate."

Stanley turned back to Mr. Hoskinson. "Yesterday when Mrs. Praetzel visited, she was accompanied by her grandmother, Harriet Locke. Mrs. Locke knows your condition and she knows that Aleta can interpret your wishes. On top of that, she's just retired, so she may have some time available. What you may not know, Mr. Hoskinson, is that she retired from Atherton Bank located in Oakland, California where she was a Vice President in the Trust Department. She handled a trust of considerable size personally and I can give you four personal references as to her ability and integrity."

As he was speaking, Mr. Hoskinson's head began nodding.

Stanley finished with a question. "If the court appointed her, would you approve?"

The nod was vigorous.

"Your Honor, I believe I can reach Mrs. Locke and we can settle this matter within the hour," Stanley said. "In the meantime, I believe Mr. Hoskinson has another matter to bring up. I believe it has something to do with Mr. Johanson."

The nod was vigorous again and the judge ordered Stanley to make the call while she questioned Mr. Hoskinson herself.

"Is it this matter relevant to this hearing, Mr. Hoskinson?" Judge Davis asked.

Hoskinson nodded.

"Mr. Johanson, please enlighten the court as to what Mr. Hoskinson is referring."

"His will."

Hoskinson nodded.

"Mr. Hoskinson, do you want to change your will?"

The head nodded and the eyes looked over at his lawyer. Mr. Johanson nervously adjusted his tie.

"Did you ask your lawyer to make the changes?"

Hoskinson nodded.

"Mr. Johanson, is this true?"

"Yes, Your Honor. I have the new will with me. There is only one section that was changed. That was the section pertinent to the method his sons would inherit."

"Do you have a copy of the old will with you?"

"Yes, Your Honor."

"Let me see it and the new will, please."

The judge began comparing the wills. Stanley went over and put his hand on his wife's shoulder. He could tell that Aleta had calmed down.

She looked at him questioningly. He shook his head. She didn't know it, but he still felt a tenseness in her body. Dr. Cook had said stress could bring on another stroke. He knew if he took her from the room and Mr. Hoskinson was left alone, she would only fret. The situation had to be resolved with her present.

Aleta was puzzled by Stanley's action, still she felt good that Stanley had managed to extricate himself from a responsibility he didn't want and still help Mr. Hoskinson. She felt a great deal of empathy with Lars Hoskinson's situation. She'd brushed against it too recently not to have the fear it engendered quickly reawakened by seeing someone else robbed of the power to form words. She had come out of that dark hole within days. The pit he was in was deeper. He might never climb out.

When Judge Davis finished scanning both wills, stopping only at the changed sections to study them carefully, she nodded at her clerk who prepared to again take down what was said.

"Mr. Hoskinson, I am going to read aloud just the changed portion of your will. If you find the change acceptable, we will proceed to have you sign the new will now."

Mr. Hoskinson said something and Judge Davis said, "I'm assuming that you are saying that you cannot use your right hand; however, a mark with your left properly witnessed will suffice."

Mr. Hoskinson nodded and the judge read the changed section aloud and added the gist of the portion completely deleted.

It was then Aleta discovered that Mr. Hoskinson had pitted his sons against each other with the winner taking over control of all nine lumberyards.

The new will gave his eldest son, Cliff, the five lumberyards in Illinois and Indiana and Neil, the younger son, the lumberyards in Iowa and Ohio.

As the will was being signed the door opened and Chief Lyle West and Harriet Locke entered. Both were dressed in camouflaged hunting gear including heavy boots and winter jackets.

Lyle, seeing Judge Davis, apologized, explaining that the call had indicated that the matter was urgent. While he was speaking Harriet rushed over to her granddaughter.

"Are you alright?" she asked.

Stanley answered, "She is fine, Mrs. Locke."

Harriet nodded. She guessed that Stanley had invoked that weird order of his. Now was no time to make a scene so she kissed her granddaughter lightly on the forehead and stepped back.

Judge Davis stated that there was one more matter before the court.

"Mrs. Locke," she said, addressing Harriet, "Mr. Hoskinson has asked the court to appoint someone to handle his financial affairs. It has been suggested you might be willing to serve the court in this capacity. It appears you have the qualifications to do this."

"Am I to assume that Aleta has not lost her ability to understand him?"

"Correct."

"Then the answer is yes."

"I protest this appointment," Oscar Johanson declared. "What's to keep her from absconding with Mr. Hoskinson's money?"

Laughter greeted the suspicion. It was Lyle West who spoke up. "Because Mrs. Locke has been dealing in other people's millions for years without absconding with a cent."

West's statement attesting to Harriet Locke's trust worthiness tickled a faint recollection in Oscar Johanson's memory of some trustee of the now famous Tontine Trust who had moved to Willow Glen to retire. Could this be the woman standing in front of him outfitted like a hunter. He had a difficult time putting this person together with his stereotypical image of a female financial wizard. It didn't fit. Still, even in hunting gear she had a decisiveness he wasn't used to in older women. She'd said yes without a moment's hesitation.

The granddaughter appeared much weaker. Her adherence to her husband's wishes harked back to an era before he was born. He knew the Catholic Church imposed such restrictions on its priests and nuns at certain times, but this was a modern woman, a California attorney no less, and they were in a court of law. Then he remembered that she was willing to go to jail to support his decision. That took a different kind of guts.

He wasn't the only one impressed. Chief Peets, who'd never seen the like of what was happening in this room was glad no one was looking at him as he knew he was gaping much of the time. Ed Ornstein, standing in the far corner, was enjoying the whole scene. He'd come from California on Trust business with Aleta and was present when she and Stanley met. It had been a wild ride since then.

Mr. Hoskinson realized that while Aleta had indeed brought her husband, this man knew how to handle his wife, him and the court. He would not anger him again.

Stanley leaned over and whispered in Aleta's ear. She glanced at him and he nodded. She rose and took her former place at the front of the bed.

"Mr. Hoskinson," she said clearly. "Do you have any other business to bring before this court?"

The old man relieved that she was again his interpreter managed a short question.

"Your Honor," Aleta said turning to address the judge. "Mr. Hoskinson would like to know when the power of attorney orders go into effect?"

"Immediately," Judge Davis said.

Her clerk extracted two prepared forms filled in the blanks and handed them to the judge to sign.

Mr. Hoskinson again spoke.

Aleta repeated his concern.

"He also wants to ask if I can authorize his being moved. It appears his doctor recommended therapy but his sons didn't want to spend the money given the poor prognosis, so they moved him here. He heard the doctor say therapy could possibly restore some of his speech."

"You may order that," Judge Davis replied, "as well as any other therapy he wants and any other aid he may desire."

"I need to transfer money to the hospital to guarantee payment," Harriet said to Lars Hoskinson. "Your insurance may not cover this transfer from this home to a hospital on the basis of your desire."

Hoskinson uttered a long string of syllables, none of which Harriet understood. Aleta, however did.

"He agrees to prepaying the hospital. He also wants to transfer the money in his checking to an account only Mrs. Locke can access."

Johanson objected vociferously. "Your Honor. His sons should have access."

Hoskinson shook his head violently.

"It appears the answer is no," Judge Davis said. "All these matters have the court's approval. Court adjourned."

Her clerk stopped recording and the two left immediately.

Hoskinson continued speaking. Aleta translated.

"Now he wants everyone to leave but Mr. Ornstein and me."

"Lyle, can you drop me at the bank?" Harriet asked. "I need to take care of this matter immediately."

"Chief Peets," Aleta said, "will you arrange for the ambulance? And choose Mr. Hoskinson's location in the hospital? And see to his protection until we can hire a bodyguard?"

"Yes, Ma'am," Peets said. "I'll do all that."

Hoskinson uttered a short couple of syllables.

"I will accompany Mr. Hoskinson to the hospital," Aleta told the chief. Stanley heard her.

"Call me when you need to be picked up," Stanley said, closing the door behind him.

Hoskinson began to speak before the door was completely shut. It didn't matter. No one in the corridor could understand a word he was saying.

Aleta translated quickly.

"Something's going on at some of my lumberyards. My bookkeeper argued with me about what he called a foolish competition. He said I'd rue the day I set my sons against each other."

She translated his words for Ed and then added, "But that's over. He's the reason I finally changed my will. He was a good man with sound judgment. And this was the first time I hadn't listened to him."

Aleta translated and Ed took over the conversation.

"Was?" Ed asked. "He's dead?"

"He had a massive stroke."

"When did he first notice something was wrong?"

"He didn't say anything was wrong. It just wasn't right. Neil was making too much profit."

"Where was it coming from?"

"Increased lumber sales."

"So he's a good salesman."

"I been in this business a long time. Lumber sales are steady. They can go up when there's a surge of building, but, there ain't none in Elyria."

"You had the sales figures checked against the inventory?" Ed asked.

"That's the first thing I had the new bookkeeper do. Whatever Neil is doing, he's doing it off the books."

"Just Neil?"

"Yeah, until about four months ago, the two boys were neck in neck, then Neil's net profit started to rise in all his lumberyards."

"What if I concentrated on one lumberyard?" Ed asked. "Chances are the same thing's going on in all of them."

"Start with Elyria, Ohio. That was the first."

When Stanley and Aleta arrived home a little before six, they were greeted by three exuberant Chessies.

"Grams, are you here?" Aleta called as Stanley took her cloak from her shoulders and hung it up.

"No, the dogs came over by themselves," she called back. "We're back in the utility room looking at the ducks."

Aleta rushed back and looked at the row of dressed ducks. "Wow! You had a great day!"

"Sent a couple home with Lyle along with a loaf of Bertha's homemade bread."

Stanley joined them.

"So that's what I smelled when I came in. What else is cooking?"

"Spaghetti, and I'm staying for dinner," Harriet announced, "since I had a hand in making it. Bertha wanted to finish up dressing the ducks."

Bertha washed her hands in the laundry room sink while Harriet finished bagging the ducks destined for the freezer as well as the ones that would be refrigerated until Saturday's party.

"If you're going to have parties all the time, you need a second refrigerator," Harriet said.

"I can take three home with me," Bertha said, putting three wrapped ducks in a paper bag.

"So, did Ed take the job?" Harriet asked, picking up two ducks and taking them to the refrigerator.

"Yes," Aleta said. "But Stanley told me I shouldn't talk about it."

"Well, Ed will tell me if he needs my help," Harriet said as Stoney followed her walking on his rear legs, sniffing the ducks which she was holding away from him. "Yes, Stoney, these are your ducks. And yes, I gave Morgan his. No, I didn't mix them up. And no, you aren't eating any, at least not until after Saturday night when, if you are very good, you might get some leftovers."

"Bertha, before you leave, where are the scissors?" Aleta called when she saw her housekeeper at the door.

"In the pencil holder," came the reply. "Good night."

"Thanks for doing the ducks," Aleta said. "That was a big job."

"It was fun to be doing some again," Bertha said as she closed the door.

"Should we eat first?" Harriet asked.

"I'm too curious about the package addressed to me," Aleta said, plucking the scissors from the holder. "I can't guess what it is."

Harriet took the salad out of the refrigerator. "Oh, Stoney, doesn't like one of your packages."

"Really?" Aleta asked. "Which one?"

"The square box."

"Well, we'll soon find out what's inside," Aleta said heading toward it from across the room. Stoney was already nosing it, growling.

"He's growling at it," Aleta laughed. "What is it, Stoney?"

When she reached for it, the big dog knocked her hand away.

"Boy, Grams, he really doesn't like it. He won't let me touch it."

Harriet left the kitchen area where Stanley was helping her set the table.

"Show me," she said.

Aleta extended her hand with the scissors in it toward the box.

Stoney growled and pushed it away.

"Try without the scissors," Harriet suggested. "Maybe they have a smell on them he doesn't like."

Aleta put down the scissors and then reached for the package. Stoney growled as he shoved her hand aside.

"Maybe he just doesn't want me to open a package," Aleta suggested.

"See if he'll let you pick up the other one."

Aleta reached for the slender box from Marshall Fields and Stoney didn't object.

"I guess he knows its silver," Aleta said. "And he's not into silver."

"It's something else," Harriet said. "He's acting odd."

"Think maybe we should call someone?"

"Like who?"

"Like Milani," Aleta said. "Suppose this time someone sent us a bomb in the mail? I mean, think about it. When we were handling the Dobbins case, that guy put a bomb under our car."

"He's in jail," Harriet pointed out.

"He could've gotten someone to do it."

"Why?"

"Revenge."

Stanley, who'd paused to listen, came over and looked at the package. He immediately opened his cell phone. "Tom," the two women heard him say. "We think someone may have sent us a bomb... Aleta, back away... The dog won't let her open the package... No, he let us open another one... Okay."

He turned to the two ladies. "He said we should take the dogs and leave the house until he gets here."

"We can't just put it out?"

"He doesn't want us to touch it."

"What about supper?" Aleta worried. "It'll burn."

"It's on low. It won't burn," Harriet said. "Let's go."

An hour later, Tom Milani joined the three for supper. "It's Rachel's choir night. I get leftovers," he explained. "Besides I love home baked bread."

"They're sure it's a bomb."

"They'll call me when they know more; but no one ties a package with wire inserted in twine except a bomber.

They'll try to remove the wrapping without exploding the bomb, but my guess is that there aren't any good prints."

He took a forkful of spaghetti before asking, "Stanley, why'd you call?"

"We told him the dog was acting funny," Aleta replied.

Milani, his mouth full, raised a brow in query as he looked at Stanley. "Is that it?"

"There was no postmark. And the mailman would have left it in the box," Stanley replied. "And the zip on the return address was wrong."

"Who wants Aleta dead now?" Tom asked.

"Why Aleta? " Harriet inquired.

"The package was addressed to me, Grams," Aleta said. "Could it have anything to do with Mr. Hoskinson?"

"Or Bertha," Stanley added.

Aleta protested, "It can't have anything to do with Bertha."

"This Hoskinson…," Tom began, and then interrupted himself, "Nobody who bakes like this can have a bad bone in her body."

"That's your stomach speaking," Aleta laughed.

"Don't the dogs like her?"

"Yeah," Aleta admitted. "They really do."

"Ed Ornstein says the dogs always know."

"Now, you're taking advice from a P.I.? "Stanley joshed.

"When it's good advice, I am. Besides, West says Ed's one sharp cookie and I do listen to West."

"So that just leaves someone connected with Hoskinson," Stanley mused. "But why Aleta?"

"Maybe whoever tried to kill him before doesn't want him able to communicate. Maybe he knows something."

"How about it Aleta. A death threat releases you," Stanley said.

"All he knows is that one of his sons is making too much profit."

"That sure isn't a good motive to kill someone," Milani said. "Maybe he doesn't know what he knows."

Chapter 5

The next morning when Stanley was helping Aleta dress, he noticed she seemed depressed and asked her what was troubling her.

"I really brought trouble upon us, didn't I?"

"Well, if it's any consolation, you didn't bring it. Trouble seems drawn to you. That's all."

"If you had known…," she began.

"I did know."

Slowly, Stanley began unbuttoning her blouse.

"You're really upset," Aleta said. "You're suppose to be helping me dress, not undress."

"Your grandmother's dogs are out," Stanley murmured kissing her on the neck just under her ear.

"We haven't time!" she protested.

"You aren't the only one who can fool with the clocks."

"Why did you do that?"

"Because I knew you were upset last night and would mention it when I was rushing to leave."

"How much time do we have?"

"Enough for me to convince you that I truly love you and am not angry with you about anything."

Aleta sat down on the edge of the bed. "Go ahead. I'm listening."

"Lay down. I want to communicate with you while you're completely relaxed."

"I'm only half dressed. And you aren't dressed at all."

"Don't worry. Dr. Cook was pretty specific about no sexual activity with your shoulder still healing."

Gently cradling her, Stanley helped her lay back on the bed. He kissed her gently on her lips. It was a long, sweet kiss and she relaxed in the love it conveyed.

She opened her eyes when he finished and she murmured, "I'm convinced."

"You want me to waste the rest of my plan?"

She saw the twinkle in his eyes. "You won't do it even if I say yes."

"No more than you did," he grinned. "Today it's my turn."

"Sex isn't the end all," she whispered as he kissed her on the neck.

"No, it isn't," he murmured. "It just adds emphasis to the spoken word."

"Emphasis is good," she said. It was the last utterance she made for twenty minutes.

"I smell coffee," Stanley announced rising.

"But Bertha can't be here. It's too early."

Aleta woke from her dreamlike state with a sharp query, "What did you do to the clock?"

"Pushed it ahead an hour."

"If it's not Bertha, it must be Grams."

"Rats!"

"What's wrong?"

"I wanted to talk. It was important."

"Go ahead. If she needs us, she'll knock," Aleta said.

"She expects us to dress first."

"About yesterday…," he began hesitantly.

"Oh, you mean the thing in the room," Aleta remembered aloud, "I figured you had a reason."

"I did it because I thought you'd reached your stress limit."

"Maybe you need to let me test my limit."

"And risk another stroke so soon after the last one?"

"Life is going to get stressful. I need to be able to handle it."

"Aleta, you will be eventually. But right now you have limits. At mother's house I sensed things were going awry. You have no idea how I've regretted not stepping in."

He saw her struggling to pull up her slacks and decided he'd help her dress first.

"My stroke wasn't your fault," she declared.

"Actually, it was. You stress out more over me than anything else. Do you think that I'm going to fallout of love with you if things get rough? Think about that today, will you? It's the key."

"So you're saying that if I stop worrying about you, I won't have another stroke?"

"I may regret saying that," Stanley said. "This is not a license to divorce me, just to stop worrying that I'm fragile."

"Fragile! That's not how I see you!" Aleta objected vociferously.

"Yes, it is. Sunday you were sure I couldn't handle my mother. Yesterday, you were afraid I couldn't handle Hoskinson's demands."

Aleta was silent. Could he be right?

He slipped her arm back into its sling and said, "Now go see why your grandmother's here while I finish dressing."

Pensive, Aleta entered the kitchen.

"Oh, good, you're up," Harriet said cheerfully. "I'm flying to Elyria this morning. You know it took two pots of coffee before you realized I was here. So there's plenty. I've already filled my thermos."

"When did you decide to fly to Elyria?"

"Last night. Martha's loaning me her plane and pilot," Harriet said. "I'll be back for your party."

"Couldn't this trip have waited until Monday?"

"Ed's meeting me." She went on, "We'll fly back together."

"I thought you were going to go to the hospital with me to go over Mr. Hoskinson's financial affairs with him," Aleta protested weakly.

This was too sudden a change of plans.

"Ed found another set of books," Harriet said. "Tell Mr. Hoskinson I'll see him Sunday," Harriet said as she poured a cup of coffee into a mug and headed for the front door.

"Where are you going?" Aleta asked.

"To give Joe a fresh cup of coffee," Harriet said.

She opened the door and handed the mug through the narrow opening.

"Joe? Who's Joe?" Aleta called after her.

"Milani has given you a bodyguard," Harriet said closing the door and walking back into the kitchen.

"I don't want a bodyguard!" Aleta exclaimed angrily.

"It's going to happen. Stanley insisted."

"Stanley did? No wonder he…"

"He what?"

"Skip it."

"Sex, huh," Harriet said with only a slight hint of a smirk. "Used to work with your grandfather every time."

"Grams!" Aleta protested, shocked.

"Your father wasn't conceived immaculately."

Embarrassed, Aleta said, "Tell me my bodyguard isn't wearing a uniform."

Harriet couldn't help herself. The smile just erupted. "Full uniform. I think Milani even made him shine his badge."

Aleta groaned.

"It gets worse," Harriet said. "You're going to ride everywhere in a squad car."

"Ugh!"

"Tom's looking forward to your party. Rachel is buying a new dress. He's going to do everything he can so Rachel can wear it," Harriet commented lightly.

Aleta remained dour. "Bet Joe wishes he'd never joined the force."

"On the contrary, the men drew straws for the privilege of guarding you. You're the closest thing to a crime wave this town has seen in years."

"Milani tell you that?"

"Joe did. He's only got you for four hours. He's hoping you'll go somewhere."

"Grams, do people tell you everything?"

"Gotta go," Harriet said, picking up her thermos.

"Stanley says I think he's fragile."

"You always do that?" Harriet returned irritated.

"What?"

"Bring up what's bothering you just as someone's about to go somewhere. It's as if you're afraid of the response."

"That's what Stanley said a few minutes ago," Aleta retorted. She hated when people told her what she habitually did.

"No wonder you fussed so about the bodyguard," Harriet commented.

Aleta's annoyance increased. "Well, do I think that? He says that's the reason I had my stroke."

"If I were you, I'd weigh what he says carefully. The man is an astute observer of what makes people tick."

"But fragile? I don't think that!" Aleta exploded suddenly. "I couldn't! He's wrong."

"Well, he could be. He's only human, after all."

"That's a terrible word to apply to a man!" Aleta charged, her anger still gripping her tight. "I would never call him that."

"As I recall, he used the word, not you."

"To tell me how I saw him," Aleta countered.

"He's the one you need to talk with," Harriet concluded, putting on her coat.

"I can't do that. That would make it seem important."

"He already thinks that."

"But I don't want to hurt him," Aleta protested.

"He brought it up. Ask him to elaborate. That won't hurt."

"You don't understand," Aleta charged.

Harriet walked over and kissed her granddaughter lightly. "See you Saturday."

When Stanley emerged from the bedroom, he found Aleta alone at the kitchen table. She was cradling a mug of coffee.

"She left," Aleta stated gloomily.

"So we can talk?" he asked hopefully.

"She knew I was upset and she left anyway," Aleta muttered.

"She didn't leave you alone," Stanley noted.

"She left me with a man who thinks I think he's fragile and told me to talk about it with him."

"So she did leave us so we could talk."

"She went to Elyria."

"She left?"

"That's what I said," Aleta said. "You don't ever listen to me, do you?"

"Whoa!" Stanley exclaimed. "What page are we on?"

"Does it matter?"

"Yes, it does. I can't do anything if we're on your grandmother's page. So turn back to my page. Why does the word 'fragile' bother you so?"

"Because you aren't!" she shot back angrily.

"Talk about denial," Stanley said. "I hit a nerve, didn't I?"

"I hate being misunderstood!" Aleta declared, her anger rising.

"You feel misunderstood?" Stanley asked calmly.

"Don't patronize me!" Aleta shot back.

"I think I take back what I said," Stanley said with a hint of a smile. "I guess you don't think I'm fragile after all."

"That's better," Aleta said, calming down at once.

"At least not all the time," he added.

The sound of a car driving around the house to the rear alerted both of them. Aleta looked at the clock.

"Bertha's early," Aleta observed.

"Good!" Stanley said.

"Good?" Aleta queried. "Good as in now we can stop talking and I can leave early or good as in I can sit down and have breakfast with my lonely wife."

"I rather liked the breakfast on a tray by the door," Stanley said.

"Not today," Aleta said with mock sternness. "Sit!"

Bertha, who entered through the back door, upon seeing both Praetzels seated at the breakfast table, threw her coat and purse on the washer and hurried into the kitchen, apologizing.

"Grams woke us early, Bertha," Aleta explained. "Stanley just agreed to have breakfast at the table with me this morning."

"Coffee, Sir?" Bertha offered, seeing that it was ready.

"Yes, please. And pancakes."

While Bertha flew around the kitchen, Stanley told her about the package that contained a bomb.

"Will we be getting more of those, Sir?" she asked politely.

"I'm only telling you about this so all my warnings will make sense. No one comes in this house for any reason. The police guard outside will accompany Aleta today."

"Yes, Sir. But what about the delivery of party supplies Mrs. West ordered? They're supposed to be delivered today."

"What party supplies?" Aleta asked.

"Tables, chairs, table cloths, candles, you know."

"I thought we were having a buffet."

"Mrs. West changed that. It's a formal sit down dinner with four tables of six and we need one more guest."

"We could just have an odd number at one table," Stanley suggested.

"No we can't," Aleta said firmly. "Tell Mrs. West to invite Bessie Dobbins. Evelyn can pick her up."

"Yes, Ma'am," Bertha said. "And the delivery?"

"I'll talk to Chief Milani," Stanley said.

Aleta Praetzel walked into Lars Hoskinson's hospital room a few minutes after eight. His doctor was already making notes on his chart.

Aleta introduced herself and said that she had Mr. Hoskinson's medical power of attorney.

"You won't mind if I check with his sons," the doctor said coolly.

"Court ordered," Aleta said. "Yesterday."

"Exactly who are you?"

"His interpreter," Aleta replied. "I can understand him. He has some questions."

"Listen, lady…"

"Mrs. Praetzel."

"Listen, Mrs. Praetzel, I am not revealing privileged medical information to you without some proof."

"Isn't it in his chart?" Aleta said. "He was moved back to the hospital on my authority."

"I'm going to check this out with his sons."

"We already know their wishes are contrary to his."

Dr. Cook appeared at the door. "Excuse me, Dr. King, may I talk with Aleta for a moment?"

"You know her?"

"She's my patient," Dr. Cook said. "By the way, Aleta, how are you today?"

"Fine, thank you," Aleta replied.

Dr. King then noticed a scar on her head. That, together with the sling, made him nod his head knowingly. A patient with a mental problem, he surmised. Dr. Cook would remove her with a few words.

To his surprise Dr. Cook didn't escort her out. Instead he walked across the room and shook Mr. Hoskinson's hand.

"Good morning, Mr. Hoskinson. I'm going to need to borrow your interpreter."

There was a barrage of garbled sound. Dr. Cook looked at Aleta who responded.

"He says he needs me. His doctor won't listen to me and he wants his therapy to start today."

"Brice, can I help here?" Dr. Cook asked.

Impatient, Brice King said, "You can remove your patient from this room.

"Brice, remember how you told me you'd like to meet one of the ladies of that big Tontine Trust?"

Dr. King surveyed the young woman standing in front of him. "They are all older women," he said knowingly.

"That they are. May I present their lawyer, Mrs. Aleta Praetzel, granddaughter of Harriet Locke," Dr. Cook said. "And, Brice, she really does have Mr. Hoskinson's power of attorney. I wouldn't mess with her. Her husband's Stanley Praetzel, her mother-in-law is Judge Davis, her best friend is Lauren West and she is one of my grandmother's special friends."

Aleta watched Brice King's face slowly drain of color.

"Stanley was worried about you."

"He called?"

"Well, you are not even a week away from your own stroke. Last night had to be stressful."

Mr. Hoskinson muttered a few nonsensical words.

Aleta turned to him. "Someone sent a package to my house with a bomb in it. It was addressed to me."

"This gift of yours, Aleta, have you tried it on anyone else?"

"I haven't been led to," Aleta said.

"I've got a stroke patient who is panicky but I don't know about what. No one even knows her name. She's homeless. Maybe you could see if you might be able to understand enough to help us help her."

Mr. Hoskinson mumbled a long string of syllables which Aleta promptly translated.

Dr. Brice King noted every order on the chart. "I'll have the therapists start today," he said.

Mr. Hoskinson mumbled a short spiel of unintelligible sounds and Aleta answered his directly.

"She flew to Elyria this morning. Ed found a second set of books."

More queries poured forth in a jumble of sound that was beyond the sharpness of either doctor to make sense of.

Again Aleta responded directly. "Chief West got a court order from the judge and took Grams to your house to gather your financial records. She'll talk to you Sunday."

Minutes later Aleta entered another hospital room.

The sight of a strange woman accompanied by a police officer in full uniform frightened the women in the bed. Her gaunt weathered face paled. Her eyes widened in fear and she babbled an incoherent word. Her body was writhing under the restraints.

"What's your dog's name?" Aleta asked calmly.

The writhing stopped. More sounds tumbled out.

"King," Aleta repeated. "No I'm not from Animal Control. I do like dogs though, so I can see that he's cared for. Where is he?"

More sounds were spit out.

Aleta turned toward the officer standing beside her, repeated her words and asked Joe if he knew where that was. He replied that he did. The woman in the bed became agitated again and more unintelligible words spilled out.

"Don't worry," Aleta replied. "He's not going to take him to the pound. I'm going to find a temporary home for him."

More utterances poured out.

"I wouldn't trust me either if I were in your shoes. It's scary not to be able to communicate. I know. But Dr. Cook will tell you that I'm good with dogs and I keep my promises."

Dr. Cook nodded his affirmation. "She's a friend of mine. She loves dogs."

The woman began to cry and her next words brought tears to Aleta's eyes. She took the woman's hand. Don't worry about your pup. We'll go get him immediately."

"Aleta, in case you've forgotten, you have only one good arm. And Joe here might scare the pup. Take someone who knows dogs with you."

"You're right. I need help. I'll call Lauren."

"Isn't she getting ready for your party?"

"It's a Lab pup," Aleta said.

"Call Lyle," Dr. Cook said. "That's his job."

"What's his job—to rescue puppies?"

"To serve and protect. And you're serving my patient by protecting her puppy," Dr. Cook said. "Tell him I ordered it. Doctors can order police chiefs around, you know."

Aleta smiled impishly. "No, I didn't, but I'm going to love getting his reaction to that statement."

Lyle met Aleta and Joe near the abandoned railroad depot. The three entered the dilapidated building and moved through the shadowy interior to a door at the far end. They heard a faint whimpering on the other side.

"I'll open it," Aleta said. "You be prepared to catch him if he runs out. His name is King."

But the dog didn't run out. It stood by the wreck of a bed, tethered, tail wagging tentatively. A plastic dish was tipped over near his head. It had been chewed lightly. Aleta guessed it was his water dish.

She bent down and petted him gently while Lyle untied the rope securing him to the bed. The pup licked her hand.

"He needs a vet," Lyle said.

"He needs love and food," Aleta declared.

"And a bath," Joe added.

The two looked over at him and then at each other.

"You carry him," they chorused.

"Me?" Joe protested. "I'm on duty."

Lyle glared at him and Aleta snickered.

Joe was immediately apologetic. "I'm sorry, Sir. Of course, so are you. Of course, I'll carry him."

"Gently," Aleta said.

He bent down and picked up the pup. He did it carefully and carried the pup to his patrol car. He laid him on the floor in the back. Aleta climbed in beside King and stroked his head. He laid his head on her foot.

They drove straight to her house. His replacement was waiting for him at the door. Joe picked up the pup and followed Aleta inside.

Joe whispered as he went inside, "You're in for a wild ride, Gary, unless she's too worn out to keep going."

"Hope not," Gary said.

He wasn't to be disappointed. Aleta reappeared immediately. "Come on, we have to go to the pet store and get some things."

"Yes Ma'am," he said eager not to be stuck standing outside the door for four hours.

They rode in Gary's squad to the pet store near Stanley's office and she bought everything from shampoo to a large bed for King to sleep on.

"What's your housekeeper doing with the pup now?" Gary asked as he loaded the trunk.

"Feeding it cottage cheese. Petting it. Letting it follow her around," Aleta replied. "Making friends. I think she wants to keep it."

"Won't it be hard on it to be left alone all day?"

"Oh, Bertha will bring him to work," Aleta said. "King's a nice pup. After we drop this stuff off, we need to go back to the hospital."

"Good," Gary exclaimed.

"You're full of energy, aren't you?"

"Yes, Ma'am."

When they arrived at the house, Joe's patrol car was still parked near the house. Before Aleta could worry, Joe emerged from the house in shirt-sleeves and offered to help carry stuff in.

"Why are you still here?" Gary asked handing his counterpart the dog bed and the dog food.

"Milani says I should stay and supervise the delivery of the party stuff," Joe replied. "Bertha is sponging off my coat. It got muddy."

Gary carried in a second bag and a medium-sized dog crate. Joe was sent back out to get the exercise pen which was in a large box.

Bertha ordered the two cops to unpack it and then disappeared into the bedroom to help Aleta.

They heard her scold Aleta when the two emerged a bit later. "You need lunch, Ma'am. Everyone will be upset with me if you don't eat."

Aleta paused. "You're right. They will be. Fix me a milk shake."

Bertha bit her lip and murmured, "Yes, Ma'am."

Ten minutes later Aleta was on her way back to the hospital.

"I need to talk to the homeless woman who owns the pup. Maybe I can get her to give him up."

"Can't you just take him? He was in pretty bad shape."

"She did her best by him", Aleta said. "She cares about him."

At the hospital, to Gary's surprise, Aleta was greeted warmly by the nursing staff and taken straight to the stroke victim's room.

"Good afternoon," Aleta said. "I forgot to ask your name."

The woman muttered a few syllables.

"Stella Lemay?" Aleta repeated. The nurse wrote it on her chart.

The woman spoke again.

"I'm sorry, but while I can understand you, the others can't. I don't know if it was because I had a stroke this week or something else. And I don't know how long I'll have this gift. I need to tell you about your pup and ask you to do him a favor."

Slowly, Aleta went over finding him and where she took him and the person who fell in love with him and would like him for her own.

"She's a working woman, but he will go to work with her everyday. She lost her husband recently and she needs someone to talk to, to take care of, to love. She will be good to him. He is already following her everywhere."

The woman babbled a few words. Try as he could, Gary could make no sense out of the syllables.

Aleta took the woman's hand and said, "Bless you. You truly have saved this pup's life. Because of you, he will have a good future."

The woman spoke again.

Aleta smiled and turned to the nurse. "No Jell-O. She hates Jell-O. She loves pudding, especially chocolate pudding."

The woman nodded then spoke again.

"And whoever feeds her should ask her if she likes the food. She dislikes certain foods. And she can think. She wants you to know that."

The nurse jotted notes on Stella's chart.

"Will she get speech therapy?" Aleta asked.

"She's indigent," the nurse said softly.

"Put her down for all the therapy she needs," Aleta said.

"Her dog is picking up the tab. Tell Dr. Cook. He'll understand."

"What will I understand?" Wayne Cook said entering the room.

"Do you want speech therapy?" Aleta asked Stella.

The head nodded.

"Will you work hard?"

Again there was a nod.

Dr. Cook smiled. "Then you shall have it Stella."

"Her dog's paying for it," Aleta said. "One good turn deserves another."

"And where exactly do we send the bill," Wayne Cook grinned.

"To my house, of course. King is my housekeeper's dog. It's one of the perks that comes with being employed by us."

"Does Stanley know this?" Wayne asked knowing full well Aleta's word was enough.

"Stanley will do whatever I ask."

Wayne grinned. "So he's one of us after all."

Aleta eyed him askance. "Just what does that mean?"

"I came to ask a favor," Wayne said. "A colleague of mine, Dr. Chesney would like you to speak to a special patient."

"Wayne, I don't know if I can talk with all stroke victims. I may only be able to understand when there's a life at stake."

"A dog's life?"

"I think God likes dogs," Aleta quipped. "He counts the feathers on birds."

"Well, let's hope this patient has a bird or a dog or a fish," Wayne commented. "Will you try?"

Aleta turned to Stella. "Even if I can't understand you tomorrow, I'll come back and tell you how King is doing, okay?"

Stella nodded.

Gary followed the two to another floor wondering how much danger this woman could be in here. Still, crazies could pop up anywhere, so he kept his guard up. Milani had said that he hoped the presence of one of his officers in full uniform would deter a would-be assassin.

Wayne escorted Aleta into a private room. A tall white-haired man was holding the patient's hand. He turned as they entered.

"Dr. Chesney, Aleta Praetzel."

The doctor shook Aleta's free hand as Wayne Cook helped her remove her cape. Gary waited outside the open door. He blocked it with his body.

The woman uttered a few syllables.

"I'm glad to meet you Elizabeth," Aleta said. "I'm guessing Dr. Chesney told you I can understand the speech of some stroke victims."

The tall man gripped Wayne Cook whose height matched his own and began to weep.

The woman spoke.

Aleta turned toward Dr. Chesney. "This is your wife?"

Unable to speak, he nodded.

"She says she cannot nod her head," Aleta said. "I'm not sure how to let you know... wait... yes, Elizabeth that would work."

Aleta faced the doctors.

"She says to watch her eyes. She'll blink once for yes; twice for no."

The two men moved close to the bed. Aleta told them she'd simply repeat the woman's words as she heard them. They nodded mutely. For Dr. Chesney this was fervently wished-for, prayed-for miracle. For Dr. Cook this an unbelievable experience.

"I have a living will, Bernard. I didn't tell you about it because I know you couldn't bear to discuss the inevitable."

Aleta paused. "Ask her to affirm what I'm saying."

She blinked several times.

"Elizabeth, blink just once for yes," Dr. Cook urged.

He was rewarded with a single blink. Aleta went on to tell her husband where the will was. Then she told him how much she loved him and while she couldn't speak, she heard every wonderful thing he'd said to her. Finally, she said that if she died, she was ready. He needed to honor her wishes when the time came."

Aleta interrupted herself. "Give him a chance to talk with you about that."

The woman mumbled.

"Yes, I'll explain. She wants you to read the will and tell her how you feel. She knows she can only answer by blinking, but it's communicating. She wants to communicate with you."

The woman blinked once.

"Now I'm going to give you one more signal," Aleta said. "Blink three times for 'I love you.'"

The woman spoke again.

Aleta laughed. "She's added another phrase. Four blinks means, 'Do it my way.'"

Dr. Chesney managed a rare smile. "She is the bossy one."

Elizabeth blinked once.

"She agrees with you," Dr. Cook said smiling.

"One more thing," Dr. Chesney said, "I need to know if she's in pain."

"Ask her," Aleta said. "If she blinks once, ask her where and how much. I'll come back tomorrow between eight and nine and see if there's anything she forgot."

Dr. Chesney walked them out. His eyes were brimming with tears.

"I didn't know if her mind was still working. I can handle things now. Rudimentary though it is, we can communicate. You will stop in tomorrow, please, even if you lose this ability. She will understand that, I know. She will want to see you."

"If I'm alive, I'll be here," Aleta said. "The cop with me isn't just for decoration. I realized after I promised Stella I would return; I have to be careful about such promises."

Wayne Cook stepped in. "Someone tried to kill her yesterday."

"Why on earth would anyone do that?"

"Because I'm talking to a stroke victim who knows something someone doesn't want anyone to know."

"Why not kill him?"

"That was tried. He was put under police protection. I guess now I'm the threat."

"If there's anyway I can help, let me know."

"Glad you said that," Wayne said. "Now I know who to call seven months from now."

Dr. Chesney looked at Aleta and raised a brow. "You're pregnant?"

Aleta smiled as she nodded.

"Well, congratulations. If you decide you need a real expert, call me."

"She's my patient," Wayne said, "but I'll send you one in a month."

"Who are you deigning to share?" Chesney grinned. He looked at Aleta. "He loves his patients and the most we ever get to do is to consult."

"Well this time you get the patient," Cook said. "I can't handle her pregnancy."

"I'd never thought I'd hear you say that. What's wrong with this one?"

"She's determined that I deliver her baby."

Chesney cocked his head. "You never turn anyone down. Oh, I get it. She's rich and you don't take rich women. Well, send her over. If you want, I'll charge double and send you half and you can assist if you're free."

"That sounds fine. Wait until I tell Yancey. She'll be ecstatic."

"Your wife?" Dr. Chesney asked, his surprise evident.

"Yep, and it's all Aleta and Stanley's fault."

"How's that?"

"Well, first Lauren and Lyle decided to have another baby, and as usual. Yancey said, 'Good for them,' and then Aleta got pregnant and, just like that, she changed her mind."

"What about her golf?" Aleta asked.

"She decided after watching the wave of young teenagers doing well on the circuit that she wants to raise a girl and train her. So I guess we'll keep producing until we come up with a girl that has a talent for the game. Considering neither of our sons does, we may have to have several girls."

"Oh, you poor man," Aleta said tongue-in-cheek. "You are going to get that big family you've been dreaming about. Poor, poor you."

"Are you sure she's pregnant?" Dr. Chesney asked politely.

"She took five pregnancy tests even though I could have told her in a day or two," Wayne Cook said. "She's so excited she is marvelous to live with."

When Dr. Chesney went back to his wife's bedside, Aleta asked Dr. Cook about Elizabeth Chesney's condition.

"It's serious," was all he would say.

When she entered Lars Hoskinson's room, he greeted her with a long series of sounds.

"You need to remember I'm neither your employee nor your child, and I will not be scolded by you."

An apology followed and Aleta accepted it.

"Were there any queries your doctor had you couldn't answer with a yes or no?"

He directed her to a clapboard.

"Good," Aleta said. "Let's answer them."

Hoskinson settled back and responded to each question watching Aleta note his reply on the pages clipped to the clapboard. It went relatively quickly.

When she finished, Aleta said, "Now what do you know that I need to know. Who's trying to kill us and why?"

Hoskinson denied knowing either who or why.

"You'd rather see me dead than give me a hint," Aleta said angrily.

He said all he knew he told Ed Ornstein in her presence and added. "I'm sure it's not Cliff."

"Well, that's something," Aleta said. "What were you planning to do before you had your stroke?"

"Go to Elyria and then Des Moines. I'd know what was wrong if I spent a couple days in each store."

"Neil?" Aleta queried.

"Possibly. Or his managers."

"Two managers in states not close to each other?"

"Okay, it looks like Neil but, he's only at each location one day a week and the sales are up for days after each visit. On top of that, he doesn't know anything about bombs. Neither does his wife. She's a real dummy that one."

"How'd your first therapy go?" Aleta asked.

"Didn't do much."

"They have to evaluate where you are."

"Asked me to do a lot of things I couldn't."

"With your arm?"

"And hand. I couldn't even squeeze the ball. It just fell outta my hand. I didn't get to try much."

"Are you willing to practice?" Aleta said.

"Yeah."

"I'll be right back," she said. When she returned, the therapist was with her. He stuck the ball in Mr. Hoskinson's hand and it rolled out.

"Okay," he said. "If you're sure."

"Mr. Hoskinson," Aleta said. "I'm going to have him tape the ball to your hand so it doesn't rollout. Your brain will have to come up with new pathways to squeeze it. It's the first step to using your hand again. You don't have a lot to do with your day. See if you can find a way to squeeze the ball. If you don't, you don't, but you will have a real chance to try."

He nodded his head and the ball was taped to his hand.

"Note it on the chart," Aleta suggested, "so no one removes it. And, Mr. Hoskinson, I expect no less than two hundred tries. If you lose count, you need to start over."

The succession of sound coming out sounded like it was riding on a wave of anger.

"You said you wanted to work hard," Aleta replied. "So prove it."

"How do you know he'll tell you the truth?" the therapist inquired.

Aleta looked Hoskinson directly in his eyes. "Are you going to lie to me?"

Gary followed her out wondering where this woman the same age as he was picked up such a commanding presence. He didn't doubt Mr. Hoskinson would tell her the truth or that he would complete his task several times over so as to be able to tell her he did what she asked.

"I need to pick up some law books from Lauren West," she said. "Then it's home for me, and you get to freeze your keester standing guard. Sorry about that. I'll have Bertha bring you some coffee."

Chapter 6

Ed Ornstein was at the airport when Harriet Locke's plane, on loan from Martha Cook, landed. He told her he'd booked two rooms in a hotel in Cleveland, then drove her east to Elyria.

He handed her a yellow flyer advertising mold inspection services for a nominal fee by Mold Inspection Limited as a service from Hoskinson Lumber.

"I don't remember seeing any income from this service on the books," Harriet said.

"I had Dean check out this Mold Inspection Limited when I found the flyer," Ed explained.

"Head honcho is Neil Hoskinson. He did some further checking and found out he heads another business called Ozone Testing, Inc."

"But his profits are coming from an increase in lumber sales," Harriet said. "We can't investigate a company he owns that's separate from the lumberyard."

"That's why you're here," Ed said. "I think they're all tied in somehow. Dean is working on hacking into the financial records. I think Neil's stuff is on his computer, but the old man insisted the lumberyard books be kept the old-fashioned way. I need you to connect the two while I check the names in the logbook."

"That's the second set of books you were talking about—logbooks?"

"Yeah," Ed confessed. "I needed to get you out here before Neil catches wind of what I'm doing and shuts me down."

"There's nothing wrong with him starting up businesses that feed customers into the lumberyard."

"So long as they're legit."

"You got a reason to believe they're not?"

"Yeah," Ed replied. "Neil."

A little less than an hour later, Ed pulled through the wide double gate leading to the Hoskinson Lumberyard and parked at the side of the office in the space reserved for Neil Hoskinson.

Harriet put her navy blue hat on her head and waited for Ed to open her car door. All their moves had been carefully planned to establish Harriet as a person of authority.

Her dark blue coat and black leather gloves were part of her bank attire. She breezed through the small showroom to the office in the rear.

Perry Larson, the foreman, hurried to catch up. He arrived just as she was introducing herself to the surprised bookkeeper. Harriet told them she was there to audit the books.

"On whose say so?" Larson asked.

"Mr. Lars Hoskinson," Harriet replied. "And as you know, he's had a massive stroke. The court ordered me to handle his financial affairs."

"I want to hear that from Neil Hoskinson," Perry Larson said.

Harriet set her purse on the bookkeeper's desk and pulled out an envelope. She withdrew a single sheet of paper and showed it to the foreman.

Larson read it and then said, "This could be a fake."

"Why would I fake a court order to audit your books?"

Perry Larson could think of no reason, so he blurted out the truth, "Mr. Hoskinson doesn't like people snooping around in his business."

"His father changed his will yesterday. He is prepared to change it again upon my recommendation," Harriet said. "Stand in my way and tomorrow you won't be working for Mr. Neil Hoskinson. You'll be working for me."

"I'm gonna call."

"Go ahead," Harriet said. "Meanwhile, Miss Zeller, take the next couple of hours off."

"I want her watching you," Larson demanded.

"An auditor is not 'watched'."

"She's right, Perry," the bookkeeper put in. "That's how it is."

Harriet removed her gloves, hat and coat and sat down at the bookkeeper's desk. She looked at Ed.

"Mr. Ornstein, check the shed in the back first," she ordered, handing him the keys.

"Where'd you get those?" Larson asked.

"Mr. Lars Hoskinson, of course," Harriet replied. "Now everybody clear out. I need to get started."

Ed left at once and headed for the shed. Perry Larson let him go. He needed to get a direction from his boss. He went to his desk and picked up the phone.

He brushed past the bookkeeper and told her to wait outside.

Neil answered on the first ring. He was waiting for a call from his wife who was still at police headquarters. He'd called Oscar Johanson and told him to get him out. Johanson's associate had showed up and interrupted the interrogation before it really got underway. He asked Chief Peets if he was ready to arrest Mr. Hoskinson, and when Peets said no, the associate left with his firm's client.

Neil was surprised at getting a call from his foreman.

The man had never called him before.

Larson got right to the point. "Mrs. Harriet Locke is here to audit the books. She has a court order."

"Let me check with our lawyer," Neil said.

He was put through to Johanson when he declared it was an emergency.

"Harriet Locke is at the Elyria Lumberyard doing an audit. Can she do that?"

"She has your father's power of attorney in all areas financial which means she can go wherever he could go and look at his financial records of any of his lumberyards."

"Is there any way I can stop her?"

"My advice is not to try. This is not a woman to mess with. If you're into anything you shouldn't be, you'd better hope she doesn't find it."

"I'm not into anything illegal," Neil blustered. "And I don't like the implication."

"Then there's no reason for concern," Johanson said smoothly.

"I don't want her poking around in my business is all," Neil declared. "She shouldn't be allowed."

"What business are you talking about?"

Neil thought for a few seconds, and then decided he needed advice.

"I started up two new companies."

"In your name only?"

"Yes."

"Did your father cosign a loan or anything like that?"

"No."

"Then they're off-limits to her. She can only look at the financial records of your father's companies."

"What about papers and stuff relating to those businesses?"

"Off-limits."

Just as Neil hung up the phone, his wife Rosalie burst into the family room.

"They kept me forever. How come you got off so fast?"

"My lawyer walked me out right away," Neil said. "Can we talk about this in a couple minutes? I need to make a call."

Rosalie's face grew dark with anger.

"What's more important than what happened to me?" she stormed.

"Harriet Locke's nosing around in Elyria," Neil said. "Go pour yourself a drink and relax."

Rosalie moved over to the bar. Neil dialed Larson's number.

"Mrs. Locke can audit the books; but she's not to enter the shed."

"She already sent her man out there," Larson rejoined.

"And you let her do that?"

"She had your father's keys."

Harriet spoke up. "Is Mr. Hoskinson objecting to Mr. Ornstein entering the shed?"

"Yes, he is. He says you aren't allowed."

"Tell him I have the right to search the property for illegal substances."

"She says she can search for drugs."

"For chrissake, Larson, use that thick skull of yours. I don't deal drugs!"

"He says the place is clean."

"Let me speak with him please," Harriet said.

Larson handed her the phone.

"We're doing a spot inventory. Is any of the property in the shed a part of the lumberyard inventory?"

"None of it," Neil said, seeing a light at the end of the tunnel. "It all belongs to another venture of mine."

Harriet looked at the foreman. "You may go and ask Mr. Ornstein to report back here."

On the other end of the line, Neil heard the office door open and close and he began to relax.

"My lawyer said you can't investigate my personal business ventures."

"That is correct, Mr. Hoskinson; however, I do hope you realize that if you are using a building on this property for a separate business, you need to pay rent."

Neil was appropriately surprised by this twist.

"Rent? For chrissake, it's my property."

"Not yet, it isn't," Harriet said with authority, "But your lumberyard profit line will look even better. Your father will be impressed."

"How much?"

"What is the shed used for?" Harriet asked.

"Storage," Neil said. "That's all."

There was a pause before Mrs. Locke spoke again. Neil heard a door open and close again. Someone had entered the room.

"Mr. Ornstein," Harriet said, loudly enough so Neil Hoskinson could hear her query, "Tell me; does it appear the shed is used mainly for storage?"

"Mostly," Ed said. "But something else is going on too."

"Mr. Hoskinson, what else is the shed used for?" Harriet asked coolly.

"We pack our samples for shipping is all," Neil replied.

"Shipping?" Harriet asked Ed.

"Some evidence of that. Stuff is tagged to go somewhere. There was a microscope."

"Lab work?" Harriet asked.

Neil cursed silently. She must have some idea what he was doing, but he couldn't bring himself to tell her what she might not know.

Harriet prompted him. "This mold inspection business you have needs inspectors, right? Do you do some training in-house?"

Neil's tone brightened.

"Yes," he said. "There are lots of kinds of mold. Some is harmless. Some is not. I grow samples of both kinds to show my inspectors."

"Five hundred a month," Harriet said decisively. "Where do I send the bill? I figure you owe five months rent."

"Send it to my home address," Neil said, not daring to tell her to send it to the lumberyard.

"And the name of your company is Mold Inspection Ltd., right?"

"Correct," Neil managed to say. She knew more than he realized. But how much was the question.

"Put Larson back on," Neil said.

Rosalie was still fuming when Neil finished talking with his foreman.

"They treated me like a common criminal," Rosalie spat out. "They kept asking questions. They made me tell them about every second we spent together like I was lying."

"You stuck to the story right?"

"Yeah, I stuck to it for all the good it did," Rosalie stormed.

"They switched to, 'Where was I the rest of the day?' And, 'Where was I yesterday morning?' We didn't talk about my needing an alibi for yesterday morning."

"Where were you?"

"Getting my hair done like usual," Rosalie said. "And I had to sit in that room while they checked out my alibi, and my damn hairdresser took the day off. They couldn't find her. I was there forever."

"But you're home."

"Why did they need to know about yesterday morning?" Rosalie pressed, her tone suspicious.

"I delivered the package myself," Neil confessed.

"You went to the door and rang the bell?" she asked aghast.

"No. I snuck through the orchard and put it on the step in front of the door. When I was walking back through the orchard, a delivery truck drove up. The delivery man spotted the package and handed it to the maid along with the one he was there to deliver. It was perfect."

"That was a dumb move. Why the hell didn't you stick to the plan and mail the damn thing?"

"My friend told me that the FBI is good at finding people who send bombs in the mail. He scared me."

"So, when you was at the police station, did you tell him you have a right to see your dad?"

"Yeah. So did Cliff; but the chief said the only visitors he gets are that Aleta Praetzel and her grandmother."

"Why them?"

"Seems Dad gave them power of attorney."

"Did you call Johanson? We can sue to get it back."

"Johanson says we ain't got a snowball chance in hell."

Rosalie thought for a minute. "The money in your father's checking account, we gotta…"

She stopped when she saw Neil shake his head. "She got that yesterday—all two hundred thousand."

"We gotta tell the judge!"

"She approved it," Neil said. "Oh, and Dad's been moved."

"Moved? Where?"

"Seems this Praetzel dame put him back in the hospital," Neil informed her. "And he changed his will."

"He can't even sign his name!"

"Seems this Praetzel dame can understand him. And Dad had actually changed his will before the stroke so the Judge allowed it. No more contest with winner taking all. We get what we get."

"After all we did to show a profit. That ain't fair!"

"It gets worse. Dad hired a P.I. He's at the Elyria lumberyard now."

"So did he find anything?"

"Yeah, he looked in the shed."

"And?"

"He found out we used it for storage for the mold inspection business, and she insists I pay rent since I told her Dad had nothing to do with it."

"What the hell did you do that for? We could've said it was his idea."

"With Aleta Praetzel able to understand him?" Neil countered.

"Besides Johanson says that she can't snoop around in my affairs at all as long as Dad's not involved."

"I don't like those two messing up our plans. We need to take out Aleta Praetzel."

"Why take the risk?" Neil asked. "What's done is done."

"It ain't over. So long as she's alive the old man can change his will again. Without her around, he won't be able to."

"They didn't find nothing. There's no need."

"Can't you figure out nothing on your own? Those two at Elyria. They was playing you."

"No way," Neil declared. "I did a good selling job. It's what I do, you know."

"You gotta go to Elyria and find out," Rosalie decided.

"Then they'll know I got something to hide," Neil said. "Besides Larson's going to watch them.

Back in Elyria, when Larson left the office to go back to supervise the movement of lumber in the yard, Harriet asked Ed, "Did you get enough?"

"The pictures will tell me what I missed."

"Wish you could have gotten some samples," Harriet said. "I have a feeling that place will be cleaned out as soon as we leave."

"Why do ya think I wear these baggy clothes? Nobody notices bulges?"

Ed looked out the window.

"Looks like Larson has been ordered to see we don't go in there again. He's hanging around practically on top of the door."

"We can't present any of this stuff to Mr. Hoskinson unless we can tie it to Hoskinson's Lumberyard."

"What about the flyers?"

"So Neil offers discounted service. That's not a bad idea. We've got to tie in his scam with increased sales."

"I guess we need to interview past customers," Ed said. "The problem is I only saw the last pages in the log. Those are the next marks."

"Did you see the name of the inspector?"

"Just initials: E.W.," Ed replied. "Say do you have the payroll records?"

Harriet pulled up that book. "No E.W."

"How about five months ago?"

Harriet flipped back to June. "Edward Winslowe, with one 'e'. He was a part-timer."

"That's our guy," Ed said. "How many Edward Winslowe's can there be in the phone book?"

"None," Harriet said. "He's a college student."

"How do you know that?"

"My nephew added an 'e' to his name to stand out. His son's name is Edward."

Ed was properly taken aback. "Shit!"

Harriet raised an eyebrow at his exclamation.

"It could work in our favor," she said.

"But you could be exposed," Ed pointed out.

"Maybe it's time."

"Maybe for you it doesn't matter anymore. Your friends all know, but what about your grandchildren?"

"Aleta's okay with it," Harriet responded. "Still she and Stanley are being circumspect. I don't think they've told anyone besides his parents."

"And the one that's getting married?"

"It'd ruin things for her. Her fiancé isn't like Stanley."

"Do you want to stop our investigation here," Ed asked. "We could move our investigation to Des Moines."

"We may not get lucky again," Harriet replied. "In fact, Neil may be calling his other yards as we speak. He could make it impossible for us to uncover anything given our time limits."

"Any way to do this without Edward?" Ed asked.

"Let me do a bit more looking in the yard books," Harriet said. "You concentrate on the computer logs. If we can't find anything by noon, then we look up Edward."

Back in Willow Glen, Rosalie was still arguing with Neil about taking out Aleta. "What do you think will happen if those two nosing around uncover something?"

"I've been real careful. Didn't even use names, only initials in the new bookkeeping system."

"Why keep any records?"

"Hell, Rosalie, I gotta know if any of the contractors is reneging on our deal," Neil retorted. "I don't trust them sonsofbitches."

"That Locke woman could find something. And what'll your old man do if he finds out how come we suddenly got money?"

"Cut me off," Neil said, stating the obvious.

"So, don't it make sense to take precautions?"

"We can't do another package in the mail," Neil said. "They'll be looking for that."

Rosalie smirked. She had him.

"Car bomb," she said. "We get him to make two—just in case. This time we use a car bomb," Rosalie decided. "Can your friend make a car bomb?"

"Sure, I guess, but I can't attach it to the ignition or anything like that and he won't do that."

Get him to put it on a timer. Then all you gotta do is tape it under the car. Jesus, do I have to do all the thinking around here?"

"How do you know...?" Neil started but Rosalie interrupted him.

"Call him. We gotta have it tonight."

"How do we...?" Neil started again.

Rosalie cut him off.

"We gotta do some—what do they say when an army sends a guy out to scout things out?"

"Reconnaissance," Neil answered.

"Yeah, that. We gotta do that."

"How..."

"Don't you got a single damn idea how to do anything? Do I gotta do all the thinking?" Rosalie asked querulously.

"I been finding stuff out," Neil quipped.

"Like what?" she challenged.

"She goes to the hospital everyday in the morning," Neil said, "between eight and nine."

"How the hell did you find that out?" Rosalie said peeved because he had actually done something he'd promised to do.

"I called the hospital and asked when the doctor was there. I wanted to talk to him and I wasn't going to pay for a damn office visit. She said Dr. King makes his rounds between eight and nine."

"So why the hell do we care?"

"Because I figured this Aleta dame would be there when he was."

Rosalie smiled. "Good thinking. So we go over to her house tonight..."

Neil stopped her. "We said anything about going over there? Last time I was there, there were dogs."

"Where?"

"Inside the RV, but they could be let loose at night."

"We gotta go over there and see," Rosalie said. "After we get the bomb. When it's almost dark."

"I ain't going up against them dogs," Neil said adamantly. "We wait for her in the hospital parking lot. Do it my way or do it yourself."

"Okay, we do it your way."

Meanwhile, at Hoskinson's lumber yard in Elyria, at quarter to twelve, Ed got up and wandered over to the window.

"Hey, he's gone."

"Larson?"

"Yeah," Ed said. "Should I give it a try?"

"Go for it."

He was back in a few minutes. He closed the door behind him.

"You look upset," Harriet noted.

"I am. I was too late. The log's gone. So are the samples in bags. I found a couple that'd dropped on the floor and been kicked under the shelves. I took photos again."

"I guess we are going to have to look for Edward."

The door behind Ed was flung open. A voice preceded the appearance of a slim, young black man, "Hey, Perry, where's the log?"

Ed spun around. His recovery was immediate, "Edward Winslowe? We were just coming to see you."

"What are you doing here? Where's Mr. Larson?"

Harriet rose from behind the desk and extended her hand. "Hello, Edward. It's good to see you again."

"Aunt Harriet?" he stammered without thinking.

Ed reached behind him and closed the door. He thought he saw a flicker of motion in the showroom but he couldn't be sure.

"You alone?" he asked.

"Yes, Sir," Edward said, suddenly realizing what he'd said.

Ed slipped past him, stepped out and looked around. He saw no one. He waited and listened. His waiting paid off. After a few minutes, Miss Zeller emerged from the washroom.

"Oh, Miss Zeller," Ed said. "I opened the door thinking it was you. It was a young man who says he's some sort of mold inspector. Do you know what he's talking about?"

Embarrassed, Miss Zeller stammered, "We offer a service but, I don't know much."

"Isn't he on your payroll?"

"Neil pays him from an account I don't do the books for."

"You only deal with lumberyard accounts?" Ed asked. "No crossovers?"

"No. Mr. Hoskinson is very careful," she said, eyeing the closed door suspiciously.

"So you know nothing about his new business ventures?" Ed went on.

"No, I don't."

"Does Mr. Hoskinson have another office?"

"I don't know about that," she said edging toward the front door.

"You can go now Miss Zeller," Ed said. "We'll be here one more hour."

"What about him?" Miss Zeller said frowning at the closed door.

"He came in looking for a log book."

"It's not there. It's in the shed," she said tartly.

"I assume he looked in the shed first," Ed replied.

"Well, it won't be in the office and he shouldn't be poking around in there," she came out boldly. "It's not his place."

"I'll see he leaves immediately," Ed said.

She relaxed. "Sometimes they get uppity and go where they don't belong."

He noticed the scowl, the pursed lips and knew she was going straight toward Larson and complain. He took a bold step. "You heard him call her Aunt Harriet, didn't you?"

"I don't eavesdrop!" she declared, reddening.

"Mrs. Locke sponsors a great many college scholarships. All the recipients call her Aunt Harriet. It's a term she likes."

"But it's not right!" Miss Zeller said. "He should know his place."

"Mrs. Locke obviously doesn't share your view," Ed said coolly. "I don't argue with my employer."

Miss Zeller opened the door murmuring that she'd be back in an hour.

Ed joined Harriet and Edward in the office. They both cast inquiring glances in his direction and he repeated the conversation.

"I'll stick to the story," Edward said. "It is true, after all."

"Edward has a great memory for names and places," Harriet said. "I have a customer list for us to work from."

Ed turned his laptop around showing a page of Neil's log for Mold Inspectors Ltd. "Recognize these initials?"

"Sure," Edward said, going over to a file drawer and pulling out a folder. He took out the top sheet and handed it to Ed. "Those are the initials of the contractors we recommend."

Ed took the paper and scanned it.

Edward Winslowe glanced at the screen. "Something's wrong?"

"What's wrong?" Ed asked.

"Those aren't sale receipts because there's no odd cents. So what kind of receipts are they?"

"Interesting observation," Ed said. "You tell me."

"Some kinda cut to Mr. Hoskinson for selling their services?" Winslowe suggested.

"That's my guess," Ed said.

"I thought we weren't connected with the contractors," Edward said. "At least we aren't connected with the ozone company."

Ed punched in a few keys. When he brought up Ozone Specialists, Inc., Edward's jaw dropped.

"I... I didn't know...," he stammered. "It's a con, isn't it?"

"We believe it is," Ed said.

"But ozone kills mold. Neil showed me."

"Yes, it does," Harriet said, "but only the mold it can reach."

"But it's a gas," Edward argued. "Gas seeps in everywhere."

"That's a logical assumption; however, it doesn't," Harriet said. "It would take pressure to displace air inside the dry wall, wall cavities, floor cavities, ceiling cavities to say nothing of inside upholstered furniture. And those are the places the worst kind of mold exists."

"At least it gets at some of the mold," Edward said. "That's something."

"There's a trade-off," Harriet said. "It damages plastic and rubber components to appliances and electronics. It eats up exposed extension cords."

"I'm sure the people are warned," Edward said. "Well, almost sure."

"And ozone is a health hazard," Harriet finished. "And the mold kill only lasts three months."

"It doesn't sound like such a good idea," Edward said.

"But the remodeling is okay, right?"

"Only if it's necessary," Ed said.

"I take good samples," Edward said. "I took some courses. I'm certified."

"You're certificated," Harriet pointed out kindly. "There are currently no certified mold inspectors. The business is in its infancy."

"We send the samples to a lab. We don't do our own testing," Edward Winslowe declared.

Ed looked at Harriet. She nodded, and he pulled a bag out of his pocket.

"Yeah, that's a sample I took," Edward said, without opening the bag. "See the mark on the end. I do that so I can identify mine. Mr. Hoskinson said he might hire another inspector. I didn't want my samples mixed up with his."

"I wish you had a copy of all the people you did inspections for," Harriet commented.

"I do," Edward said. "I thought you were only interested in spot checking."

"Your having a list makes a difference," Harriet said. "We can do something now."

"You can't," Ed said. "Hoskinson only hired us to investigate."

"Let's go see some of the people who've been customers of Mold Inspection, Ltd.," Harriet said. "Then we'll talk."

Young Edward Winslowe found out the truth at the first stop when the gray-haired widow showed him the lab results which were attached to the plastic bags across the top of each seal of which he'd written her name. He read the result and then looked at the piece of wood inside. He turned the wood over several times.

"This isn't the sample I took," he blurted out.

Harriet stepped in quickly, "Mrs. O'Brien, I'm from the main office of Hoskinson Lumber. We're checking out how the samples are processed. You'll be glad to know we found no fault in Mr. Winslowe's sampling techniques which is why we're going to ask you to allow him to take five new samples. We will submit them for a recheck and this will be a free service."

"Well, I guess so," Mrs. O'Brien said. "Only the contractor is coming this afternoon with his estimate. What'll I do about that?"

"We believe, in your case, the samples were mixed up and that you don't need extensive repair."

"Mr. Hoskinson guessed it would cost me about twenty-seven thousand dollars," Mrs. O'Brien said. "I applied for a loan against the house, and I guess I'll be paying a mortgage for another twenty years. I'm looking for another job but there aren't a lot for women my age."

"Tell the contractor that you won't sign a contract until the lab work is redone," Harriet said. "If he gives you trouble, call me at this number."

She wrote her cell phone number on the back of Lars Hoskinson's business card.

"I can be reached through the main office when I'm not travelling," she added.

When they left, Ed Ornstein split off to check out the contractors. Harriet and, her nephew Edward visited another dozen homes making each homeowner the same offer. No one refused. The possibility of escaping a huge bill was incentive enough to win over even the most skeptical.

Each asked different questions, which Harriet fielded smoothly. Edward listened intently and toward the end of the first group, he found himself taking the lead.

On the fourteenth call, they ran into Ozone Specialists setting up a tent. Harriet walked boldly up to the foreman and said, "This has been postponed. There's been a mistake."

The homeowner emerged and Harriet consulted with the old man briefly. He recognized Edward Winslowe who smiled but didn't speak. Moments later, the old man nodded.

Then he told the foreman of the tenting crew to get the hell away from his house.

"The thousand isn't refundable," the foreman shouted at him as he ordered his men to take down the tent. "If you don't let us proceed now, you'll have to pay the full amount when we come out again."

"You didn't tell me the ozone would eat up my electrical equipment," the old man yelled back. "Or that it might hurt my dog."

"Who says?"

"This lady does," the old man said. "And she's got a paper that says so, too."

Harriet ushered the old man into the house. When they emerged, he went over to Edward and shook his hand.

"Thank you for remembering me," the old man said.

"Yes, Sir," Edward smiled. "I'll be back an Tuesday to get those new samples."

"No charge, right?"

"Absolutely."

"Hoskinson, he's a good man," the old man said.

"Mr. Hoskinson is a good man," Edward said.

When they were back in the car, Edward asked Harriet what had happened to turn the old gentleman away from the anger he could see building.

"I gave him his deposit back," Harriet said.

"That's it?"

"It's amazing what a good feeling ten one hundred dollar bills can instill in one."

"Cash?"

"While he was an easy sell, he grasped the truth pretty fast. He was ready to storm into the lumberyard to give Neil a piece of his mind."

"How long are you going to be here and do this?"

"I have to leave tomorrow afternoon."

"We'll never get done," Edward said.

"For some it's too late," Harriet said. "The house has been gassed or the floors ripped up. I haven't figured out what to do in those cases yet. A quality check is within our purview and we can explain that, but I'm walking a tightrope here. I can't make Lars Hoskinson liable."

"Why not?"

"Because, like you, he has a reputation that's important to him," Harriet explained. "Our first aim is to stop the scams. After that I need to persuade Mr. Hoskinson to consider his options."

"Those people should sue."

"I know you're angry at being used," Harriet said. "Take the position that this is a quality control check and you won't know the results until the lab results are back."

"But I know they were conned!" Edward exclaimed.

"People aren't going to appreciate you telling them that," Harriet said. "You've been angry ever since I told you."

"They should know!" he declared adamantly.

"What I'm worried about is them thinking you were part of the scam and take it out on you. My verifying that your work is not suspect is important, wouldn't you say?"

"Yes, Ma'am," Edward agreed reluctantly. "But I'm having a hard time agreeing that Mr. Hoskinson is a good man when it's not true."

"But it's true. Mr. Lars Hoskinson is paying you fifty dollars to take the recheck samples and that's a good act."

"He is?"

"And he will stop his son from expanding this nefarious business using his other lumberyards if I can show him proof of what's really happening," Harriet said. "Are you with me?"

"But what about these people. I live here."

"You think about what you want me to do and I'll listen," Harriet said. She paused and then added an admonition, "In the meantime, you sit on that temper of yours."

Back in Illinois, when Neil Hoskinson arrived home after picking up the two home-made bombs, there were a string of messages on his answering machine from angry contractors in Elyria.

He began calling back immediately. The stories were all the same. Contracts were either cancelled or put on hold pending a reinspection of the house.

What was going on?

Neil told each one it wasn't his idea and explained that his father had had a stroke, was off his rocker, and had hired this professional auditor who had overstepped her boundaries.

"It'll be taken care of," he promised Artie, his fourth caller, as he had the first three.

"When?" Artie had insisted. "I got a crew ready to work. I can't afford delays."

"Just do what you do when rain hits. Stop work until the weather clears," Neil said. "Gimme a few days."

He turned to Rosalie after returning his last call. "She's even talked a couple customers out of ozone tenting with the crew right there ready to go."

"How'd she know where to go?"

"That no-good black kid I hired was with her."

"Didn't Larson grab the log?"

"Yeah, he did," Neil responded dourly. "Who knew the kid would remember where he'd been?"

"If this gets out, we could be sued!" Rosalie jumped in. "God, we could lose everything. We gotta stop her!"

"We need a pro," Neil said. "That guy at the Home you get your drugs from. Get hold of him."

"He won't do it."

"But he knows guys who will. We don't."

"Those guys will cost."

"Won't cost as much as a couple lawsuits."

"What about the kid?"

"I'll take care of him personally," Neil declared his rage rising. "That sonofabitch is gonna have one last lesson in loyalty."

"We already paid five hundred for these bombs," Rosalie pointed out. "And we got a plan."

"Yeah, you're right," Neil agreed. "We go ahead tomorrow as we planned."

Rosalie glanced at her watch. "Maybe I can still catch Dean before he leaves work."

"Tell him we'll spring for dinner."

"Why do that?" Rosalie said. "He's gonna want money for doing this."

"Because we need him," Neil said. "God, Rosalie, you don't understand about business lunches at all do you?"

"Sure, I do," Rosalle said. "But this is different. It won't be good to be seen together."

"Set it some place outta town," Neil told her, disgust riding his words.

"Don't get snippy with me!" she snarled.

"Don't let your penny pinching do us in!" Neil warned. "Dad always said I couldn't see that saving a dollar could cost me two, but he ain't never met the likes of you. We're gonna be dealing with pros. You let me do it."

Rosalie fumed silently. She didn't pick up the phone. She was waiting for an apology.

The only sound in the room was the ticking of the clock. Rosalie stared at it daring him to wait.

But Neil was angry, too. He waved his arm around. "You wanna lose all this?"

Scowling, Rosalie snatched the receiver from its cradle and punched in the number. She waited while the receptionist ran out and caught Dean in the parking lot.

"This is Mrs. Hoskinson," Rosalie said. "Neil and I wanna take you to dinner. We got a proposition for you. Some place outta town."

She listened, murmured a yes and hung up.

"Scotty's Ribs twenty miles west of Willow Glen," she said. "In half an hour."

Chapter 7

"I'm home," Aleta called then rambled on when Bertha appeared, "I got more puppy food and biscuits. I figured you should have stuff for here and your place. I got an extra couple of bowls too. And a bed."

"Thank you, Ma'am," Bertha said. "I'll pay you back as soon as I cash my check."

"It doesn't work like that," Aleta said. "If I buy it, I pay. I don't spend other people's money."

"But it's for my dog," Bertha protested.

"It's food and a bed for a guest in my house," Aleta said firmly. "I assume you already packed stuff to take home."

Stanley emerged from the bedroom. "Don't argue with her, Bertha. You can't win."

"Yes Sir," Bertha said. "Thank you, Ma'am."

"How come you're home so early?" Aleta asked.

"Quarter to six isn't early, is it, Bertha?" Stanley countered.

"Supper is ready," Bertha said politely. "King and I will be going now."

"Ten tomorrow, Bertha," Aleta said.

"Good, I'll have time to take King to the vet for his shots."

"Don't have him give him the DHLP and the rabies at the same time. He's not strong enough yet."

"Yes, Ma'am. Lauren told me the same thing. She made the appointment."

"Lauren was here?"

"She brought over same gruel for the puppy. She said it would be easier on his stomach. I'm slowly mixing in the puppy kibble," Bertha explained. "She came over to check on the table arrangement and bring over the cloths and candles and extra silver."

"Wow! This party is moving right along without me."

"Isn't that how you wanted it?" Bertha asked a slight frown creasing her forehead.

Stanley stepped in. "That's how I want it. That's how it should be this time. And thank you for seeing that Mrs. Praetzel does no work."

After eating, Aleta said, "Which do you want to do first: fool around in the bedroom or build a fire in the living room and talk?"

"You pick," Stanley said as he cleared the table and put the dishes in the dishwasher.

"You aren't going to say you have work to do?"

"I have all weekend. Tonight I'm yours."

"Start the fire then meet me in the bedroom. I want to get into something comfortable."

"What are you going to be doing?"

"Lighting the candles."

"I guess I know the order of things now," Stanley observed dryly.

When Stanley entered the bedroom ten minutes later, both their robes were laid out an the bed along with his pajamas and her nightgown. She'd done more than light candles.

He showed his annoyance indirectly, "At least you didn't close the drapes."

"I left them open on purpose," Aleta said. "I told Gary to tell the next man on that no one was to pass by our windows at night. I told him we liked the view."

"And you trust them?"

"Of course," Aleta said sweetly. "Besides you remember Dr. Cook's orders. No sexual activity."

"That didn't stop you last night," Stanley said. "You are an extremely creative lady."

"Well, tonight, we're going to be really good. We aren't even going to get in bed until it's time to go to sleep."

"I'm going to hold you to that," Stanley said as he sat down and unlaced his shoes and pulled them off.

"How about me first?" Aleta queried slyly.

As expected he jumped up and rushed to where she was standing. As he slipped her arm from its sling and unbuttoned her blouse, she suddenly told him to put her arm back into the sling.

Puzzled, he did as she asked.

"Now you stand right where you are," she said. "Tonight I'm undressing you."

"With one hand?"

"So I do it very slowly," she quipped. "Do you care?"

Before he could answer, she kissed him and her right hand began undoing his shirt buttons as their lips were still engaged.

Twenty minutes later he completed unbuttoning her blouse. This time he kissed her as he began the process. He paused long enough to comment, "You are a mischievous little minx, aren't you? Dr. Cook has no idea how narrowly you define sexual activity."

"The emphasis is on activity," she whispered. "My left shoulder didn't twitch the whole time."

"We are going to dress before we go sit before the fire, aren't we?"

"I'm still thinking about that," Aleta mused teasingly.

"What's to think about?" Stanley said. "I can't think rationally when you're naked."

"That's good to know," she said as he had her step out of her slacks. She steadied herself by putting a hand on his shoulder.

"As if you didn't know," he charged.

"Put my arm back into the sling," she said.

"First your gown."

"I like the nude idea. There are whole groups of people who talk and eat while nude."

"We aren't nudists," Stanley argued. "And I'm not interested in becoming one."

"We've never tried it—I mean on our own volition. I know we were forced once. I think we should replace that image with a good one."

"Aleta, we have men parading around our house."

"One man," his wife retorted. "And he's not parading around."

"I like clothes," Stanley said. "Being naked unsettles me."

"That does it!" Aleta shouted gleefully. "We go nude."

"No we don't."

"Would you object if I did?"

"No, of course not!" he shot back and then softened his tone. "You are beautiful. I love looking at you."

"Well, tit for tat."

"What does that mean?"

"Didn't it occur to you that I might enjoy the same thing?" she asked. "Come on indulge me."

"Sorry, Aleta, not in this."

"Okay, put on my gown and robe and then the sling," she said. "I knew you'd say no. I love a man who's a tad shy."

Stanley reddened but in the candlelight Aleta didn't see it. Still she sensed that he'd stiffened. However, he remained gentle as he redressed her.

"You don't like the word shy?"

Stanley didn't reply. Instead he busied himself with restoring her arm into its sling. Then he hurried to dress himself.

"I'll get us some coffee," he said a bit tartly.

"I'd like that," she responded softly. "Please don't be angry. I don't think shyness is a bad thing. I'm shy a lot."

"You're a woman," he bit back.

"Hey, fifty percent of your genes carne from your mother."

"That's irrelevant," he snapped.

"Go get us some coffee," Aleta said. "I need to calm down."

Stanley stormed into the kitchen, and Aleta sank into a chair and pouted. This wasn't going as she planned. One little word and everything was ruined. She wondered how can we have a meaningful conversation when one of us goes off mad because of one little word? It wasn't even a bad word. A lot of men are shy. What's wrong with that?

She heard Stanley rattling the cups in the kitchen.

"Don't break anything," she shouted.

"I know what I'm doing!" he shouted back.

"Some of the time," she muttered, "but not all of the time."

"I didn't hear what you said," he shouted.

"Never mind," she spat out.

He emerged from the kitchen. "Don't 'never mind' me. What did you say?"

Aleta looked at him. She suddenly didn't want him angry any more. "It's not worth repeating."

He walked over to her and knelt down. "I don't want to fight with you."

Tears burst forth and Aleta brushed them away angrily. "I didn't use to cry so much."

"You're pregnant," Stanley commented. "I'm sorry I was impatient."

"Will you give me the dictionary?"

"Sure, why?"

"I think I came up with the wrong word."

"I can tell you what shy means," Stanley said. "It means bashful, easily frightened, even a bit timid."

"How come you can rattle off the meaning?" Aleta asked, then eyed him suspiciously. "You looked it up didn't you?"

"I'll get the coffee."

"I want the dictionary. I don't think of you as timid. I need to find the word I think…"

"What's been said has been said."

"Not when I don't have full control over my words. Let me do same searching."

"That could take all night."

"Not necessarily. I think the right word will surface as I look at the wrong ones," Aleta said. "We got any lemon squares left?"

Stanley brought her the dictionary. When he returned with the lemon squares and coffee and moved the coffee table over so she could reach them, Aleta was busy flipping pages.

He sat in a chair, sipped his coffee and waited. She had used a word he disliked, but she had not meant to hurt him. She had even said she liked the quality. Maybe she had indeed used the wrong word.

"I found it!" she exclaimed happily. "Modest. I think I planned to say 'modest' and my brain hopped over to 'bashful' and from there to 'shy.' But the word I wanted was 'modest' otherwise defined as 'reserved.' I like a man who's reserved, meaning using restraint in one's words and bearing. That word fits you. It's a quality that stands you in good stead. You think before you act. Me, I'm impulsive. I'm sorry I used the wrong word, and I'm even sorrier I didn't realize it. I know what I think, and my brain just didn't put that together with what I said. I guess it's true. I defend myself vigorously even when I'm wrong."

"So now are we ready to talk about why you think I'm fragile."

Aleta's jaw dropped. "Where'd that come from?"

"That last part about defending yourself vigorously when wrong. It had a double meaning."

"I thought we settled that this morning."

"No, we didn't," Stanley observed, "but let's move on to why I said it. I want to take whatever steps are necessary to keep you from the stress that apparently triggered your first stroke."

"I can't believe I think you're fragile."

"You do know that all people have a breaking point— men, as well as women."

"Yes, I know that."

"I think you believe you saw me broken," Stanley said. "And, in fact, you did. But it didn't happen when you think it did. Still, that doesn't matter. The point is I did give up. When the kidnappers separated us and I could no longer protect you—that's when it happened."

"I thought what happened before…"

She stopped because Stanley was shaking his head.

"The point is I think you believe that I'm now weak like a piece of china cup whose handle has been glued back on."

Aleta listened with a new openness. What Stanley was saying she began to realize was how she did feel.

"The point is I'm not a china cup. I'm a human being. While the cup handle might never be as strong as it was originally, a man who's been broken and recovered is stronger, not weaker."

"But in the hospital…," Aleta let her words trail off. He knew the question.

"We explored my humiliation, and you helped me deal with that."

"You did the same for me," Aleta said softly.

"The break was repaired before that. I almost didn't take your advice and crawl to safety. I wanted to die. Well, most of me wanted to die. There was apart of me that refused to let the break be complete. I hung on with the tiniest bit of self that I had left. I let it carry me through. I rebuilt the rest. You've been a large factor in that."

"Me?"

"Tonight should have proved it to you."

"Tonight? The fight?" she asked, surprised.

Stanley laughed. "I've never been afraid to fight with you. It was before that. If you dig down, you'll realize I didn't give in to what you really wanted to do. If I can stand up to you, I can stand up to anyone, including my mother."

"Arguing doesn't bother you?" Aleta pressed.

"I'm a rational man. If you convince me, I'm ready to change my mind. You're basically a rational woman although I'm not so sure if that is a possibility."

"Women are rational."

"By their definition," Stanley said. "Their base point is different, however, so given the same facts, they draw different conclusions than men."

"So if I'm rational, I can sway you?"

"To a point. You were being rational about there being nothing wrong with nudity. While I may agree that there isn't, my deeply ingrained modesty doesn't allow certain behaviors on my part."

"You know, when Mother comes for a visit, she's going to insist I do something about my scar."

Now it was Stanley's turn to be caught off-guard. "Where did that come from?"

"New subject," Aleta announced calmly. "You finished with the other, didn't you? I mean you want me to trust you not to fall apart when the pressure's on, right?"

"Right," Stanley replied a bit shakily. "At least I think… I mean you sound like you got my point."

"Trust me. I did," Aleta said. "But feel free to remind me anytime. You have the power."

"Granted graciously by you," Stanley smiled. "I love a woman who keeps her promise."

"So what do I do about my mother?"

"She's your mother."

"She's persistent and she can make me feel bad about myself.

"Mothers have that power," Stanley said. "I trust you'll work it out."

"How did you learn to handle your mother?"

"I don't handle her. I just don't let her handle me."

"You let me handle you," Aleta accused.

"You're my wife. You aren't trying to change me."

"I am too. What about breakfast?"

"Hey, you're right I need to establish that habit."

"And how about my letting Bertha go before six so you have to come home."

"Another healthy habit," Stanley said. "I need help on those and I love your creativity."

"Suppose I told you to change your nose."

"You wouldn't."

"My scar's the same thing."

"And the choice is yours. No one else's."

"Why do I keep going over this?"

"Because you aren't sure what to do," Stanley said. "Ask yourself what you really want."

"I want my hair the way it was."

"That might not happen."

"I don't want to wear a wig."

"So, there's your answer. You wish your hair were the way it was, but a wig isn't a good substitute in your mind."

"My mother won't understand."

"So what's different about that? She doesn't understand you now. But she loves you. Just go with that and keep your own counsel."

After a few quiet moments, Aleta asked, "Are we ready for gossipy stuff?"

"Let me get us some more coffee and then I'll be set."

Chapter 8

The following morning, Harriet and Ed met with a local contractor in an Elyria café. Guy Ginsberg ordered a large stack of pancakes, bacon and eggs while Harriet and Ed settled for a medium stack of pancakes, orange juice and coffee.

Ed envied Guy his lean muscular frame and realized the man worked hard. He guessed he did much of the work himself. He was a hands-on type of contractor. Ed presented Guy with a couple of estimates of repair work taken that Harriet had procured from Edward Winslowe's clients the day before. All were Xerox copies with names and prices deleted.

Guy, however, wanted to know what was going on and what this had to do with Cook Construction. His blonde brows shaded deep blue eyes that didn't miss the nuances of non-verbal exchanges between these two.

Harriet eyed Ed questioningly and he smiled and shrugged. Guy waited for the bullshit.

Harriet picked up the ball. "I see my friend Martha's reputation has extended beyond Illinois."

"You actually know her?" Guy asked, surprised she would be so blatant.

Harriet laughed. "We are actually very close friends, but I don't usually trade on that fact."

"Is she coming out here?" he asked wondering why these two were in Elyria.

"At ninety, I think she's done expanding," Harriet said.

"She is quite a woman," Guy said.

"You help me and I'll get you a personal interview with her, and you can pick her brain."

"Deal!" Guy said enthusiastically, then suddenly sobered. "You're putting me on."

"Would you like to see her plane?" Harriet asked. "She loaned it to me to make the trip."

"Really?"

"We'll take a quick trip to the Cleveland airport right after breakfast," Harriet said.

"All this for just looking at some small job estimates?" Guy asked.

"There's more," Harriet said. "I'll tell you about that on the way to the airport. But first, I need a rough estimate on these jobs."

The pancakes arrived and Guy studied the proposed renovations while downing his huge breakfast. He took out his calculator, and by the time he finished his coffee, he had scribbled estimate totals on the bottom of each of the six pages.

Harriet, who had memorized each of Neil's contractors' estimates watched in awe as Guy's numbers came in a quarter their totals.

"Are you sure you allowed for contingencies?" Harriet asked.

"Put the twenty percent in already."

"Bet you're outbid a lot," Ed said.

"If this were a bidding on these jobs, I'd lower this a bit. You said that all you wanted was an estimate as to a reasonable cost for these jobs."

"If we sound a little wary," Harriet said, "it's because the contractors hired for these jobs estimated four times what you did."

"And they were accepted?" Guy said.

"Would you have bid these jobs?"

"Not all of them. A couple are too small. Too much hassle. Not enough return."

"Eight thousand is too small?" Ed asked.

"It's a two thousand dollar job at most, not eight," Guy corrected. "But I'd have suggested a couple of men who would do it for two and do a good job, too."

"Ed, I need to be at Edward's house at nine. If Mr. Ginsberg can drive you, you can call our pilot and ask him to give you a spin around Cleveland in Martha's jet."

"And our talk?" Guy said.

"After your plane ride," Harriet said. "I have same business to take care of now."

At the Praetzel house, Aaron Ponce arrived a full half-hour early for his shift as Aleta's bodyguard.

Rumors around the Station were that their charge was impetuous. From what he'd gathered, Aleta Praetzel would use whoever was handy to drive her. He planned to be handy so he wouldn't be standing outside the house his whole shift.

Like his counterparts, Aaron was in his late twenties and happy in his work. He was slightly smaller than his fellow officers, but even though Alan Peets towered over half the men, Chief Milani and Chief West were men of modest stature. Aaron was not muscular but he was lithe and strong. He could outrun and outshoot any man in the department. His marksmanship was closest to that of Lyle West, who was the gold standard of shooters.

Next year he planned to take the sergeant's exam and hoped to move up. Peets' transfer wasn't permanent, but if it became permanent, one of the sergeants would move up and there would be an opening. It would mean more pay, and with a new baby he could use the extra money.

As he predicted, Aleta Praetzel emerged from the house at ten to eight and said simply, "Let's go."

Aaron opened the door to his patrol car, Aleta asked his name, and over the next fifteen minutes she asked about his family, his hobbies and his goals.

"Tell me when you pass the exam and we'll celebrate," she said. "I'm taking the Illinois bar exam the end of February, so I understand how important passing these exams are."

"I thought you were a lawyer."

"I am—in California. I'm a House Attorney in Illinois. That means I can only practice law within the framework of the corporation that pays my salary."

"Doesn't that keep you busy?"

"It did for a while, and it will again when the projects near completion, but right now the architects and contractors are in charge."

"So who are we going to see in the hospital?"

"Just people who've had strokes and can't speak very intelligibly."

"Why do they need a lawyer?"

"They don't. I'm an interpreter."

Aaron didn't notice the cars parked on the road leading to the hospital parking lot.

Aleta, however, with her penchant for numbers gathered the license plate numbers of the whole row of cars and repeated them to herself as Aaron drove to a space reserved for Police cars near the emergency entrance. The two walked straight through to the elevators.

She had Aaron write down the numbers, explaining that a memory test she'd taken had her repeat words after ten minutes. She wanted to see if she could remember the string of license plate numbers after twenty minutes.

"What'll that prove?"

"That my memory's coming back," Aleta said. "I had a stroke six days ago. On Monday I couldn't remember any sequence longer than six numbers."

"You've got a string of thirty numbers here."

"Yeah, it's getting better."

"How long do you suppose she'll be inside?" Neil asked as Rosalie parked next to the patrol car.

"Set it for ten after nine," Rosalie said.

"You're guessing."

"I figure if she leaves early, we could run into the car. You know, have an accident."

"That's a dumb idea," Neil said. "We need to have an alibi. I thought we'd go somewhere and have breakfast."

"I got it," Rosalie said. "Call the desk. Tell the nurse you wanna see her at a quarter to nine, but if you don't show by nine, she don't gotta wait because you ain't gonna make it."

"I'll set the timer for nine fifteen," Neil said. "She might wait an extra five."

"Okay, only hurry. We gotta set up our alibi."

The nurse passed on the message to Aleta when she approached Mr. Hoskinson's room.

"Did he say who he was?" Aleta asked.

"No, he just said he had to get back to the nursing home but he'd call you at this number at quarter to nine. He said it was about something that happened the morning Mr. Hoskinson was attacked.

Aleta hesitated then turned.

"Then I think I'll check on the other two people first, so I'll be back an this floor to take the call."

Aaron reported the call to Milani who called Peets. Milani sent another two units to the hospital to check out the floor Hoskinson was on.

The reports from his men came back negative.

"Stay there until Aleta leaves. Escort her all the way out. Then follow her until she's back home."

Aaron was informed of the plan by radio. He was standing outside Stella Lemay's room listening to the woman babble incoherently and Aleta answering what he could only suppose she thought were her questions.

It took him a few minutes to realize King was a dog. The first clue he got that Aleta understood the woman came when Aleta asked the old lady if King had had his rabies shots. The old woman mumbled something, and Aleta commented that he was going to the vet today and that was the first shot he was getting. The conversation lasted for another five minutes before Aleta left. She stopped a nurse and told her that Miss Lemay liked tea with a little milk in it and loved ice cream. The nurse replied that she'd put that down an her chart.

Aaron waited outside Elizabeth's room while Aleta talked with Dr. Chesney, the obstetrician who had delivered his baby just a few months prior. He wanted to say something but he couldn't think of anything, so he stuck to his job which called for him to be silent and watchful.

The doctor had a few questions for his wife, and Aleta appeared to act only as an interpreter, talking in the first person. He realized she was repeating Mrs. Chesney's words exactly as she spoke them. With the doctor speaking to his wife through Aleta, he began to believe she actually understood the mixture of sounds being uttered by the ailing woman.

Mr. Hoskinson's visit she saved for the end. The minute she appeared, Aaron saw the man's face light up. He held up his hand with a ball taped to it.

"How many times?" she asked.

He mumbled something and she responded, "You had to start over several times didn't you?"

He nodded and seemed happy about it.

"I'm not untaping it," she said, "because it'll roll away when you sleep."

He muttered something.

"Of course, you're tired. And, if you tell the therapist you've had enough, I'll be angry."

More muttering and more exclamations. It seems Mr. Hoskinson wanted faster results. Aleta called in Aaron and told him to look at the paper. She rattled off the first ten numbers without stumbling and then stopped. She explained to Mr. Hoskinson what she was doing.

"I used to be able to do thirty numbers," she said, "and I could retain then for several hours; but now I'm down to ten. I don't like not being able to do what I once took for granted, but I was told that you can get a lot of your ability back. The brain has the capacity to go around the damaged pathways and make new ones. You've only just begun to hack out a new trail in your brain. Once it's completed, you'll have some of your former abilities back."

His mutterings sounded bitter. Aaron was amazed that he could tell that. All he had to do was believe that the man's brain was functioning to be able to feel his emotion.

"I'm not feeding you a bunch of bull crap. I'm better. I know you've got a harder path; but you've got grit. No man builds up such a fine business without a lot of determination. And wasn't the first year the hardest? A baby's first steps are the hardest too. So are the first movements after a stroke. It'll get easier."

There was a long sequence of sounds, and Aleta nodded as he was speaking. Finally, she said, "I gotta go. I'm having a party tonight. Ed will be there, so I expect we'll both see you tomorrow. "

"It's five past nine," Aaron said.

"Well, I guess he's not going to call back. Let's go," Aleta said. "What's with the reinforcement?"

"Milani thinks the phone call was suspicious."

"He thinks someone might have called me to pin me here so someone would know where I was."

"I don't know, Ma'am," Aaron said.

"I'm going to Lauren West's house before I go home," Aleta announced. "I hope you don't have instructions to take me straight home."

"No, Ma'am," the young officer replied.

As they drove out of the parking lot, Aleta pondered the reason for the strange call aloud. "If it was someone trying to pinpoint my location, then the danger is over, isn't it?"

"It would seem so, Ma'am," Aaron said.

"But didn't the caller know that such a call would alert the police?"

"Not all criminals are smart," Aaron pointed out.

"But this would be really dumb, like waving a red flag, unless there was another reason for the call," Aleta contended.

"What other reason?"

"Turn here. Left three blocks down."

"Yes, Ma'am."

"I guess to pinpoint the time I would leave," Aleta said. "But nobody knows I'm going to Lauren's but me and Lauren, so maybe someone planned an ambush for me on the way home... only how would they know which way I was going? The answer is they wouldn't. Boy, I never thought I'd say this, but I'm stumped."

At that moment Harriet Locke had just entered Edward Winslowe's house and embraced Edward's mother. She was shaking hands with his father, Ezekiel Winslowe, when she saw the numbers on a digital clock flipping with each number being one less than the one before. She paled visibly until she saw the tires of a car turning.

She immediately called Ed and shouted, "Pull over and leave the truck."

She heard Ed order Guy to stop. The tires screeched and she heard the men scrambling to get out as Ed explained to Guy that there might be a bomb.

The minute she heard him say it, she realized, the bomb was elsewhere.

Aleta!

Quickly, she dialed Aleta's cell.

"Are you in a moving car?" she asked.

Suddenly, Aleta knew.

"Aaron stop the car!" she yelled.

"We're almost there."

"Stop!" she screamed.

Aaron jammed on the brakes. The cell phone flew from Aleta's hand. Her seat belt kept her from hitting her head.

The patrol car following them screeched to a halt but not fast enough to avoid hitting the car Aaron was driving.

Aleta pushed the lock on her seat belt and then reached over and released his.

"Get out and run," she yelled as she threw off her belt, yanked open the door and grabbed the phone from the floor.

"What's happening?" he said looking around.

"A bomb!" she shouted. "Trust me! Use those legs!"

She stepped out as the words hit him. The terror in her voice was contagious. Aaron threw open his door, leaped from the car and ran straight toward the huge trees along the curb.

Jerry Fawkes watched the sudden flight from behind the windshield of the patrol car whose bumper had hit them.

"Come on, guys," he said as he opened his car door and began to get out. "I didn't hit…"

In Elyria, Harriet screamed as the explosion blasted over the cell phone. She dropped the phone and the family gathered around to listen to the sounds, which despite being from two states away, terrified them.

On the quiet tree lined street in Arborville, everybody was too close when the bomb went off.

The side window of Jerry Fawkes's patrol car shattered peppering his face with broken glass as the force of the explosion threw him back against the steel of the door opening, and he lost consciousness.

Aleta, who had started out a few steps ahead of Aaron couldn't run as fast in her long cape, and she was the second one thrown by the blast. She was lifted into the air and cast down onto the street. The impact of the blast slammed her down on her right side and slid her forcefully along the rough pavement until the curb and her shoulder met, breaking the latter without even cracking the old concrete. Her head snapped down against the hard ground and she lost consciousness.

Almost simultaneously, the blast threw Aaron down on the grass in the parkway and he slid along head first. His trajectory slowed enough so when his head hit the huge tree trunk, he didn't lose consciousness.

I made it, he thought, his brain processing that fact with lightning speed.

The next thing his brain processed was sudden excruciating pain as the car door blown higher into the air descended on his legs. He screamed in agony and fainted.

Lyle West rushed out of his house, his radio to his ear, alerting all units with the call, "Officer down."

A huge fire in the middle of their quiet street brought people half-dressed to the sidewalk, some to gawk, some to help.

When Chad Redden leaped from his patrol car in the midst of telling dispatch that Aaron had stopped the car and was running away. The sound of explosion blasted over the radio waves and Milani knew about it almost before West did.

Milani heard West's calls for help and he heard the distant sirens respond. He went to the hospital to wait. He needed to be there when his men arrived.

Chad Redden called to a muscular man in his undershirt to help him carry the unconscious Jerry Fawkes away from his patrol car. They carried him far enough away to be safe should the second car catch fire.

Chad bent over Jerry and ascertained that he was breathing and his heart was beating. Lyle West called to Chad. After telling the man in the sleeveless undershirt to keep an eye on the comatose officer, Chad ran to Chief West's side.

Lauren who had run out of the house upon the heels of her husband followed Lyle to where Aleta lay still. Lyle, after making sure that Aleta wasn't bleeding rushed over to Aaron who was pinned under the car door. He was joined by Chad Redden. They saw that Aaron was bleeding profusely and decided that first they needed to fashion a tourniquet near the top of his leg. Then together with two neighbors the four men lifted the car door carefully off Aaron's leg and set it in the street.

The first ambulance arrived immediately afterward, and Lyle told the paramedics that Aaron was first. He told Chad to stay with the comatose officer and let him know if his condition got worse. Both could hear the sirens of a second ambulance as the fire department rolled in.

Lyle went back to Aleta. She was beginning to stir.

Don't move," Lyle said. "Lauren, stay with her."

He went back to directing his arriving officers as the fire engine rolled in. The fire dominated the scene, and people poured out of houses, running toward it from blocks away.

Lyle directed his officers to keep the crowd back and clear the street for the emergency vehicles. One of West's officers was sent into his house to keep his children inside and safe.

When Lyle moved back near Lauren, she said, "You've got to call Stanley."

Lyle walked away and made the call.

"Stanley," he said, "how close are you to picking up the package?"

"About twenty minutes. Why?"

"There's been…"

Stanley's heart leaped into his throat.

"Is she dead?" Stanley choked out.

"No, but she's hurt. I don't know how badly. She's just coming to now. Lauren is with her. I'm only a few feet away. There was a bomb. The paramedics took away the officer who was driving her. He'd lost a lot of blood. The man in the car that was following is still unconscious. It happened practically in front of my doorstep. Here comes the second ambulance."

"What should I do?"

"Pick up her gift. Then come straight to the hospital. Lauren will stay with her until you get here. I'll keep in touch."

When he moved back, Lauren asked how soon Stanley would be there.

"He's in Chicago picking up a special gift for Aleta. I told him to wait for a few minutes and get it. He'll come straight to the hospital."

Lauren scowled and Lyle knew what she was thinking.

"Trust me," he whispered.

It surprised and annoyed Lauren that Stanley didn't drop everything and come. There was no gift that was that wonderful. She was peeved that Lyle didn't know that.

"Stanley?" Aleta whispered.

"He's in Chicago. He's on his way," Lauren said in a calm voice, "I'll stay with you until he gets here."

"It blew, didn't it?"

"It was a spectacular explosion," Lauren said, forcing a smile. "I wish you'd been able to watch it."

"Me too," Aleta murmured. "My arm hurts."

"Your injured arm?"

"My good arm. It really hurts."

"The paramedics will be here in a second. Just hang in there."

"We gotta have our party," Aleta said.

"One thing at a time," Lauren cautioned. "First we need to move you out of the driveway."

The paramedics moved in, removed Aleta's cloak and put a neck brace an her.

"The other arm is injured too," Lauren said.

"We'll take care of it," the paramedic said.

Lyle leaned in.

"Dr. Cook will meet you at the hospital, Aleta. Just hang on."

"With what?" Aleta quipped, gritting her teeth. "Left arm doesn't work. Right arm doesn't work.

"Your brain still works," Lyle returned. "Lawyers need brains. Everything else is extra."

Aleta was turned and strapped onto a backboard. As the paramedics loaded her onto the gurney, Lyle took Lauren off to one side.

The two were back at the ambulance door before the driver closed it.

"Lauren goes with her," Lyle said.

"You know the rules, Chief," the paramedic said, climbing in the back.

"Aleta's under police protection," Lyle said. "A cop rides with her. Those are the rules."

"Your wife's not a cop."

"I just deputized her," Lyle said. "Lauren, get in."

Lauren climbed in and Lyle swung the door shut. She heard the siren from the other ambulance start up as they passed it. She was glad they would get there first. Aleta needed Dr. Cook now more than ever.

As they drove away, Lyle called Stanley. "She's on her way to the hospital."

"Why did it take so long?"

"They had to immobilize her arm."

"She broke her other arm?"

"Looks that way. But she's conscious and making jokes."

"Any other injuries?"

"The cape protected her skin, but I'll bet she's pretty bruised."

"Who's taking care of her?"

"Wayne went over. He'll meet the ambulance at the hospital."

"The baby?"

"I don't know," Lyle said. "Lauren went with her in the ambulance. I'll get over there as soon as I can. It's a miracle they weren't killed."

"I'm getting ready to leave now. I'll be there in about forty-five minutes."

"I'll call as soon as I know more. Drive carefully. Chances are you won't be able to see her for at least an hour even if you're here."

Dr. Cook met the ambulance at the door. When he saw Lauren, he raised an eyebrow. He knew the rules.

"I'm deputized. I get to stay with her. She's under police protection," Lauren said, a hint of pride in her tone.

Dr. Cook took Aleta's hand lightly as she was wheeled into an examination room.

"I gave away your bed," he said.

Aleta managed a wry smile. "I'm not staying. I have a party to go to."

"I'm afraid we'll need to cut off the blouse," he said.

"Just leave both arms," she quipped.

"I see your brain is still working," Dr. Cook said. "Let's see if everything else is."

"I didn't fall on my left shoulder," Aleta announced like a child proud of having obeyed an order.

"I'm proud of you," Dr. Cook said. "Not only that, you managed to survive. Let's put things in perspective here."

"Stanley was in Chicago when it happened," Lauren inserted. "He's on his way. Lyle told me he'll be here in forty-five minutes."

Aleta looked over at her friend as the nurse removed her slacks. "He knows I'm alive, doesn't he? I don't want him to kill himself getting here."

"Lyle told him you were making jokes," Lauren reported.

"Dr. Cook, what about my driver. Is he okay?" Aleta worried.

"He has an injured leg. It's pretty bad."

"Oh no," Aleta cried. "He's a runner."

"They may not be able to save it."

"Have them call in a specialist. I'll pay for it. Save that leg."

"I'll talk to his doctor," Dr. Cook said.

"Do it now!" Aleta insisted. "I can wait."

Dr. Cook turned to the nurse. "I want an MRI. But, Aleta, you aren't going home tonight."

"I am too!" Aleta declared. "I have a bed reserved at home and two nurses to take care of me."

Dr. Cook grinned, "And there is that duck dinner I get if I say yes, right?"

"Absolutely. The table is already set, isn't it Lauren?"

"Four tables of six," Lauren said.

"I'll check on Aaron," Dr. Cook said. "Lauren, stay with her."

"Really?"

"Policemen have privileges," Wayne Cook said. "I wouldn't give up that badge if I were you."

Lauren looked at the badge Lyle had grabbed from a nearby officer and pinned an her shirt. Lyle was a man of forethought. He never broke rules. He knew how to use them. He went up another notch in her estimation. He must know what the gift is and think it would delight Aleta. He had gone to her first even though he sent the cop to the hospital first. He had his priorities straighter than she did.

She walked beside the gurney and once the group was in the elevator, she inquired, "You aren't claustrophobic, are you?"

"I'm developing MRI-itis," Aleta said. "It's like a rash that won't go away."

Just as Aleta was sliding into the huge tube, Dr. Cook reappeared. He gave her one last piece of advice, "Think of the most pleasant thing you did yesterday."

"Can you read my mind with this thing?"

"No, I can't. Why? Are your thoughts going to be x-rated?"

"You better believe it."

"So much for obeying my orders," he quipped.

"My left shoulder stayed out of it."

"That I can't buy."

"Ask Stanley."

"Shush, Aleta. I need to get a good picture."

"Okay," she whispered.

Dr. Cook didn't say another word. He stood behind the technician and watched the images appear on the screen.

Lauren stepped outside and called Lyle who immediately called Stanley.

"Good news. The baby is okay. Aleta is asking to go home tonight. It's not a definite 'no' yet. It depends on the MRI."

"I'm only twenty-five minutes away."

"I'm stuck at the scene," Lyle told him. "Tom is at the hospital with his men. Lauren is with Aleta. I deputized her so she is able to accompany her everywhere."

"Thanks," Stanley said gratefully.

Aleta was rolled into the treatment room where casts were applied and was told someone would be with her shortly. Lauren went with her.

"I think something's broke," Aleta said to her friend.

"That's my guess too."

"What do you think my chances are of going home?"

"Fifty-fifty."

"So you have no idea."

"You got it."

"Didn't he say anything when I was having the MRI?"

"He pointed to a few things, but didn't say much. I stepped out for a few minutes to call Lyle so he could call Stanley. Stanley was about twenty minutes away then. He should be rolling up any minute."

Dr. Cook poked his head into the room. "How are you two doing?"

"What's broken?" Aleta said.

"I want you to think about a cast that holds your arm in the air like this?"

"Oh no!" Aleta exclaimed.

"Think about it because unless Stanley gives me same satisfactory answers, that's what you're going to get."

"Stanley?" Aleta gasped. "Why him? I told you the truth."

"You two wait here and pray," Dr. Cook said closing the door with a grin.

The grin was still there when he entered the waiting area.

Stanley relaxed. "Looks like good news."

"Pretty much," Cook said. "Slight concussion. Broken clavicle. No damage to the fetus. She'll have a lot of bruising appearing in the next few days. You don't hit the pavement hard enough to break a bone without surrounding tissue damage."

Cook then held out his hand, "Good to see you, Mr. Locke. If I can count on you to help, maybe I can let her go home as soon as I bandage her arm and fit her with a sling, but it depends."

"We'll do anything," Robert Locke said.

Stanley nodded his acquiescence.

"Stanley, I can't stress too strongly that it will take six to twelve weeks for the break to heal. She must not use that arm for anything. I told her I'd put her in a cast with her arm in the air if you couldn't guarantee she'd obey my orders."

"She's obeyed them with her other arm," Stanley said. "It hasn't been easy for her to submit to Bertha helping her with bathroom chores, but she did."

"What about sex?" Cook asked glaring at the young husband.

"What did she tell you?"

"To ask you to explain how you engaged in sexual activity without her shoulder being compromised by your activity."

Stanley flushed as he glanced at Aleta's father.

"You have no idea how creative a daughter you have, Mr. Locke. But, I never... I wouldn't... honest... she did manage to... um... Wayne, could I talk with you privately."

Robert Locke backed out of the room, muttering, "Creative, huh. That doesn't surprise me."

When her father was gone, Stanley, his face still bright red, told Dr. Cook exactly how creative Aleta had been.

Wayne Cook put his hand on Stanley's shoulder. "Don't fret. My wife's just as creative. I just had to be sure Aleta did, in fact, follow my orders."

The color in Stanley's face began to fade. "She'll obey whatever orders you give. I'll add my order to it. She won't play around if I tell her not to."

"It will be worse than it was. She could do a lot with one arm. She'll not be able to do anything now. I don't dare take the other sling off. She'll overuse the arm if I do."

"I understand."

"You have full-time help at home?"

"Day-time only."

"I want her to walk every day but someone will need to accompany her and keep an arm around her waist. She can't afford a fall."

"Her father plans on staying as long as necessary. With two of us around all the time, we should be able to care for her."

"She promised me that duck dinner if I would let her go home. What doctor could resist such an offer?"

"So, you're going to let me take her home?" Stanley asked, surprised.

"She was going to sign herself out. And I need her under your control until she realizes how crippled she is," he said. "Oh, and she needs a blouse."

"I'll send for one. When can I see her?"

"As soon as I'm done."

A few minutes later, Dr. Cook entered the room where Aleta was waiting.

"Am I going to get to go home?" she asked.

"Stanley told all," Dr. Cook answered, his eyes twinkling.

"He didn't!" Aleta exclaimed flushing.

"I told him about the cast I was preparing for you. I don't like to be disobeyed."

"But I didn't."

"So he told me."

"He didn't go into detail?" Aleta queried fretfully.

"Sorry, that's privileged."

Aleta's worry switched to anger. "What do you mean 'privileged'?'"

"You're a lawyer. You understand privilege," Dr. Cook said calmly. "Now do you want that cast I described before or do you promise to obey all my orders?"

"No cast," Aleta said, reigning in her vexation. "I'll do whatever you say."

"I'm going to put on a butterfly bandage to hold your shoulder in place and a sling to take the weight of your arm off your shoulder. Now having said that, let me tell you that every time the arm is lifted out of the sling to scratch your nose or rub your eyes or stick a cookie in your mouth, you are defeating the purpose of the sling and asking the broken shoulder to support your arm."

Aleta nodded solemnly. "No using the arm."

"Pretend you don't have it," Dr. Cook said.

"How long?"

"Six to twelve weeks."

Aleta paled, but then she had an idea.

"What about my other arm?"

"You can't use that arm either."

For a second Aleta didn't speak. Then her words burst forth. "Oh, my God! What am I going to do?"

"Finally!" Dr. Cook exclaimed. "You've finally got the picture. The answer is nothing."

"What about turning pages," Aleta said. "I can turn pages can't I? I'm studying for the bar."

"You can turn single pages. If you need to flip a number of pages, you ask for help."

"You're asking me to live like a helpless invalid!"

"Aleta, you are. Accept it!"

As he bandaged her arm, Dr. Cook told her he would be checking her before during and after the party.

"Expect it," he ordered her.

"Yes Sir," Aleta responded wryly. "You're the boss."

"Should the party be short?" Lauren asked.

"Actually, the longer the better. I don't want Aleta to sleep tonight, and it will be easier for her to stay awake with company around."

"So the party's a good thing?" Lauren pressed, still unsure if anything should be changed. "There will be twenty-four people there. I could cut it down."

"Don't change a thing."

Dr. Chesney entered the room. "I heard you'd been hurt. How are you?"

"Broken clavicle," Aleta said. "I won't be able to do much. I'd like to visit your wife tomorrow as planned. I'm not sure though whether I can still understand her. Concussions do things to the brain."

"She won't care. She'll just be happy to see you," Dr. Chesney said warmly. "What about the baby?"

"It's okay," Aleta said. "My head and shoulder took most of the impact. Sometimes I'd like it not to be my head."

Dr. Chesney smiled. "Take care of yourself."

Aleta giggled. "That's a big order. Besides Dr. Cook said that's the one thing I can't do. I can't even sneak a chocolate bar."

"Come tomorrow and I'll feed you chocolate."

"You've got a deal."

"If you visit anyone in the hospital, I want you in a wheelchair," Dr. Cook said.

"Whatever for?"

"Don't argue. Just do it. And use a wheelchair if you go shopping. It'll protect your from being jostled. I'll tell Stanley."

"I'm feeling more like an invalid by the second."

"Good!" Dr. Cook exclaimed.

A nurse entered carrying a handful of blouses and two sweaters. Dr. Cook examined them and commented that they wouldn't do because to put any of them on would involve twisting one shoulder or the other.

"You need a hospital gown type of blouse," he concluded.

"Send me home in one," Aleta said. "Lauren, I'll need a pin to hold the back closed, and I'll need my slacks on. That'll work for now."

Dr. Cook nodded his approval.

"Lauren, who can sew a blouse for me in time for my party?"

"Julia Danielson makes a lot of her clothes. Her daughter Kim is your size," Lauren replied. "I'll ask her."

"Something silky and bright," Aleta said, then flipped to a new topic. "Dr. Cook what happened with Aaron's leg?"

"The doctors are going to try to save it."

Chapter 9

Chief Alan Peets called in the entire Oakwood police unit immediately after Milani's phone call. When they were assembled, to their surprise he took roll. Two were missing. Kirk Boyes was on guard duty at Tri City Hospital, so he was excused.

"Anyone know where Ernie Wilson is?" Peets asked.

Rob Finch offered to call him again and tell him it was important.

"Were you with him when he got the call?" Peets asked.

"Yes Sir. We're roommates."

"And what was his response? Your job depends an you telling me the truth," Peets said sternly.

Rob, who'd only been on the force a few months, still hedged, "Well, Sir, I believe he thought he'd get the same instruction when his shift started."

"Why did you come in?"

"You ordered us in, Sir."

"Correct answer," Peets said. "He's right about one thing. When he reports in he'll be given instructions. The first one will be to turn in his badge."

"He's fired?" Rob stammered.

"Correct again," Peets said. "Now, down to business. Some of you may have heard about the car bombing in Arborville. Two officers were injured, one critically. The person they were protecting was also injured. These men were friends of mine from Willow Glen, but even if they weren't, we are partly responsible."

There was a murmur of dissent.

"Our perp, the one who tried to smother Mr. Hoskinson, was not nailed by us. That's our failure. The victim of the car bombing was lured by a phone call promising her the name of our perp. So we are tied in directly."

Murmurs of concern swept the room.

"We are going back to Oakwood Home and we are going to interview every resident and every staff member. Someone there knows something. They may or may not know they know it. I want everyone interviewed twice, each time by a different officer. You are not to compare reports. All reports will be turned in to Officer Peterson who will assign each of you your next interview. Some interviews will take longer than others. Take whatever time is necessary. Remember some are sick people. Some are old. Some have memory problems. Don't concentrate on the attempted smothering. Concentrate on anything unusual happening at the home. I want recorded observations. We will pull them together later and then hopefully have a direction for our investigation. Above all, don't try to prove anything. This is information gathering."

Hank Peterson spoke up. "Most of these men have never interviewed anyone other than for a traffic violation."

"Good point. Remember, men, these are witnesses not violators of the law. Treat them with respect at all times. No quips about anyone being crazy or senile or operating on a different wave length."

"You want all of us to go?" Rob ventured.

"Two cops were almost killed. Anyone who doesn't care about that can hand in his badge," Peets announced.

There was a general murmur of assent. The men were behind the project. This man appeared to have a plan—one they could understand.

Peets called out over the hubbub, "Stop and get your assignments from Officer Peterson before you leave."

Hank Peterson looked slightly bewildered until Peets handed him two lists. "Patients and staff. Alternate everyone between the two. Just go down the lists as the officers come to you. That's your order."

Hank nodded and went to the supply cabinet and took out a stack of forms. He put the name of the person to be interviewed and the designation of patient or staff on top and then handed the form to the officer next in line. Peets was pleased with this plan. The men would descend upon the home one or two at a time.

Before he left, Chief Peets took Hank Peterson aside. "If any man turns in a careless report or is abusive in any way, send him back to me and go on without him. I expect you will need to send me a few men for reassignment. This won't be everyone's forte."

Twenty minutes later Nick Viguetta stood before his chief. "Hank Peterson said you had a new assignment for me, Sir."

Not having any idea why the man was sent back, Peets sent him to relieve Kirk Boyes and guard Hoskinson at the hospital.

He could tell that assignment wasn't to his liking either.

As the reports came in Hank Peterson noticed that Don Wishnefsky's and Ned Zimmerman's reports were lengthy and full of underlined quotes. He sent each of them to reinterview the people Nick had done. Neither was told about the first interview.

Ned Zimmerman approached the cook and found she didn't speak much English. He asked others in the kitchen if they knew Spanish. One woman did. He called her over and began his interview. The woman translated the questions into Spanish and then repeated the answers. He asked her a wide range of questions and found that while she didn't speak the language she had noted a number of odd things, mostly that one of the attendants regularly met people behind the building when he took a smoking break. Since she was the person in charge of the garbage, she was in the alley frequently. She couldn't understand most of the words, so she didn't know what was going on.

At the other end of the building Don Wishnefsky listened to Nellie Carlson in the farthest room from the entrance complain about not having any visitors. He sympathized with her, and she began to list her other complaints.

"They stick me in a room with a person with Alzheimer's. They expect me to watch her. That's what I think. All them others…"

"What others?"

"Alzheimer's patients is in rooms by themselves. Why can't I get a regular person? There's plenty of them here. I can't get around, so the days get long, and it would be nice to have someone to talk to who could remember some of what you just said."

"Do you have an idea why your roommate isn't in a room by herself?"

"No visitors. That's why."

"What do you mean?"

"She's been here forever and she never gets no visitors. The others are all new, except maybe the couple at the end of the other hall. Any ways, they got visitors."

"Regular visitors?"

"Lots of family. And they don't recognize anyone. I asked the nurses aides, and they said they're as bad as the one I got, so I can't even get her switched. I still asked because even family give me someone new to talk to. But they said no."

"You ever see any of the visitors?"

"No. Nobody ever stops by. There's this one who wears black and red all the time. I think she's a slut come to do someone in here. She goes out this door a lot. It's closer to the cars, so a lot of them do that when it's raining or really cold."

"You're very observant," Don Wishnefsky commented.

"You know what else? All of them's alike."

"The visitors?"

"Yeah. They're all women, the kind what have time for a hairdresser. Not busy with kids. Nails done up just so. They come regular. Always in the middle of the day so none of them works. And none of them never misses their regular days."

"They have regular days."

"Yeah, that red and black one comes every Thursday except last week, but she was sure in a hurry to leave when that siren went off. Scared the bejabbers out of me, I'll tell you. I would've run too if I had legs that work."

"Can you handle a wheelchair?"

"Not a regular one. I could handle one of those electric ones, but I ain't got no one to give me one."

"I need to go now. Would it be alright if I stopped by once in a while to visit you?"

"You would do that?"

"Sure, maybe on Tuesday or Thursday next week."

"I'll be here."

Ned Zimmerman and Don Wishnefsky hit Hank Peterson's station within seconds of each other.

Both started right in with, "I think I got something. Can I take it to the Chief?"

Hank Peterson shook his head.

"You let Nick take in his report," Ned challenged.

"My report too," Don said. "He needs to see it right away."

Hank Peterson told them to wait. He went outside.

"Hey, Chief, I got two eager beavers who think they've got something good. Same two people Viguetta reported knew nothing. What do you want me to do?"

Peets thought for a few minutes. He didn't want everyone vying for a chance to hand his report in personally, but he couldn't believe that would happen. The men weren't really comfortable with him, so he couldn't see them in a shoving match to go one on one with him. That these two dared to break out of the group told him he might have found his first candidates for promotion.

"Send them over, but no one else until they come back."

"Yes, Sir," Hank said.

Peets decided he should move Hank up in rank. While he was only acting chief, why should he act like he was a fill-in? Why not act as if he were permanent? Even if his tenure only lasted a few months, he could give it his all. A big case might not come along again during his tenure. He'd never have a better chance to test the mettle of his men. Two had already fallen by the wayside. Balancing that with temporary promotions made sense to him. They would be made on merit. He knew life was more complicated than that, but hell, he would never be permanent, so why not do the job the way he wanted to do it. He had nothing to lose.

The two stood silently in his office while he studied the reports of each.

"I assume you shared these on your way over," he said when he finished.

Both nodded.

"Good!" he said and saw tenseness leave the faces of each.

They're scared to death of me, he surmised. This took guts.

"Well, I'm pleased," he said. "Now, what would you suggest we do next?"

"Keep on with the interviews," Ned Zimmerman said. "There are probably others who noticed Arnetti's activities. Also, I'd search to see if Arnetti has a record. He might be a conspirator in the attack, or at the least, he's probably dealing drugs."

Peets looked at Don Wishnefsky.

"Me?" Don said, then when Peets affirmed his query, went on. "First I'd take Nellie Carlson flowers."

"Why?" Peets said his brows raised in surprise.

"Because she's lonely, but it would allow me to return periodically and become a regular visitor so that if we needed more information on Arnetti or intended to devise a sting, I'd be in place."

"And when this operation is over?"

"I'd work to see that she gets an electric wheelchair that will let her mingle with the other residents. And I'd keep visiting her."

"What would you do to further this investigation?"

"I'd check all the regular visitors, beginning with the ones on Thursday. I believe our killer-to-be is one of them."

"I like all the ideas you both presented. I'm going to make you two lead detectives on this case. When all the reports are in, you'll read them and decide whom you personally want to re-interview. Until then, Ned, you go back and check the employment records of all the employees. Don, you get hold of the visitor's log and go through it. Find out how soon after these Alzheimer's patients were admitted that visitors started arriving. Ned, I want to know not only when Arnetti is on, but exactly what his duties are. Tonight you will go over the reports together with Hank Peterson. If Hank wants you to interview anyone because he's not satisfied with the reports, do it. He's still in charge of gathering information. Pinpointing the culprit is important, but proving it is critical. We can't arrest without evidence."

The two were nodding energetically at nearly every statement. Peets could remember feeling such excitement when he first started. Such enthusiasm was exciting. For the first time he began to feel good about being here. He had the beginnings of a crew.

"I'm going to a dinner tonight. Chief West and Chief Milani are going to be there. I will check with you by phone during the evening."

When they were on their way back, Peets filled in Hank Peterson and then told him that he wanted to promote him temporarily to sergeant. "I need you to deploy the men when they finish the interviews. Send the night shift men home now to rest."

"How long do you want Viguetta to stand guard at the hospital?"

"Let me get back to you on that," Peets said.

As soon as he disconnected from Peterson, Chief Peets headed straight for the hospital. He needed to talk with Milani personally.

Milani was downstairs with several of his men waiting for news. Aaron Ponce was still in surgery. Jerry Fawkes was in intensive care still in a coma.

Peets walked up to Milani and said, "I need to talk someplace where we won't be disturbed. And I also need to check on my man on the third floor."

"The one you sent over to guard Mr. Hoskinson?"

Peets nodded.

"I think he's in the lunch room," Milani said.

"How about we go sit and talk in Mr. Hoskinson's room?"

"I'm game. Waiting's a bear." He turned to one of his men. "Beep me if there's any news."

Chief Peets greeted Mr. Hoskinson. "I know you can't speak but I'm going to hold up fingers, each representing ten minutes. I want to know how long the guard's been gone. As long as you nod your head, I'll keep going."

He held up one finger and said, "Ten." Then two fingers and said, "Twenty." At thirty, another nod. At forty, a shake.

"A guess?" Peets asked.

Hoskinson shook his head. Peets looked around and spotted a clock on the wall.

"Thank you," he said. "Mr. Hoskinson, Chief Milani and I have some police business to discuss, and we wonder if it would be okay to talk in here. You may repeat anything you hear to Aleta if you wish, that is, if she can understand you after the bombing."

Mr. Hoskinson eyes widened with fear.

"I'm afraid it happened, Sir, right after she left you this morning. She survived. Chief Milani here has one man on the operating table and one in a coma in intensive care."

Milani spoke up. "Aleta warned the officer with her, and they both got out of the car, but they didn't get far enough. She has a broken clavicle and a concussion, and she's badly bruised."

Peets added, "The good news is she's still going to have her party."

Hoskinson nodded strongly.

"I'll give her your good wishes."

Again the old man nodded.

"Tom," Peets said as he took a seat where he couldn't be seen from the door, "I fired a man today."

Tom Milani sat down where he also wasn't visible from the corridor.

"Cause?"

"I ordered them all in. He ignored me."

"That's cause," Milani said.

Hoskinson nodded his head.

"I'm about to fire a second man," Peets said.

"Mr. Hoskinson's guard?"

"Dereliction of duty," Peets said.

"That's cause in my book, too."

"We're reinterviewing the people at the home. We may have some new leads. Two of my men turned out to be sharp investigators. I put them in charge of the investigation. Another is an organizational whiz. I'm moving him up to temporary sergeant. He's going to handle the scheduling. He's the one that sent Viguetta back to me because his reports were useless. I sent him here. I figured with so many of your men around that Mr. Hoskinson would be safe."

Peets turned to the old man. "Don't worry. Your next guard will do a good job because I'm counting on you to tell me if he doesn't. Deal?"

The old man nodded his head.

"You said you had new leads," Milani prompted.

"There's a drug dealer operating out of the home," Peets replied. "One of the staff. I think we can nail him through his clientele and then maybe get at Mr. Hoskinson's attacker through him. I really want to nail him on the drug charges though. I've got a man inside. What I need to know is whether you think I should move prematurely on the hope he'll crack and give us Hoskinson's attacker."

"Don't do that. We're already sure we know who it is, but we haven't an ounce of proof. Get him solid before you move in," Milani said, then added, "I'm doubling the men on Aleta, and one stays with the car."

"You aren't locking her up?" Peets asked, surprised.

"Lock up Aleta Praetzel against her will. That'd be career suicide. The whole family are a bunch of lawyers, for Pete's sake."

Peets grinned. "You're taking my name in vain?"

"I hear hard shoes coming down the hall," Milani said. "Let's see how long it takes him to discover us."

Hoskinson uttered a few syllables and Viguetta poked his head into the room.

"Sorry, old man, no one can understand you, so don't bother."

"He says you've been gone forty minutes," Peets said from his chair in one corner of the room.

Nick Viguetta whipped around and stammered out, "Uh, Chief. I just went to the john. I ain't been gone no forty minutes. More like forty seconds."

"How long would you say we've been here, Chief Milani?" Peets asked. Nick Viguetta turned and saw that the chair in the other corner had a man in it, too.

"About twelve minutes I'd say," Tom replied. "What I don't understand is how he mistook the cafeteria for the john."

"I guess he's not too bright."

"He saw you fire a guy today, didn't he?"

"Yes, he did."

"I guess he thought you had a limit on the number of people you could fire."

"Guess so."

"Hey, look, I made a mistake," Nick Viguetta whined. "We all make them. I didn't take my job as serious as I should. I'm sorry. Everyone deserves a second chance."

"I believe in second chances," Peets said. "Don't you, Chief?"

Nick looked at Chief Milani as he nodded.

"Then I get a second chance?" Nick asked hopefully.

"You already had it," Peets said. "This was your second chance."

"What did I do wrong? I interviewed the damn people Hank gave me. One was a cook's helper who don't speak English. The other was an old lady who about chewed my ear off about not getting any visitors. She rattled on and on. If I'd have gotten a better draw I would've come up with something. I know I would've."

"Well, so far they're two of our best sources of vital information, which we have thanks to the two men who interviewed them after you."

His immediate shock, Nick covered up with an accusation. "Who could tell? I guess I just don't get the experience I need. And that's your fault."

Peets smiled. Milani had seen that smile before. Peets was moving in on the kill. He sat back to enjoy the moment.

"I agree with you, which is why I didn't fire you then," Peets said. "Instead I gave you a second chance. Everyone knows what guard duty is. Sorry Officer Viguetta, you lose. I'll take your badge and your gun, please. You're fired."

Hoskinson made a funny sound which both chiefs agreed later was laughter.

Chapter 10

The Oakwood mayor, Louise Oppenwall, appeared unexpectedly in Chief Peets' office two hours after he fired Nick Viguetta.

"You fired two police officers today," she charged.

Peets took his eyes off the reports on his desk and looked squarely at the gray haired, thick-bodied business woman.

"Yes, Ma'am, I did."

"Both said you're a racist and that you're making room for black officers."

"I'm not planning on doing any hiring," Peets said. "I believe the new Chief of Police should do that. I'm just cleaning house."

A bit mollified, the mayor toned down her approach. "Any more firings in the works?"

"Ma'am, here are the reports received from my men in the field today. I see only two that are totally unsatisfactory. What is your opinion?"

She picked out four more. "These are pretty worthless as well. You can't fire a man because he doesn't get anything from a witness."

"Every witness was interviewed twice, Mrs. Oppenwall,"

Peets said as he sorted through the papers in front of him. He paired the reports with the witnesses. Each of the four reports she had selected was attached to one of two witnesses. "It would seem that these two people were not forthcoming with either of the officers assigned to interview them."

"You can't say that. It could be the officers," Louise pointed out.

"All four?" Peets asked.

"It's possible."

Peets then laid down the second report of each of the four officers. The second report in each case was detailed and quite extensive.

"I see your point," she admitted "What about Nick Viguetta's reports?"

"Here are Nick Viguetta's reports on two different witnesses. Here are the second reports on these same two witnesses," Peets said.

"He mentioned something about not being given proper instruction. Ernie Wilson claimed the same."

"Ernie Wilson failed to report for duty when ordered."

"He said he didn't know there was an emergency. In fact he claims that it wasn't a real emergency, that you were doing Chief Milani a favor."

"He refused to follow an order," Peets said. "The order was clear to every other man on the force."

"Well, since there was no emergency…"

"There was an attempted bombing in Willow Glen and then this morning a bomb took out two police officers and the person they were protecting. And it all started here in Oakwood. An attack on a police officer is an emergency in any policeman's eyes."

"But they weren't Oakwood's officers. We've always liked being autonomous," Mrs. Oppenwall pointed out.

"The chief of both Arborville and Willow Glen are not interfering with my investigation in any way," Peets said coolly. "However, I stepped our investigation up a notch when I realized that we might be able to stop this madman before he turns back around and strikes here again."

"Why are we guarding someone in Tri City Hospital?"

"Because he's still in danger."

"He's no longer in our jurisdiction," Louise Oppenwall observed, remembering Nick Viguetta's argument.

"If you were attacked and the attack failed but you wound up in the hospital, I would put a guard at the door to your room."

"I'm an Oakwood citizen."

"Am I to assume that the people residing in the Oakwood Nursing Home are not residents of Oakwood?"

Brought up short, Mrs. Oppenwall stammered slightly. "No, you're right."

"Whether I placed Officer Viguetta to guard a citizen of Oakwood or a citizen of another town, he had an obligation to follow orders and protect the man. He was not fired because he was an ineffective investigator. He was fired because he left his post for forty minutes. That's dereliction of duty."

"So, how many more are we going to lose?"

"None, as far as I can see. The inexperienced ones are ready to be taught. And I'm willing to teach them."

"Both Wilson and Viguetta claim no one respects you."

Peets smiled. "Well, if they don't they're doing a damned fine job of hiding their disrespect. Their work at the Home has uncovered a major felony as well as real clues as to who is responsible for the murder attempt in the Home and the bombings in Willow Glen and Arborville. You said autonomy is precious to this town, but I can tell you what's even more important—respect. If we crack two big cases, this police department will move into equal status with the ones in Arborville and Willow Glen which is a place Oakwood has never been. Isn't that what you'd really like to see happen?"

"Carry on," Louise Oppenwall said.

"I am promoting three men who've proven themselves to be worthy of recognition and capable of stepping up. I do understand that these are temporary promotions as I am acting chief, but while I'm here, I will choose the men I want to help me direct the current investigations."

"You'll get no more guff from me, Chief Peets," Louise Oppenwall stated firmly. "You obviously know what you are doing and you've answered all my questions. I apologize for my gruffness earlier."

"Ma'am, you had every reason to be concerned. I'm very pleased you brought your concerns directly to me. Feel free to approach me any time you think an action of mine is questionable."

As soon as she left, he called his wife. "Eloise is the party still on tonight?"

"Lauren called to assure me it was."

"Good. I need a party."

Chapter 11

When Lauren saw how delighted Aleta was to see her father, she forgave Lyle completely. Aleta's grandmother arrived while Aleta was still in the hospital. After touching base with Aleta, Harriet drove Lauren home to get her car. The party was still on.

After dropping off Lauren, Harriet Locke drove straight to Aleta's house. When she came in, her son Robert met her.

"We have an errand to do," he said. "Go say hi again and then goodbye. Tell her we'll be back shortly."

Harriet walked into the bedroom where Aleta was sitting, waiting.

"Are you okay?" she asked. Her granddaughter wasn't one to sit still.

She grinned. "Stanley told me to stay put, so I'm staying put. He's getting my lunch. What about you?"

"Your dad and I have an errand to run," Harriet said.

"He told me," Aleta said. "He said he was staying all week, and, Grams, he didn't lie. He told Mother he was coming to see me. He told her he wanted to see for himself if

I was okay. He promised he'd call her. He's already called her twice.

"The first time he told her about the party. She said that I couldn't be too badly injured if I could throw a party. He told her it was a sit-down, formal dinner for twenty-four people. That seemed to alleviate her worries even further.

"On his second phone call he told her about Bertha. He really praised her cooking and said that she referred to me as 'Ma'am.' Mother was very impressed.

"Eventually, he's going to tell her he's going to stay awhile. Sort of a vacation. He says she doesn't really want him underfoot right now, so she won't mind. Anyway, since he's going to be here all week, we've got lots of time to talk."

"Then I'll run along," Harriet said. "The sooner we're done, the sooner we'll be back."

"Grams, don't worry. Stanley's here. Bertha's here. And Lauren's coming over to deal with the delivery of the flowers. She plans to help Bertha with the ducks."

Harriet stopped worrying when she heard Stanley giving instructions to Bertha. Evidently, he was going to lay down with Aleta after she ate. He told Bertha that he needed to practice feeding Aleta in private. Bertha could have pointed out such a task didn't take much practice, but she didn't.

Harriet decided she wouldn't either. Getting Aleta to rest was a good idea. When Stanley added that he was setting his wristwatch, in case he dozed off, she left.

In the car as they drove down the driveway, Robert asked his mother, "Why are you smiling?"

"Because Aleta chose herself a good husband. She didn't shop much, but she knew when she'd found a gem."

"You shopped for her," Robert quipped. "You and Martha Cook. I can see you're pleased as punch with yourself."

"So what's so important we had to get it now and not Monday? I don't work anymore you know."

"Aleta's wheelchair."

"I didn't know she needed one."

"Dr. Cook told Stanley she wasn't to go to the hospital or shop unless she was in a wheelchair. He doesn't want her to fall and he doesn't want either shoulder bumped. It's pretty hard to protect both sides of your body at once."

"Are we renting one?"

"Mom, you know Aleta. You tell me."

"She'd send it back. And she'd figure on using the hospital wheelchairs which she'd have to wait for which she might not do if the delay is too long."

"And she'd say we could shop during the off hours when there'd be fewer people," Robert added, "And then she'd argue that she doesn't really need one."

"So we're buying one."

"And a van to fit it in."

"A van?"

"I want you to pick one you'd like to use for the dog show stuff."

"Who's buying this van?"

"You are."

"Why me?"

"Because Aleta likes the familiar. Once she's been driven around in it for a while, she'll want one just like it. She can buy it from you. If you decide to keep it, she'll buy a twin. Right now it's important to protect her. It's not easy to get Aleta to do what's good for her."

"You do know your daughter. It's a good plan."

"How much money do you have available?"

"A hundred thousand in my checking account," Harriet replied evenly.

"So much?"

"To cover unexpected medical costs, of which there have been a lot lately," Harriet said. "But no dealership is going to take my personal check."

"I figured as much," Robert said. "I have a back-up plan."

"A credit card?"

"And have Marian see it? There are some things she doesn't need to know. How wealthy you are is one of them."

"Does Paul know?" Harriet asked, referring to her other son.

"He's the one who told me."

"And his wife?"

"Doesn't know. We can keep your secrets, Mother, all of them. It's in our blood, you know."

"Your father would be proud of both of you. So would your grandfather."

"Van first I think," Robert said. "We need something to take the wheelchair home in."

"What's your back-up?"

"Mrs. Cook."

"Martha's not coming?" Harriet gasped, thoroughly taken aback.

"Isn't she?"

"Robert, she's over ninety. She can't go shopping for a van."

"You're not a big shopper yourself. We're going to a Chrysler dealer. She's already called. He'll have several models ready to go."

"When did you arrange all this?"

"I called Martha from the hospital. She was delighted to help us surprise Aleta."

"You said I was to buy it."

"That hasn't changed. Only we three know it's for Aleta. As far as Aleta's concerned, it's a loan. We can't overwhelm her and Stanley. Neither can think in the long term right now. I'm sure she thinks this'll all pass in a week."

"She'll hate your going home."

"I'm not leaving."

"What about Jayline's wedding?"

"I'm not needed until the day. Marian has enough credit cards to pay for two weddings."

"What'll you tell Marian?"

"As little as possible. She needs to enjoy the wedding. In a week I plan to tell her I'm flying home with Aleta and Stanley for the ceremony and that will calm her worries about Aleta's condition."

"Aleta said you didn't tell her, but I wasn't sure."

"So far I've come up with enough activity that she's stopped worrying."

"Aleta won't be able to fly back for the wedding. She won't be healed enough."

"Stanley and I are flying her back. And you too."

"Is his father going to pilot you?"

"I'm taking flying lessons," Robert said. "I have a month. Stanley knows how to fly. I'll be able to take over once we're in the air. I take my first lesson Monday afternoon. I can drive Aleta to the hospital in the morning and take her for walks after my lessons."

"You sure came up with a lot of plans since landing," Harriet commented, not displeased.

"One has to in order to stay ahead of you women.

"Aleta will want to be at Jayline's wedding," Harriet said. "But she'll be worried about her mother's reaction."

"I'll prep Marian a couple days in advance," Robert said. "If her reaction is too bad, I'll threaten to cancel Aleta's appearance. Marian will never permit that. She'll pull herself together.

"Who'll be the co-pilot on the trip back?" Harriet asked.

"I'll be the co-pilot," Robert said.

"Marian will want to come."

"By then Aleta will have a routine and Marian will find out how self-sufficient her daughter is. Our visit will be short."

He had no idea how few of his well-conceived plans were going to be realized as he envisioned them.

Meanwhile, back at the house, Stanley had fed Aleta an egg salad sandwich and a glass of milk, brushed her teeth, removed her soiled slacks and dressed her in soft cotton sweat pants. He undid the pin holding the back of the hospital gown together and then he helped her lay down on the top of the bed covers.

"You can sleep," he told her. "I'll be right here if you need anything and I'll wake you every two hours just as Dr. Cook ordered."

He hung up his suit and donned a sweat shirt and pants. Aleta smiled. Stanley would never lie down in his suit.

He gently crawled onto the bed beside her, careful not to touch her.

"If you put your hand on my heart," she whispered. "You can tell if it stops."

Stanley placed his hand gently on her chest but felt nothing.

"Not on top of the sling, Stanley. Underneath. I have a blouse on, so it's okay."

The hand moved under the sling.

"It feels good," Aleta said quietly. "As if we're connected."

"Don't worry about the party," he murmured and his breathing slowed down.

She didn't have to look at him to know he was asleep. She closed her eyes and joined him.

Two hours later, Bertha became concerned.

"They've been quiet for a long time." she said to Lauren.

"I thought he'd come out and check on things."

"Maybe they're both asleep," Lauren said.

"Mrs. Praetzel is supposed to be roused every two hours," Bertha said.

"Go check," Lauren said.

Bertha went over and knocked softly on the door. There was no answer.

"Go in," Lauren coached.

Bertha tiptoed into the room. She looked over at the couple lying so still on the bed.

She went straight toward the side of the bed nearest where Aleta lay. She saw Aleta watching her and was discomforted.

"Take the tray," Aleta whispered. "Let him sleep."

"Yes, Ma'am," Bertha whispered turning and picking up the tray.

She'd seen Stanley's hand which was under the hospital gown.

Bertha walked out quickly, red-faced.

"How is she?"

"Awake, but Mr. Praetzel is asleep," she reported. "I'm sure he'll awaken soon."

"Does she want company?" Lauren asked.

"Oh no! Ma'am," Bertha exclaimed. "No one should go in there. If he's not up in two hours, I'll wake him."

She rushed into the kitchen and looked through the kitchen window as she set down the tray.

"The florist is here," she announced with relief.

An hour later, Stanley woke up and realized where his hand was. He slowly pulled it out and looked at his watch.

My God, he thought. It's been three hours. Why didn't my watch go off?

He leaned over and kissed Aleta on the cheek. Her eyelids remained still. He kissed her on her neck. Still no movement.

His fear mounting, he kissed her on the lips. No response. He put his hand back under her blouse to feel her heart.

"That's better," she whispered. "You can kiss me awake now."

"You little minx. You scared me. I thought you'd slipped into a coma."

"Bertha came in after two hours," Aleta said smiling. "She saw your hand on my heart. I think she was embarrassed."

Stanley rolled away. "She's not the only one. Aleta, you have got to stop getting these damned concussions!"

"Is that an order?"

"It is if I thought you could help it."

"Help me up. I want to see how things are going."

"Let me get dressed."

"You can dress later when I get dressed. We're a matching pair right now."

He came over and helped her up.

Stanley hesitated at the bedroom door. "You know having the master bedroom open straight into the living room isn't such a great idea, after all."

"You can make any changes you want."

"I thought we should add another bathroom," he suggested. "While we were sleeping, no one could use the bathroom. That's pretty inconvenient."

"Probably we should add another bathroom right away. Bertha would like that."

Stanley opened the door.

"Good, you're awake," Lauren said. "We've got to clean up your bedroom and set up the flowers. Go sit somewhere."

"Dad and Grams aren't back yet?" Aleta asked.

"Bertha, come give me a hand," Lauren called. "I still need to go home, get dressed and pry Lyle away from his work."

"What about my blouse. Did Julia finish it?" Aleta asked.

"She's sewn you several. She'll be here any minute."

"But no word from Dad?"

A horn honking coming up the driveway alerted them all.

"Julie wouldn't honk," Lauren said, running to the kitchen window. "It's someone in a new van followed by your Lexus."

"Dad bought a van?" Aleta said. "For a week?"

"I don't think it's his," Stanley surmised. "He took your grandmother with him. Has she been talking about getting a van?"

"She likes the RV," Aleta replied. "And her Jeep's still parked next to it. It's brand new."

Everyone went to the picture window. The van was driven right in front of the window but back far enough so Aleta could get a good look from the house. Stanley, however, slipped on his coat and ran out to take a closer look and to ask his father-in-law what was going on.

Robert Locke jumped out and Stanley climbed into the driver's seat while Aleta's father stood outside talking to him through the window. Harriet parked behind the van and hurried into the house.

Aleta heard her greet the two police officers standing outside. She looked at Lauren. "When did the police get here?"

"They followed you home. There are two more at the gate," Lauren said. "Those two are from Arborville. You've got the heads of three police departments coming for dinner. It's not just you they're guarding."

"Oh," Aleta said softly. "Okay then."

"How do you like my new van?" her grandmother asked.

"Why did you get it today?" Aleta asked, her suspicions rising.

"Your dad was here and he wanted to get your wheelchair and I thought, why not now instead of later. I realized I needed a van when Lyle and I went duck hunting."

That explanation satisfied Aleta. She had wondered how long it would be before her grandmother found her new jeep too small for her needs.

"You said wheelchair," Aleta remembered. "I don't need a wheelchair. I can get one at the hospital when I go, and you know I never go shopping anyway."

"Dr. Cook meant anytime you're going to go where there's a crowd."

Aleta's temper rose full force. "I'm not sitting in a wheelchair at my own party!"

"Aleta, be nice. Your dad is just following Dr. Cook's orders."

"He rented it, didn't he?" Aleta asked hopefully.

Harriet Locke eyed her granddaughter knowingly.

"He bought it. I sat in it. It's quite comfortable."

"I don't care. I'm not sitting in a wheelchair tonight. And that's final!"

"They're bringing it in," Lauren announced. "And here comes Julia."

The door opened and Aleta saw her dad's beaming face. He thinks he's bought me a real gift. That upset her even more. Now she was going to hurt him when she refused to use it. But she was not going to give in. She was not sitting in it at her party. She scowled as she watched the men unfold it and check it out.

"Try it out," her dad suggested when they ascertained that it was okay.

If her arms weren't already in slings she would have folded them, so all she could do was not move, no one would dare force her. That much she knew. It was a stand-off.

Stanley waited for Julia and escorted her into the house.

"Whose wheelchair?" Julia asked.

"It's for Aleta," her father said.

"Why?" Julia inquired, puzzled. After all Aleta was standing in the center of the room.

"I don't need it," Aleta declared.

"Dr. Cook ordered it," her father explained. "She's to use it when she goes to the hospital to visit those friends of hers and anytime she goes out where there's a crowd and she might get bumped."

"Like tonight," Julia said. "Good idea. Nathan will be delighted. He's been hankering for someone else to share his experience."

"I'm not sitting in it." Aleta stated emphatically. "And no one can make me."

Stanley walked over to the chair and positioned it behind her.

"Sit!" he ordered.

She felt the edge of the chair behind her legs. Without another word, she sat. Surprisingly, the scowl disappeared. Part of obeying was not to do so with a disgruntled expression.

Robert Locke shook his head in disbelief. "I see now where my mistake was. I should have married her off when she was two."

"Are those my blouses?" Aleta asked Julia.

"I made a sheer one for tonight. It has a silk lining, but the outer part is fuller, so you can wear it later when you begin to show. The silk lining can be let out," Julia said as she held up the blouse. "I made the neck plain because you're wearing two slings, and I let the blouse colors make it dressy. Do you like it?"

"It's beautiful," Aleta said smiling as tears welled up.

Stanley wiped them away with his sleeve. "She cries a lot lately."

"I'm going," Julia said. "I'll be back at six."

"Me too," Robert Locke said.

"Dad, where are you going?"

"To shower and shave and change," Robert replied. "Stanley's parents are putting me up."

"I need to air my dogs," Harriet announced, "so I'll be going."

"I'll be back a little before six to help Bertha with the appetizers," Lauren said. "We eat at seven."

"It you don't need me, Sir," Bertha said. "I'd like to take King for a run. Then he'll be ready to be put in his crate until I leave."

"How'd he like the pen?" Aleta asked.

"He didn't mind it after a bit. He enjoyed the toys. Those hard rubber ones are great to chew on, and he thought that ball that spilled food was fun."

"Sorry about your having to keep him closed in all day," Aleta said.

"He likes it better than being left home alone, and I've walked him often enough, so he's had a good day. He's still pretty weak, so it's not like he's up to a lot of activity."

When she and Stanley were alone, Aleta said, "Wheel me into the bedroom. I understand I'm on TV."

"That's why the guards," Stanley told her. "Whoever tried for you knows he missed."

"Surely, they won't try again tonight."

"Both Lyle and Tom are making sure they don't even think about it," Stanley said wheeling Aleta into the bedroom and turning on the TV.

"You can get up now," Stanley said.

Aleta rose. "You're going to order me to use the wheelchair, aren't you?"

"Yes, I am," Stanley said soberly. "I didn't know how handy your wedding gift to me would be. It was quite a gift."

"It has no expiration date," Aleta responded.

Stanley put his hand around her waist and gently drew her to him and kissed her.

On the road outside from the rise that allowed them full view of the house, Neil had stopped the car when he heard a horn honking in the driveway to the Praetzel house.

"Who would've guessed the bitch could've lived through such a blast?" Rosalie said. "People are pouring in. How come she's so damned popular?"

"That's a wheelchair," Neil commented. "Didn't we see her walk on TV?"

"No, some damn man lifted her out of the wheelchair," Rosalie snarled. "Don't you never pay attention to nothing?"

"She hopped a little," Neil said. "I'm sure of it."

"I know what the hell I saw!" Rosalie snapped. She was in a foul mood. "The woman should, by rights, be stone cold dead."

Neil responded irritably, "You saw what you saw. I saw what I saw. But now she needs a wheelchair. That makes her an easier target and that's good."

"Let's go," Rosalie said. "We can't be late. You remember what I told you to say."

Neil sighed. "Tell me again. You're going to anyway."

"No fooling around with my sister on this trip."

"I'm renting a car for her in your name, and she's going shopping in Cleveland. We'll eat dinner together and that's it"

"That don't bother me. It's after you close the damn door at night."

"I can go alone if you're worried," Neil said. "Or we can stay in different hotels."

"She needs to be me," Rosalie said.

"Stop worrying. I don't find your sister attractive."

"She's fatter than me," Rosalie commented.

"Yes, she is. And she's not sexy. You are," Neil said hoping that would placate her.

He didn't like the plan but he couldn't come up with another. They had to get rid of Dean Arnetti and quick. Dean had told Rosalie that the Oakwood cops had returned to the nursing home and were asking a lot more questions.

That's what Rosalie would take care of on Monday. She'd live in her sister's apartment for the four days he would be gone. That way their house would be empty. She planned to drive her sister's car and wear one of her sister's coats. Her sister lived in a suburb of the City in a large apartment building. They weren't close. Her sister was doing this because Rosalie gave her a charge card with five thousand dollars left on it. Rosalie's sister wanted a new wardrobe desperately. And she shared Rosalie's lack of patience.

Dorothy knew something underhanded was going on, but she didn't care. Rosalie had never shared a dime with her before, and God knows she needed help now and then.

This is payback time, she thought, and I'm spending every cent.

The bar was ten miles out of town and the pair spotted Dean at a rear booth. He was alone.

"Where's the man we're suppose to meet here?" Neil asked as he slipped in on the opposite side of the table.

"I'll take my thousand," Dean Arnetti said. "Then you'll meet him."

Rosalie dug an envelope out of her purse. Dean opened it and counted the hundreds. Then he reached into his packet and withdrew a key.

"Your man is waiting for you in the room this key fits."

Neil turned it over. "There's no name on it."

"It's a duplicate. The motel is the second one on the right thirty miles up the road. Room six."

"We need the name of the motel," Neil insisted as Dean tucked the envelope in his coat pocket.

"The name's appropriate to the job," Dean said as he rushed off.

"What a bastard!" Rosalie exploded. "The sonofabitch ripped us off."

"We know where to find him," Neil said. "Let's go check out the motel."

Thirty miles up the road there were a series of motels clustered around a major intersection on the outskirts of Rockford. The first in the line was a Motel 6, the second was tiny with the dubious title of Dead Quiet Motel.

The key fit the lock, and the pair entered room 6. The man was in the bathroom. He came out drying his hands on a towel. He was not the rough-looking man they expected in such a sleazy motel. His disguise was subtle: glasses, heavy eyebrows, false teeth, slick straight dark hair.

"Spread the dough on the table," he said.

Rosalie took out a second envelope and spread out thirty thousand in five-hundred dollar bills.

"Ten apiece," she said referring to the marks.

"What the hell…," the man began.

Neil stopped him.

"It's for Aleta Praetzel only, as agreed."

"What do you mean?" Rosalie started up. "We need three done."

Neil produced another envelope. "This is for the other two."

The man slipped the new envelope into his pocket without counting.

Neil pulled out a couple news articles. He had circled the face of Aleta Praetzel.

"She's in a wheelchair," Rosalie added.

"We're flying to Cleveland tomorrow afternoon. We'll return Wednesday. It's got to be done while we're gone," Neil said.

"You say she's got cops on her?"

"One, maybe two," Rosalie said.

"She go anywhere?"

"She goes to the hospital every morning," Neil put in.

"Even Sunday?"

"Dammit, we don't know what's in her brain. How are we supposed to know that?" Rosalie snapped. "We've been watched a lot. We figure the cops'll slack off if we leave town."

It wasn't the reason for the trip, but it sounded good so Rosalie spit it out the minute she thought of it.

"If I gotta kill a cop, it'll cost another ten."

"That's robbery!" Rosalie protested.

"You agree or it's no go," the man said. Slade Lacaze could tell he was dealing with a woman who hated to part with a cent. He would've turned down the job except for the fact that Aleta Praetzel had done in his half-brother, and he was thinking of taking her out anyway. This idiot woman didn't know what a deal she was getting and still she quibbled.

Neil had the final say. "A couple cops got hurt when a car bomb went off and all hell broke loose. But the extra ten is yours if you take down a cop."

"Good enough!" Slade said. "Now the other two?"

Neil slipped him two more newspaper photographs. Ed made the paper when he married Beatrice; Harriet Locke was photographed at a charity event with Martha Cook.

"No police on them?" Slade asked.

"Not so far," Neil said. "Can you do all three?"

"Consider them done," Slade said.

Chapter 12

What Neil and Rosalie Hoskinson didn't know is that Slade Lacaze had scouted the job immediately after Dean Arnetti approached him and had already figured out that the big party would be a good time to hit all three. The cops would be worn down from a long evening of guarding. Aleta and her husband would be tired and easy to sneak up on.

He didn't care if the Hoskinson's had an alibi or not. What mattered was getting the job done. All the garbage about the hospital was for the bitchy woman's benefit. If he hit tonight, she wouldn't be sure whether he'd done it or not.

Neil had given him a newspaper clipping that mentioned the hospital but no home address, so Neil would wonder if the man he hired did the job or someone beat him to it.

He climbed into his car and drove to the motel outside Willow Glen where he'd set up shop. He set his clock and laid down for a nap.

At the house, once dressed, Aleta asked Stanley if she could walk through the house while it was empty and read the place cards. He agreed. It was quiet enough for her not to have to sit in the wheelchair just yet.

It was while they were looking at the cards set on the plates that Bertha opened the laundry room door and King bounded through pulling the lead from her grasp. He made a beeline for the family room and jumped up on Aleta.

Surprised, she lost her footing. Were Stanley's hand not on her waist, she would have gone down. The bump was a slight one to her left shoulder which was partly healed.

She yelped in pain.

Bertha rushed in apologizing.

"Don't blame the pup," Aleta said, "I just wasn't ready."

"How's your shoulder?" Stanley asked.

"It hurts," Aleta said. "Now, at least, I know Dr. Cook knows what he's talking about. Let's get the chair."

"I'm so sorry, Ma'am," Bertha repeated. "He got away from me."

"Bertha, it was an accident. No damage was done. And I learned my arms are more fragile than I thought, so it was a good thing."

"If you want, I can leave him home until you're better."

"I have a better idea," Aleta said. "I use the chair even at home and he gets to come here with you. I like King. I'd miss him."

"Yes Ma'am. Thank you Ma'am."

Lauren was surprised to find Aleta in the wheelchair when she arrived.

"There's no one here," she commented.

"The dog nearly knocked me over," Aleta said. "It happened so fast, and I was so unable to catch myself. If Stanley hadn't had his hand on my waist, I would have crashed. As it is I bumped my so-called good shoulder and, boy, is it still not healed."

"So you're taking no chances," Lauren remarked. "Not a bad idea. How do you like the seating arrangement?"

"Odd."

"What's odd?"

"Your parents with the Danielsons and the Tobiases."

"That one was easy. My parents are good with handicapped people, and they like to meet new people. The Danielsons and the Tobiases are friends, so they will enjoy being together. Come on, ask me about the rest."

"Why Ed and Beatrice at your table with Peets and his wife?"

"She will feel like the biggest outsider, so sitting at the table of the hostess will calm her feeling of not belonging. Ed is comfortable anywhere and Beatrice is sparkly. Lyle wants to know Peets better, and it wouldn't hurt for Peets to get to know Ed."

"You put Tom Milani at another table. Why not put him with Peets?"

"Because he already knows Peets. Rachel will enjoy being at a table with the power houses, Martha and Harriet, as well as your in-laws, who are eager to know the chief guarding you."

Lauren went on. "Wayne is at your table because Yancey is pregnant so you two have something in common besides your medical condition. Evelyn and Bessie are an odd pair, and you and Stanley know them both. The Cooks know neither and they like meeting new people too."

"What about my dad?"

"His plate is here and will be set on any table he chooses to join. I want him to feel as comfortable as possible," Lauren finished.

"Remind me to have you hostess all my parties."

"I'd love to," Lauren said. "This has been a lark."

"The first cars are arriving," Bertha announced.

"That'd be Evelyn and Bessie with the pies, Beatrice with the potatoes and Madge with the rolls. She'll need help with Nathan."

"I'll go," Stanley said.

"Never mind," Lauren said. "Lyle is here. Bertha, are the hor'doeurves ready?"

"First batch is in the oven."

"Stanley," Lauren said as she turned. "Where'd he go?"

"He said he'd forgotten something," Aleta said, nodding toward the bedroom.

He reappeared with a box and a roll of adhesive tape. Curious, Lauren came over to watch.

Aleta looked at her husband quizzically as the door opened and people began coming in. Stanley told them to put their coats in the bedroom, but everyone stopped instead to see what Stanley was doing. They watched fascinated as he taped the little fingers of Aleta's two hands together.

"What are you doing?" Lauren finally asked.

"She moves her hands automatically when she talks. This will remind her not to," Stanley explained.

"What's in the box?" someone else asked.

"A token to take out the sting of my taping her fingers. I planned to do this before anyone got here, but... well I didn't."

He opened the box. The women oohed as he picked up the sparkling diamond necklace and fastened it around Aleta's neck. One hand went up to feel it, and the taped finger on the other hand kept it down.

"It's lovely, Aleta," Julia said. "I'm so glad I didn't put a collar on the blouse."

"It's perfect," Lauren said. "The band circles your neck perfectly lying just far enough down to frame your face just right."

Beatrice nodded in agreement, "I wish I had a neck like yours that would carry such a piece so beautifully."

Aleta, flushed with happiness, decided Stanley had done the perfect thing. He'd made her taped fingers inconsequential. No wonder he won so much in court. He paid attention to emotional details.

I wonder if working with children in crisis made him such an empathetic person. He seemed to know what to do instinctively, yet she wasn't sure it was instinct. He spent a lot of time in thought.

By the time the first group had put the food in the kitchen, others were streaming up the driveway. The two police officers at the gate checked everyone's name against the check list. Robert Locke's wasn't on the list; a call was made, and Milani answered it from inside the house.

"Aleta, a man at the gate says he's your father."

Aleta laughed. "He is. He's staying with Stanley's parents. I thought West's men were on the gate."

"My men are fresher," Milani said. "We took over."

The Peets arrived and Alan, noticing Tom Milani's coat on the rack, put his there, too.

As he passed Tom Milani, Tom looked at him and said, "I was telling Kurtz that I got a phone call from Louise Oppenwall about you today."

"Is it something that I should hear?" Peets asked politely.

Eloise headed for the bedroom to lay down her coat and purse.

"She just wanted to know who I'd gotten to replace you. I told her no one," Tom said. "Then she asked me if I had a second choice. I told her no one measured up to you. You were the best I had to offer."

"You have two other good men, who would do a good job heading up the Oakwood force," Peets said.

"They don't hold a candle to you, and I know it even if you don't," Tom said. "Lyle, tell them about your call."

Peets looked surprised. "She called you too? And I thought she was satisfied with the job I was doing. Who did you suggest?"

"No one," Lyle smiled. "I told her she already had not only the most experienced man on any local police force, but one with connections."

"Connections?"

"I told her you were a guest at our party tonight."

"That's when she called me," Judge Davis said, joining in.

"I must have been last on her list," Kurtz West said. "I guess all criminal defense attorneys study their opponents' weaknesses. I told her I usually give your cases to someone else in the office because it's almost impossible to catch you on a technical error."

Peets shook his head. "And all this time, I thought you thought I wasn't a worthy opponent, and so I tried harder."

Kurtz West grinned. "You won almost every case my office handled. Didn't that tell you anything?"

"It never occurred to me," Peets admitted.

"Well, she got the picture," Kurtz West said.

Eloise joined the group once she realized the conversation centered on her husband. She took his arm when he asked his next question.

"Did she say why she wanted to replace me?"

"I don't think she does," Lyle said. "I think she was testing the waters."

"She still has the town council to consider," Peets said.

"Kurtz is wrong," Judge Lydia Davis said, "which he is rarely. Mine was the last call. She told me that she was planning to propose to the town council that they offer you the chief's job permanently."

"What do you think his chances are?" Tom Milani asked.

Peets wanted desperately to know; now, when he was in the company of people who believed he deserved the job.

"I could call her," Bessie Dobbins said timidly. "She and I are friends—sort of. She stood up for me when no one else did. I also know two people on the new council."

"What do you think, Mom?" Lyle asked. He knew his mother understood social politics.

"Bessie, you shouldn't call her. She's already made her stand," Lyle's mother interposed. "Call your two friends on the council. They're the ones that need citizen input."

"I'm not technically an Oakwood citizen," Bessie said.

"But Oakwood wants to annex your property still, doesn't it?"

"Yes, they do, but I like the county sheriff, and I don't like what the fire department did to my house."

"Are you going to sue?" Judge Davis injected.

"I don't think so," Bessie said. "I don't want to spend anymore time in court, Your Honor."

"You can call me Lydia outside of the courtroom," Judge Davis said.

"Even if they hired Chief Peets, I might not want Oakwood to annex me. I'm still angry about what the fire chief did to my house."

"Politically, you have a bigger stick than you think you have," Judge Davis said. "Use it wisely."

"Where'd Aleta go?" someone asked.

"Dr. Cook took her into the bedroom to check on her," Lauren said. "As soon as he's done we can eat. Mr. Locke, where would you like to sit?"

"With Nathan," Robert Locke said. "I haven't even begun to pick his brain."

Lauren laughed. "While Mr. Locke is picking Nathan's brain; Jason will be carving the duck at his table; Lyle, at his; and Harriet, at hers. I figure our hunters are experts in carving what they shoot. Aleta's table has a hunter, but one slightly handicapped being unable to use either arm so since Wayne professes to be an expert with a knife, he gets to do the honors. This time we get to watch him at work."

Everyone was laughing when Dr. Cook wheeled Aleta back into the living room.

"We missed something," she said. "Hey, I got a puzzle. There's another pregnant lady at this party besides Lauren and myself. Guess who?"

"Don't anyone look at me!" Julia said. "Eight is enough."

Aleta looked at Eloise, "Can you guess?"

Eloise was taken by surprise. "Are you psychic or something?"

Aleta responded quickly, "I prophesy, but not about this."

Then she paused.

Her smile broadened as she added, "How far along are you?"

Peets stared at his wife. "You're pregnant?"

"Some detective you are," Lyle quipped.

"Tell them when I told you," Lauren jibed.

"End of the second month. How's a man supposed to know?"

"So, Yancey, your turn," Aleta said.

"Just took the pregnancy test. Took five of them. I couldn't wait for Wayne," Yancey burst out. "They were all positive."

"That's four baby showers," Aleta said. "Lauren, then me, Eloise and then Yancey. What an exciting spring we're going to have."

Lacaze rose from his motel bed at seven. It was nearly dark outside. His disguise packed in his travel bag, he changed into a black knit outfit with a hood that covered his face. He grabbed his rifle case and left that motel room permanently.

He parked on a side street near Stanley Praetzel's place. Then he walked down the perimeter of the property two doors away. His boots were calf high and meant for rough walking. He cut across the field at the far end of the Praetzel properties. He chose a section of the fence directly behind the barn, cut the barbed wire fencing and stepped through. He walked straight down a rut, his ankles turning on a clod of dirt every few steps.

As he expected, the police personnel were concentrated around the house. He progressed unseen to the back of the barn. He entered the dark interior and headed for the ladder to the left, gratified for a cloudless sky and a bit of moonlight.

Sitting in the shadows under the eaves near the front opening in the loft, he assembled his rifle by feel and watched for patrols. He had a clear view of the house from where he sat.

Quite a party, he thought as he snapped his rifle shut and looked through the telescopic sight. Perfect!

Two men with flashlights approached.

Hurriedly, he buried the rifle case in hay. Then he slowly scooted as far as he could get under the eaves.

He saw the beams shining up through the slats from below. These guys were good.

They approached the ladder to the loft.

"The string's in place," one said.

Slade's hand had touched it going up and carefully avoided it. He wasn't sure it wasn't connected to some sort of alarm or noise maker.

"Go up anyway," the other said.

No, don't, Slade wished silently, burying his face in the straw and holding his breath. He froze in place not daring to breathe. The light seemed to linger on his back.

His face was buried in the straw, but his eyes were open. He waited for the light to move away so he could breathe. He hoped he wouldn't cough.

"See anything?" the cop below yelled.

"Just shadows I guess," came the reply. "Shine your light up from below."

"All I see is straw," the man on the ground said.

"I guess I'm spooked over nothing," the other said.

Slade lifted his head and watched the two walk away toward the house. He brushed hay from his face and his rifle. Lying down, he looked through the telescopic sight and saw an empty living room. He moved over to the other picture window. The bedroom was empty too. Considering the activity in the kitchen, everyone was eating somewhere. They'd drift back into the living room when they were finished, and eventually he'd have a clear shot at his target. He had but to wait.

The conversation at all the tables had been lively. Lyle, acting as host, since Stanley was busy feeding Aleta, kept the wine glasses full. The duck was prepared with a special orange sauce and consumed with murmurs of appreciation, as were the prepared side dishes.

While the tables were being cleared for dessert, Aleta whispered in Stanley's ear. He rose immediately and wheeled her out of the room toward the bedroom. It was then many realized just how helpless Aleta now was. While they watched Stanley struggling to maneuver the wheelchair away from the table and through the kitchen, the question arose as to why Aleta didn't walk. Lauren explained that earlier the puppy had jumped on her. Stanley had caught her but the bump hurt.

"No wonder she's stuck to the chair like glue," Dr. Cook said. "I knew it couldn't be me."

"Well," Robert put in from the far table as soon as the pair was out of hearing range, "she objected to the chair when I brought it in and nothing I said could get her to even try it. Then Stanley told her to sit and she sat. Boy, that's something I'd like to learn how to do."

General laughter greeted his comment.

Slade spotted the wheelchair enter the living room, and lifted his rifle just as the chair disappeared into the bedroom. He waited for it to reappear in the bedroom window. When it didn't, he wondered how it could have traversed the bedroom without him seeing it. He swung his rifle back to the living room and searched.

Puzzled he kept searching the far reaches of the open kitchen to see if the man showed up.

As soon as they entered the room Aleta asked Stanley if she could stand and kiss him as a thank you for the beautiful necklace.

"Let's take care of business first," he suggested.

Aleta's head bowed.

"I'll be too embarrassed then," she murmured.

"Embarrassed," he asked, his surprise evident.

"I'm not modest, only," she said. "I'm bashful."

Stanley almost laughed aloud, but he heard the pain in her voice.

Gently he lifted her head and kissed her tenderly. He paused long enough to say, "I'll expect payback when I'm old and gray."

She giggled. "In your dreams."

Stanley smiled at her. "A man needs dreams."

"I love my necklace," she whispered, kissing him softly until he embraced her and the softness turned to passion.

When their lips parted she said, "That's for my million dollar necklace."

He smiled wryly. "You aren't going to pry the cost out of me that way."

"It almost makes up for you taping my fingers together."

"Almost?"

"It's a crazy idea. I'm surprised at you."

"It just hit me, and I went with it without thinking. I'll take off the tape if you want."

"No," she said firmly. "Then everyone will think it's a foolish idea."

"I think they do now," Stanley confessed.

"But since I went along with it, they're not sure," Aleta agreed. "So let's not touch the tape until everyone's gone."

"Even I think it's a dumb idea in retrospect»' Stanley admitted.

"Don't even suggest it when we go back," Aleta said. "This conversation is private."

Aleta took off quickly for the bathroom, and Stanley hurried to catch up.

Her sudden movement caught Slade Lacaze's eye and he swung the rifle around. Before he could steady it, she was gone from view.

He sighed contentedly. At least now he knew where she was. So, she could walk. That was a surprise. He resolved he wouldn't be caught napping again.

He wondered briefly what person who could walk would choose to use a wheelchair. It made no sense.

He looked up at the moon and searched the sky for a nearby cloud. It was a cold, clear November night.

Too cold, he thought, blowing on his fingers. His gloves were fingerless. He had no intention of leaving his gun or the case.

He glanced over. Where the hell was the case? He felt the mounds of straw all around. How could he lose it? He hadn't moved that much.

As he moved his boot hit something hard and he remembered. He'd laid it in front of himself when he was squeezed under the eaves. How could he have forgotten that?

His focus returned to the task at hand. He adjusted his elbows and looked through the sight. He knew the level her head would be. He put his finger on the trigger.

"I can squeeze off two rounds," he decided.

The man exited first and Slade took aim.

Chapter 13

Aleta was talking non-stop and Stanley knew she was trying to hide her embarrassment. He figured the best thing to do was to accept her way of handling it.

"Peets was sure surprised," Aleta commented. "Eloise thought I was psychic. The only reason I called on her was so she could guess the only woman left in the room that it could be. Who knew?"

Stanley laughed lightly, "Well, until tonight, no one. Are you coming?"

"I can't get over how beautiful this necklace is," Aleta said. "But so much money."

"The jeweler assured me it was an investment."

"And I suppose he showed you earrings to match."

"They're on lay-a-way," Stanley said.

"Stanley!" Aleta retorted. "Lay-a-way?"

"Isn't that what they call it when a jeweler says he'll hold them for your approval."

"Stanley, you've been rich too long. Lay-a-way is when you have to make payments to buy something."

"They're on lay-a-way," Stanley said poker-faced.

"You forget I've seen your bank statements."

"I thought we'd go see them whenever one hand is free enough for you to hold them up to your ears."

Aleta took one more turn in front of the mirror. "It sparkles all the way around. It's perfect!"

"You said that."

"Don't make me come up with a new word because I can't right now."

Stanley was suddenly worried. "You're okay, aren't you?"

"Strokes don't start with one not being able to locate a word. That's how they end. Mine is still ending."

"One would never know it."

"Unless one was me. I never had to search for a word before speaking. Never in my whole life."

"And soon you won't again," Stanley said. "Come on. People will think we fell in."

Aleta giggled.

She exited and turned around. "Am I all together?"

"You look great," Stanley said.

In the barn loft, Slade Lacaze tightened his grip on the gun and began to squeeze the trigger.

"Come on," Slade whispered to himself. "Just a little further, Aleta Praetzel."

Aleta came out and walked in front of the window looking out as she did so.

It was a clear night with a half moon. The air was still. The leaves were mostly on the ground. The early frosts had killed the remaining summer annuals. The ground was hardening. When the winter snows came, low temperatures would keep the frozen moisture in abeyance until spring.

"I haven't ever lived through a winter before," she said, pausing abruptly.

The rifle moved back into position. The movement was slight but it caused Aleta's eye to catch the glint of the metal barrel.

Her mind, unable to come up with words, was, however, capable of assessing what the glint meant. Given the recent attempts on her life, Aleta reacted instantly.

Before Slade's finger squeezed enough to fire his first round, Aleta's brain had already told her what to do.

Words failed her. But her response was not going to be a verbal one as it had been last time. This time there was literally no time for words.

Her abrupt stop had placed Stanley half a stride in front of her. With no warning she tackled him, butting him in the chest with her folded arms. She fell on top of him. The two landed hard.

Stanley hit his head just after the rifle bullet broke the window and buried itself in the pile of coats on the bed. The second shot followed the first. It sailed through the broken window silently travelling a bit further and burrowing through the coats and into the mattress underneath.

The fall pushed a scream from Aleta's throat and those startled by the bullet and breaking glass were electrified by the yell.

Lyle West was on his feet first and shouted, "Tom, Alan, get that guy. I'll take charge in here." The two men plucked their coats and guns holsters from the hall rack and left the house still slipping into both. Tom issued orders to his men who had already started running toward the sound of the rifle crack. They were weaving in and out of cover, not certain the man wasn't still in position to take out the first man that got too close,

Lyle West meanwhile shouted at everyone to stay put.

"Doc, you're with me," West said.

It was Robert Locke who moved into the kitchen and told Bertha to leave the kitchen and then looking back at the living room window told everyone to move to a spot where they could no longer see it. The other men followed his lead. The professionals were in charge.

Chief West and Dr. Cook found Aleta lying on top of Stanley flat on the floor. West glanced outside and noticed a number of men converging on the barn.

"Safe?" Cook asked.

"I'll shield you," West said moving on the outside of the doctor. "Can we move them?"

"Not until I have some idea where they were hit."

Aleta breathed. "Not…"

"You weren't hit?" Dr. Cook asked.

Aleta shook her head weakly.

"You hurt?"

Again Aleta shook her head again.

Together West and Cook lifted Aleta off Stanley and moved her to the side of the room and laid her down. Stanley remained in place.

"Hit him hard," Aleta croaked.

"You just sit there and catch your breath," Dr. Cook said.

West radioed for an ambulance.

Cook picked up his bag which he'd tucked under the night stand.

"You came prepared?" West asked.

"I examined Aleta earlier, remember?"

Within minutes the ambulance siren was heard.

"How close was the ambulance?" Cook asked.

"Pretty close," West admitted. "Tell me what you need."

"A gurney and oxygen," Dr. Cook replied.

Lyle came out to open the door for the paramedics. He saw the frantic faces of the two fathers.

"No one got hit," he said as he followed the paramedics back into the room.

West helped one of the paramedics lift Aleta into the wheelchair. The oxygen soon restored her ability to speak. As soon as she could breathe she shook her head, but no one took off the oxygen mask. She tried talking through it but all attention was on Stanley.

An oxygen mask brought him around as well. He looked up at Dr. Cook, his eyes full of questions.

"Aleta's okay. She's back in her chair," Dr. Cook said looking over. "Trying to yell at me it looks like."

Stanley continued to look confused.

"I want to take you to the hospital," Dr. Cook added. "I want to take a look at that head of yours."

"No way!" Stanley responded. "I bumped my head. That's all."

"I should check you out. You were unconscious for several minutes."

Aleta yelled through her mask and Dr. Cook finally realized that she couldn't remove It. His attention went to her hands.

"Who did this?" he asked, removing her mask so she could speak.

"Stanley," Aleta said. "And if you think he needs to go to the hospital, he goes."

"How are your shoulders?"

"Actually, they feel okay," Aleta said surprised that they did.

Dr. Cook picked up her taped fingers. "This is why. Your hands would have gone up automatically when you started to fall. You'd have wrecked at least one if not both shoulders with such a fall. This bit of tape was a brilliant idea!"

"Stanley always has brilliant ideas except when it comes to doing what's good for himself," Aleta quipped. "You don't let him talk you into releasing him until he's okay."

Stanley took the mask from his face.

"I can't go. We are having a party."

"I may need to keep you," Dr. Cook warned.

"You let Aleta come home," Stanley argued.

"You were here to watch her."

"She can watch me," Stanley said, his mind seemingly clearer. "We've got friends we can call on to help."

"The guests will be here awhile," Lyle put in. "The bullets are buried somewhere in this pile of clothes."

"The bedroom's getting cold fast," Stanley observed looking over at the window. "How'd that break?"

"I'll tell you all about it in the ambulance," Dr. Cook promised. Gasps of surprise came from the group when they saw who was on the gurney.

Lyle West pushed Aleta out of the bedroom and ordered everyone back into the family room telling them that the shooter could still be on the grounds.

"I'd like to go with Stanley," Hubert Praetzel said.

"Not possible. The bullets hit the coats and we have to find them," Lyle explained.

"I'll go coatless."

"Stanley wants you here," Aleta said. "Dr. Cook said he'll allow Stanley to return if there are people here to watch him. I assumed you'd do it."

"Absolutely," Hubert Praetzel said.

"Aleta, how are you dear?" her grandmother asked.

"I got a new bump on my poor banged-up head," Aleta said. "Aside from a new sore spot, I'm fine."

Lyle wheeled Aleta back to her place and others crowded around with questions.

Bertha poured her a cup of coffee and her dad sat beside her pulled over the slice of pie already set down at her place and cut a piece with a fork.

"No bite," he said as he raised the fork to her mouth.

"I'm all grown-up, Dad," Aleta responded tartly.

"Which means your teeth are bigger," Robert Locke shot back.

Laughter erupted and the party began to be a party again.

Two hours later one of Milani's patrol cars delivered Dr. Cook and Stanley to the front doorstep of the house where the party had spread out into the living room.

When the two entered the house, everyone turned.

"What's the verdict?" Robert Locke asked.

Dr. Cook smiled. "Don't play football with Aleta."

"I could have told you that," her father shot back.

"But," Dr. Cook went on, "If ever a bullet is headed your way, she's a great person to have by your side."

Stanley went over and sat beside his wife. He was unusually silent, but he managed a smile. He turned down her offer of pie.

"Are you alright?" Aleta asked wishing she could touch him at least.

"Just a headache," Stanley said.

"Is it bad?"

"It's getting worse," he admitted.

"Maybe an aspirin would help," Aleta suggested.

"No aspirin," Dr. Cook said, taking a bite of his pie. "The headache will either subside on its own or it won't. I need to know."

Peets motioned to Milani and West to follow him. He led them to the far corner in the back of the family room well away from the group.

"What Dr. Cook said," Peets started when the three were out of earshot. "Do you believe one of those bullets was meant for Stanley?"

"There were two shots," Milani pointed out.

"I'm not sure we'll ever know," West added.

"That's why I put a man on him," Milani said. "Just in case."

"Let's take this backwards," Peets said.

"The shooter got away," Milani said. "I hate to start there."

"Why?"

"He was just too fast," Milani concluded.

"Over that plowed field in the middle of the night?" Peets scoffed. "And Milani's men were spread out across the field in back."

"So?"

"So we know where he didn't go," Peets said. "Once you've eliminated the possible, what's left?"

"The impossible," West said. "But if he had run from the barn across the flat space to the orchard, someone would have seen him. Besides no one could run fast across the field. It's just been plowed."

"So he didn't run," Peets said. "Let's assume for a minute we're dealing with a highly skilled pro. Wouldn't he have an escape route figured out in advance?"

"If he didn't run," Milani said, "what did he do?"

"What soldiers do when they are in battle," West concluded, following Peets line of reasoning.

"He crawled," Peets guessed.

"Once at the orchard, he had lots of cover," Milani finished.

"We never got even a glimpse of him," Peets said. "How much you want to bet he was in black head to toe?"

"That would mean he was a pro," Milani said.

"How did the Hoskinsons get hold of such a high-priced hit man?" West asked. "Most ordinary people have no access to that kind of pro."

Peets offered his take on that.

"We're investigating a man at the Oakwood Home that we think is dealing drugs. He might have found them a hitter."

"Can you move on him yet?" Milani asked. "We need something to bargain with."

"Monday's the soonest we can move," Peets said.

Ed Ornstein joined the group. "You've just figured out we're dealing with a pro, huh?"

The men turned when he spoke. "What do you know?" West asked.

"That Neil Hoskinson's got a lot at stake and he's got the bucks. And Aleta's not the only target."

He had the attention of all three chiefs.

He then explained the scam Neil was running.

"Let me see if I got this," Milani asked. "He sends an inspector to a house for a fraction of the usual price and that's his foot in the door. Then he switches samples and ships off moldy samples which he's manufacturing in his storage shed and takes the lab results from these back to the owners and promotes the use of one of the contractors who charge four times the normal fee for such work. He gets a cut. If the people won't go that way, he offers a bogus ozone testing scheme and pockets a hefty profit from that since he owns the company."

"Yep. That's it pretty much," Ed said. "He's got four lumberyards with this scheme at various stages of development. Elyria was the first."

"How much could he be making?" Peets asked, "A couple thousand out of each venture. A pro would take a year's profit or more."

"I got it on good authority that he's socked away half a million in four months at one site only—all tax free. You do the math."

"He'd take out everyone who's a threat," West said. "And we thought it was only about Hoskinson's will."

"So who are the other targets?" Peets asked.

West answered. "Has to be Harriet Locke and Ed here."

"We're the ones who know, and Aleta's the one who can get old man Hoskinson to shut down his son's scams."

"Does Neil know you know?" Milani asked.

"Oh yeah. Harriet began shutting him down today. We flew home before she finished."

"Then why didn't the shooter wait until we were all back in the living room?" West asked. "He could have taken out all three."

"You know," Tom put in, "he could've been after both Aleta and Stanley. Wives tell husbands things."

"I'll accept that premise. Stanley stays under protection too."

"We need them somewhere we can keep an eye on them without using two police forces," Milani said.

"Protective custody?" Peets asked.

"The hospital," West said. "Neither of them is well enough to be away from medical care. Wayne hasn't left Stanley's side since they came back. Something's going on."

"Can we do that?" Peets asked. "Use the hospital that way?"

"Let me ask Dr. Cook to join us," Tom suggested.

"Get Bertha to serve us some coffee on your way," Lyle said.

Peets' mind began churning as soon as Tom left. "I would approach Justice and see if they can suggest pros who specialize in this type of hit."

"Tom has contacts in the City he could tap to see if there's a new hitter in town," Lyle said.

Bertha arrived with a tray holding a carafe of coffee, sugar, cream, spoons and cups. She set it in the middle of the nearby table and the men sat down.

West told Dr. Cook that the suspected hit man was a high-powered hitter and the three chiefs had decided that the only safe place for the two young Praetzels was in the hospital.

"He wouldn't stay," Dr. Cook said. "He has that right."

"But you can readmit him if he shows any signs of getting worse, can't you?" West asked. "Use Aleta to force the issue. She was pretty adamant about that earlier."

"He appears to have recovered. All I have to go on are suspicions. It wasn't enough for him. He insisted on getting back to Aleta."

"Did you notice," Ed said, "that even though Stanley's back, Aleta's father is still holding her coffee cup?"

"That's not enough," Milani said. "We need both of them in the hospital."

"I could run another test to check her shoulders, but that would only take an hour," Dr. Cook said.

"When she told us the story," Ed said, "she said she felt like vomiting right after she fell, but she was on top of Stanley so she repressed the urge."

"I'd say it would have come up anyway," Dr. Cook said, "but we're talking about Aleta here. However, that's enough of a symptom for me to take her back. I can keep her for a day. Stanley will want to go with her and I can talk him into letting me readmit him for observation as well."

"I can guard them in the hospital easier than here," Milani said. "How long can you keep them?"

"Monday morning."

"That's a start," Milani said.

"I suggest we transport them in an ambulance," Peets said, "with a police escort."

West spoke up, "We need to remember the hit man is a sniper. He has a specialty. He won't switch MO's. We need a room whose window faces no high buildings."

"Fourth floor looking east. 402 is a double," Dr. Cook said. Nothing but farm land for miles."

"I need the rooms on both sides empty as well," Milani said.

"You order it and the staff will arrange it."

"West, since you're Stanley's best friend, how about you handle it," Milani said. "I'll call the ambulance and pull same of the guys outside for escort duty."

Peets lingered behind and asked Ed, "Are you going to your office? I understand you have quite a computer set up."

"I do. Do you have some stuff you wanna know unofficial like?"

"Just some ideas I have. They could be nothing."

"Let me give you directions," Ed responded. "We've got the whole night."

Lyle walked into the living room with Dr. Cook.

"Stanley, your wife didn't tell Dr. Cook all her symptoms. He's going to take her to the hospital. You are going as well."

"But he's okay," Aleta said. "And so am I."

"Who's been caring for you exclusively before the shooting?"

"Stanley, of course," Aleta said and then made the connection. "Stanley, why didn't you take over when you came back?"

"My stomach's a bit unsettled," Stanley admitted.

"We'll both go," Aleta decided.

"Good!" Martha Cook exclaimed. She turned to her grandson. "Wayne, can you keep them until Tuesday morning?"

"Why?" he and Lyle West chorused.

"Because I can replace not only the bedroom window with bullet proof glass but this big window and the windows in the kitchen and family room. I can have motion sensor lights installed on the barn as well."

Milani walked into the room as Martha was speaking. "I can have my men oversee the work. I like it."

"What about my cases?" Stanley protested. "I can't stay past Monday morning."

"I'll get postponements for you unless you think Kurtz West or I could handle them," his father said.

"My God!" Stanley exclaimed. "I can't think what ones are coming up."

That he couldn't remember them frightened Aleta, but she responded as if this was not abnormal.

"Call his secretary," Aleta said. "She'll know."

Harriet came over. "Aleta, do you want me to keep your necklace for you?"

"There's a box," Stanley started.

"It's probably been moved," Harriet said as she unclasped the glittering necklace. "Don't worry I'll find it."

Aleta spoke up.

"Dad, I'd like you to come to the hospital at eight thirty. I have people I promised a visit."

Chief Milani and Dr. Cook reacted with equal fervor simultaneously.

"You aren't leaving your room!" they chorused.

The two men looked at each other. They were on the same wave length.

Aleta instantaneously switched her objective. "He can go tell them personally why I'm not there. It's important. I promised."

Dr. Cook looked at Chief Milani. "What about visitors?"

"Parents only," Milani said looking at the gathering.

"Sorry, folks, but my men need to have a short list."

"That's not fair!" Aleta protested. "He gets two visitors to my one."

"For heaven's sake, Aleta," her father scolded. "You...,"

Aleta interrupted his lecture.

"I want Grams on my list."

"Okay, okay," Milani acquiesced. "But that's it."

"Lydia, when you come, can you bring some leftovers?" Aleta said. "Like pie and duck."

Stanley's mother chuckled. "Just that?"

"Rolls and potatoes, too," Aleta added.

"They will feed you," Lydia mentioned with a wry smile.

"If it's anything like last time, no one will be allowed to send me any flowers or candy or anything really neat to eat, but leftovers from tonight's dinner are above suspicion, right, Chief?"

"Bring her the leftovers," Milani sighed. "Now, Aleta, if I allow this, you'll stay in your room, right?"

Aleta realized Milani was bending as much as he could to appease her.

"I will," Aleta promised.

Robert Locke kissed his daughter goodnight and told her he'd see her in the morning. The ambulance siren announced its approach.

"Don't feel guilty," Harriet whispered in Aleta's ear. "It's been a great party with a good ending. We all want you safe more than anything else."

An hour later, while Dr. Cook was supervising MRI's on both his patients, in the basement of a ramshackled frame house to the west of Willow Glen, Chief Alan Peets was looking over Ed Ornstein's shoulder as he was giving Peets a demonstration of his computer's capabilities by searching Rosalie Hoskinson's family history.

"She was too nervous when I asked her about them," Alan Peets said. "She's hiding something."

"You think she has a relative in the joint?"

"If she has, he could be the contact."

"She has a sister," Ed announced.

"She said she was an only child."

Intrigued Ed brought up the sister's driver's license photo.

Peets stared at It. "It looks like her."

Ed began pulling up other sites while Peets mused, "Why hide a sister? See if she was ever arrested."

"It may take me a while," Ed informed Peets. "The sister was married more than once."

"I'll wait," Peets said. "I have nowhere more important to be."

"I won't tell your wife you said that," Ed said.

"You're here," Peets reminded him.

"You don't tell my wife I feel the same way," Ed remarked. "Besides I give her enough attention and judging from your impending fatherhood, I gather you don't neglect Eloise either."

"How did Aleta guess?" Peets asked. "I had no idea and I live with the woman."

"Leave it to Aleta to make things lively," Ed said.

"I guess we'd better keep her around then," Peets concluded.

"Right," Ed said and went back to work.

In the double room on the fourth floor of the hospital, Stanley was asleep when Aleta was wheeled in and moved from the gurney to her bed. She got a brief glimpse of Stanley before she found herself on her back, her pillow blocking off her view of the other bed.

The nurse began to pull the curtain that separated the two beds. Aleta stopped her, telling her that she didn't mind if she was awakened by them checking on her husband no matter how often.

When the nurse left, Aleta looked through the open blinds at the clear November sky. Still too excited to sleep, she tried to talk with Stanley, but he didn't wake.

A nurse appeared a short time later and her touch on Stanley's wrist woke him. Aleta felt better immediately.

"Aleta?" he inquired.

"She's in the next bed," the nurse said. "Now you rest."

When she left, Aleta began to talk, but Stanley interrupted her.

"I need you to do something for me," he said.

"I can't get up, Stanley," she replied regretfully.

"I need you to promise me something."

"Anything," Aleta responded, eager to assuage his anxiety. She could hear a tremble in his voice.

"I want you to obey Dr. Cook's orders as if they were mine."

Aleta felt a sudden tightening of her stomach. "Stanley, you're scaring me."

"Tell me you'll do it."

"I want to know why," Aleta pressed.

"Because I'm ordering you to," Stanley said.

"Okay," she replied. Obeying was a given. "Now will you tell me what's going on?"

"Thank you," was all she heard.

Whether he was asleep or feigning sleep Aleta couldn't tell, but he didn't respond to any of her queries.

Something was going on. She was sure of it. Something was wrong. Dr. Cook had told her that her MRI looked good.

She'd asked him why he kept doing MRI's. She'd understood CT scans were usually done.

"MRI's are better. They're much more expensive, but you can afford them, and since you aren't insured, I only have to answer to you and Stanley, and he insisted when you first came in that you were to have the best."

"Well, he's to have the best too," Aleta declared.

"I didn't give him a choice," Dr. Cook smiled.

"You did his MRI first," Aleta said. "Why?"

"He was ready before you," Dr. Cook replied.

And Aleta had been satisfied with that reply. But now she realized she'd forgotten to ask the results of Stanley's MRI. She thought back to the moment.

"Stanley's in your room waiting," he had said next. "I need to get some sleep."

Immediately, Aleta showed a friend's concern. "Tell Yancey I appreciate the loan of her husband."

"I will," he said, "although she's probably already asleep."

Having said that he left her.

When Aleta remembered that her fear subsided. Dr. Cook would never have gone home if anything had been wrong with Stanley.

Relaxed, she fell asleep. She was vaguely aware that the nurses were coming in frequently to check on Stanley, but nothing in their tone alarmed her.

The quiet roll of wheels awakened her. She kept her eyes closed. She vaguely heard the nurse say something about the needles not hurting, and she wondered what that was about. Nobody needs more than one needle for an IV.

Puzzled, she kept her eyes closed. She could think better. Logic told her that if she opened her eyes the nurse would realize she was awake and listening.

"There," the nurse said. "You're all set."

A second person joined the first. The curtain between the beds was pulled.

"Where's Dr. Cook?" she heard the new person ask.

"Asleep," the nurse replied.

"At home?"

"In the lounge downstairs."

"Has Dr. Taekman arrived yet?"

"No. We were to wake Dr. Cook as soon as he arrives," the nurse replied. "And I think I hear the chopper now."

Aleta's eyes opened. She watched the chopper approaching from the east. Fear gripped her. Stanley was in serious trouble, and she was being kept in the dark.

A few minutes later, Dr. Cook appeared beside her bed.

"What's going on?" Aleta asked.

"Stanley has an extradural hemorrhage. That's a ruptured blood vessel in his head. We need to do a craniotomy immediately to drain the hematoma and repair the ruptured artery," Dr. Cook explained. "I have a neurosurgeon flying in from Cook County Hospital."

"But you let him come home?"

"I didn't let him do anything. He signed himself out of the hospital," Dr. Cook said. "Now, did Stanley ask you to do something for me?"

"Yes, he said I was to obey you as if you were him."

"Okay then, you stay put. I don't want you getting out of bed for any reason."

"I...," Aleta began. Abruptly she swallowed her protest and said, "Yes, Sir."

Dr. Cook left immediately.

"What side?" Aleta heard a nurse ask.

"Left," came the response.

After a few minutes, Aleta heard the snip of scissors followed by the buzz of a razor.

Her stomach tightened.

She hadn't asked enough questions. Who was this Dr. Taekman? Obviously the operation was serious enough to call for a specialist. She could barely remember the name of the surgery, but she did remember that Dr. Cook said they were going to drain a hematoma and repair a blood vessel. He couldn't do that without opening up Stanley's head.

And it didn't sound like it just involved peeling back the scalp. That he wouldn't need a specialist for. How deep was the surgeon going to go? What kind of risk was there? What danger was there to Stanley's brain?

Just before she left Madge told her they'd be praying for both of them. But she knew that group. As soon as they'd made their request they'd add, 'Thy will be done.' She didn't want God's will done. She wanted Stanley back alive and without any brain damage.

The idea flitted into her head that this new gift of hers would come in handy if Stanley lost his ability to speak.

"Oh, no!" she exclaimed silently. "No, God, I don't want that. I want him back whole. Take me instead. Yes, I know You don't bargain, but I wouldn't be able to stand it if I lost him."

And he would? Came the thought.

"No, of course he wouldn't," Aleta answered, still without speaking aloud. "He loves me as much as I love him. He'd lose twice because he'd lose the baby too. I would at least have that."

Aleta paused as her mind reviewed what she had just thought.

"Okay, God, I take it back. I don't want him to suffer that much, so if you're going to take one of us... Oh, God, I can't say it. I want Stanley to live and I don't care if he's whole. I just want him to live."

Are you trying to bargain with me again, said the inner voice.

"Of course, I am. I'm sorry," Aleta murmured. This time her words were whispered. "Oh, God, please, let him live."

And what will you do in return? Came the question.

"Anything," Aleta whispered. "Anything."

It's just a question, came the thought. I don't bargain.

"You want something, don't you?" Aleta queried silently. "You who don't need anything want something. What could I possibly have that You want?"

Aleta's mind stopped there. She waited expectantly.

The story of Abraham and Isaac came to mind.

That doesn't apply, Aleta told herself, but she knew it did.

"You want me to put Your will before mine, don't you? I know You do. And You want me to be willing to let Stanley die, don't You? In fact, You want me to love You more than him."

"But, God, he's real and he makes my heart sing. I wouldn't be able to handle the loss. Don't you know that? Besides I thought we didn't need to sacrifice anymore. Isn't that what Jesus dying was all about—the end of sacrifice? Just show me my sin and I'll repent."

Aleta paused and the thought came to her. She repeated it softly.

"You want me to obey you without question as I do Stanley? That's it?"

She frowned. "Don't I do that now?"

And the minute she said it, she realized that she reluctantly did what God asked. If it became difficult, she knew she wouldn't.

"But You're so vague," she protested. "Stanley is so clear. I always know what he wants.

"Yes, I know, if I ask, you'll give me another sign. It always seems clear to me at the time, but later I think that maybe You didn't speak to me after all. That it was all my imagination."

Aleta thought for a minute.

"You are how You are," she said aloud. "But why me?" Another Bible passage rose in her thinking.

"To him to whom much has been given, much will be required," she murmured. "Well, You have given me everything I could possibly want. Am I willing to let it go if you ask? Everything but Stanley. I can't say I'm willing to let go of him. That would be a lie."

Suddenly, incredibly tired, Aleta closed her eyes and hoped to sleep past whatever decision she needed to make when the nurse walked into the room to check on her.

"How's my husband?" she asked.

"No word yet. It's a long operation," the nurse said. "I don't expect we'll hear anything for several hours."

"What exactly is a craniotomy?" Aleta asked surprised that she remembered the word.

"I'm perhaps not the best one to ask," the nurse replied. "I'm sure Dr. Cook will explain it all to you when it's over."

"The artery that's ruptured isn't easy to get to, is it?"

"It is a complicated operation," the nurse said writing on the chart and turning to go.

"One question," Aleta said. "Yes or no answer."

The nurse turned.

"Do they have to go through the skull?"

"Yes," came the reply and then the nurse was gone.

What was I thinking, Aleta berated herself. You can't repair a blood vessel through a small hole. Why didn't I ask something that would tell me more?

He could die, she thought suddenly. Opening up the skull means you expose the brain.

Is that why Stanley gave me that order? He knew how risky the surgery was.

He doesn't think he's going to make it, Aleta concluded.

Despair took over rapidly. As she slid down into the deepest depression she'd ever known; she began to understand why suicide seemed so reasonable to people at times. It didn't matter that there were people who loved her. It didn't matter that she was pregnant. The light in her life was about to go out, and she would be plunged into the darkness of grief.

She'd known grief before, but nothing like what she was about to face. She'd never before loved anyone so deeply, so completely. She couldn't fathom living without Stanley. Always she'd worried about the both of them being killed, but those worries were instantaneously aroused and almost as quickly dispelled. There was something almost exciting about existing in fear and suspense, but this was different. There was no excitement here. Only loneliness and fear.

Never before had she felt so alone and so helpless. Even the horrors that had been visited upon her when they were kidnapped had been mitigated because she'd shared the experience with Stanley. But now he was gone. And there was no one.

She was alone in a room where all she could see was the night sky. And she found no peace in the sight.

She could ask the nurse to call someone, but she knew it wasn't people she needed. She needed to know Stanley was going to be alright. No one could assure her of that.

Stanley was truly in God's hands, and she didn't even know how to pray. How could she have been given the gift of prophecy and the gift of understanding and be so confused as to how to approach Him who gave her those gifts.

It occurred to her that she'd been pretty flippant about the relationship, accepting the protection of the one gift and the pride that accompanied the other without any comprehension of the magnitude of either.

Talk about being full of oneself, she mused. As if somehow it was me in charge.

Well, I'm not in charge now. And my gifts are as useless as I am.

"Oh, God, please forgive me," she prayed. "Please."

Her eyes closed and slowly she slipped into a deep sleep.

Chapter 14

Aleta awoke just as the sky was beginning to lighten. The stars had faded into the grayness of the pre-dawn sky. She could see nothing outside now. The only reality was the bed on which she lay.

Her shoulders ached. She wondered why. They hadn't ached yesterday. Could Stanley's crazy finger taping have kept her shoulders in a better position for healing? It wasn't as if she was supposed to raise her arms anyway. Movement at this stage was detrimental to healing.

She lay very still and listened. She was alone in the room. Stanley wasn't back yet. Was the operation over? Was he dead?

"The answer, God," she said softly, "is yes, I choose You above all."

She didn't know where her statement came from, but she realized it was not a lie. Stanley's love was a reflection of God's love.

She no longer felt alone.

A short time later, the door to her room opened and the light was turned on. Dr. Cook reached inside her sling and took her pulse. "Hmm. Same beat as your husband's?"

Aleta's heart began to beat faster. "He's okay?"

"He'll be fine. Dr. Taekman is a fine surgeon," Dr. Cook said smiling. "All went well. He'll be ready to go home, in a week. He'll have faint headaches for a while, but they'll go away eventually."

"You cut open his skull," Aleta said. "And…"

She couldn't finish.

"You want to know if we messed up his brain?" Dr. Cook said. "The ruptured artery was a couple layers closer to the surface, so the answer is no. We didn't mess up his brain. It's the same as it's always been. If you wanted us to change anything it's too late now."

Dr. Cook was ready for a quip in response to his banter.

Aleta's wit was always primed and ready. This time he was surprised.

Aleta's tears began to flow.

"God, you gave him back to me," she murmured.

"I gather you were worried," Dr. Cook said, immediately matching her mood. "Stanley said you would fear the worst. I disagreed. I guess he was right."

"I need the tape on my fingers again," Aleta said.

Again Dr. Cook was taken aback. "Whatever made you come up with that?"

"My shoulders hurt," Aleta explained. "Now that I'm not going to bury him, I may as well feel good all over."

Wayne Cook shook his head as he chuckled. There was no outguessing Aleta.

He stepped outside the room and she heard him ask the nurse for adhesive tape. The nurse followed him back into the room and watched as he taped the little fingers on each hand together.

"If that helps, we'll keep doing it," he said.

"When will Stanley be back?" she asked.

"In a couple of hours."

"Shouldn't someone call his parents?"

"Already did. I told them they wouldn't be able to see him until eleven. That should give you two a bit of time alone first."

"May I get out of bed yet?" Aleta asked, thus reminding him of his order.

"Not today," he said. "It's Sunday. I need my day of rest and, if you're mobile, I won't get it. So you stay put."

Aleta smiled. "I owe you. Today is part payment."

"Part payment for what?" Lyle West said, entering the room.

Aleta's face lit up upon seeing him. "I thought I wasn't supposed to have any visitors."

"I'm not a visitor," Lyle said. "My men are on your door. I told them to call me when you were awake."

"I thought Milani's men were guarding these two," Dr. Cook said.

"They have Stanley. I have Aleta. Peets has Hoskinson. With a pro involved we stepped up our security," Lyle said.

"They woke you up?" Aleta inquired.

"Who was sleeping?"

"You have on your uniform."

"I have a spare at headquarters. When one wants to roam hospital corridors, a chief's uniform is almost as good as a doctor's coat in gaining access in off-hours," Lyle explained. "Now let's get to why I'm here. Wayne, what did you do to Stanley?"

"You knew?"

"Our men report to us regularly," Lyle replied.

"Have you seen him?" Aleta asked.

"What's left of him," Lyle teased.

Aleta blanched.

"He said he didn't touch his brain," Aleta claimed, her voice tenuous.

"He made a hole big enough to take it out and toss it around the operating room a few times."

Dismay joined the shock her face was displaying.

"He wouldn't. He didn't," Aleta protested.

"Now that Aleta's prepared for the worst," Lyle smiled wryly. "Why not describe what you did do? And I want all the details."

Aleta nodded, the color returning to her face.

Dr. Cook told them.

Aleta would have lost her breakfast had she had any when he described cutting through the layers of skin, muscle and membrane and how the cut portion is hinged back and laid on the skull. Imagining the drilling of a series of holes in the skull made her cringe but she tried to hide her reaction. Then it got worse. It seems the next step was to saw the skull between the holes and then the flap of the skull was also lifted back on a hinge. The artery was repaired and everything was put back.

"So you didn't leave a hole?" Aleta asked and then felt stupid for half believing Lyle's joking.

"He's got everything he had yesterday," Dr. Cook said, "except half a head of hair. I even gave him a scar to equal yours."

"But his hair will grow back, won't it?" Aleta asked.

"He'll have a fuzz before he leaves the hospital," Dr. Cook said. "You worry about the strangest things."

"You have no idea," Aleta remarked. "No idea at all."

"Which is why I'm here," Lyle said. "I need to pass a puzzle past Aleta. Is she up to it, Doc?"

"She's up to anything so long as it doesn't involve her moving out of that bed or using either arm."

"Wow!" Aleta exclaimed smiling. "That gives me a lot of options."

"I only need her brain," Lyle said.

"It's all yours," Cook said. "I'm going home. Don't worry, Aleta. I'll be back this afternoon."

"If you're going home, Stanley must be doing well," Aleta commented.

"I told you he was."

"Your actions are more persuasive than your words," Aleta grinned. "However, I will stay put as I promised."

Lyle pulled up a chair and presented the puzzle of Rosalie Hoskinson lying about having a sister.

While that discussion was taking place at the hospital, miles Dean Arnetti's cell phone rang. He answered with a surly hello.

"No names," Slade Lecaze warned.

"Do you know what time it is?" Dean growled.

"Ship the crap. I need info."

"Whatcha calling me for?"

"You work at the hospital, don't ya?"

"At the Convalescent Home," Dean corrected.

"So you gotta know what's happening," Slade pushed on. "I gotta know how bad they was hit."

"Who?"

"Don't be a shithead."

"You did her last night?"

"She went down only I'd swear it was before not after. The ambulance was there before I made it to my car, so I couldn't follow it."

"I ain't getting into this. Not for no measly thousand."

"How'd you like to lose that thousand and a piece of your anatomy?"

"Shit!"

"I'll call back in two hours."

"That ain't enough time," Dean protested. "And I don't want you calling me at work."

"I thought you was off Sundays?"

"They're short-handed," Dean said.

"Okay," Lacaze relented. "You call me."

Two hours later Dean Arnetti snuck outside supposedly for a smoke. He dialed Slade Lacaze's cell.

When Slade answered, Dean yelled, "Do you know how much I had to layout for this information?"

"Why is that my business? You're lucky I don't take the rest."

"You missed her!" Dean gloated.

"So why the ambulance?"

"To take him to the hospital. He was operated on last night. A chopper brought in a brain surgeon."

"What about her?"

"Seems she had a concussion. She's on the fourth floor. She's got police guarding her. They both got police guarding them. You ain't getting nowhere near them."

"Which side of the hospital is the room on?"

"I saved the best for last. She's on the side that faces nothing but miles of flat farmland."

"You sound too happy. Whose side you on anyways," Slade snarled.

"I gotcha the dope, didn't I? Cost me too," Dean snapped. "This is it. I'm done."

Slade Lacaze immediately put in a call to a friend in Ohio. He'd used Buddy Horvat before and split the fee. Buddy was eager to do more jobs for Slade. The man was careful and sharp.

"I need you on this job," Slade said without preamble.

"Half as usual?"

"I only charged half."

"What'd ya do that for?"

"Special circumstances," Slade said. "But I'll give you the whole bundle."

"Must be really special circumstances," Buddy concluded. "But you been good to me. I'll do it for my usual cut."

"How soon can you get here?"

"One o'clock. What airport?"

"There's a little one north of Willow Glen, Illinois," Slade said. "With a little luck we could be done by tonight. I'll tell you then if I need you for the others."

"Others?"

"She's primary."

At exactly eight o'clock that morning, Robert Locke walked into his daughter's hospital room. He noticed the empty bed beside hers and came over and kissed her on the forehead and said quietly, "I'm sorry you had to go through that alone."

"He's going to be alright, Dad," Aleta said. "But Dr. Cook told me he'd told everyone not to show until eleven."

"He did, and I'm only here to deliver messages. I had to promise not to visit until the Praetzels could come. It's a weird arrangement; but these men are working hard to protect the two of you, so I can live with their rules."

"I can't write anything down, so you'll have to remember what I tell you."

"Don't worry, I'll remember," her father assured her.

"You won't be able to understand them at all, but they'll understand you. Stella will want to know about King. Dr. Chesney is going to help Dr. Cook deliver my baby. It's his wife who's sick. He will probably be there. Mr. Hoskinson will just want to know what happened to me."

One of the guards opened the door and said, "Time."

"See you at eleven," Robert Locke said.

"Don't worry. I'll be fine," Aleta assured her father. "Stanley won't really be ready to see anyone until then."

Shortly after her father left, the door opened and in walked her grandmother.

"Grams?" Aleta questioned. "How long have you got?"

"As long as I want I guess," Harriet Locke said.

"No one stopped you?"

"I expected them to, but no one did. It was as if I was invisible. Strange."

"Why are you here?"

"I have a message."

"A message?"

"I don't understand it, so why don't you tell me what's going on."

"You mean with Stanley?"

"I mean with you and God."

Suddenly, Aleta's face crumbled. "Oh, Grams, I'm so confused. I think I told God He could take Stanley; but when I found out Stanley was alive, I was so happy I think I betrayed everyone."

"What exactly did you say?"

"I told God I chose Him first. But…," she stopped, her voice failing her.

"And you believe He was asking you to give up Stanley?"

"That and being rich."

"That sounds right," Harriet said.

"But I still have Stanley, and I'm still wealthy."

"God didn't take Isaac either. Abraham just had to be willing to let go of the one he loved the most," Harriet explained. "The greater the love, the bigger the choice."

"But it wasn't a real test was it? It was just my imagination, wasn't it?"

"If you believe you were being asked to do this?"

"Yes, but…"

"Then you were. Once you've let go, you've let go. Physically letting go is no proof. We release our obsessions inwardly."

"How do I know…? I mean, I am so grateful Stanley is alive, I'm not even sure I was being totally honest with God. I've always been so proud of my honesty, and here I made the most important decision of my life, and I think I mucked it up. I'm not proud of myself at all."

"Now the saying I came across on the internet makes sense. It popped up today and I wrote it down. And then I felt that I should bring it here," Harriet said. "Here it is."

She held out the paper so Aleta could read it.

"'The beloved of the Almighty are the rich who have the humility of the poor, and the poor who have the magnanimity of the rich.' It was written by the poet Saadi in the early thirteenth century," Harriet said.

"The last part. That's Stella. She needs to hear this," Aleta said. "Will you read it to her and say I sent it?"

"Of course," Harriet said. "You do realize that this experience has changed you, don't you?"

"It has?"

Ah, my dear Aleta, the fact that you don't see means it's real," Harriet said tenderly. "Just think about the first part of that quote. I'll go now. I'll be back later. Stanley is leaving the ICU. He'll be here in a few minutes."

"How…?" Aleta began, but her grandmother was gone.

Within minutes, the gurney carrying Stanley was rolled into the room.

"Aleta, are you okay?" he asked the minute he was completely transferred from the gurney to his bed and the nurses had left them alone.

"I think so," she replied tentatively. "It's been a strange night. How about you? Are you okay?"

"I was worried about you," Stanley confessed.

"So was I. I was sure you were going to die."

"So what did you think of doing?" Stanley asked knowingly.

"Going to the roof and jumping off," Aleta confessed.

"I forbid you to ever have that thought again."

"Too late," Aleta said. "God has already done that. We had an encounter, He and I. Grams says I'm changed. I hope you still can love me."

"Aleta, does my having a huge scarred head change how you feel about me?"

"Of course not!" she exclaimed.

"So your psyche was scarred," Stanley said. "God didn't destroy you. If anything, He would have refined you."

"But you liked the rough edges."

"I loved the stone beneath the rough edges. Rough or smooth, I love you."

Aleta let her tears flow. "You can't see, but I'm crying. I wish I could kiss you, but I promised to stay put. I'm telling you this so you'll know how I feel. Please believe me."

"What I believe is that God left your heart intact. I'm sorry I can't come over there and hold you, but I'm under orders too."

Suddenly, Aleta giggled. "Don't tell me we're both relegated to using bedpans."

"Do you suppose if I don't drink any water, I can hold it in until tomorrow?"

"You've had an IV in your arm for hours. You're sunk," Aleta said with a wry smile. "So am I. They actually stand over me holding the glass until I drink enough."

"This should humble both of us."

"God wants us that way."

"What way?"

"Grams brought me a saying she found on the internet this morning. She just walked right in here. I don't understand it. The guards actually timed my father, but they didn't notice her come or go."

"So what was the saying?"

"The beloved of the Almighty are the rich who have the humility of the poor and the poor who have the magnanimity of the rich."

"That's not from the Bible, is it?"

"God inspires poets and writers outside of the Bible," Aleta responded evenly.

"That He does," Stanley agreed.

"He tested me and I think I flunked, but He let you live anyway."

"He let me live to spite you?" Stanley quipped. "I'm punishment?"

"Oh, for Heaven's sake, Stanley, that's not it. You're misunderstanding me completely."

"Am I?"

"Yes, you are," Aleta declared. "It was an Abraham-Isaac thing."

"Which one was I?"

Aleta rushed on, "Let me think of another analogy."

"So, I'm Isaac, huh?"

"Grams says that a sacrifice is only meaningful if it's of something precious."

"Nice recovery, but maybe the next time you and God are going to have an encounter, you could tell me so I can fly to Australia."

"Australia?"

"It's far away but not as cold as Antarctica."

"I think He's probably disgusted with me. There won't be anymore encounters."

"Good Heavens, Aleta, you had one this morning."

"I did?"

"Your grandmother managed to get past all the guards to bring you a poem. You know if you can't recognize the still small voice, we're going to have a lot of thunder claps in our lives because, believe it or not, God likes you, and He's not done with you."

Aleta was silenced by his words and the authority she heard in his voice.

Stanley waited for the comeback. It didn't come.

"You mean, for once, I got in the last word, he mused. She has changed.

Chapter 15

At ten thirty, Dr. Chesney entered the room, a small box tucked under his coat. "You really have been put out of commission haven't you?" he said genially.

He walked over to Stanley and introduced himself as he pulled the box out from under his coat.

"How's Elizabeth?" Aleta asked.

"She passed half an hour ago," he said sadly. "We both knew it was only a matter of days. One of the reasons I'm here is to give you the chocolates I promised you this morning. Your dad had some. Thank you for sending him. He told us some fascinating stories about you. Elizabeth had a good time listening to him. You've made all the difference in our last few days. I will be forever grateful for the gift you shared with us."

Murmurs of sympathy followed his speech.

He turned to Stanley. "Do you like chocolate?"

"Love it."

"Then I'll bring more in a couple of days. I understand the police are refusing to let anyone bring you anything at all."

"They're being careful," Stanley said.

Dr. Chesney opened the drawer in the night stand. "You can ask your visitors to feed you them," he told Aleta. "I know the nurses won't."

"You let her go, didn't you?" Aleta queried softly.

"I had her directive in hand," he replied.

"Sometimes the most loving thing we can do is choose to obey when we don't want to."

"She deserved to have her wishes honored," he said and then left.

When the door closed, Stanley observed aloud, "There goes a man whose heart has been torn out."

"What will he do?"

"Grieve and go on," Stanley said. "That's his only good option. To do otherwise would dishonor his wife's memory."

"I don't know if I could," Aleta said.

If the time ever comes, you'll find the strength," Stanley declared confidently.

Again Aleta was silent.

At eleven o'clock all four allowed visitors crowded into the double room. Stanley's mother tried not to break down when she saw him.

Stanley seeing her distress said, "Go ahead and cry, Mother, it's been almost two hours since anyone cried over me."

Lydia laughed as she began to bawl. Hubert held his wife close and said, "Mother, he's alive. And he is still Stanley. We haven't lost him."

"I know," she sobbed. "I know, but I can't help myself."

Aleta spoke up. "I didn't cry until he was out of danger either."

"I had an interesting time with your friends," her father said. "The Chesney's were so easy that I knew how to talk with the other two."

"Elizabeth Chesney died this morning," Aleta reported. "Dr. Chesney came by and told me. Your visit made their last morning together enjoyable."

"I'm sorry to hear that," her father responded.

Harriet interposed, "Stella Lemay died as well. I was with her. I'd just read her the poem and I took her hand and she squeezed it and just like that she was gone."

"What about Mr. Hoskinson?" Aleta said, suddenly upset. "He seemed fine," Robert Locke said. "He wanted to communicate something to me, so I tried to find out what."

"How'd you do that?"

"I played twenty questions'."

"So what did he want to say?"

"That you were good with numbers."

"Oh, yes, I remember. I had tried to memorize the license plate numbers of all the cars parked on the street as we entered the hospital parking lot. I made Aaron write them all down and then when I was in Mr. Hoskinson's room I tried to repeat them. I could only remember ten. I was telling him that there was a time when I could have remembered the whole group. I said it was frustrating to lose an ability, even one as trivial as that."

"Hoskinson went on," Robert said. "I couldn't get much more than that it was about his son. Since I didn't know their names, I was stymied."

"What would my remembering numbers have to do with his son?"

"License plate numbers," Stanley put in. "Dad, have one of the guards outside radio Lyle West."

"I don't remember the numbers now," Aleta pointed out.

"You had the patrolman with you write them down," Stanley reminded her.

Between them West and Milani tracked down the notebook and identified all the license plates. West sent men out to interview every car owner, hoping one or more of them could remember the car or the people who parked it along the street Saturday morning. He also sent a unit to bring in Neil and Rosalie Hoskinson for questioning.

It was after twelve before the police unit pulled up in front of the Neil Hoskinson house. The car was gone and it appeared that no one was home. The unit was told to wait.

When one of the residents remembered seeing a couple sitting on the road leading to the hospital early Saturday morning and said he was annoyed because the street was for residents and the hospital had a huge parking lot and people didn't have to pay so why didn't they just go park there.

After that report came in, West persuaded a judge that there was enough evidence for a search warrant for Neil Hoskinson's house and car. The judge also ordered the phone company to turn over their phone records.

While Neil Hoskinson was helping Rosalie's sister, Dorothy pack her clothes in Rosalie's suitcase, Rosalie moved the second of two car bombs from the trunk of their car to the trunk of her sister's car.

An APB was issued for the Hoskinsons. They were wanted for questioning. Still Neil drove to O'Hare and parked in long term parking without being stopped. He boarded the plane with Dorothy who was excited at having a charge card with a five thousand dollar limit. Her only restriction had been that she had to spread her charges over the entire trip.

Rosalie meanwhile moved her schedule up a day once she discovered that Dean Arnetti was working that Sunday.

The sooner she got this done, she thought, the better.

At one o'clock, while Slade Lacaze waited in the tiny parking lot outside the Willow Glen municipal airport and Rosalie Hoskinson completed her change of wardrobe and left Dorothy's apartment, Neil Hoskinson and Rosalie's sister Dorothy boarded their flight to Cleveland.

Slade pulled a case out of his trunk and had Buddy take off immediately. Once in the air, Slade assembled his assault weapon,

"Thought you didn't use those," Buddy said.

"Have to. You're going to hover while I shoot and this time I need a spray to do the job."

"Hover? Where?"

"Target's on the fourth floor in the local hospital."

"Which side?"

"East."

"Which room?"

"Don't know. I went up there. It's one of those at the north end."

"You gonna shoot up all the rooms."

"I'm guessing the cops cleared out the ones on each side."

"Hope you're right."

"You just put me in front of the middle room. I shoot and we leave. Piece of cake."

As they approached the hospital, Buddy noted that the hospital had a helipad on its roof. Therefore they were used to choppers coming and going. That fact buoyed up his spirits.

Buddy flew over the helipad and hovered for a few minutes. "You set?"

"Ready," Slade said shouldering the gun. "Let's do it."

Buddy flew up and out as if leaving the pad. He descended slowly on the northeast corner of the hospital and moved forward along the line of windows on the fourth floor.

Just as they reached the second large window, Slade shouted abruptly, "Turn off!"

Buddy turned away and flew straight east.

"Cops!" Slade exclaimed furiously.

"You didn't expect cops?"

"Yeah, guarding the door," Slade said angrily pulling in his gun and dismantling it. "These were two standing at the foot of her bed. Chiefs, I would guess from their hats."

"She's got police chiefs guarding her?"

"They weren't guarding her. They had their backs to the window," Slade said still vexed. "And if I'd sprayed the place I'd have killed two police chiefs and not even touched her. I can't believe her luck."

"When do you want to try again?"

"Tonight, when it's dark."

"You said they had their backs to the window," Buddy commented. "That means they didn't see us. Oh, I know they saw the chopper, but not your gun."

"If everyone still thinks she's safe, a piece of luck come our way too," Slade observed.

"As you said," Buddy enthused, "A piece of cake."

Inside the room, Lyle West and Tom Milani were telling Aleta they needed to talk with Lars Hoskinson and they had tried on their own but gotten nowhere.

"We just can't come up with the places Neil might go," Tom Milani said.

"We need you to come to his room with us," Lyle said.

"I promised to stay put."

Lyle turned to Stanley. "Will you give her your permission?"

"It's not me she promised."

Tom Milani exploded. "We're trying to save her life here. We need some cooperation."

Lyle inserted his question quickly before Milani got any angrier. "Who did you promise, Aleta?"

"Dr. Cook."

Milani threw his hands in the air and turned away. "This is crazy!"

Lyle went to the door and had one of his men radio a unit to pick up Dr. Cook at his home.

"He's not going to be happy," Aleta commented.

Stanley just smiled. Aleta, determined, didn't give in.

Lyle took Tom out into the hall.

"Why couldn't you just phone him?"

"I needed to make an impression." Lyle responded.

"He won't cooperate if he's angry." Tom argued.

"He would have insisted on checking her out before he gave an order for her to move. I know him. He was upset about letting Stanley almost get away from him."

Lyle's explanation calmed Tom Milani.

"I'm not up for this," Tom said.

"With Aleta, you don't try to bust down the door. You ask for the key that will open it."

Dr. Cook arrived less than fifteen minutes later. He was escorted to the fourth floor and, when he saw both police chiefs outside Aleta's room, he began to smile.

"Stop grinning!" Lyle said. "She won't leave her bed. She says you said she had to stay put.

"I did."

"Since when does Aleta obey anyone besides Stanley?"

"Since Stanley told her to," Wayne grinned. She was a pain, this Aleta, but she was fun too.

"So undo it," Lyle said. "We need to take her to see Hoskinson. We need some answers."

"Bring Hoskinson up here."

"We can't get hold of his doctor," Lyle informed Wayne.

"Yeah, he takes his days off seriously. He goes where there's no phone service."

"We need this information," Milani put in. "We need it now. We've got to stop whoever is still out there. If we can find Neil Hoskinson, he might be persuaded the jig is up and give up the man he hired."

"I'll take her down," Wayne said. "And I stay with her the whole time. If that's not acceptable, she stays put."

"Acceptable," Lyle said.

Tom nodded.

"You do realize she might not be able to translate anymore. She's had another concussion."

"You think it knocked the ability out of her?" Tom asked.

"I'm just warning you, that's all," Dr. Cook said. "Now let me check out Aleta. If she's okay, I'll send for a wheelchair."

Twenty minutes later, the four of them were entering Lars Hoskinson's room. To their surprise Alan Peets and Ed Ornstein were there.

Peets quickly explained, "Ed wanted to deliver his report but he couldn't get past my guards. Mr. Hoskinson seemed to want to hear it. I was just leaving."

Mr. Hoskinson's eyes lit up when he saw Aleta. He uttered a long string of syllables and all three police chiefs held their breath waiting for her answer. When they saw her about to respond, they relaxed.

"Yes, my dad told me which is why we're all back here. It seems your son's license number was in the group of numbers. How did you know?"

A string of syllables followed the query.

"They weren't yours. The police checked. The car is registered to him."

Another unintelligible response followed.

Aleta addressed the chiefs. "He's guessing that when he had his stroke, Neil had the car reregistered in his name. He's guessing that Neil will tell Cliff that he OK'd it."

"But he didn't?" Lyle asked.

The old man nodded.

"Interesting," Lyle commented. "Mr. Hoskinson, we can't find Neil. We ran out of guesses you know. Tell us what we didn't think to ask."

The syllables that spewed forth made Aleta smile.

"On Sundays Neil flies to either Iowa or Ohio to check on his lumberyards. He likes to arrive early on Monday morning. He thinks that keeps his employees on their toes."

"Does his wife go along?" Lyle asked.

The old man shook his head.

"What does she do?"

Again he shook his head.

"Does she get together with her sister?" Peets asked.

A jumble of sound accompanied a slow shake of the head.

"I didn't know she had a sister," Aleta translated.

"She told us she didn't have any living relatives," Peets said. "Do you know any reason why she'd hide a sister?"

Hoskinson shook his head.

"Just one more thing," Lyle said. "Do you know where he stays when he's out of town?"

The huge volume of words were tinged with vexation. Aleta translated the words minus the wrath.

"Neil refuses to economize. He stays in the best hotels in the area. And eats at the most expensive restaurants he can find. It'd be worse if I let him take his wife along. She's a real spend thrift."

"Thank you, Sir," Lyle said. "You've been a big help."

The old man uttered another phrase. Aleta translated it exactly.

"Please catch him before someone dies."

"Sorry, Sir. Someone already did," Lyle said. "One of Chief Milani's men, but you may have saved the lives of others."

Dr. Cook wheeled the chair around and took Aleta out of the room.

"Ed might have needed some help," Aleta said, her protest unusually mild.

"I went as far as I'm prepared to go," Dr. Cook said. "You and Stanley are more fragile than you think."

"We're stronger than you think," Aleta argued.

"Stanley isn't. And he needs you nearby to stay put. I can't order him as I did you, so you have to do as I ask so he'll do what he needs to do."

Aleta nodded. "You've got it."

"And I want one of those chocolates you've got in your night stand."

"How do you know I have any left?"

"Because your parents wouldn't have raided your little stash."

"But you would?"

"You called me away from my Sunday nap. You owe me."

"Lyle called you," Aleta pointed out.

"Lyle doesn't have any chocolates."

"One piece, but you've got to give me one too."

Aleta was smiling as she was wheeled into the room. She saw Stanley's worry vanish as soon as he saw her. Dr. Cook was right. Stanley's condition was delicate.

"I can still translate," she said happily. "Neil flies out of town on Sunday."

"No wonder they couldn't guess," Stanley said.

"I won't be going back," she announced as Dr. Cook eased her back into bed. "This was a one-time deal."

She noted gratefully that Stanley's face appeared to relax even more. He needed her here.

Dr. Cook opened the drawer and handed Stanley a chocolate, fed Aleta one and then ate one himself.

"These are my favorites," Dr. Cook commented as he put the box back.

"You can have another," Stanley offered.

"Aleta and I made a deal for one," he grinned. As he was leaving the room, he pointed at Aleta and said, "My order still stands. You stay put until I see you tomorrow."

Aleta nodded. Nothing would make her leave her bed, she resolved. Nothing.

Chapter 16

Harriet Locke arrived at the hospital too late to see Aleta in action, but when she entered Mr. Hoskinson's room, she asked Ed if he'd told Mr. Hoskinson what they found out.

Mr. Hoskinson mumbled something and looking at him, Harriet guessed, "You have some ideas what you want to do, don't you?"

Lars Hoskinson nodded.

She paused because Ed was shaking his head.

"Dr. Cook is not letting her out of bed again," Ed said.

"Ed, don't you have a tape recorder in your stuff?"

The short pudgy fingers reached into his pocket and he grinned sheepishly. "I always carry one, only recording Mr. Hoskinson didn't make sense since only Aleta knows what he's saying."

"Well, turn it on," Harriet said. "Mr. Hoskinson let me make my suggestions. And Ed will record what I say and your reply. Then I'll take the tape to Aleta. This will be slower, but we will be able to communicate."

Mr. Hoskinson nodded.

Harriet continued.

"It could be argued that the repairs were necessary to stem the spread of the mold. In almost all cases, mold results from faulty construction, so correcting the problem is not a bad thing. However, with no bad mold present in the house in the first place, the actions taken after the inspection are fraudulent. We need lab results to prove that. Edward Winslowe is gathering new samples."

Mr. Hoskinson spoke into the tape recorder that Ed held directly in front of him.

"We stopped some clients from moving ahead pending the recheck. We will not be liable on these no matter what the recheck shows."

Mr. Hoskinson nodded.

"The question is what to do about those people who are in the middle of or finished with the recommended procedure to rid their houses of mold.

"Whether or not the report is honest or fake," Harriet went on, "the ozone fix is bogus."

Lars Hoskinson spit out some angry words.

"Let me answer the two questions you might have here. Remember, Aleta will straighten me out if I'm wrong."

Hoskinson nodded.

"Since Neil owns the ozone tenting company outright, do you have any liability?"

Hoskinson shook his head .

"I'm not a lawyer and I think you have a case against having any liability. However, it could be argued that the ads and the inspector carried your endorsement which would make you liable."

Another string of angry syllables poured forth.

"Let me give you my suggestion as to how to avoid a lawsuit," Harriet said. "Reimburse the customers for any damaged electronic and other equipment. Ozone does in fact kill mold and Neil worded the contract carefully. He only claims it kills mold for three months. But he forgot to put in any warning about destruction to personal property."

Hoskinson talked at length.

When he stopped, Harriet went on. "Now this next is a suggestion that I'd like to implement immediately whether or not you decide to reimburse people far anything. Have Mr. Ornstein and Mr. Edward Winslowe interview the ozone customers and find out what if any damages were incurred. This can be done as a follow-up procedure by Hoskinson Lumberyard to see if the service should be continued. They can document the extent of the damage and that will prevent bogus claims at a later date."

Mr. Hoskinson nodded.

"You agree on this step?" Harriet asked.

Mr. Hoskinson nodded as he spoke into the tape recorder. "Now, you might wonder who Mr. Edward Winslowe is. He's an upstanding, Negro college student who…"

Harriet was stopped by a string of angry exclamations. Ed wondered why she mentioned Edward's race.

Harriet waited until he finished and then said to Ed, "Rewind back to when I was so rudely interrupted."

Ed did as he was told. Hoskinson continued to spiel out angry syllables.

"Now," Harriet said nodding at Ed to record again. "I do not know what you are saying; but I can guess you are objecting to Mr. Winslowe purely on the basis of his race."

She held up her hand. "Don't say a word until I finish. He was hired by your son to do the inspections. He has been helpful. He is incensed that he was drawn into a fraudulent scheme. I suggest you not anger him further by dismissing him when he is doing an outstanding job helping to clean up this mess.

Hoskinson nodded mutely.

"And you will never use a disparaging word about any race in your speech. Aleta has my permission to cut off this tape the moment you do," Harriet said. "Do you understand me?"

Hoskinson nodded although the part of his face not paralyzed looked bewildered.

"No, Mr. Hoskinson, we do not think as you do, do we, Mr. Ornstein?"

"The lad is smart and has a way with people. They trust him. He's got a good heart," Ed said. "Some white folk ain't worth shit. Some black folk is pure gold."

Hoskinson mumbled a few words which Harriet assumed was an apology.

"Now you need to tell Aleta what you want to do about this whole mess," Harriet said. "But before you do, let me tell you we don't know how far Neil has gotten with setting up this operation in his other three yards, so be sure to address that issue."

Harriet sat down in the chair and stared out the window at the farmland, brown stubble evidence of the last harvesting of the season. Bales of hay were stacked neatly in fields waiting transport. A few squares of still green grass were being grazed by black and white cows. Northern Illinois, like its neighbor to the north was dairy country.

The sun was rising toward its noon time zenith. A few scattered clouds were far away. It's brightness made Harriet avert her eyes. Just as she did so a dark cloud shut off the blinding brightness.

"Where'd that cloud come from she wondered. It was dark. The others were small and white.

The shadow it threw on the earth gave Harriet a chill. The old man seemed to be done.

She stood up. "Are you finished?" she asked.

He nodded.

"We'll talk after Aleta translates this," Harriet said. Strangely, he shook his head.

Puzzled, Harriet stared at him.

"You want me not to come back?" she asked.

He nodded.

Ed looked as puzzled as she did.

"What does he want?" he asked.

Harriet tried a direct question. "Do you want me to continue?"

The old man nodded vigorously.

"But not come back here," she posed thoughtfully. Suddenly her face brightened.

"You think Neil is there and will undo what we've done?" she queried.

Hoskinson nodded his head vigorously.

"Ed, let's call Martha and see if we can borrow her plane again."

The old man's head nodded again. Then he pointed at the phone.

"Yes, we can call Aleta," Harriet said.

"Ed, I'm packed. Are you?"

He nodded.

"Then I need to tell Aleta and give her this tape."

"You won't get past the guards," Ed warned.

"Move my suitcase to your car," Harriet ordered giving him her car keys.

Harriet walked up the stairs to the fourth floor and straight down the hall, past both guards and into Aleta's room.

"She's asleep," Stanley whispered.

"Play this for her when she wakes up. Mr. Hoskinson made some comments. I need to know what he said."

"Are you leaving?"

"That's what I came to tell her. I need to fly to Elyria immediately. I sense danger. Ed is going with me. Some of the explanation is on the tape."

"I understand," Stanley said. "Don't worry. We'll be fine."

Harriet put the recorder in Stanley's hand and squeezed it.

"You're a good man, Stanley."

Buddy landed the helicopter at the Willow Glen airport and asked, "We gonna just wait until night or you wanna go after them other marks?"

"Let's check out where they are," Slade said.

He directed Buddy to fly over the Praetzel house.

"She lives in that RV," he said.

"There's a cop guarding the place," Buddy commented.

"She's not there. Her jeep's gone."

"Where next?"

"She could be at the hospital," Slade said.

Within minutes they were over the parking lot.

"There's a jeep," Buddy said.

"Let's go back and get the car. I can pick her off when she leaves the hospital."

"There are three roads out of there," Buddy commented.

"Which one do you want to use?"

"A helicopter makes planning easy," Slade said. "That one. And we'll sit facing it. I'll have a clear shot at her approaching the jeep."

"You got it," Buddy said.

"You helped me," Slade said. "Half is yours."

"Thanks, man."

Twenty minutes later, they were parked exactly where planned. Slade moved to the back of the car, and took his rifle out of its case. Buddy watched the jeep.

"There's a little fat guy fussing around the jeep." Buddy reported.

Slade put the telescopic lens to his eye and waited for the man to turn.

"That's our other target," he announced. "Keep an eye on him."

"He's taking a suitcase out of the back," Buddy said.

Slade finished assembling his rifle. He looked out the side window as Ed was opening the trunk of his car and put the suitcase in the trunk.

"You got him in your sights?" Buddy asked.

"Yeah, but something tells me she's going to join him," Slade said, pulling in his rifle. "We're going to wait."

"He's climbing in the car," Buddy said. "Looks like he's gonna pick her up at the Emergency entrance."

"Back up just enough to keep him in sight," Slade ordered. "Don't move any closer though."

Slowly, Buddy eased the car back. He stopped when Ed's car was in full view.

"He ain't getting out," Buddy commented. He heard a grunt from the back seat. Slade knew. He didn't speak again.

Slade opened his window and sat back so his rifle barrel remained inside the car. He shouldered the gun and zeroed in on the balding man in the driver's seat.

When she comes out of the hospital and I take her out, Slade reasoned, he'll get out to go to her aid. That's when I'll nail him. One, two. Good plan.

He moved his rifle slightly and zeroed in on the emergency door.

The emergency doors swung open. Someone was coming out. Slade moved his rifle into position and pressed his finger lightly on the trigger. His eye followed the first head out the door. A uniformed cop.

That didn't surprise him. Of course there'd be cops on the entrances. They had the Praetzels upstairs.

He moved the rifle over to just beyond the shoulder of the tall man who was standing sideways signaling to someone. Slade didn't dare to take his eye away from the doorway. She would be exiting any second now.

He caught a glimpse of her gray head and then suddenly it was blocked by the tall cop who hurried to open the car door for her. His body continued to block her as she entered the car and he leaned over to speak with her briefly as the car was started. He stood beside it, then moved with it as it rolled forward.

Slade pulled his gun inside as the car turned and went down a line of parked cars.

When the siren started up, he jumped. His focus lost, he watched as his targets fell in behind a squad whose flashing lights cleared the main road leading from the hospital.

"Follow them!" Slade shouted, quickly dismantling his gun and putting it in its case.

Buddy turned the car around and sped across the parking lot. He was able to keep track of the flashing lights from several blocks back, so following the two cars was easy. When they hit open country, he stayed well back.

Slade was muttering obscenities in the back seat. Buddy picked up the reason for Slade's anger by the time they hit the city limits. Evidently he'd been told these two weren't under police protection.

"Looks like they could be headed for the airport," Buddy commented.

"How fast can you get in the air?" Slade asked.

"Pretty fast."

"What are the chances they're catching a chopper to O'Hare?" Slade asked.

"That'd be my guess," Buddy replied.

"Can we catch another chopper?"

"Sure. My chopper's fast," Buddy said. "I can even catch a small plane."

"Then I'll take them out in the air," Slade declared.

"I know a shortcut," Buddy offered.

"Use it."

"Hang on," Buddy said, turning down a gravel one lane road that led between two fields.

Buddy pulled into the parking lot next to the airfield just minutes ahead of the police car whose siren had been turned off. The blue lights were still flashing however.

Slade grabbed the rifle case and followed Buddy across the field to his helicopter. They passed behind a Cook Construction Company jet warming up on the runway.

"We'll be able to take off after the jet," Buddy said as they climbed into the chopper. "Whatever they're planning to catch isn't here yet."

A small plane circled the field.

"I'll bet that's their ride," Buddy said.

To the surprise of the two men in the chopper, the patrol car entered the field with the car the targets were in close behind. The patrol car stopped near the steps leading to the open door in the side of the medium-sized jet. Two uniformed officers jumped out, guns drawn.

"What the...?" Slade exclaimed.

Ed and Harriet left the car and hurried aboard the jet. One of the officers climbed into the car while the other one removed two suitcases from the trunk and took them to the plane. The steps to the plane were withdrawn, the door shut and before the cop was back in his patrol car the jet started down the runway.

"Go! Go!" Slade shouted.

"It's a jet!" Buddy threw back. "I can't catch a jet."

"Take off anyway. The cops are watching."

Buddy did so.

Inside the jet, Ed looked at Harriet. "How you feeling?"

"Okay," she replied.

"Danger passed?"

"It appears it is."

"So there's a contract on us as well," Ed concluded softly.

Just before five, Robert Locke breezed through the door. "Talk about guarding you. These guys mean business. I'm on the list, but still they checked me out. I guess Dr. Cook gave orders that you weren't to have any more visitors. I told them I had his permission. Fortunately, Lyle believed I wouldn't lie."

"They let Harriet breeze right in," Stanley commented. "No problem."

"How long ago?"

"A little while after Aleta got back. She was asleep so…"

Robert Locke went to the door. "How come you let my mother through without a hassle?"

"No one has passed through until you came, Sir," one guard said.

Robert Locke reentered the room. He knew Stanley had heard them.

Immediately, he apologized, "I wasn't checking up on your story. I was just curious why she could come and go and I couldn't."

"She was here," Stanley said. "She left this for Aleta. She said she was leaving town."

"She did leave. She and Ed flew to Ohio. She called me and told me to take care of her dogs," Robert said. "I guess she must've been here, or you wouldn't have known that she left town."

"Well, I'm glad I wasn't hallucinating," Stanley grinned. "Although if I was, conjuring up a tape recorder would have been quite a feat."

Robert looked over at his daughter. "How long has she been sleeping?"

"All afternoon," Stanley said. "The nurses said not to worry. Dr. Cook was expecting she might."

"He said I could feed her supper," Robert said. "I must admit I begged."

"She'll be delighted," Stanley said. "Wake her with a kiss. She likes that."

Robert went over and laid his hand high on Aleta's forehead. He stroked her head lightly and then gently kissed her.

"Stanley?" she murmured.

"Don't you wish," her father joshed.

Aleta's eyes flew open, "Dad!"

Instantly, her eyes went over to the bed beside hers. "Stanley, you're still here."

"You didn't sleep that long!" he quipped. "It's suppertime. Your dad came to help you eat."

"And to bring you all the latest news," Robert said.

The cart carrying the supper trays could be heard coming down the corridor. Robert pressed the control that lifted the back of the bed. He stopped when Aleta was upright enough to eat. Stanley used his remote to raise his bed even further. At exactly five minutes past five, the nurse entered with the first tray.

At exactly five minutes past five, Dean Arnetti left the Oakwood Nursing Home and put his hand on his car door handle. The timer hit the zero at that second, and the blast blew Dean across the parking lot. He landed at the base of a huge oak. His car door flew almost as far. Dean didn't notice. His eyes were open, but they saw nothing. His blood was everywhere but in his body, which lay beneath the tree like a tossed-aside rag doll, limbs askew, head tilted awkwardly to one side. He died instantly.

On the fourth floor of the hospital, several miles away, the nurse, startled by the sound, dropped the tray she was carrying. While the nurse apologized and called for the janitor, sirens could be heard screaming in the distance.

Aleta looked at Stanley fearfully.

"The explosion is south of us," Stanley said. "It can't be anyone we know. Besides your grandmother is in Ohio."

"Ohio?"

"She and Ed flew there while you were sleeping. She said this recording would explain.

"Whose dinner is on the floor?" Aleta asked, Stanley's explanation bringing her back to the present.

"Yours, of course," Stanley said smiling. "They always bring you your tray first. I'm no longer resentful of that fact."

"Dad, he'll share," Aleta announced as the nurse entered with a second tray.

"I will bring another tray," she said.

"Meanwhile, we'll share his," Aleta reiterated.

"We monitor…," the nurse began.

Robert Locke stopped her. "I'll see she only gets half. Okay?"

"That's not exactly… oh hell…," the nurse muttered as she left.

"Can you find out about the explosion?" Aleta asked.

"If I leave, they might not let me back in," her father said.

"Never mind," Aleta decided. "It's just I can't believe it's not somehow connected to the other bombings, which means it's connected to us somehow."

Robert Locke held out a piece of meat, and Aleta took it off the fork and began chewing.

The door opened and the nurse entered with their second tray.

"Where was the explosion?" Aleta asked.

"Some car in the parking lot of the Oakwood Nursing Home," the nurse reported.

"Anyone hurt?" Aleta pressed.

"One dead. Another staff member was getting in her car, and she's been brought here. Her injuries are minor."

"Who was killed?"

"Don't know who. Someone who worked there. Now who would want to blow up a person who worked in a nursing home?"

Aleta, who was chewing on a roll, tried to swallow it too fast and wound up coughing. Her father watched her helplessly.

The nurse realized at once what was happening.

"Just cough it out!" she urged. "We can clean you up afterward."

Robert stood up and stepped back. The nurse moved Aleta around on the bed and positioned herself behind her. Aleta coughed and spit, and the nurse gave her a minute to discharge the piece of bread. When it didn't come out, the nurse put her arms under the slings and in one quick movement caused the bit to come flying out.

Aleta took a deep breath and coughed a few times. Her eyes watered. The nurse offered her water, and Aleta took a sip. The nurse then repositioned Aleta in her bed and left.

Aleta tried to talk but coughed instead.

"Take it slowly," her father said kindly. "We'll wait until your throat is clear."

Stanley continued to eat. If he said anything, Aleta would insist on replying.

After a few more slow sips, Aleta was ready to continue. "It was Rosalie. She has a sister. She lied to Peets about her. Did I tell you that?"

"You think her sister would do this for her?" Stanley asked.

"No, but I think her sister might go to Cleveland in her stead," Aleta said. "Dad, can you call Peets?"

"Not Lyle?"

"It's Peets' case, and he's the one who brought up the sister, so he's already suspicious."

"I'll do that for you," her father said, "but after you've done eating."

"I can't, Dad. I'm full."

"Well, I'm not," Stanley said, hoping if he continued eating Aleta might want more.

Stanley played the tape Harriet had left. It didn't matter that Robert was there. He couldn't understand a word of the man's garble anymore than anyone else.

"He wants to change his will again," Aleta reported.

"But there's no proof of any wrong doing," Stanley said between mouthfuls. "Or is there?"

"He says he's not completely blind. He wants to do it immediately."

"I'm not sure Mother can clear her calendar again," Stanley said. "I don't know if Dr. Cook would let you go to his room to act as translator"

"I'm not needed. His wishes are recorded. I can translate them and dictate them to Dad, and he can call Johanson. Then your mother can read the new will to Mr. Hoskinson, and he can sign with witnesses as before."

"That could work," Stanley said.

When Aleta finished the dictation, her father asked, "Can he cut one son off completely?"

"He's got to leave him something," Stanley replied. "For it to stand up in court, he has to show he knowingly cut Neil off."

"Dad, can you tell him what Stanley said? Tell him I suggest he leave Neil the car he's already claimed as his."

"Is that a good idea?" her father asked. "He's letting him have what he's already taken."

"Think of the irony," Aleta said. "It's as if he chose his own inheritance."

"Can I take the recorder?" her father asked. "If he has more he wants to say, I can record it. I won't be able to get hold of his lawyer until the morning anyway, and I'll be back here to feed you breakfast."

"Stanley will...," Aleta began.

"...be confined to bed until mid-morning at least," her father said. "So do I get to feed you breakfast, or do you want some nurse to do it?"

"Yes," Aleta said, slightly abashed.

Chapter 17

"I can't believe how drowsy I am," Aleta commented after her father left.

"You have a right to be tired," Stanley soothed. "Emotions tire one out and you lost two friends today."

"You're right," she said. "I wish this headache would go away."

"You're stressing over all that's happening," Stanley said. "Close your eyes and relax and it'll pass."

Aleta did as he suggested. Within minutes she was asleep.

Stanley lay quietly listening to her breath. Two hours later the gray of dusk gave way to the black of night.

A nurse came in to check on him and turned on the light. He didn't protest even though he had enjoyed the flickering of the distant stars. Soon Aleta would awaken, and she would want to talk. Stanley dozed lightly as he waited. The light interfered with his ability to see the sky. The room was so quiet. He had the television remote on his night stand, but he was afraid he would wake Aleta. Later, perhaps, they could watch a movie together.

The clock ticked away the minutes. Shortly before eight o'clock, Stanley began to worry. He rang for the nurse. "Please call Dr. Cook," he said.

"Is something wrong?" she asked.

"I'm not sure," Stanley said. "But he said you would call him if I asked. He wrote it on my chart."

The nurse picked up the chart. Dr. Cook had indeed written those exact words. The nurse hurried away.

Dr. Cook entered his room twenty minutes later.

Stanley plunged into his concern without apology. "She said she was terribly drowsy. This was after she'd slept all afternoon. And she's been sleeping since her father left."

"Anything else?"

"She choked on some food," Stanley said, "but that was because she was talking while eating. Afterward, she complained of a headache. I thought she was tired and emotionally wrung out, but now I'm not so sure I was right."

Dr. Cook took her pulse and Aleta stirred. "How are you feeling?" he asked gently.

"I have a terrible headache," she said, then furrowed her brow. "Why are you here?"

"Stanley called me," Dr. Cook said. "He was worried. Is your headache worse than it was before you fell asleep or is it the same?"

"Much worse. Can you give me something?"

"I'll take care of it," he said and turned to the nurse. "Set her up for an MRI."

The nurse left immediately to fetch a gurney.

Aleta paled. "What's wrong?"

"That's what we're going to find out."

The sound of a helicopter approaching prompted Aleta to ask, "You didn't send for a specialist, did you?"

"No," Dr. Cook said. "That would be premature."

"Quick!" Aleta shouted. "Get us out of here!"

"There is a…," Dr. Cook started.

"Now! Carry me!" Aleta demanded.

"Guard!" Dr. Cook shouted as he scooped Aleta into his arms.

Both policemen appeared.

"Get him out of here now!" Dr. Cook ordered as he rushed around Stanley's bed and sped toward the door.

One cop held the door open for the doctor while the other hastened to help Stanley to rise. The second cop whipped his arm around Stanley's waist, yanked him from the bed and charged out of the room.

The spray of bullets swept the room just as Stanley and the cop exited. Several bullets caught the officer holding the door. As he fell, he pushed the door closed with his foot.

The sound of the rapid repetitive fire of an assault weapon electrified the staff into action. A gurney was pushed toward the doctor, and Aleta was placed on it. A second gurney was provided for Stanley. Once he could let go of his charge, the officer called in the shooting.

Blankets were spread over both Aleta and Stanley as Dr. Cook ran to check the fallen officer.

He opened the man's shirt.

"Lyle had you wear a vest," Dr. Cook exclaimed.

The man nodded. The wind had been knocked out of him.

"You're going to be sore," Dr. Cook said, "but not dead."

The cop smiled. "Not dead is good."

Sirens could be heard converging on the hospital. They were followed shortly by the whirling blades of two police helicopters hovering over the hospital.

Dr. Cook went over to Stanley. "You understand I must check out Aleta immediately, don't you?"

"I'm okay," Stanley said. "Honest. The officer practically carried me. It was quick but not rough."

"I will check back with you," Dr. Cook promised.

Having said that, Dr. Cook ordered an attendant to take Aleta downstairs for an MRI. "I'll be with you shortly," he told Aleta.

He had to alert Dr. Taekman again. And this time he had to make sure Dr. Taekman would be allowed to penetrate what Dr. Cook sensed was a blockade around the hospital. He needed him here to help him diagnose what was happening to Aleta.

He called Lyle on his private cell and explained the situation to him. He received a promise that Dr. Taekman's chopper would be allowed to land on the hospital helipad.

Dr. Taekman took off immediately and arrived before Aleta was finished with the MRI. The two doctors studied the images for a long time.

"All I see is the one hematoma," Dr. Taekman said finally. "And you say it is not in an area you were called upon to treat?"

"This is the area of the of the stroke," Dr. Cook said. "And here is the concussion from the explosion. And here is where she hit her head when she fell last night. But how did I miss this one?"

"Sometimes when we know where the injury took place," Dr. Taekman said kindly, "we focus our attention in that area."

Besides you know these subdural hematomas can take months to show up. And since you didn't know about an injury to that area, you didn't check."

"I pulled her last MRI," Dr. Cook said. "I can see it now. I didn't look hard enough."

"She showed no symptoms," Dr. Taekman reminded him. "Why would you look? You had no history of trauma to that area and no symptoms to clue you in."

"Will you help me talk to them?" Dr. Cook asked.

"Of course," Dr. Taekman said. "Just remember we caught it in time. The prognosis is the same."

"Let's tell Aleta first," Dr. Cook said.

Dr. Taekman did a double take when he saw Aleta lying on bed in pre-op with both arms in slings. He raised a brow as a silent query.

"Bullet wound that was damaged further by the kidnappers," Dr. Cook explained pointing at the left shoulder. "The right is a broken clavicle."

Dr. Taekman went to take hold of a hand and noticed the taped fingers.

"This is different," he said with a grin.

"Stanley's idea," Aleta said. "It saved my shoulders further injury when I fell."

"Do you know who I am?" Dr. Taekman asked.

"You're the doctor who operated successfully on Stanley. I assume I need an operation as well."

"Yes, you do" Dr. Taekman replied. "You have a subdural hematoma and…"

"You have to go deeper, right?"

"Correct. But we still won't be touching the brain itself. We need to remove the blood clot and repair the ruptured blood vessels."

"More dangerous?"

"A little."

"Prognosis?

"The same as for your husband. Good."

"And Dr. Cook isn't telling me all this because he's feeling guilty, right?"

"You presented no symptoms until now, and Dr. Cook had no history of a trauma to that area of the head," Dr. Taekman said matter-of-factly. This was a no-nonsense woman.

"You mean it's not the same area as either of my recent bumps?"

"Correct."

"Well, the kidnappers threw me down a couple times, but I didn't have such a bad headache then."

"Sometimes it takes months after a head injury for the blood to accumulate enough to cause pressure on the brain." Dr. Taekman explained.

"But when Dr. Cook looked at my earlier recent MRI, he saw the beginning, correct? That's why he's so upset, isn't it?"

Dr. Taekman hesitated and Aleta plowed on.

"I'm not angry. We all make little mistakes. The point is you're here and he called you and I have as good a chance of recovering as I did this morning, don't I?"

"That's true," Dr. Taekman agreed.

"If Dr. Cook had spotted the hematoma a week ago, would I have had to have the same operation? Wouldn't my prognosis be the same?"

"Yes."

"He doesn't miss much you know," Aleta said.

Dr. Taekman smiled. "He's one of the best."

"That I do know."

Dr. Taekman patted her tape-joined hands. "You are a remarkable young woman."

"Dr. Cook, you need to do something for me," Aleta began and, seeing the worried look on his face, insisted, "beside forgiving yourself for being human."

Dr. Cook smiled.

"That's better. I need happy surgeons working on my head," Aleta quipped. "Tell Stanley no one is to know. Dad would tell my mother, and she'd fly out here, and please don't put me through that. You owe me that much."

"Stanley may need company," Dr. Cook said.

"Lyle knows what's happening. He has to be here anyway, so he's free. He can keep Stanley company."

"Who's Lyle?" Dr. Taekman asked.

"The chief of police who's clearing up the mess and heading the investigation."

"He's free?"

"He's Stanley's best friend. He'll make himself free."

"Give me the authorization," Aleta said. "And Dr. Cook since you'll have time while Dr. Taekman busy fussing around under my skull, would you fix the scar along the top of my head. I think Stanley would like that."

As they left, Dr. Taekman asked Dr. Cook, "Does she have any idea how busy you'll be?"

Wayne Cook grinned. "Oh, she knows. Just wait until we talk with Stanley. You'll see how special this couple is."

The conversation with Stanley followed along the same lines. The only variation was that Stanley didn't mention needing Lyle's company and said that while it didn't bother him, the scar on her scalp bothered Aleta.

"You mean you don't care if it's fixed or not?" Dr. Taekman inquired.

"I care because Aleta cares. Women are sensitive that way. I've gotten used to it and, actually, I think it's neat. I like uniqueness."

"We may not be able to do anything about it," Dr. Taekman said somberly.

"I won't be disappointed if you don't; however, please don't make new hairless scars. I'm not sure Aleta could handle more than one."

"That we can do," Dr. Taekman said happily.

"It'll take several hours at least, maybe longer," Dr. Cook put in. "You're not to worry if it takes longer than your operation did."

Lyle West walked in as Dr. Cook was speaking. "You wanted to see me?"

"Aleta told me to tell you to keep Stanley company since you'd be hanging around here anyway."

Taekman was pleased to see the wry smile appear on the police chief's face. "Since when does she command anyone but Stanley? We've got our own redheaded wives who do enough of that."

"So, you'll do it?"

"Of course," Lyle said. "But I'm gathering there's a part two to this request."

"She doesn't want anyone to know about her having an operation."

"For how long?"

"Through Monday." Stanley put in. "Her father's coming in the morning. Lyle, you'll have to set up a no visitors policy again. This time without exceptions."

The two doctors left, and Lyle began to ask questions when one of his officers knocked on the door.

"Sorry, Sir. It's Judge Davis. She insists on speaking with you."

"I guess I set up that policy now," Lyle said turning toward the door. "Anything you want me to tell your mother?"

"Tell her Dr. Cook says I'll be able to walk around a bit tomorrow. She needs progress reports," Stanley said. "What about Lauren?"

"With an attack on the hospital, she won't expect to see me for a couple of days," Lyle said, then disappeared.

He reappeared within seconds.

"You aren't representing any member of the Hoskinson family are you?"

"No."

"Aleta can't, correct?" Lyle asked.

"Correct. And I'm not connected in anyway other than as her lawyer."

"Okay," he said and then told the man standing post he'd take all calls in Stanley's room.

"Go on Alan," he said. "Have you got her yet?"

He looked at Stanley and whispered, "We know Rosalie's in town."

"But no photo?" Lyle said. "Any description at all…? White… That's it…? How about the helicopter pilot…? That's something, but my guess is that he's long gone… Send it here anyway."

Stanley realized that his mouth was hanging open as if he were a baby bird waiting to be fed. He closed it before Lyle glanced his way and began to talk.

"Only one on the list of hit men works with a chopper pilot," Lyle told him. "No name. Just a nickname: 'The Sniper'. No description."

"If Rosalie saw him, so did Neil," Stanley said.

"He's in Ohio and we aren't ready to make an arrest. He'd be back before we could process the extradition papers."

"You know what would bring him back instantly?"

"What?"

"If Ed told Neil his father was ordering his will changed on Monday and that he was going back on Tuesday to witness the signing because Judge Davis is demanding that the same witnesses witness the new will."

"She wouldn't do that, "Lyle pointed out."

"He doesn't know," Stanley said. "And he might be persuaded that now is the time to bargain."

"Peter." Lyle called. "Get me a land line in here."

"I still have a guard?" Stanley asked.

"Of course. My men. I sent Milani's to guard the operating theater."

"What is Milani doing?"

"He's in Chicago visiting his old contacts to see if they know who the hit man is."

"I thought you had identified him."

"He's a prime suspect; but, we aren't ruling out other possibilities."

"Speaking of contacts, what about George Sciretta? He doesn't want anything to happen to Aleta," Stanley suggested.

"I hate to start exchanging favors with the Family he works for, but you could if you wanted to," Lyle said. "You know him about as well as I do."

"It's Aleta who knows him."

"Does she know who he is?"

"As far as she knows, he's just a bookkeeper who owns the Bulldog she handles."

"He interfered when you were kidnapped," Lyle said. "That's why we're sure it's out of town talent. George has evidently persuaded the Family that Aleta is not to be touched."

"He's got to know who's under attack," Stanley retorted.

"It was all local stuff until now," Lyle said. "Isn't Aleta scheduled to show his dog soon?"

"She was until the explosion took out her other arm."

"Want to bet she didn't call him?"

"I know she didn't. She was too busy with the party."

"So call and tell him what's happened to her," Lyle said.

"I can do that," Stanley said. "She'd want me to do that."

"Does Aleta have his home number?"

"Yes, but…"

"Peter, get me Sciretta's home number."

"You know it?"

"Of course," Lyle said.

Peter handed his chief a slip of paper. Lyle dialed it and handed the phone to Stanley.

"George, this is Aleta's husband, Stanley. I know it's late; but, Aleta wanted me to call you and tell you… Actually, she didn't ask me to; but, she would if everything goes well… She's having emergency brain surgery right now… A couple days ago the car she was riding in exploded. She'd just gotten out. She was blown to the street and got a concussion. We thought she'd be alright and then late night a sniper took a shot at her through our bedroom window. She fell on me and we both hit our heads. I was operated on last night... Yes, I'm doing okay... Tonight we were in my hospital room and that same sniper came down in a helicopter and sprayed the room with bullets. A cop was hit only he had on a vest. Aleta wasn't hit; but, the doctor did an MRI and found that all this knocking around caused a blood vessel to break open... Yes, she has the finest specialist in Chicago doing the operation... The police know who did the car bombing and are closing in on them... Local people... It's the sniper that has us worried. No description on him at all. Just his nickname: The Sniper... Yes, the police are working on it. Chief Tom Milani is in Chicago right now looking up his old contacts, hoping someone can give him a description of the man... What...? Duffy's Tavern on the Southwest Side...? Sure, I'll tell him... I'll tell Aleta you wish her well. She'll appreciate that... Yes, I'll let you know how the operation went. Goodbye, George."

"Peter, find the exact location of Duffy's Tavern," West ordered, "Southwest Chicago. I need it now!"

Lyle took the phone and called Tom Milani. "Someone in Duffy's Tavern will have information for you... Start driving southwest... Yes, I know whose territory that is... Peter is looking up the exact location... I'll have him call you as soon as he finds it... Just take whatever you're given and beep me... I'll call you back from the roof... No radio transmission on this one."

As he was waiting, Lyle called Dean Lundgren and got Ed's number at the hotel. He called Ed next, told him about the sniper attack, assured him there were no injuries and told him the plan to get Neil back as fast as possible.

Harriet got on the phone before Lyle could hang up.

"Let me speak to Aleta," she demanded.

"She's asleep," Lyle said. "She's the one who told us what Mr. Hoskinson wanted to do. Stanley and I thought up this plan just now."

"She wasn't hurt?" Harriet asked.

"Not a single bullet touched her. Dr. Cook carried her out..." The minute Lyle said that he knew he'd said too much. Stanley motioned Lyle to hand him the phone. "Grams, it was a frightening experience. Dr. Cook finally had to give her a mild sedative. We're more or less quarantined here for the next twenty-four hours while the police try to track down this hit man... Yes, I'll tell her. Goodbye."

"Is she going to fly home?" Lyle asked.

"I don't think so. I think she'll check with her son or my parents," Stanley responded.

"I hope she doesn't show up here," Lyle said. "Rumor has it she can become invisible at will."

"That's nonsense!" Stanley declared.

"I hope so because if she can, there will be no hiding anything from her."

"Don't even entertain the possibility," Stanley said then scowled. "It's too late. You already did, and my brain has already assimilated the concept... My God, Lyle... She's been living practically on our doorstep for months... She couldn't have... It's not possible... My God... I'd tear my hair out but I can't afford to lose any more..."

"You must have a hellava sex life," Lyle commented, grinning shamelessly. "I'd like to be a fly on your bedroom wall. They have those great eyes you know..."

"You try it and I'll swat you!"

"Do you even own a fly swatter?"

"I'll buy one."

"I've got two. I'll give you one."

Lyle's beeper went off.

"I need to go up on the roof and call Tom," Lyle said. "Peter, come here and sit with Mr. Praetzel."

The tall, blonde officer dutifully came into the room and sat down. Stanley noticed his name tag.

"You're a sergeant."

"Yes, Sir, I am."

"I would have thought this duty would be relegated to someone lower on the ladder."

"Second in command tonight," Peter said. "Chief West wants someone to handle things unobtrusively when he's busy."

"He gave you a lot of orders."

"He does that," Peter smiled. "But there's no one I'd rather work for. He never wastes my time."

"Interesting observation," Stanley mused. "Why do you suppose he asked you to sit with me?"

"So he will know exactly where I am when he comes back."

Stanley laughed and Peter joined him.

Lyle walked in on them as they were exchanging Lyle stories. Peter jumped to his feet.

"You were supposed to cheer him up, but not at my expense."

"Yes, Sir," Peter said. "Sorry, Sir."

"I knew I could count on you," Lyle added smiling. The young man relaxed. "Get Dean Lundgren on the phone. Tell him to fax me a photo of Henry Fonda."

"Yes, Sir," Peter said without a question.

Stanley's curiosity was fully aroused. "Henry Fonda?"

"That's the description of our mysterious sniper, a young Henry Fonda."

"You can't circulate a picture of Henry Fonda," Stanley said. "The media will grab hold of it, and you will be sued big time."

"I won't even look at it," Lyle said. "You'll look at it and describe the man in the chopper."

"I didn't see him," Stanley protested.

"You saw more than you think you did. You'll make subtle changes when you describe him to our police artist."

"You have a police artist?"

"Sure, we do. We're as complete as any big city department. Of course, each man doubles as something else."

"And who is your artist when he's not drawing?"

"Chief of Police."

"Do your parents know?"

Lyle laughed. "Yes, they know. It was my father's biggest fear that I'd opt to be an artist."

"I thought he was afraid of you becoming a cop."

"His second biggest fear."

The next half hour Stanley tried to describe the man in the faxed photo and Lyle sketched. Before he showed it to him for the first time, however, he made Stanley tear the faxed photo up and make his corrections to the sketch from memory. When Stanley was done, Lyle called in Peter French and asked him what he thought.

"Not a very good likeness of Henry Fonda," he said.

"Can you see a resemblance?"

"Some."

"Fax it to Chief Milani and Chief Peets. Xerox copies for our men. It's a rough description but it's better than none," Lyle said.

Peter took the sketch and hurried away.

Lyle looked at his watch.

"Two hours into Aleta's operation. Got any idea how we should spend the next three or four."

"What will your men do with the sketch?"

"Peter will organize those not assigned to the hospital to take the sketch around to the hotels in the area. We could get lucky."

"You don't think he's long gone."

"He hasn't fulfilled his contract. It's a matter of honor now."

"We don't need Neil to come home early, do we?"

"We need to see his reaction when we show him the sketch. It might promote a confession. We need that. Our case is too thin."

"Suppose he lawyers up?"

"I'm assuming the two best lawyers in the county— your dad and mine—will turn him down."

"And if their alibi scheme is to work," Lyle added, "he needs to show up with Rosalie."

"You think like a cop," Stanley observed.

Lyle smiled. "It helps."

"Are you worried about our fathers taking over my cases?" Stanley asked.

"Dad said your mother was going to walk them both through the procedures this afternoon," Lyle responded. "They plan to ask for a continuance if they feel they're losing."

"They haven't caught the orientation yet. It's not a win-lose situation. It's either a win-win or a lose-lose."

"Wish we could watch them," Lyle said. "My father has always been so unflappable."

"Both my parents are like that, although I will admit that Aleta has flapped them a bit."

"A bit?"

"A lot," Stanley grinned, then abruptly turned serious.

"God, I don't know what I'll do if I lose her."

"Well, she's alive now. Let's go with that," Lyle said. "Tell me how do you feel about being a father? I still remember seeing my first born for the first time. I'd been hoping for a son so I was ecstatic."

"A son?" Stanley said. "Camay's your oldest."

"She and Josh are children from Lauren's first marriage. It's a long story."

Stanley smiled. "I've got hours."

"You promise Harriet isn't standing here listening," Lyle joshed.

"Don't even go there!" Stanley ordered. "Besides it's PG rated."

"Well, not exactly," Lyle said. "It's rated R for violence."

"Those redheads don't come easy, do they?" Stanley grinned, his curiosity sitting on top of his worry. "So give. I want every detail."

Chapter 18

In the suite near the top of one of Cleveland's finest hotels, Harriet put down the receiver after talking with Stanley.

"He's lying," she stated flatly.

Ed was sprawled out in a chair opposite Harriet's, slowly sipping his coffee. The two had just finished a late supper in their suite and were discussing the day's events when Lyle West's call came.

"Stanley doesn't lie." Ed responded.

"He just did," Harriet said. "He said Aleta couldn't come to the phone because she was asleep."

"Why is that a lie?"

"He went on to say that Dr. Cook had given her a sedative. Aleta would never take a sedative no matter how upset she was."

"Maybe this attack was scarier."

"Scarier than having a bullet plow through your scalp? Scarier than having two whiz past your ear? Scarier than having the car you're riding in blow up?"

"Choppers can be scary," Ed observed. "And this one was in her face spitting bullets at her."

"I don't buy it," Harriet said. "They don't want me to come home. It must have been Aleta's idea. I caught both Lyle and Stanley off guard. Lyle let slip that Dr. Cook was in their room checking on Aleta when the attack occurred, and Stanley tried to cover the slip."

"You could call your Son," Ed said.

"That's the last person Aleta would tell. She doesn't want her mother out here."

"We could go back," Ed said.

"Aleta doesn't want me back or Stanley would have told me what was going on and asked me not to say anything."

"So, Aleta wants you here?" Ed asked.

"That's my guess."

"So what do you want to do?"

"We have a task," Harriet said. "Let's do it and stay out of everyone's way. We want the police to concentrate on protecting Aleta and Stanley and not have to worry about us."

"You gonna call your son?"

"No, we play this Aleta's way."

"What I wonder is why Neil didn't make his move today," Ed mused. "He was in the office."

"So was his bookkeeper. Edward recognized her car when we passed by," Harriet added.

"You were born here," Ed said. "A minor hack could find that out, especially if the bookkeeper didn't swallow my explanation."

"Considering how much work it took for Dean to come up with the records of Neil's two companies, I'd say Neil is a few steps up that ladder."

"What are you going to do?"

"Warn Robert and Paul."

"It's still two hours earlier on the west coast," Ed said.

"You're right. I need to tell Paul right away. There's no telling when Neil might choose to expose me."

"If he does," Ed cautioned.

"If he doesn't, Rosalie will," Harriet said with certainty. She dialed Paul's number.

"I'm going to bed," Ed said. "See you in the morning."

Harriet waved at him as she spoke to her son, "Paul we have a catastrophe in the making."

Ed shut the door.

Chapter 19

Back in Tri City Hospital's intensive care unit, Aleta Praetzel opened her eyes at the sound of Dr. Cook's voice.

"It's one," he said. "It went well."

"My head is fixed."

"Didn't touch your brain," Dr. Cook said, "so I'm sure it still has all its quirks intact; however, we removed the clot and repaired the broken blood vessels."

"So it's fixed?" Aleta reiterated.

"I think that's what I just said," Dr. Cook said.

"Not quite. You told me what you did and you told me what you didn't, but you didn't tell me it was all fixed."

"You're right," said a new voice. "It was worth the wait."

"What?" Aleta asked.

"I told him he should be here," Dr. Cook said. "I told him he would be in for a treat."

"I'm a treat?"

This time Dr. Taekman answered. "You are indeed. We fixed the scar, by the way."

"So what didn't you fix?"

"What isn't there yet," Dr. Taekman said.

"There's no inop... inable... er... no brain tumor you decided you couldn't take out?"

"No brain tumor," Dr. Taekman said. "Everything looked great. You have a great brain."

"It still has a limp," Aleta pointed out.

"Everything is fine Aleta," Dr. Cook said. "You are still pregnant."

Tears welled up in her eyes. "I didn't lose him?"

"Or her," Dr. Cook said.

"Stanley wants a boy," Aleta said. "I think he should get what he wants."

"You do know that you can't choose," Dr. Taekman said.

"One can always choose what one wants," Aleta said. "One doesn't always get it, however. Thank you for fixing my scar."

Dr. Taekman chuckled. "You're welcome, Ma'am," he said amused by her mental quickness. "Please call on me again if your head needs fixing. And take care of that brain. It's a gem."

"A girl likes to have other things about her be appreciated besides her good looks, which, in my case, unfortunately, have been misplaced."

"Stanley is going to be so pleased," Dr. Cook said.

"Did he survive?"

"He seemed okay when we spoke with him, but I'm afraid he's not ready for you yet."

Aleta frowned.

"Do I look that terrible?"

"No, but he's been through a terrible ordeal," Dr. Cook said with a twinkle in his eyes. "I'm not sure he's ready for a charged-up Aleta."

A groan came from a nearby bed. A nurse went over immediately. Words were exchanged.

"Why isn't the nurse understanding what the woman's saying?" Aleta asked.

Dr. Taekman began to answer but Dr. Cook stopped him.

"Can you understand the woman, Aleta?"

"Yes, of course. Can't you?"

Dr. Taekman again opened his mouth, but Dr. Cook was quicker. "No, Aleta, we can't. Tell me what she is saying."

"She has a sharp pain in her leg," Aleta said and then uttered a string of foreign sounding words. The woman looked over at Aleta and responded.

"Her left leg," Aleta said, "just below the knee."

Dr. Taekman and Dr. Cook rushed over, checked the woman's chest and leg, and told the nurse to call the woman's physician.

Dr. Cook turned to Aleta. "Tell her we are sending for her doctor."

Aleta told the woman that her doctor was being called. What followed was a long exchange which the doctors gathered was not about the leg.

Dr. Taekman asked, "Aleta speaks Romanian?"

Dr. Cook smiled. "Evidently today she does."

"I thought you said she could understand stroke victims."

"That was yesterday," Dr. Cook said. "I'm not sure exactly what is happening, but she very well might have saved this woman's life."

"Her baby is home alone," Aleta said. "She left him to go get some milk. She tried to tell the paramedics but they didn't understand her. Neither has anyone else until now. I have her husband's work number."

"Give it to me. I'll pass it on to Lyle," Dr. Cook said.

"There is a family nearby who can take the baby and watch him. She thought she'd be right back," Aleta continued, "but she doesn't know their phone number. Her husband will know."

"Give me the number."

"Promise me…," Aleta said. "You know what I want Lyle to do."

"I'll tell him," Dr. Cook said.

Aleta gave him the number.

As soon as the woman's doctor came, Dr. Cook went straight to Stanley's room. Dr. Taekman followed him. He listened as Dr. Cook told Lyle the whole story.

"So she's back," Stanley said happily.

"It would appear so," Wayne Cook said. "With a whole new gift. But, she is not to get involved. Do you understand? I want her to take a month off. One week here, three weeks at home. She isn't to stir out of the house. I know she has a new wheelchair, and I want her in it if she's not in her bed, but it's not to leave the house."

"You said she could walk with…," Stanley began. He was interrupted.

"I'm not ready to be reasonable just yet," Dr. Cook said distinctly perturbed, "Give me a week of no trauma and I might reconsider my restrictions."

"I gather she's still going to be without the use of her arms," Stanley said.

"You may need to hire a full time nurse," Wayne Cook said.

"We have Bertha and me and her dad.

"You are to do nothing!" Wayne Cook said. "You've both had serious operations. Bertha will have her hands full handling the house. Her dad will be a big help; however, I still want a nurse checking on her daily. I tell you what. I'll set up a visiting nurse. She can take care of bathing her and checking her vitals."

"It all sounds good to me," Stanley said. "But you're going to have to tell Aleta."

"She's your wife."

"She's your patient," Stanley countered. "And I'm your patient too."

"You win," Wayne said, his rancor gone.

"She wants to go to her sister's wedding the end of the month."

"No way!"

"That one's going to be a tough sell," Stanley said. "I'm glad you're the one who's going to do it."

Dr. Taekman was grinning when he and Dr. Cook left the room. "I gather Aleta isn't so easy to deal with. She seemed reasonable to me."

"That's it. She's a reasonable woman," Wayne Cook exclaimed. "She's a lawyer besides. She can out argue and out maneuver any man we know."

"What'll she do if you just order her to do as you say?"

"Right now, she'll obey it."

"Now?"

"Stanley told her she has to obey me without argument, so she will."

"She obeys him?" Dr. Taekman asked.

"Yes."

"Then why is he worried?"

"Because he knows her obedience is a gift and while he believes she will okay whenever he asks, he is using this gift sparingly. So far, he only uses it in life-saving situations."

"You have the most interesting patients," Dr. Taekman said.

"Some of them are."

An hour later, Aleta was wheeled back into the room she was going to share with Stanley for a week.

"I look terrible, don't I?" she said.

"Not to me," Stanley replied. "You're breathing."

"If I'd known how easy you were to please, I wouldn't have bothered to tell them to fix my scar."

"So they did?"

"You aren't upset, are you?"

"Hey, I like having one more head scar than you do."

"Were you alone most of the night?"

"Lyle stayed all night," Stanley reported. He picked up a sheet of paper from the night stand and held it up. "A sketch of our assailant."

"Henry Fonda?"

"That's the word we got from a knowledgeable source."

"You called George Sciretta."

"You know?"

"He's too rich to be a bookkeeper," Aleta said. "And he's too circumspect to work for a known company. Men always spit out that information right after their name."

"He sends his best wishes."

"I like him."

"I think he wants it to stay that way."

Lyle walked in.

"Don't you ever sleep?" Stanley snapped.

"Hey, there's no way you two could be having sex," Lyle retorted. "So what's to interrupt? Anyway, I have an idea... Oh, by the way, we're moving you back to your old room."

"Isn't that rather dangerous?"

"Aleta wouldn't last an hour in this room with the blinds closed. Martha had her crew install bullet proof glass. She doesn't want her grandson killed while he's taking your pulse."

"She must know about my operation, then," Aleta said.

"She doesn't tell," Lyle stated.

"The bullet proof glass isn't your idea," Stanley said . "You came in with an original thought."

"I have no idea how our killer will strike next. But we're guarding every possible access to this floor; however, there are always ways. The easiest is to tamper with the food."

"We have to eat," Stanley said knowing he was stating the obvious.

"Suppose we had all your food prepared by Bertha and brought here by one of your visitors and no one else? And they are to add no treats bought in any store."

"You're being pretty paranoid, aren't you?" Stanley asked.

"The man is sharp. I'm trying to anticipate him. Once I take care of the food situation, I'll turn my attention to the next weakest spot."

"What did you tell our parents?" Aleta asked.

"That I needed twenty-four hours to set up my surveillance."

"You shouldn't be risking your reputation on a personal desire of mine," Aleta commented.

"I don't mind," Lyle said. "Besides when I call on your families to help with the food thing, my reputation will improve some."

"Why no phones still?" Aleta said.

"In case someone wants to threaten you. If no one can speak with you directly, our assassin won't go that route."

"Tom Milani's wife Rachel is making lunch and dinner today," Lyle said. "Madge sent over rolls with me. I had the hospital staff move a refrigerator into your room. Milani will stock it when he comes at noon. Accept nothing from anyone but Milani or me no matter who brings it in. Dr. Cook said if you need shots or an IV, he'll give them personally."

"You've thought of just about everything," Stanley said.

"These ploys will be a deterrent for a day or two. But no defense is foolproof. Please be suspicious of everything."

"So now what?" Stanley asked.

"Milani is taking over at nine, and I'm going to bed and sleep for twenty hours."

"I guess we'll see you this evening then," Stanley said.

"Right!"

Before he left the hospital, however, Lyle supervised moving the pair into the room with the bulletproof glass. He then joined them for breakfast, feeding Aleta himself.

"You've made me feel safe, Lyle," Aleta said when they finished eating. "Thanks."

An hour away in a hotel in downtown Chicago, Slade Lacaze ordered breakfast and then took a shower. Buddy Horvat stirred but didn't waken despite the noise of the shower and the local news on the television.

Glimpses of the number of police cordoning off the hospital told Slade that access was going to be difficult. Everyone entering the hospital passed though a metal detector and purses were searched. That was a step not usually taken. Instinct told him to investigate a bit further before proceeding.

He opened his laptop; grateful that their pursuers were so slow, Buddy was able to set down long enough for him to retrieve his car. He looked up the Arborville Police Force and read Chief Lyle West's impressive resume.

As he was reading it, a sketch of the supposed terrorist flashed on the television screen.

His jaw dropped. When the hell did this Lyle West come up with a reasonable likeness of him? He would need a good disguise, one that didn't look like a disguise at all, in order to venture back into the tri-city area again.

He checked out the police chiefs in the other two cities. Tom Milani had the usual resume. He'd emigrated from Chicago. He had connections in the City.

Oakwood's new chief was on the internet. The mayor obviously wanted everyone to know she'd made a good choice. He was from New Jersey and probably had connections in the East. Slade believed he was unknown there; however, he wasn't happy that all three chiefs were less provincial than he had hoped.

On an off-chance Aleta Praetzel would be listed, he searched the internet and found his target had been much in the news since August. He flipped from one news article to the next until a knock on the door told him breakfast had arrived.

The smell of bacon brought Buddy to life and he joined Slade for breakfast.

"You ain't thinking of going back," Buddy asked after he'd consumed half his pancake stack.

"It's now a matter of honor," Slade said.

"Bullshit!" Buddy exclaimed. "You got a hard on to off this broad."

"She put my younger brother in jail."

"When did you get a brother?"

"Half-brother. Same mother. I was from her first marriage. He was from her third."

"You keep in touch?"

"Nope. Still, I owe him."

"So, how you gonna do it?"

"Been thinking about it. The chief of police is no dumb ass. I need information."

"How you gonna get it?"

"First we're going to plant ourselves in one of the top-floor rooms in a building that faces the hospital and do same surveillance."

"What makes you think she's still there?"

"The police. They've made the hospital a fortress. She's there alright."

"They won't put her in your rifle sights."

"I want to watch the staff on her floor. We need someone who really knows what's going on."

"Snatching someone is a lousy idea."

"I don't have lousy ideas."

"That's it?"

"So far."

Two states away, on the outskirts of Elyria, Ohio, Ed Ornstein drove into the Hoskinson Lumberyard, and he and Harriet got out and headed for the showroom where they saw Neil moving around.

He turned when the two entered. His face registered shock first, but that soon gave way to rage.

"What the hell are you doing here?"

"Your hit man missed," Harriet snapped.

"What… what hit man?" Neil retorted, recovering after a minute stumble.

"Never mind that," Harriet said coldly. "We're here to give you a heads up."

Neil scowled. He knew what she was going to say.

"I know what you've been doing, and my father's going to get an earful when I get home."

"You better hurry then," Ed interjected. "Your father's new will is ready for signing tomorrow. I've been asked to return to witness it."

Surprised and disconcerted, Neil could only utter angrily, "What kind of lies have you been feeding my father?"

"No lies," Harriet said, then aside to Ed, she hissed, "you weren't supposed to say anything."

"I think the man has a right to know," Ed grumbled.

"Just try to keep you mouth shut," Harriet shot back. "I'm in charge here."

Neil scowled. "You're wrong, I am. Oh, and that little lackey running around with you, I fired him this morning,"

"Edward was here?" Harriet asked.

"I told his mother I needed to see him first thing. She sent him right over. You can always count on those people to jump when a white man gives an order."

"Where is he now?" Harriet asked politely, ignoring the racial slur.

"Getting drunk probably," Neil replied.

Harriet guessed he was baiting her. She opted to be professional.

"What was your cause for firing him?"

Surprised at the query, Neil blurted out, "Disloyalty."

"How exactly was he disloyal?"

Neil glared at her. How dare she question him!

"None of your damned business!" he spit out. "He obeyed your orders without checking with me."

"How can that be considered disloyalty?" Harriet asked, feigning shock. "We both work for the same man."

"He interfered with my business."

"How did he do that?" she pressed.

"He persuaded the people scheduled for the elimination of mold to postpone the work. He took new samples. Said it was a recheck."

"How is that bad?" she asked evenly.

"There was nothing wrong with the test results," Neil claimed, his rage rising.

"They didn't make sense," Harriet said calmly. "That's why I ordered them."

Her statement brought him up short. It was an unexpected explanation. Intrigued, Neil asked her to explain. Deep inside there suddenly appeared a glimmer of hope that maybe she really didn't know what was going on.

"All the houses were old," Harriet stated flatly.

"So what?"

"Old houses are too drafty for mold to grow."

"Not if the lumber used for framing was infested with mold to begin with."

"You mean not properly kiln dried? Are you saying green wood was sold by your father?"

"No. No. I'm not saying that. But he didn't supply all the lumber."

"Actually it doesn't matter whether it was green wood or not," Harriet went on. "One day standing in the air as part of a house frame would have dried the wood naturally to below the 18 percent mark."

"Suppose it rained on the construction. It does that in Ohio."

"Still, the old houses weren't built as tight as today's home. The wood would have dried."

"Not if the roof leaked," Neil argued.

"That's true," Harriet conceded. "But you found mold in all the houses."

"All houses have mold," Neil said adamantly.

"That's also true," Harriet agreed. "All houses have mold, but not all mold is dangerous. As a matter of fact, of the hundreds of thousands of types of mold, there are only a couple strains that will make a man sick."

"Well, those are the ones we found," Neil claimed.

"I guess that's possible," Harriet said thoughtfully. "Certain types of mold could be indigenous to an area."

Neil nodded. Ed swallowed a smirk. Neil had no idea what Harriet had just said.

"Guess we may as well go to Des Moines today instead of waiting until Wednesday," Harriet told Ed. "Sorry to leave such a mess here."

At the first mention of Des Moines, Neil panicked. He would have trouble recovering here in Elyria, but because it wasn't a large town, the competition was limited. Des Moines was different.

"What about the samples Edward already took?" Ed asked. "We'll have to take them with us and ship them from the main office."

Neil's mind was racing. He needed to keep them out of Des Moines for a couple days. They had to go home before they dug deeper. If they went home, this investigation would stop. Ed's announcement that they only had a day prompted him to go with his hastily conceived plan. He hadn't planned to present it directly to them. He was setting it up for his father. The old man would buy it.

"I don't think you're done here," Neil said.

"Not done?" Harriet asked bewildered.

"If there was any sample tampering, it was done by Edward, not me."

"Why would he do that?" Harriet asked, her tone and manner still professional and impersonal.

"Why? Because he's a cheat and a liar," Neil spit out. "He had some scheme going on. That's the way those people are."

"So what is it you want me to do?" Harriet asked coolly. "You already fired him."

"Prove it was him, not me," Neil said.

"And how am I supposed to do that?" Harriet asked sharply.

"I took pictures yesterday. Had them developed. Got them right here. Made a copy for you."

He pulled out a brown envelope and handed to Harriet the envelope prepared for his father. She didn't open it.

"We will need to see everything personally," Harriet decided.

"Follow me," Neil said and charged past the door, bumping Ed aside.

Harriet sent a non-verbal query to Ed by raising one eyebrow. He nodded.

Inside the shed, Neil pointed to the stacks of moldy wood. "I grow molds here to teach my inspectors what to look for."

Harriet murmured her acknowledgement while Ed stepped over to get a closer look.

"And here's where Edward is supposed to put his samples for shipping."

Neither Ed nor Harriet was particularly surprised to see the bins again full of packaged samples. Neil began his spiel. The procedure he described accurately depicted what Ed and Harriet had envisioned. The only difference was that he placed the deception squared on young Edward Winslowe's shoulders.

"How come you only discovered this now?" Harriet asked.

"I don't come back here much. Ask anyone," Neil said. "Edward is in charge of the shipping."

"There seem to be a number of samples here ready to be shipped," Ed said bending over the neat rows of samples.

"That's why I caught him," Neil boasted. "I have the results from this group in the office."

"But how could that be?" Harriet asked, seemingly puzzled.

"That's the point!" Neil said enthusiastically. The two were buying it. He went on. "If the original samples are here, then the results in my office must be from fake samples."

Picking up one of the group of samples, he led the way back to the office and selected an envelope containing lab results.

Ed read the name on the top aloud. It matched the name on the sample Neil handed him.

"I must admit, I'm pretty disappointed," Harriet said regretfully. "I read him all wrong."

"What'd the little shit say when you showed him this?" Ed interjected.

"But, I didn't. I'm not here most of the week," Neil replied. "I didn't want him destroying anything before I figured out what to do."

"So, he thinks you fired him for being disloyal?"

"Yeah," Neil replied.

"Then maybe we can use him," Harriet suggested. "I can tell him I persuaded you to give him a second chance."

"What for?" Neil asked suspiciously.

"The rechecks he promised," Harriet said non-plussed. "We don't want to raise any red flags by leaving our customers hanging."

Neil's suspicions rose to the fore at the mention of the rechecks. "And where will the results go?"

"Why, here," Harriet said. "It'll be a little extra work for you, but…"

Neil burst in. "Yes! Good idea!"

"I guess we won't be going to Des Moines after all," Ed concluded. "Tell me we are gonna break off early."

"Early afternoon," Harriet predicted. "We need to a get these findings to Mr. Hoskinson today."

"Yes, yes, please do," Neil said, ecstatic at the turnaround.

"Do you and your wife want to fly back with us?" Harriet asked.

"No!" Neil shot back sharply, then softened his tone. "I didn't mean to be short. Rosalie's shopping and I can't reach her. Thanks anyway."

Harriet and Ed left abruptly. When they reached their car, Harriet pulled out her cell and told Edward she was picking him up in a few minutes. Then she turned to Ed and asked if he got it all on tape.

"Yeah, but he didn't confess nothing," Ed reminded her.

"He doesn't think he confessed; but actually he did," Harriet said.

"His father won't think so."

"He will when you show him both sets of photos," Harriet explained. "You did get some from the same spots as before, didn't you?"

"That and more."

"And the tape?"

"We almost ran out. He's a long-winded sonofabitch."

"You didn't put in a fresh tape?" Harriet scolded.

"Waste not, want not."

"Ed, we can afford to pay for tapes."

"We gonna play the tape for Edward?"

"And have him blow his top?" Harriet said. "I'm going to warn him to stay clear of Neil Hoskinson."

When Chief Milani arrived at the Tri City Hospital in Arborville around eleven with an insulated bag and a shopping bag, Slade Lacaze was already on the roof of a three story building several blocks away peering through his binoculars.

He saw him exit the elevator and pause to talk with a nurse. He zoomed in on her. She disappeared from view with him and stayed gone for a considerable period.

She became his target.

In the room, Tom took two large thermos bottles out of the shopping bag. One was coffee, the other homemade vegetable soup. Also in the bag were fresh pita sandwiches. Both Stanley and Aleta wondered what the insulated bag held.

"Dessert," was all the hint Tom would give. He went on. "Tonight you get lasagna and Lyle and Wayne are joining you."

"The 'no visitor' rule doesn't apply to them?" Aleta asked impishly as the nurse held out the spoon loaded with vegetables.

"Wayne's your doctor," Tom said surprised.

"And Lyle?"

Tom laughed. "He loves Rachel's lasagna."

"I'm going to leave this hospital a fat pregnant wife because I love it too," Aleta quipped.

"What's the status of the investigation?" Stanley asked.

"No shop talk," Aleta said. "I need to eat in peace. Besides Valerie doesn't want to know the gory details."

Stanley recognized that Aleta didn't want them to talk around the nurse. He switched the subject instantly.

"I understand you beat Lyle West out for your job."

Milani fell right into the story. "It was a close one. He had the smarts. I had the experience. It was the only time in my life I was glad about those five years on the Chicago force."

The surprise dessert was homemade chocolate pudding. "Rachel was worried about your stomach so soon after your operation."

"She knows about me?" Aleta queried.

"You? No!" Tom laughed. "She's still worried about Stanley. If she'd known about you, you'd have gotten chicken soup and Jell-O."

"I hate Jell-O," Aleta said as she finished the pudding.

Nurse Valerie Kilborne picked up the tray and left.

"When are you going to tell your parents?" Tom asked.

"Dad will find out when he comes tomorrow. Grams needs time to finish her task in Ohio."

"Will she call when she's done?" Milani asked.

"I'll know," Aleta said. "I just know she needs to be there."

"That baby you rescued earlier is with his aunt and doing just fine."

"Lyle told you?"

"The woman lives in my district," Tom said.

Aleta began to respond when she stopped mid-syllable.

"What is it?" Tom asked.

"When you come tonight," Aleta said, "bring two bullet proof vests, will you?"

"I can get them here in five minutes," Tom said.

Stanley sat up in bed. "Are we in danger?"

"Not now. But it's important that no one know about us wearing them," she said. "Absolutely no one. This is very important,"

"I don't feel comfortable moving your arms," Tom said.

"That's why you're bringing them tonight when Dr. Cook is here to put mine on. Bring them with the lasagna. No one will think twice about you carrying in two shopping bags."

"If you'd just tell me what you... um... see, I could prepare for it properly," Tom urged.

"That's just it. I don't see anything. Not really just see the bullets hitting Stanley's chest. I'm assuming I'm next. I'm never able to see myself being killed. Grams always sees me being killed and I see her being killed. That's the way it works, but she's not here now. And her mind is occupied saving someone else."

"I agree you're probably the real target," Tom said. "I'd like to tell Lyle."

"Tell him tonight when he comes."

"He might want to double the guard."

"He can do it after supper," Aleta said calmly.

"You've been cutting things pretty close lately," Tom said.

"You mean the explosion in the car?"

"That and the bullet through the window."

"I didn't get a vision or a warning those times. I saw the glint of the rifle which is why I pushed Stanley so hard. As for the explosion, that came when I was trying to figure out the strange phone call and then Grams called, and it just hit me and I acted fast. No vision."

"So this is different?"

"This involves Stanley as well."

"Didn't both of the other times involve other people?"

"You're right, but I can't explain it," Aleta said. "However, if I'm wrong, wearing vests is still a good idea."

"I'm game," Stanley said. "And Tom, there really isn't anywhere we can go. Aleta needs to be in a hospital right now."

"I'm still going to alert my men," Milani said. "I'd like to bug this room."

"Oh, please don't," Aleta begged. "Stanley and I need our privacy."

"It wouldn't help much," Stanley said. "If the assassin makes it into the room, we'll be dead before you could react."

"I need to talk with Lyle," Tom said. "I'll do everything else you ask but that."

"He's been up all night with me," Stanley said. "Let him sleep. He'll be able to think better if he's not too tired."

"Well…," Tom thought aloud. "Maybe that's best. Can I talk to Peets?"

"Yes," Aleta said with assurance. "Somehow he's going to be involved."

From several blocks away, Buddy Horvat said irritably, "Are we gonna be up here all day?"

"We're going to move when she goes home."

"Shouldn't we maybe just follow the first nurse out the door?"

"We might get one that doesn't know anything," Slade said. "That's why we're staying here so we don't miss her."

"Shit!"

Chapter 20

Nurse Valerie Kilborne left Tri City Hospital by her own special exit in order to avoid the police out front. When the tunnel to the new wing was first under construction, she'd investigated it out of curiosity. It was finished at the same time the steel girders went up as the main supports for the three new floors of the physical therapy wing. As she took the elevator to the basement, she glanced at her watch. She was late. Her cat would be upset. How did one explain to a cat that hospital routine was disrupted by the police?

She wound through the maze of halls leading past the labs and the radiation unit to the double doors at the end of one of the halls. Eventually they would provide direct access from the hospital to the new wing through the tunnel.

She pushed through the doors ignoring the "do not enter" sign and traversed the hall lit twenty-four hours as a general safety precaution. No one was to use the tunnel, but people did anyway, just as she was doing now, surreptitiously.

Slade saw her head for the elevator. He focused on the front door and told Buddy to get ready.

He calculated the time and watched as people exited. She didn't exit when she should have.

How could I have missed her? He took his eyes away from his binoculars and stared at the hospital and the cordon of police surrounding it. On the far side, in the construction area, abandoned an hour before by the crews working the site, he saw a lone figure. He focused his binoculars on the person and found his target.

She has a special way in, he realized. Talk about luck. He and Buddy were in their car in minutes. The woman was heading away from the hospital, down a rarely traveled exit road. As she was on foot, Buddy caught up to her just as she began crossing an empty intersection.

Buddy eased the car into the intersection and stopped so she could cross in front. Slade unlatched his door and Buddy moved the car in behind her. Slade leaped out, grabbed her from behind, put a knife to her throat and growled.

"One yelp and you're dead."

Valerie was too stunned to react. She was an older, plump woman who had no money. She was neither sexy nor rich. She had thought she was safe.

She dropped her purse, but the man snatched it up as he backed her into the car. A second man ripped off her glasses and slapped duct tape across her eyes. The first man pulled her hands behind her and taped them as well. The driver stuck tape across her mouth. She was set upright on the far side and her ankles were bound together. Immediately afterward, the door was shut and the car took off.

The knife pricked the skin below her ear.

"You feel that?" the man growled.

She nodded.

"I'm going to remove your tape so you can answer my questions. Do you understand?"

Again she nodded, trembling.

"Some things I already know the answer, some I don't. If you lie, I will cut off a finger."

Behind her back, Valerie clenched her hands into fists.

She shook her head violently.

"I gather you want to keep your fingers," he said.

Her nod was just as vigorous. "You don't want to know what I will do to you if you scream."

She shook her head. She could guess.

"Okay, first question. What floor is Aleta Praetzel on?" The tape was ripped from Valerie's lips. The knife poked at her neck. She leaned away.

"Fourth," she said.

"What room?"

"Same as before. Second from the north facing east." The knife dug a little hole. Blood began to flow. "Honest. They put in a bullet proof window and then put them back."

"Them?"

"Her husband."

"Was he the person in the other bed before?"

"Yes. He had brain surgery Saturday night. She had brain surgery last night," Valerie said, unable to stop her rambling. "Or rather very early this morning. She just came down from ICU this morning and then they moved them back into the room that was hit."

The knife moved away.

"Tell me about the police."

"There are two at the door to the room and two at each stairway and two more at the main elevator, one at the service elevator. They are all over the hospital and around the outside."

"So many?"

"All three cities are involved," Valerie said.

"Which police force is on now?"

"Willow Glen."

"Tonight?"

"Arborville."

"Tomorrow?"

"A mix because Oakwood doesn't have as big a force, and they had a second car bombing there yesterday, and they're concentrating on catching that person."

"How do they know there are two people involved?"

"Because one is a pro and one is an amateur," Valerie said.

"They're pretty sharp these police, aren't they?"

"They are," she replied with a touch of pride.

"I assume the guards are all wearing vests, right?"

"Yes."

"They've taken other precautions, haven't they?"

"You mean, like no floral deliveries to the fourth floor?"

"Go on."

"Visitors can't bring anything."

"Does Aleta have visitors?"

"Not yet."

The knife dug another hole. Valerie yelped and clenched her fists so tight the nails dug into her palms.

"It's true. I think her parents will be allowed to see her tomorrow."

"They weren't there when she was operated on?"

"They weren't told. We were told to hand all phone calls inquiring about either of them to the police."

"What about food?"

"The Praetzels don't eat hospital food. Today it was brought in by Chief Milani. I don't know where it came from. The soup was in a thermos. I think it was homemade."

"What about shots or medications?"

"Only Dr. Cook himself gives them those. No one else."

"IVs?"

"None."

"Isn't that unusual?"

"Yes, but they seem to be doing well. Both are confined to bed for at least another twenty-four hours," Valerie finished, hating herself for giving him so much information.

She was so afraid to die, she had rattled on and on defensively.

The police would protect the Praetzels, she told herself to lessen the guilt. There was no one around to protect her. In fact, except for her cat, no one would even know she was in trouble until tomorrow morning when her shift started.

"You have a special way in, don't you?" Slade asked. It was his last query.

"I go through the tunnel from the new wing under construction and then take the service elevator. The guard on the fourth floor doesn't search me."

"You will take us there tonight, won't you?"

"Yes," Valerie said. Anything to stay alive.

Chapter 21

At five o'clock, Harriet rang the doorbell of the house of her niece Euydice Johnson who smiled with pleasure when she saw who it was. "Karolyn said you were in town."

"Edward was to meet us here at five. Is he often late?"

"Edward? Never!"

"We'll be back," Harriet said spinning on her heels and heading back to the car. Ed had the key in the ignition by the time she closed the door.

"Do you know where we're going?" she asked.

"To the lumberyard."

"Neil must've asked him to come," Harriet said.

"They close at five," Ed said.

At the moment, young Edward Winslowe parked on the street and walked through the open gate and across the deserted yard toward the office. It was unusual for the whole crew to have cleared out by five.

He was glad they were gone. He didn't want anyone to accidentally overhear what Mr. Hoskinson and he were about to discuss.

Harriet had warned him more than once during the day to stay clear of Neil Hoskinson.

"He's got a scheme going," she warned but would say no more except to repeat her warning that Edward should stay away from him no matter what.

But Hoskinson's call had changed his mind. "I want to talk to you," he'd said when he'd called. "It's about the way I fired you and about your aunt. And yes, I know she's your real aunt. All you have to do is agree not to sue me or testify against me and your aunt's secret stays a secret."

Edward was wary, but Neil had been persuasive. He wanted a gentlemen's agreement between the two of them.

Considering the foul language that had been thrown at him that morning, Edward found being treated with a bit of respect, a pleasant capitulation. He knew he had a wrongful dismissal case and hoped Hoskinson wanted to buy his way out of it.

He wasn't going to sue because Aunt Harriet was involved and he was still regretting the slip he made when the bookkeeper was within earshot. He guessed the bookkeeper told Hoskinson, so the mess was his to clean up.

As he approached the showroom, Neil came out of the office.

"I have a plane to catch," Neil said. "So come with me. We'll talk in the shed."

Edward stopped where he was. "What did you want to talk about?"

"For one thing I wanted to offer you a good severance package," Neil said. "I know we can't work together anymore. Too many things were said."

"Mrs. Locke said something about a second chance."

"I told her that to get her off my back," Neil said scornfully.

"That doesn't surprise me."

"But she did make a point," Neil confessed. "I fired you without cause. And you could sue."

Edward was silent. So he was right about the reason for the meeting.

"And if I agree not to sue, you'll do what?" Edward said.

"Agree not to tell anyone your aunt is a Negro."

"She's not!" Edward protested vociferously.

"You want to see my proof?" Neil asked. "It's in the shed."

"The shed?"

"Men are in and out of my office all day. For my deal to be worth anything, I've kept what I discovered a secret."

"What about Miss Zeller?" Edward asked.

"I told her to believe Mr. Ornstein," Neil responded convincingly.

Neil unlocked the shed door and walked inside. Edward followed him.

"Stinks of gasoline in here," Edward commented as Neil walked to the far corner of the shed and turned on the light over a small safe. He turned the dial several times and opened the safe.

"You want to see the proof or not," Neil asked drawing out two envelopes, a large brown one and a small white one.

Edward walked toward Neil who handed him both envelopes. "The white one contains your severance package. The other is my proof. Look in both envelopes. If you agree not to sue me, then both are yours. Otherwise they go back in the safe."

Edward opened the white envelope and found six hundred dollar bills inside. Three weeks pay.

Hoskinson wasn't being very generous, Edward thought.

But it was reasonable—at least from his perspective. He kept his face averted as he smiled with satisfaction. How it must have galled Hoskinson to part with this money.

He stuffed the white envelope in his pocket, not noticing that Hoskinson was slowly backing away.

He tore open the seal on the brown envelope and withdrew a sheaf of papers. He stared in dismay at the copies of old news clippings that featured among other items a photo of his aunt Harriet winning a local spelling bee as a child and mentioning her parents by name. There was a record of her birth in the Births, Marriages and Deaths column citing county records for that week. There was her father's obituary where she was listed as a survivor.

By the time he'd scanned all the items, Neil Hoskinson was not only at the door but half-way out.

"Okay," Edward said, turning, "You've got a... what's going on?"

"I'm sealing our deal permanently," Neil said.

Shocked, Edward stood motionless while Neil's hand held out his lighter, flicked it on and tossed it on same rags in the center of the room. The flames shot up instantly.

Neil slammed the door shut and turned the key. Edward shot across the room as the fire followed the rivulets of gasoline to every corner with such speed. Edward, who'd stayed away from the central conflagration, managed to make it to the door.

He pounded on it with both fists as smoke filled the room. Coughing and eyes watering, he remembered his mother's admonition to stay away and sank to his knees. He couldn't give up pounding.

He couldn't die this way. He took the brown envelope with his aunt's history and tossed it into the fire as he sank to the floor. He pressed his face against the crack at the bottom of the door. He could almost breathe.

He heard a car start up and drive away.

He took out his pen and scrawled across the white envelope. "Hoskinson killed me."

He pushed the envelope under the door. Hoskinson was going to catch a plane. Someone else would find the envelope. He'd have the last word.

Overcome by smoke, he slipped into unconsciousness.

Neil Hoskinson was driving away when Ed turned onto the street leading to the lumberyard. They watched him squeal around a corner and disappear from sight.

"There's Edward's car," Harriet observed. "But where's Edward?"

She scanned the lumberyard. "There's smoke coming from the shed."

"Hang on!" Ed said as he jammed his foot on the gas pedal. The car leaped forward and hit the wire gate bursting the padlocks holding it closed. Ed didn't brake until they were only a few feet from the shed. The tires screeched as the brakes were applied with force. Harriet clutched her purse, and the cell phone she had just taken out as her body slammed hard against the seat belt.

While Ed threw open his door and leaped out, Harriet flipped open her cell phone and punched in 911.

"Fire," she shouted, as she unfastened her seat belt, "Hoskinson Lumberyard."

Ed and she split as soon as they left the car. Harriet ran toward the shed door while Ed broke the glass on the emergency box, pulled the alarm and grabbed the axe.

Harriet reached for the door knob. Ed shouted a warning. "You'll burn your hand. We don't know if he's in there."

Harriet spotted the envelope with a scrawl on it. Her eyes read the scrawl as her hand reached for the knob.

"He's in there," she shouted and put her hand around the knob to turn it. The heat seared the flesh on her palm and fingers. She screeched and jerked her hand away.

As Ed approached with the axe, Harriet swooped up the envelope and stuffed it in her coat pocket.

"Out of the way!" Ed shouted.

Harriet drew back as Ed brought down the axe. He hit the door panel and black smoke poured out. He managed one more swing before the smoke filled his lungs and he doubled over coughing. His second swing hit the lock and broke it.

"Help me pull!" Harriet shouted putting her good hand on the sides of the hole in the broken wooden door and tugging. Ed, his eyes watering, reached out and grabbed hold of the door and together they swung it toward them.

Through the smoke they saw Edward's prone body jammed against the door frame and simultaneously grabbed his coat and pulled. He slid out onto the tiny porch. Each took an arm and carried him down the two steps and dragged him away from the blazing shed.

The fire siren told them help was near. Still neither dared lose a second.

They turned him over. Harriet bent over and began to suck the smoke out of his lungs. Ed, coughing heavily, eyes still watering so badly he could hardly see managed to put his hands on Edward's chest and start pumping.

The driver of the fire engine seeing that the gate was smashed drove right through. Two men jumped off and ran to the two working on the young man and took over.

An oxygen mask was slapped on Ed's face and another on Harriet's. She lifted up her hand and the man saw the burned flesh.

Thus it came as no surprise to her that she and Ed were bundled into the ambulance with Edward and sped off to the hospital immediately. Both of them had inhaled too much smoke and while they were still conscious, both were in serious condition.

Chapter 22

Back in Illinois, at the Tri City Hospital in her room on the fourth floor, Aleta awoke from a long nap.

"It's almost suppertime," Stanley said when he saw her eyelids open.

"Call the nurse for me, will you?" Aleta asked.

Stanley pressed his call button. In her sleep Aleta had knocked her control out of her reach again. Dr. Cook had suggested a baby monitor so all she would have to do is call, but she rejected the idea vehemently.

Shortly afterward, Aleta, her bed raised to a near sitting position, was ready to eat.

"I'm sorry," Stanley said. "I had no idea how hard those kidnappers were throwing you down."

"I'll exchange my bump, operation and all, for all you did to save me from the fate they had planned," Aleta responded. "But I'm sorry I threw you down so hard in our bedroom."

"Did you have a choice?"

"I could have stepped in front of you."

Stanley exploded instantly. "What utter nonsense! Did they take out your reason or your memory? If you'd stepped in front of me, you'd be dead. Aleta, do I have to give you orders about everything in life?"

"No," she said, "but I didn't even think about that option. All I could think about was saving myself."

"You didn't barrel into me to save yourself. You did it to save me," Stanley yelled.

Aleta cringed. She couldn't remember him yelling at her before.

"Remember this order if you forget all others," he continued. "You save you first, the baby second and me third. Is that clear?"

"Whoa!" Dr. Cook said entering the room. "Why are you yelling at my patient?"

Stanley, however, wouldn't be deterred. "Tell me you'll remember that order Aleta."

Dr. Cook walked across the room and reached beneath the sling and took her pulse.

"You're scaring her," he announced.

"I intend to!" Stanley declared. "Aleta, say yes."

"I can't."

"What are you asking her to do?" Dr. Cook asked.

"To put herself first, the baby second and me third."

"That's not possible!"

"Of course it's possible."

"When you become a parent, you'll realize that you are asking the impossible from a mother. The child always comes first," Dr. Cook said. "It's built into the DNA."

The doctor's argument deflated the anger that had ballooned up inside Stanley.

"I will always remember the way you want it," Aleta compromised.

Stanley backed off. "That's good enough for me."

"Whatever started all this?" Dr. Cook asked.

"She's feeling guilty for not taking the bullet," Stanley said.

Dr. Cook smiled. "When women are pregnant, they sometimes let their emotions sit on their reason. Redheads are worse than most because their reason isn't normal to begin with."

Aleta eyed Dr. Cook. "Does Yancey know you say things like this?"

"She should. I've told her often enough."

"You have not!" Aleta declared.

"Well, maybe not directly," Wayne Cook conceded. "I do love her, you know."

Aleta softened her stance. "I know. And Stanley loves me. And he's not quite recovered from my operation yet."

"Now that's sound reasoning," Dr. Cook said.

Tom Milani entered with Lyle West on his heels carrying the second shopping bag. Lyle told the guards no one was to enter and he closed the door.

The vests were put on the two patients before Rachel's lasagna was brought out. Dr. Cook took over the task of feeding Aleta while the two chief's discussed how a person could possibly get into the hospital, let alone up to the fourth floor.

"We have so many checkpoints," Lyle said. "You're sure it's tonight?"

Aleta nodded.

"Did you see anything else besides the bullets hitting Stanley's chest?"

"His eyes were cold," Aleta said.

Both chief's sat up. "You saw his face?"

"Vaguely," Aleta admitted. "But the sketch is pretty dose to what I saw. It was so quick. Just a glimpse."

"He was bare-faced?" Lyle asked.

"Bare-faced?" Aleta reiterated. "You mean without a gas mark? He wasn't wearing one of those."

"Hell!" Tom said. "That takes out that theory."

"What theory?"

"That he used gas to take out the guards," Lyle said. "The men will be relieved not to have to wear gas masks. We were so sure that's how he gained entry we even brought some for you."

Aleta's face lit up. She had to swallow her food first, but the men noticed her agitation and paused.

"Yes!" Aleta declared. "We'll wear them."

"But you said…," Tom started.

Aleta rushed on to explain.

"Not because of gas, but because then our killer will have to shoot us in the chest," Aleta said. "Our heads won't be such good targets."

"I'm game," Stanley said. "I can handle one night I think… I hope… I will do it."

"You're sure it's late at night?" Lyle asked.

"It was quiet. The night light was on," Aleta said. "That's why I couldn't see his face."

"Sleeping pills are dispensed at nine," Dr. Cook said. "Lights are turned out shortly afterward."

"I'll be back at nine," Lyle said. "And you are getting a monitor in your room tonight. You won't be able to talk with those masks on anyway."

"Yes!" Stanley said, emphatically. "We will both do what you ask, won't we, Aleta?"

"Do you still have the feeling of catastrophe?" Lyle asked Aleta.

She nodded sadly.

"Well, I'm going to be on the roof," Lyle said. "Tom is going to cover the first floor. Peets will be busy arresting Neil and Rosalie Hoskinson whose flight arrives at eleven.

"But I thought you said it was Rosalie's sister that was with Neil," Aleta queried.

"On the plane, yes," Lyle said. "He'll be waiting for them at their home."

"Sounds like you've got everything covered," Dr. Cook said. "I'm ready for dessert. It's going to be a long night."

"You're staying?" Aleta asked, surprised.

"The killer might shoot a hole in one of you. At least that would be a certainty if I went home," Wayne said with the glimmer of a twinkle in his eye. "Sleeping here practically guarantees your safety."

"Beatrice baked a chocolate cake," Tom said.

"I had two helpings of lasagna!" Lyle wailed. "You didn't warn me."

"That's what you deserve for being a pig and staying skinny to boot," Tom retorted.

"I'll get my piece when I come back at nine," Lyle said, happy with his solution.

When they left, Aleta spoke so softly that Stanley asked her to repeat herself.

"Blood is going to be spilled tonight."

"Someone we know?"

"Yes."

"Did you see who it was?"

"I didn't see anything. I just know."

Chapter 23

Valerie was shoved on the floor of the back seat and told any movement or noise from her would have terrible consequences. Valerie needed to be told no more than that to remain petrified.

A blanket was thrown over her and the car made a series of stops, some quite long. The slim hope she clung to was that the leader wanted to use her later which meant they planned to keep her alive until then. Even when she heard voices nearby, she stayed still and quiet.

Night fell and the men left her for a couple of hours. She dared not move because she had no idea when they would return.

They drove a short distance and parked again. The blanket was lifted and the tape torn from her mouth. "We need more information," the voice said.

She nodded and waited.

"Where are the police located on the fourth floor?"

"At both elevators, at the staircase, in front of the room."

"When we come up in the service elevator, where will they be?"

"One at the elevator door, two to the left by the staircase, two to the right one room down, two in the middle of the hall by the other elevator."

"How many on the third floor?"

"None."

"Why not?"

"They have them at all the entrances on the first floor. They figure no one will get past those guards."

"How about the roof?"

"Same are on the fifth floor. I don't know if any are on the roof. Police helicopters are patrolling the air above the hospital."

"And the basement?"

"They have some down there but I don't know how many."

"Do you pass any when you come and go?"

"No."

"Where is the nurses' station?"

"Across from the main elevator."

A new piece of tape was torn off the roll and slapped across her mouth.

"Will you move while we are gone?" he asked.

Valerie shook her head. If she obeyed, she would wind up back at the hospital—there were a lot of cops at the hospital. All she had to do was obey for a few more hours.

The blanket was thrown over her head once more. And Valerie didn't move at all. She knew she was being watched. Only a couple more hours and this nightmare would be over.

This time the men were gone for hours. Every sound outside the car made her tense waiting for the door to open.

She relaxed when the door didn't open, but tensed immediately at the next sound. Never had she been so frightened. She thought nothing could be worse than having the man with the knife breathing down her neck, but as she waited in the dark, her future unknown, her fear increased three times over.

Suppose they decided they didn't need her. She'd told them everything. How hard would it be to find and negotiate the tunnel without her?

The more time that passed, the more certain she became that they had decided they could do without her.

By the time the car door was finally opened, she would have screamed had the tape not reminded her not to utter a sound. She froze in place, hoping her compliance would earn her the right to live.

The car moved forward and Valerie's hope rose. They were going to stick with their original plan.

In the room on the fourth floor Stanley and Aleta lay in their beds, gas masks on their faces, unable to sleep. Each dozed now and then, but the uncomfortableness of the armor and the pervading sense of doom kept both awake. They stared out the window at the grayness of clouds floating between the earth and the stars. The weather forecaster had predicted snow flurries, and Aleta wished that would happen.

A part of her hoped she was wrong; another part of her wanted to be right. But if she was right, someone was going to die. She didn't want that to happen.

I still have the language skills, she inquired. I figured only one special ability at a time. Am I wrong?

Trusting is not something I do easily, God. Well, if I made a mistake about tonight, I'm certainly paying a price for it. How can anyone stand to wear a mask? These are horrible, smelly things.

And my head hurts. It doesn't want to wear this heavy thing. Dr. Cook told Lyle that it might be uncomfortable, but it would do minimal damage.

Dr. Cook has no idea what uncomfortable is multiplied by long hours of enduring it, Aleta mused with a touch of bitterness.

She dismissed the fact that she had embraced the idea with eagerness when it was first bought up. It didn't matter that Lyle had discussed it as an idea they were discarding. They could have come up with something else.

The mask annoyed Aleta and she hated being annoyed. It was not a state she tolerated for long.

The night dragged on. The waiting wore on her. Were she able to be heard, she would have scolded someone. That she was being unreasonable occurred to her. That she had a choice was dismissed by her.

Stanley was not going to out-endure her. She could take it if he could. And he had two hands free so he could take his mask off easily. Still he sat and breathed in the rubbery smelling air and waited in the silence.

Lyle had said he would be on the roof, Aleta remembered. It was a cold night. That would be a lonely vigil. She wondered briefly why he picked that duty for himself.

That was when Aleta decided she would rather be where she was.

Buddy Horvat drove down the street in front of the new hospital wing slowly with his lights off. When the car stopped, the blanket covering Valerie was tossed on the seat and she felt a knife cut the tape binding her ankles.

Her hands remained bound and the tape across her eyes and mouth stayed in place. She stood rigid in the cold November air, grateful that her ordeal was almost over.

"You know what to do?" Slade said to Buddy.

"Don't worry about that none," came the reply.

"Remember, they have to bounce."

Valerie had no idea what the men were talking about. Their plans had been finalized before they returned to the car.

Did they think she would try to stop them, she wondered.

She felt an arm grab her elbow and move her forward. Her legs were stiff from being stationary for so many hours. She stumbled a few times but a strong, powerful hand held her upright.

Her senses told her she was on the sidewalk leading to the new wing. Just before the front door the tape was ripped from her eyes. She blinked and tried to focus. She didn't see well without her glasses.

"Don't look at us," he ordered restoring her glasses to her face.

Obediently, she faced forward and led the way to the stairway that led to the basement level and the entrance to the tunnel.

Lyle West, who had been patrolling the roof, missed the movement along the sidewalk leading to the new wing. Had he been on that side of the building he might have seen the men as they hurried toward the shell of the half finished building. By the time he was again at that side, the three were at the tunnel entrance and covered from view by the first floor of the new wing.

At the tunnel entrance the men paused and discussed whether they should remove the tape from Valerie's mouth. The argument was brief, but the leader won out. She wasn't to be trusted.

The tape around her hands was unwound. Her coat was removed so her nurse's uniform was highly visible. The tape was rewound around her wrists and the group moved into the tunnel.

It wasn't until they removed their coats as well that she realized they were dressed in green hospital scrubs. Each had a surgical mask over his face.

Valerie was told to lead the way to the elevator and to make no noise. She did so without hesitation. She was almost free. It was almost over.

Once inside the elevator, the leader whispered, his voice nasally as if his nose were plugged, "When I remove the tape, you will say only the words I tell you. Do you understand?"

Valerie nodded vigorously. Whatever he said, she was prepared to do.

"The words are 'help me,'" the leader said.

She nodded. She could say those words. Those were easy words. Her heart was already screaming them. They would burst from her mouth automatically.

The third and fourth floor buttons were punched. The elevator stopped at the third floor and she saw the men slip something under their masks. "Five minutes," said the leader. The other man gave a thumbs up as he rushed into the hall with an open cardboard box tucked under his arm.

The leader held the service elevator door open as his partner rushed toward the other elevator. He bounced two hollow balls with holes, and the gas released by the trigger mechanism rendered those at the nurses' station unconscious before they could sound an alarm.

The two elevator doors closed simultaneously and both elevators moved to the fourth floor.

As the elevator door closed, Slade took out his knife, and Valerie stood still waiting for him to cut her hands free. What happened next shocked her.

The knife was thrust into her upper arm at the precise location to sever the artery.

She screamed into the tape as the blood spurted from the severed vessel.

The tape was yanked from her mouth as the elevator doors opened and Valerie was thrust into the hall screaming, "Help me!"

The gushing blood drew the attention of the guards long enough for Slade to bounce balls in both directions.

All succumbed to the gas within seconds of the balls first bounce and the escape of the gas.

Valerie fell with them. She lay in the hall amid guards whose arms had reached out to help her, her hands still taped behind her back, her blood flowing from the wound, and with it, her life began to ebb away.

Buddy, having bounced the remainder of his balls upon exiting the main elevator, rushed down toward Slade and held the service elevator door open for their escape.

Slade stepped past Valerie without so much as a glance.

He moved to the room where Aleta and Stanley lay, one hand holding a ball, the other a gun. His scrubs were splattered with Valerie's blood.

On the hospital roof, Lyle West stared down the telescopic sight of his rifle at the car parked on the street opposite the construction site, trying to remember if it had been there all evening or not.

I'm too tired, he thought. I can't think straight.

The car wouldn't start so one of the workers hitched a ride home and left it, he deduced. There could be a number of reasons why he hadn't returned to fetch it, but Lyle couldn't think of one.

It shouldn't be there, he thought. And it wasn't there before or I would have had someone check it out.

He removed his eye from the rifle sight and looked at the construction site. They had poured over the blueprints of the hospital and investigated every possible exit, but in the back of his mind he remembered seeing the doors to the proposed tunnel between the two buildings and was told that it wasn't useable yet. He remembered dismissing it as an entrance.

But I didn't check, he remembered.

Now he wondered if he had interpreted the words as meaning that the passage wasn't complete; however, perhaps he'd made an incorrect assumption. Still, its presence was not generally known. How would Slade know about it?

Two stories down, Slade threw the ball through the door into the room where the Praetzels lay, the backs of their beds raised slightly.

Aleta and Stanley both saw the ball bounce into the room. Their ears picked up the hiss of the gas.

Stanley turned his head toward the door. Aleta closed her eyes and prayed.

Slade stepped into the room, the green surgical mask hiding all but his eyes.

Stanley saw a flicker of surprise in his assassin's eyes as his finger automatically squeezed the trigger.

No wonder Aleta only saw his eyes, Stanley thought. The mask hid the rest.

It was the last thought he had. The three rounds hit him squarely in the center of his chest, and their impact forced the air from his lungs and the consciousness from his brain. He grunted and his head fell to one side.

Two steps later Slade was staring at his primary target. To his surprise she made no move to escape. She just lay there and stared at him through the gas mask covering her face.

Why had the patients been given the masks, he wondered, and not the cops guarding them.

He had less than a minute of air left. He raised his gun and waited for a few seconds to see the fear. When that didn't happen, his anger pulled the trigger repeatedly and he didn't stop until the chamber was empty.

She slumped down. Satisfied, he raced from the room. The doors of the elevator were already closing when he slipped through them.

On the roof Lyle West radioed, "I know how they got in. The construction tunnel. Fourth floor, check in."

Lyle waited only a few seconds before issuing orders. "Peets, take two men to the basement. Tom, seal off the first floor. All others stay put."

The service elevator reached the basement level at the same time the elevator from the emergency wing did. Peets and his two men rushed out and headed toward the tunnel exit.

Slade and Buddy, however, were faster.

"Take a breath," Slade told Buddy as they reached the door. He himself sucked in a lungful of air and then bounced a ball down the hall just as two men turned the corner.

Peets heard Slade shout the order to Buddy and guessed immediately what was about to happen. He took a deep breath and watched the two men in front of him fall. Holding his breath Peets raced for the door to the tunnel.

Something on the other side resisted his opening it. He pushed harder, not daring to breathe.

He heard the footsteps of the men running down the tunnel. Desperation gave him enough strength to push harder and the door gave way slightly.

He slipped through and saw that it was a winter coat that had held the door. He ran past it down the passageway, not daring to gasp for air until he was almost at the other end. Then his body overrode his desire not to breathe and gasped in a lungful of air.

He ran through the door at the far end. The men were already running across the floor above.

"In pursuit," he radioed as he ran to the stairs, "but they're too far ahead."

"Got you covered," Lyle radioed back.

He dropped to the roof and setting his elbows on the flat surface, raised his rifle and set his focus on the sidewalk leading to the car. He didn't hesitate a second when he saw the hospital scrubs. They were heading for the car at a run. They were the killers.

He aimed and fired.

Slade Lacaze fell as the round hit him in the middle of his back. Buddy Horvat stopped dead, threw his hands in the air and knelt down.

Within seconds Alan Peets handcuffed Buddy and searched him, all the while keeping his gun trained on the fallen man.

He threw Buddy's gun several feet away and called for back-up, warning Tom that gas had been released in the hospital.

Tom Milani sent two men from the front of the building and ordered all others to don gas masks.

Peets moved over to the second man. He plucked the gun from his hand and turned him over. The eyes were open and staring lifelessly. The front of his shirt was bloody.

"One dead," Peets reported.

Lyle West descended the staircase to the fourth floor. He found the floor littered with fallen men. He checked them and found that all were alive.

He saw the nurse, hands taped behind her back, lying in a pool of blood. He whipped off his belt and made a tourniquet above the cut.

"I've got a nurse who's lost a lot of blood. Tom, send me two men to take her to emergency. Then we need to evacuate the others up here."

Lyle waited until he saw the men come down the hall with a gurney before he stepped into the room where his friends were. They were either dead or alive. With them there would be no in-between. The man was a pro who didn't care if the nurse lived or died. He also figured she'd bleed out before help arrived. Lyle guessed she was merely a diversionary tactic.

He walked into the room and Stanley, seeing Lyle in a mask, left his on. He gave him a thumbs up. Aleta smiled at him. "Did you get him?" Stanley shouted.

Lyle grinned as he nodded.

He left them and Aleta relaxed behind her mask.

Somewhere in her mind's eye she remembered that pros usually made at least one head shot. The masks had deterred him from doing that.

Her ribs hurt when she breathed. How many times had she been hit? She'd lost count after the second shot.

Two hours later, Lyle and Dr. Cook walked in without masks. Stanley tore his from his head and took a deep breath.

"I will never take fresh air for granted again," Stanley commented.

"Let me take a look at you," Dr. Cook said, removing Stanley's hospital gown and helping him out of his vest.

"I'll take that," Lyle said. "Um. Three rounds. He meant business."

"I think you have a cracked rib," Dr. Cook said as his fingers explored the chest area. "I'll take an x-ray as soon as I check out your wife."

"Let her wait," Stanley said. "I want her to think about what happened."

Aleta's mouth fell open.

"We can't do that!" Dr. Cook said.

"Take me to x-ray and I'll explain," Stanley said. "Aleta, stay put until I get back. And think!"

Lyle sat down to wait. He was tired, but this exchange had aroused his curiosity. The puzzle was one his mind was already working on.

Aleta realized Stanley was indignant about something. But about what? The vest had saved his life. The mask had deterred their attacker from putting a round in their brain. He should be grateful, not resentful.

She pouted for the first few minutes. Her eyes roamed around the room. How could he do this to her? Act as if she wasn't important. No, that wasn't it. He was angry. And he wanted her to know why without him telling her.

That's because I'd argue with you, she thought, and you know it.

So he wanted to avoid an argument. No, it was more than that. If she thought of it, she wouldn't be defensive. She'd move straight to being contrite.

"I've got it!" Lyle declared suddenly.

"What?" Aleta shouted through the mask.

"I can't believe I beat you to the answer," he said smugly.

The challenge spurred Aleta to try to think. How come Lyle came up with it and she hadn't?

It's my anger, she decided. It's clouding my reason.

But I was reasonable, she thought. I saw Stanley being attacked. I reasoned that I was the target and I protected us both. What's wrong with that?

And suddenly she knew.

"I was the target," she said not worrying about whether she could be heard. "There was no reason for him to even be here."

She could see from Lyle's face he'd arrived at the same conclusion.

"He could have asked to be moved," Lyle said.

"But he didn't," Aleta retorted. "So why is he upset?"

"Because you didn't recognize the choice he made," Lyle said.

"I saved his life," Aleta declared.

"Which was only in jeopardy because he was near you."

"Ugh! Men!" Aleta exclaimed. "They are never satisfied!"

Dr. Cook wheeled Stanley back into the room.

"We heard the end of that," Dr. Cook said. "I gather she understands."

Lyle's nod gave them both the answer. Then he added, "I'm not sure she's calm enough to examine."

"Aleta," Stanley said sternly, "your choice. You can vent your anger at me now in which case I will send these gentlemen away for an hour or…"

The violent shake of Aleta's head stopped Stanley.

"You are going to treat them with the respect they are entitled to, right?" Stanley pressed.

The nod was demure.

Lyle stepped forward and gently removed the mask. Dr. Cook drew the curtain. Then he released her arms from the splints and removed her hospital gown which had effectively covered up the vest. Lastly he removed the vest. He handed it through the curtain to West and then proceeded to examine her chest.

"Your breasts are going to be sore for a long time," he said. "Unfortunately, I think you have a couple of cracked ribs to boot. I could take you to x-ray, but I'm hoping you'll trust me on this and not want to know. I'd prefer not to x-ray you because you're pregnant."

"Would the treatment be any different?"

"Cracked ribs heal on their own," Dr. Cook said. "In your case, you are immobile enough so I won't even have to tape them."

"Why did you x-ray Stanley?"

"With cracked ribs he needs to be more careful than he might be otherwise."

"Did you get hit with the gas?"

"If I did, it hit me while I was sleeping, so I don't know," Dr. Cook said. "However, I woke up when an oxygen mask was slapped on my face. It was a... an odd way to wake up."

He replaced the gown and looked at Aleta's head. He rang for the nurse as he removed the bandage on her head.

He studied the scar on the top of her head as well as the one on the side.

"There's been a little movement of the flesh in one spot," he said.

"It still hurts," she responded.

"It's not enough to try to repair," he concluded. "I'd only make it worse. You are going to have a scar though."

"Where?"

"On the side," he said. "If you wear your hair a little longer, it won't be visible."

"And the top?"

"Looking good."

The nurse, who'd arrived as Dr. Cook was removing the bandage, returned with fresh gauze and tape.

"Make it pretty," Aleta said. "My father is coming this morning."

"Don't worry, Aleta. He's already come and fainted," Lyle called. "He saw the curtain and thought you'd died."

"My father wouldn't faint!" Aleta declared.

"Okay, he didn't faint, but he did hear your conversation, so my guess is, he's a bit prepared for your new look."

Dr. Cook pushed the drape back and Aleta smiled at her father. "I'm alive, Dad."

"Oh, my God, what happened?" he asked, too shocked to move.

"I had an operation yesterday."

"Why didn't anyone tell me?" he continued, unable to assimilate the bandaged head and what it meant.

"My choice, Dad. We need to talk. I don't want Mother to know."

"For heaven's sake, Aleta, why not?" he gasped, too surprised at her request to do more than react.

"Because Jayline is getting married in three weeks and this is her time. Don't ruin her wedding. Please, Dad."

"I can't keep this from your mother," Robert Locke said, finally crossing the room and reaching under her sling taking hold of her hands as he kissed her gently on her cheek.

"Think of it as my wedding gift to my sister. I want her happiness to be unspoiled. I'm alive, Dad, so why distract Mother from Jayline's big event."

"You're making some sort of sense," her father said, backing away slightly, "but I know it won't seem reasonable when I face your mother."

"I'll tell Mother when the time is right," Aleta promised. Her voice was resolute and strong.

"What changed you?" her father questioned leaning back and staring at his daughter. "You've always asked me to be your intermediary."

"A lot has changed," Aleta said. "I don't want you to have to be the middle man anymore."

She turned to Lyle. "I want a phone in here at ten. I'm going to call my mother and tell her about Stanley. She won't even ask about me."

"She'll offer to come out," her father predicted.

"And I'll tell her that I want her for a long visit after the wedding. She can fly back with us."

"That'll help," her father said.

"I love you, Dad. Now go ply Dr. Cook with the questions I know you're dying to ask. And yes he called in the best neurosurgeon in Chicago to do the operation. He took good care of me and I want you to trust him."

"Does this mean, we're back on hospital food?" Stanley asked Lyle.

"Well, Aleta has to be fed, so if you have your family bring food when they come, that's your choice," Lyle said then added. "I know Lauren would like to do lunch if you'd let her. The ladies would love to spoil you both, and if that happens, I'll be here too."

"You've got a deal!" Stanley said.

Lyle left, and before either of them could think of what to say, he popped back in again.

"Dr. Cook says only family except for Lauren who's coming to feed you lunch. It seems you two are going to be here another seven days."

"I have cases!" Stanley protested.

"That's why," Lyle commented.

"Tell him, Stanley will not sign himself out or I will to," Aleta said.

Stanley sighed heavily, "We do it his way."

Lyle left a little surprised. There were rules in this relationship he didn't understand.

Aleta commented as an aside and at the same time as a concluding statement.

"It's over. We survived and there's nothing more to fear."

"Didn't your grandmother go to Elyria with Ed?"

"Yes, but they had separate agendas."

"Suppose they didn't?"

"Grams would have told me."

"Like you told your dad?"

"I guess she wouldn't have," Aleta said. "So what could happen?"

"You think about it," Stanley said. "Then we'll talk."

"Let's see if it does happen first," Aleta said realizing to what he was referring."

"It's your family. We do it your way."

Chapter 24

A little before noon the next day, Lauren showed up with lunch. She gasped at the sight of Aleta's head and apologized immediately.

"Lyle didn't prepare me well enough," Lauren said as she busied herself unpacking the lunch.

"Where's Lyle?" Aleta said. "I need a phone. I told him that yesterday."

"He said he'd be right along," Lauren replied.

"Something about needing to meet a helicopter. He said we should start without him."

The sound of the approaching helicopter drew all eyes to the window. It was a medical helicopter and Stanley murmured, "Wonder who's leaving?"

On the roof, Lyle West and Dr. Cook met the chopper.

As soon as the gurneys were in the elevator going down, Lyle took Harriet's good hand and said, "I need to apologize for Stanley and me."

The oxygen mask prevented Harriet from responding. Dr. Cook looked up from reading her chart. "You keep the mask on. Lyle can anticipate your questions."

"We're putting you on the fourth floor," Lyle said, "but Aleta won't be able to visit you for a few days."

The door opened and the two were wheeled into separate single rooms. Dr. Cook accompanied Ed and Lyle picked up from where he left off as soon as Harriet was settled in her hospital bed. He told Harriet about the operation that had followed the attack finishing with the assurance that Dr. Cook would answer all medical questions and promising he'd return as soon as the doctor finished with her.

He walked down the hall and entered Aleta and Stanley's room.

"I see you're almost done," he said. "Good. I have some business to discuss with both of you."

Lauren gave him his plate and he began eating urging them to finish up. Stanley watched his friend's face closely.

Lyle was troubled. The news couldn't be good.

"My phone?" Aleta asked petulantly.

"Dr. Cook said no," Lyle replied.

"I'm surprised he's not here," Stanley said.

"He would be except that two new cases came in by helicopter that demanded his immediate attention."

"People were flown here?" Aleta murmured surprised.

"From where?"

"Ohio," Lyle replied. "They live here and wanted to be near their families."

Aleta's mind put the puzzle pieces together. "Grams?"

"She was one," Lyle said.

"Ed?" Stanley asked, half-knowing the answer.

"He was worried about Beatrice leaving Emma and the pups. He knew she'd fly out the minute she heard."

"What happened?"

"Smoke inhalation when they rescued a young man from a fire at Hoskinson Lumberyard," Lyle said. "Your grandmother burned her right hand when she grabbed the hot doorknob. Considering how hot it was, it's a miracle the young man wasn't dead."

"So he's okay?" Aleta asked.

"Serious smoke inhalation, but he regained consciousness this morning," Lyle said. "Ohio is trying to extradite Neil on charges of attempted murder and arson among other things. If Edward Winslowe dies, they're going for murder one."

"What does Edward Winslowe have to do with Neil Hoskinson?" Aleta asked.

"He worked for him," Lyle replied. "Now, let me get to…"

"But, I want…"

Aleta's interruption was overridden by Stanley. "Go ahead, Lyle. Aleta, put your curiosity on hold, Lyle has something serious he needs to tell us."

"Time for me to go," Lauren said, rising.

"No, stay," Aleta said. "I have a feeling about this."

Lauren sat back down.

Lyle signaled her to leave. Lauren rose again and Aleta told her to wait a moment. Lyle nodded and Lauren remained standing.

"Rosalie wants to be included in the financial conference Mr. Hoskinson is having on Friday," Lyle began. "She says she has evidence of some malfeasance on the part of Mr. Hoskinson's advisors."

"She used the wrong word," Aleta replied. "Grams and I hid a personal fact from Mr. Hoskinson. That's all."

"That's it?" Lyle blurted out.

Aleta chuckled. "You didn't think we'd done anything illegal, did you?"

Lyle reddened. "No, I really didn't, but whatever it is, her lawyers agree that that fact alone could result in Mr. Hoskinson requesting a new financial advisor and thereby change his financial decisions."

"I need to be at the meeting," Stanley declared. "Mrs. Locke may need legal representation."

"You know what this is about, don't you?" Lyle asked.

"What I do or don't know is privileged information," Stanley said. "You know that."

"Ah, yes," Lyle sighed. "Police chiefs aren't supposed to trust people, but I can't help it. I do trust you."

"We should tell them," Aleta said. "Lauren, sit down."

"It's your call," Stanley conceded. "But didn't you promise your grandmother...?"

"She won't object," Aleta said, "It's all going to come out anyway."

"Mother could have everything said during the court proceeding sealed."

"Lyle, when the Hoskinsons come to the hearing, will they be guarded?"

"Of course."

"Can we request that there not only be just two guards?" Aleta asked, "but that the guards be men we choose?"

"It could be arranged," Lyle said cautiously. "The others can wait outside."

"You remember Edward at our second wedding, don't you, Stanley?"

Lauren gasped, "You had a second wedding?"

"In Grams' home town," Aleta said. "All her relatives came. It was quite wonderful."

"Who was your maid of honor?" Lauren asked, slightly miffed that she hadn't been asked.

"Grams," Aleta smiled. "Her relatives loved it. My mother didn't know about it. Neither did my sisters. My dad was Stanley's best man and Uncle Paul walked me down the aisle. The real wedding was the one where you were the matron of honor."

"Why two weddings?" Lauren asked. "I don't get it."

"Our second one was in an all-black church. The only white people present were Stanley and his parents."

"And you and your dad and…," Lauren started when Lyle's head shake stopped her.

"Your grandmother is mixed race?" Lauren questioned.

"Yes," Aleta said. "I don't know how light Gram's mother was. She could have been passing when she met Gram's father. Gram's brothers and sister are quite dark. All married other African-Americans. Grams has twelve nieces and nephews and thirty great-nieces and nephews. And everyone came along with their spouses and in-laws and I think a lot of friends. The church was packed."

"I wish I'd been there," Lauren said. "It sounds like it was grand."

"So Edward is a relative?" Lyle asked.

"Grams' great nephew," Aleta said. "She's helping him through college. She's done that for a lot of them. A lot of them are educators like her father. She's very proud of that."

"Being of mixed race isn't the anathema it once was," Lauren said.

"Grams doesn't mind for herself," Aleta said. "Her friends all know. My sisters and cousins don't know."

"Why did your grandmother tell you?" Lyle asked.

"Grams wanted me to be a lawyer for the Tontine Trust and Martha Cook suggested Stanley as the local lawyer to work with me. Anyway, all the members of the group were aging, so the members each took their share to fund a public project; however, each had a private matter that needed protecting. Grams decided it was time for everyone to know about those matters. Stanley and I, as the Trust lawyers, sat in on the disclosures."

"How did Rosalie Hoskinson find out?"

"I'm guessing something happened on the visit and Neil picked up on it and then told his wife."

"How can this Rosalie hope to use this against you? This is the twenty-first century," Lauren observed.

"Some circles are still operating in the nineteenth century," Aleta responded soberly. "And that's the social circle my mother has aligned herself with."

"So what about your sister, the one who's getting married?" Lyle asked.

"Same social circle as Mother," Aleta replied.

"Isn't your sister marrying a graduate of an Ivy League college?" Lyle asked.

"Not only that," Stanley added. "He has a position in a firm dealing with estates and trusts. Social standing is critical in his position."

"He might not be willing to jeopardize his social standing," Lyle remarked.

"Then he doesn't deserve Jayline," Lauren declared.

"I don't think Dad has a choice anymore," Aleta said. "Rosalie is going to be sure this gets out."

"What'll your mother do?"

"Divorce my father," Aleta stated flatly. "There are same things she wouldn't be able to stomach. This is one."

"You don't know that," Lauren said. "She could surprise you. Your dad's a great guy."

"Let us know if we can help," Lyle said.

Aleta frowned as she stared out the window. All three knew it wasn't Lyle's comment of which she was disapproving. She was thinking.

"See you tomorrow," Stanley said. "She could be like this for an hour."

The two laughed and departed.

When she stirred half an hour later, Aleta's first query was directed at Lyle who'd long since left. "Lyle, why did Dr. Cook decide we can't have a phone in here?"

"I can answer that," Stanley said. "Because if we did, you'd get no rest at all. You are recuperating from major surgery in case you forgot."

"Tomorrow I want a phone."

Chapter 25

That evening when Stanley's parents entered the hospital room, Lydia took one look at Aleta and dropped the bag she was carrying and rushed toward Aleta.

"Oh, my stars, child, your poor head! Does it hurt? It looks dreadfully painful. We don't have to stay if you'd rather we not. My God, why didn't you warn us, Stanley? What's wrong with you anyway?"

Aleta jumped to Stanley's rescue.

"Hey, it's okay, Mom. I'm alive. And the part of my brain that thinks Stanley is beautiful still works."

Lydia burst into tears.

Bewildered, Aleta looked at Stanley for an answer.

"You called her Mom," Stanley said.

"It just slipped out," Aleta said. "She's acting like a mother."

A new burst of tears was the older woman's response.

"Hey, Mother," Stanley quipped, "I was operated an too."

Lydia brushed him off. "You look fine."

Stanley looked at his father.

"Dad, would you care to give me a bit of sympathy?"

Hubert smiled at his son. "Face it. Aleta upstaged you again."

"Let's eat," Stanley said, "and Mother can explain to me why it was my fault she wasn't prepared for how Aleta would look."

Lydia wiped her eyes and glanced at her son. "It just is."

Aleta giggled. "I love that line. I haven't used it yet."

"After you have a child, you'll use it a lot," Lydia commented.

"Why don't you think up a girl's name for us?" Aleta asked.

"I thought your mother had come up with a pretty one," Lydia queried.

Stanley spoke up. "She's worried about her mother's reaction when her dad tells her about his heritage."

"If she loves him, it won't matter," Lydia declared.

"Dad would have told her long ago if that were true," Aleta noted a little sadly. "I wanted him to tell Jayline before she marries, and now, it appears he has no choice."

"Does he have to tell her?" Hubert asked.

"Something came up," Stanley replied. "It's probable that Grams secret won't be a secret any longer."

"Oh, good heaven!" Aleta exclaimed. "Mom, your friends. I forgot about the impact this could have on you. Oh, I'm so sorry."

Lydia moved closer and reached in and took hold of Aleta's hands. "Never think you need to apologize to us for your heritage. We are proud to call you daughter."

Tears sprang into Aleta's eyes.

"Don't cry," Lydia said, "or I'll start up again, and I never cry."

Aleta smiled wryly, "Never?"

This time Stanley came to his mother's rescue. "Aleta told Lyle and Lauren West today," he said. "Neither of us wanted them to find out from someone else. Robert's in a real bind over this."

Stanley's father spoke up. "Now is the time for him to put money in trust funds for his daughters."

Lydia eyed her husband disparagingly. He defended himself lamely.

"Well, he's been thinking about it," he said, taking a big bite of his breaded veal chop.

"Good suggestion," Aleta said. "Jayline's future plans should be safeguarded, no matter what happens."

"He's been talking about retiring. He should do that immediately, then there will be no sizeable income to attack and he may be able to resolve the money issue with a generous settlement and…"

"Hubert!" Lydia exclaimed sharply. "You're burying the horse before it's dead."

"You and I have met Mrs. Locke," Hubert said, this time without apology. "Do you see another outcome?"

"She's Aleta's mother," Lydia pointed out.

All ate in silence for several minutes. Finally, Stanley's father spoke up. "It was inappropriate for me to bring up this matter here. I apologize, Aleta."

"No need," Aleta responded. "We're family. Families discuss what other members should do all the time."

Lydia smiled. The statement warmed her. This girl had changed and she loved her more than ever.

"You know what I'd like to do?" Hubert ventured. "I'd like to give your dad a chance to talk over his choices."

"Oh, do it!" Aleta urged. "Dad needs a friend right now."

"I'll do it tonight," Hubert promised. "Don't you worry about it. You didn't do anything to cause this."

"Oh, Aleta will find some way to blame herself," Stanley predicted.

"No, I won't, Stanley. Your dad's right. None of this is happening as a result of any choice of mine."

Stanley's eyes shone with pride. "As you can see," he quipped. "Dr. Cook fixed the reasoning part of her brain while he was there."

Aleta snapped back with a touch of humor, "Just be glad he didn't monkey with the part that thinks you're wonderful."

"You've mixed up your anatomy," Stanley shot back. "That part's in your chest not your head."

"I'm not wrong," Aleta declared. "My heart loves you; my brain thinks you're wonderful."

"I stand corrected," Stanley conceded.

And again Aleta let him have the last word.

The next morning Aleta waited for her father nervously. Despite what Hubert Praetzel had told her, she'd worried all night.

She had shared bits and pieces with Stanley, at first but as his responses became slower she remembered that he was still recuperating and he'd not slept at all the night of her operation, so she worried silently and let him sleep.

"You're still worrying?" he asked when he woke up.

"I feel so helpless," she said.

"If you'd accept that fact, maybe God won't break a leg," Stanley retorted. "What does it take for you to let Him handle things?"

"I let God handle lots!" Aleta declared and then laughed at the absurdity of what she had just said.

"My father is a good listener," Stanley said. "And he's not personally involved other than as a friend."

"I wish Grams were well," Aleta said.

"Me too," said her father entering with breakfast, "But she's not, so I kissed her goodbye and promised we'd talk later."

"Where are you going?"

"Home," he replied. "I need to talk with your mother and sisters, but I'll be back before you're ready to leave the hospital. I wouldn't miss your recuperation for anything. It's going to be a kick."

"I'm not going to be difficult," Aleta countered.

"No, but you're going to test the boundaries every day. Stanley is going to need all the help he can get."

"Are you sure, Dad?"

"Hubert and I had a long talk last night and I think he helped me come to grips with what has to be done."

"Isn't there still a chance...?"

"Aleta, I'm a realist," her father said. "And while it's possible she'll opt to stay married in name only, I won't do that."

"Poor Jayline," Aleta murmured.

"I'm sorry about that," her father said. "I do feel I made the wrong choice in not telling all of you as soon as I found out."

"Did Stanley's dad talk with you about setting up a trust fund for Jayline?"

"We talked about a lot of things. He's going to the Bay Area with me as my friend and lawyer."

Stanley burst in, "Dad hasn't done divorce work in years."

"Actually, he's helped a few friends."

"What about my cases?" Stanley asked, suddenly flushing over his lack of sympathy.

Robert replied evenly, "Your dad arranged for Kurtz West to handle them alone for a few days. Kurtz has cleared his calendar. They're still postponing some of your cases»'

"Yeah, the dull ones," Stanley grumbled. "I know those two."

"Your father told me to tell you that all your clients are sticking with you," Robert added with a hint of a smile.

"When's your flight?" Aleta asked.

"As soon as Hubert checks out the plane."

"He shouldn't fly all that way alone," Stanley protested.

"He's not," Robert said. "I'm sitting in the co-pilot's seat. There are long straight stretches that I can fly."

"With only a couple of flying lessons?" Stanley asked still perturbed.

"I'm a fast learner. Hubert said he'll give me a couple lessons on our way. It'll break up the trip. We may even land a couple of times so I can learn to take off. That'll give us both a break. We're looking forward to this trip."

Stanley smiled. "Dad does like to play hooky."

Robert turned to Aleta. "I have to tell your mother personally. I really have no choice. I hate to leave you."

"Don't worry about that," Aleta said. "Is there anything you want me to tell Grams when I see her?"

"Just tell her whatever happens is not her fault," Robert said. "And I'm glad I'm her son."

Within an hour of leaving the hospital Robert Locke and Hubert Praetzel took off. Hubert, true to his word, taught his friend many things about flying. They made two stops before landing in a small airport in the North Bay.

They headed straight for Robert's office in a rental car because Robert needed to take care of several matters before he told his family he was in town. First he met with his partners. He told them he wanted to retire.

"I brought my lawyer," Robert said. "Let's talk buy-out."

Next the pair stopped at Harriet's old bank, and Robert arranged to set up trust funds for all three of his daughters with Paul as trustee.

Then they visited Paul at his office and talked.

"If things get uncomfortable at home, you are welcome to stay with us," Paul offered warmly. "We have plenty of room."

"Have you told Andrea?" Robert asked.

"She said it made me more special."

"What about the kids?"

"Paul Junior said, 'So what;' and Lettie said, 'Cool!'"

"I told them they couldn't say anything to anyone and they couldn't see why not, but eventually they agreed to do as I asked. Their mother explained that their cousins hadn't been told yet and they weren't to ruin the surprise."

"It'll be some surprise alright," Robert muttered. "I'm not telling my wife I'm in town until Thursday. I have a lot of legal matters to take care of."

"Have dinner with us tonight," Paul suggested enthusiastically. "The kids would love to see you."

When Robert hesitated, Hubert jumped in, "We'd be glad to. We can tell you all about what's happening with Stanley and Aleta. They've had an exciting couple of days."

"See you at six," Paul said as they parted.

Chapter 26

Robert called his wife early Thursday morning and told her he'd flown in to tell her and their daughters something extremely important.

"Jayline has a fitting," Marian protested, "and Jocelyn can't miss school."

"This is important," Robert said. "Have Jayline cancel her fitting, and tell Jocelyn she can stay home from school."

"I most certainly will not!" Marian stated flatly. "You can see Jayline when she'd done with her fitting."

"Have her come straight home," Robert said.

"I'll tell her you have something important to tell her, but she may have plans."

"Tell her it has to do with her wedding," Robert said. "That'll bring her straight home. Where will you be?"

"With Jayline, of course," Marian said.

"I'd like to talk with you alone."

"Whatever you have to say can wait until tonight when the girls are in bed."

"Never mind," Robert said, defeated. "I'll see you when the fitting is done."

When he hung up, he turned to Hubert. "I'm going to need you to come with me."

"Won't that inhibit your wife from being able to express herself?"

"Unfortunately, no," Robert said. "Come as my lawyer. Please."

"Of course," Hubert said. "I gather the divorce is certain."

"I believe I was living an illusion," Robert said sadly. "Protect me from giving away the farm. Remember I want to share what I have, but not give up everything; except…"

"Except what?"

"Never mind. I'll never have that choice."

"So are we going to wait at your house?"

"No, we're going to pick up Jocelyn at school."

"Will that make her angry?"

"Jocelyn is a bit like Aleta. She'll enjoy the break in routine."

Jocelyn bounced into the back seat beside her father, said hello to Mr. Praetzel and asked, "Where are we going?"

"To give you a plane ride," Hubert Praetzel said.

"Whee!" Jocelyn said "I'll take it. Later you can tell me why you're bribing me."

"I have something unsettling to tell you," her father said.

"The secret?"

Robert raised his brow in query while Hubert smiled inwardly. She was like Aleta.

Jocelyn prompted him, "The one I'm not suppose to know about. Lettie told me."

"Lettie?" Robert gasped. "Paul's Lettie?"

"Do I know any other?" Jocelyn quipped.

"What did she tell you?" Robert asked.

"Do I still get my plane ride and the day off?"

Robert laughed. "You do."

"Lettie said Grams is African American. Is that true? Are we part Negro?"

"It's true," her father said.

"Cool!"

"That's what Lettie said," her father remarked. "I don't understand."

"It makes me secretly different from all the other girls I know. And I don't have to do any shit to be different. I am. That's boss!"

"It has a down side."

"Yeah, it means I won't have to marry a jerk like Scott."

"You don't like your sister's fiancé?"

"What's to like? He's a prick."

"You can marry anyone you like," her father said.

"Oh Dad, you are so retarded in same ways. Mom is obsessive about who is right for us. Even Aleta had a jerk of a boyfriend until Grams took her away and introduced her to a real person. And I'm not as strong as Aleta."

Her father put his arm around her and gave her a hug. "I think you're stronger."

"Are you going to get a divorce?"

"That's possible."

"If you do, can I come and live with you?"

"I'm planning to move to Illinois."

"Where Aleta and Grams are?"

"Yes."

"Can I come? Please," Jocelyn begged. "Can we bring my horse?"

"Your friends are here," her father said. "Your mother will want you to stay with her."

"Don't you like me either," Jocelyn asked, her voice trembling with emotion.

"Either?

"Well, you love Aleta and Mother loves Jayline. Grams loves Aleta. So it's Aleta two; Jayline, one; me, none."

Robert put his arms around his youngest daughter.

"My poor baby bird," he murmured. "Don't you know how precious you are to me? I'd give anything to have you with me, but your mother won't allow it. And you've grown up white. I don't want to take that away from you."

"Suppose I could show you how Mother really feels?"

"Your mother will be angry and upset. She could be goaded into saying things she doesn't mean, so don't try it. I know what's best for you. But never, ever doubt my love. It's real."

Later in the air, Robert gave up his co-pilot's seat to his daughter. Her enthusiasm for flying soared to new heights once in the front with her hands on the controls. She asked about everything and forgot none of what Hubert Praetzel told her.

He let her take over briefly and she squealed the whole time she was in control. Both men found her enthusiasm delightful.

It was too short a ride home as far as Jocelyn was concerned and she said so.

The silver BMW in the drive told them all that Marian and Jayline were home.

Jocelyn tittered, "She's going to be so pissed."

"Watch your language," her father cautioned, but Jocelyn was already out the door. She raced up the path and threw open the door.

"Guess what!" she gushed. "I got to fly an airplane."

"You mean ride in one," her mother corrected.

"No. I sat in the pilot's seat and drove—all by myself. It was excellent."

Marian took out her annoyance at being kept waiting on Robert.

"You won't let her get a driver's license until she's eighteen and you let her fly a plane."

"Hubert was in the other seat," Robert explained.

Marian softened her tone when she realized Mr. Praetzel was standing behind Robert. She had been very impressed by Stanley's parents, enough so that she reluctantly agreed Aleta had married well.

"I'm surprised Aleta and Stanley aren't with you," she said.

"That's one of the things I wanted to tell you," Robert said. "Both have had surgery on their heads to repair broken blood vessels."

"Brain surgery?"

"They suffered concussions and had hematomas that had to be drained," Robert said. "The surgeon never went into their brains."

"So how long's that going to take to heal?" Jayline asked. "They won't be wearing bandages or anything at my wedding?"

"Hush, dear," her mother said. "We can have them sit in the back."

"Aleta has both arms in slings besides," Robert said. "She can't use either hand."

"Oh, Mother, she will have to eat with her mouth. That's gross!"

"Someone feeds her," Robert said.

"Like a baby!" Jayline wailed. "She'll get all the attention. Mother! It's my day!"

"She's not coming," Robert responded evenly. "She doesn't want to ruin your day."

"She should be there," her mother said. "We can keep her out of sight."

"Her doctor won't let her travel," Robert said.

"She can fly," Marian said. "They're used to dealing with handicapped people."

"No she can't," Robert said.

"Thanks, Dad," Jayline said.

"You said you had something important to tell us," Marian snapped. "I hope that wasn't it."

Jocelyn danced around. "He's gonna tell you a family secret. It's boss."

"Jocelyn, show Mr. Praetzel the patio," Marian said.

"Sure, Mom," Jocelyn replied. "Come on, Mr. Praetzel, she don't want her dirty undies to be hung on the line."

"Jocelyn!" her mother snarled. "Behave."

"Come, Jocelyn, let's go look at the view," Hubert Praetzel said. He wouldn't be needed until later and he personally felt Marian Locke should have a chance to explode.

Robert made both his wife and middle daughter sit down and then carefully explained that the secret was about to be revealed by a vindictive woman who wanted to hurt his mother. The two listened as he told them briefly about her family's decision that she was to leave home and never return.

"She'd murdered someone?" Jayline asked.

Her father shook his head and continued. "They did it because they wanted her to be treated like a white woman. That would never happen if she stayed with her family. It took a lot of love for them to say goodbye and a lot of courage for her to leave and not look back. I'm very proud of my mother and the family that raised her. They were learned people of high moral character."

"So why did she have to go?" Jayline asked. "I don't get it."

"She looked white," Robert explained. "Her family is Negro.

Marian blanched. "Negro?"

"You're kidding, right, Dad. She's as white as you and me."

"She grew up black," Robert said.

Jayline shook her head. "This isn't funny, Dad. Do you have any idea what this would mean if it were true?"

"You're going to need to tell Scott."

"Tell Scott? Don't be stupid! I can't tell Scott. He doesn't want a nigger for a wife."

"Don't use that word!" Robert ordered sternly.

"You made me one, and you tell me to live with it, and then order me to watch my tongue. How dare you do this? How dare you do this two and a half weeks before my wedding."

"Circumstances arose…"

"Shut the hell up!" Jayline screeched. "You just ruined my life."

"It didn't matter to Stanley."

"He's a freak!" Jayline screeched. "Scott isn't. Scott can get any woman he wants. He isn't going to want me now. Neither is anyone else! I'll be ostracized!"

Jayline began to cry. Marian moved over and put her arms around her daughter.

"We had plans, Mother, great plans. What am I going to do now? What'll I tell Scott? I can't tell him the truth."

"Don't tell him anything," her mother said. "Your father married me without telling me."

"I didn't know when I married you," Robert said. "And basing a marriage on a lie is a big mistake."

"Can't we keep it a secret?" Jayline said. "Grams and Aleta are half way across the country. The people there don't know about us. If Dad doesn't say anything…"

"It's going to come out," Robert stated flatly.

"Why should I suffer for something you did?" she cried. Her tears began to flow again.

"Me?" her father whispered.

"You should have known," Marian accused. "She's your mother. You probably did know, but decided to ruin my life anyway."

"Marian, I…," he said rising and moving toward her.

She cut him off. "Don't touch me. Never touch me again. I will not be fondled by a Negro."

"Mother!" Jayline wailed. "What are we going to do?"

Jocelyn burst back into the room.

"I'm missing the fireworks!" she exclaimed. "I told you they'd be pissed.

"They're beyond that," Robert said evenly.

"And why shouldn't we be?" Jayline yelled, her face contorted in rage. "He can't stand for me to be happy. He has to fly out here to tell me to tell Scott I'm part nigger."

Jocelyn grinned. "That word'll freak Scott out. He sure won't marry you now. He don't want no black babies."

"Mother, make her stop! My life's ruined, and all she does is joke about it. Well, little sister, I'm not in this alone. Wait until you are ready to get married. It won't happen."

"Aleta got married."

"Yeah, to someone I wouldn't touch with a ten foot pole," Jayline sneered.

Jocelyn snapped back. "He wouldn't want you that close. God you're such a toad!"

"Look who's talking, metal mouth."

"They'll come off and I'll be beautiful and you'll still be a toad."

Jayline burst into tears again.

"I want to die. I'd rather be dead than have a drop of Negro blood!" she stormed, jumping up and heading for her room.

"Stop!" Marian said. "You don't have any Negro blood in you."

Jayline whirled around, jaw open in disbelief.

"This was a joke?" she gasped in dismay.

"It's no joke," Robert said.

"I have a secret of my own," Marian said. "Your father isn't your biological father."

"What?" chorused Robert and both his daughters.

"I found out about his mother's parents once when I brought Aleta over to her house," Marian said. "I was furious, and well, there was this married man who was a good listener and well, we fell in love. You're his child, Jayline. That's why the two 'J' names. It was the initial of his first name. The affair lasted until after Jocelyn was born.

Both of you are one hundred percent white. Only Aleta carries her father's blood."

"That's not true, Marian," Robert protested. "You were never unfaithful."

Jayline grabbed onto the opening. "I'm not related to Grams? Who's my father?"

"I promised I'd never tell," Marian said.

Jocelyn's eyes filled with tears. It was her turn to be upset, "Dad's not my dad?"

Robert embraced his youngest, "You are my baby bird. You are mine. I know it in my heart."

Jocelyn snuggled against her father's chest and let his arms fold around her. Still the tears wouldn't stop. She believed her mother. She was devastated.

Hubert touched Robert on the shoulder and nodded toward the patio. Jocelyn, however, wouldn't let go, so Robert took her with him. Hubert lowered her voice. "Don't argue with your wife."

"But Jocelyn believes her," he said, pushing Jocelyn far enough away to look in her eyes. Jocelyn's eyes were full of pain. "I can't have that!"

Hubert made Jocelyn sit down. "I can prove to you that you are your father's biological daughter with a DNA test; however, your sister seems to need this to be the truth. So what do we do? Prove your mother is lying and destroy your sister or you chose, without proof, that your father is your real father."

"I don't want to live a lie."

"You won't be," Hubert Praetzel said. "I see the same spirit in you I see in Aleta and her grandmother. You didn't get that from your mother."

Jocelyn's tears stopped. She sniffled. "Really, I'm like them?"

"And the link between the two is your father," Hubert said. "Do you still want to live with your father?"

Jocelyn hugged her dad, "Oh, yes. Please."

"But if she's not mine…"

"She is yours," Hubert said staunchly. "I saw Marian's expression through the patio doors when you told her. She didn't know."

"But she could have had an affair," Robert began, then hesitated nodding toward his daughter.

"Don't you remember her reason?" Hubert asked.

"Sure, she found out… oh I see… if she knew, then why was she shocked?" Robert said. "She'd have berated me for my timing."

"She's weakened her position as far as custody of Jocelyn is concerned."

"I thought she'd strengthened it."

"How important is Jayline's wedding to your wife?"

"As much as to my daughter."

"Let me speak for you," Hubert said. "Now after setting up the trust funds and after the property is divided, how much will you have to negotiate with?"

"A million, maybe. But then I'd really be broke."

"How much of that are you willing to give to keep Jocelyn?"

"Every cent," Robert said. "You can put me so far in the hole I'll never get out no matter how hard I try."

Hubert smiled. "Obviously, I have free rein here. Now trust me."

"Oh, Dad, please. Trust him. Please don't leave me behind. I'll sell my horse even."

"Hubert, see if we can avoid that," Robert said. "Aleta has a barn and pasture land."

When the three returned to the room, Marian announced, "I want a divorce."

Hubert nodded lightly and said, "That's why I'm here."

"Oh no," Marian said. "I'm not negotiating. I want it all."

"California grants you half. It's a no-fault state."

"But he's at fault," she argued. "I've been deceived horribly for years."

"And you allowing him to raise another man's children wasn't deception?"

"He thought they were his."

"But they weren't, were they?"

Marian looked at Jayline, her face again flushed with happiness. She was stuck with her lie.

"Sadly, no. They weren't."

"We agree to an equal division of all assets and liabilities."

"I want alimony."

"He resigned from his firm yesterday."

"They bought him out?"

"Yes."

"I get half."

"Done," Hubert Praetzel said. "The buy out is going to be paid out over the next ten years, so that will give you a sizeable annual income for a decade."

"I still want alimony," Marian insisted, "and child support."

"Robert would like Jocelyn to live with him."

"That's not going to happen," Marian said. "He just wants to get out of paying child support."

"And what amount are we talking about here?"

Marian couldn't think fast enough, but Jayline could.

"Five thousand a month."

"Does that sound reasonable to you?" Hubert asked Marian Locke.

She nodded.

Hubert did his mathematical calculations aloud purposely. "She's sixteen now. Child support at sixty thousand a year for two years is one hundred twenty thousand. How much alimony do you want?"

"Same amount," Marian said, "for twenty years."

"That's a little over a million dollars."

"A million two," Jayline piped up.

"It's yours only if you'll take the lump sum and only if you let Jocelyn chose with whom she wants to live," Hubert said.

Jocelyn who'd been listening to the negotiation intensely cried, "No! No! Dad, you can't do that. You'll be so deep in debt, you'll never crawl out. I'm not worth that much."

"She gets to choose," Marian said. "And I accept the terms as outlined."

"I'll draw up the papers. We sign the preliminary document tonight," Hubert said.

"I choose Dad," Jocelyn said abruptly. "That means he doesn't need to pay child support, right?"

"It would seem you are correct," Hubert Praetzel said.

"But that's not much help is it Dad?" Jocelyn said. "We still won't have anything."

"You can still choose to stay with your mother. I won't hold it against you."

"I want to fly back with you," Jocelyn said with steely determination. "I want to see Aleta."

"But the wedding," Marian whined.

"I'll fly back with Dad and Grams. Jayline won't want anyone knowing about the divorce until after the wedding. Right, Jayline?

The young blonde bride-to-be didn't hesitate a second.

"Mom, we need to keep this quiet until afterward. And Mom, you should book a cruise, sort of a vacation, right afterward."

Marian ignored the latter suggestion. She looked at her youngest daughter.

"I don't get it," she said. "You're giving up everything. Your father won't be able to send you to college."

"I guess I'll have to work my way through," Jocelyn flipped out. "Dad and I will scrub floors together. Isn't that what people like us do?"

"Jocelyn!" her father said sternly. "Don't make fun. You and I both will respect your mother's sacrifice. There's no doubt in my mind she loves you as I do."

Jocelyn looked bewildered and her father kissed her lightly on the forehead, "Aleta will explain it to you. Let's go pack for your trip."

Chapter 27

The following Friday half a week after Robert Locke's departure, at Tri City Hospital the early morning quiet was disturbed by the rattle of the food cart. Stanley woke and looked over at his wife who was still sleeping. He sat up and waited for a few seconds before slipping his feet into his terry cloth hospital slippers.

He stood and wavered for a couple of seconds, letting his legs know they were again in business. It was wonderful to be upright again. He thought Dr. Cook was going to keep him in bed forever. He knew that his not being allowed to walk had more to do with Aleta's condition than his.

He walked over to the window and stared out. It was going to be a beautiful, clear November day.

He decided to wake Aleta before going to the bathroom. Better she be wakened by a kiss than the flush of the toilet.

He walked over to the bed and gazed at his wife with a previously untapped sadness. She was too young, too beautiful, and too innocent to be so injured. He leaned over and gently kissed her on the lips.

She murmured and licked her lips. He put his hand under her covers and slipped it down her belly and kissed her again.

Her eyes flew open. "Stanley, remember where we are!"

"Everyone's busy delivering breakfast trays," he responded, leaving his hand where it was and kissing her again.

"Not doctors," came a voice from the doorway.

Startled, Stanley withdrew his hand and straightened up. Both stared at the man walking into the room.

"Dr. Chesney!" Aleta gasped.

"I just delivered a beautiful baby girl, and I thought as long as I was here, I'd check in on my newest patient."

"But I'm Dr. Cook's patient."

"You're part of an exchange program," Dr. Chesney said, taking Aleta's wrist and staring at his watch. Stanley rushed into the bathroom.

"Dr. Cook traded me?"

"For every rich patient he sends me, I take one clinic patient with pregnancy complications. He had three such patients come in this month, so I got you and Lauren West and Yancey."

Aleta's jaw dropped.

"He traded his wife?"

"I'm good, you know. Expensive, but good."

"I don't believe you," Aleta said. "You don't work that way."

"That's the second bet Dr. Cook won this morning," Dr. Chesney said. "Your pulse is up. Sex is good exercise. Keep it up."

"You want us to have sex."

"Hey, if couples didn't have sex I'd be out of business."

"What was the other bet Dr. Cook won?"

"He said you had an active sex life."

Aleta blushed. "Now tell me why he is sending the three of us to you?"

"He said he wanted to share the wealth."

"Try again."

"He said he's so busy with your shoulder and head injuries, he's afraid he might miss something in your pregnancy."

"You're getting warmer," Aleta said. "That's part of the truth."

"The bottom line is that most people get head bumps and they heal without complications. Both of you needed surgery. He is sure your pregnancy will become complicated somewhere along the line. He wants me to be thoroughly familiar with you just in case."

"I can go along with that," Aleta said. "Did you bring me any chocolates?"

"They're in my locker. I'll deliver them after breakfast," Dr. Chesney said, obviously amused. Then he added, "I'm ordering some blood tests."

"I've had blood tests."

"I'll be checking for other things," Dr. Chesney explained as he drew the curtain. "I'll do a full exam when you come in for your first prenatal check, but right now I want to do a preliminary exam."

Stanley lay back on his bed and tried telling himself that he hadn't been caught doing anything wrong.

For God's sake, I'm married, he scolded himself, but the embarrassment clung.

Suddenly, the curtain was opened. "Everything looks good," Dr. Chesney said. "So what do you want? Boy or girl?"

"Stanley wants a boy," Aleta said. "I'd like a girl."

"Good!" Dr. Chesney grinned. "I love unity."

"Unity?" the two chorused.

"You both want the baby," he said and left.

"I like him," Aleta said. "You should have seen him with his wife."

"I wish I had. Then I wouldn't be so upset about him seeing me with you."

Instead of being upset with him, Aleta grinned. "So, Dr. Cook won a bet on you and me. Makes me feel understood."

"I could do with a little less understanding," Stanley muttered.

Stanley's mood remained dour until Robert Locke walked in with breakfast.

"Dad, what happened?" Aleta asked and Stanley realized his wife was about to deal with something far more serious than a momentary embarrassment.

"It went better than I expected," Robert Locke said. "I'm broke, your mother's rich, Jayline is happy and Jocelyn is moving here with me."

"Moving here?" Aleta gasped. Her eyes lit up. "You're going to live here? Where?"

"Jocelyn is bunking in with Mother in her RV until Mother's house is finished. I asked Mother whatever made her build a four bedroom five bath home. She said she was 'told' to do it. Is she getting senile?"

"Prophetic," Aleta said.

"I thought she was just able to predict catastrophe."

"Evidently our gifts have babies," Aleta giggled.

"Anyway, she and Jocelyn are going over to pick out her bedroom and talk about colors," Robert said. "I think Mother is looking forward to family life again."

"So Scott accepted Jayline's mixed heritage," Stanley commented. "I guess I misjudged him."

"He doesn't know."

Stanley's shocked look made Robert hasten to explain what had happened.

"Mother did that?" Aleta asked. "I don't mean cheat. I mean she would lie to save Jayline's marriage to Scott? Didn't Jayline see what Mom was doing?"

"No," her father responded sadly. "As a matter of fact, Jocelyn believed her too. Your mother was very convincing."

"But Jocelyn's here."

"She's here on faith," Robert said. "By the way, can she use your barn for her horse? She was willing to give him up, but I told her we'd board him at your place."

"He won't be happy alone, Dad," Aleta said. "Horses are social animals."

"No one else rides," Robert said.

"Rescue groups are always looking for places for horses. Jocelyn could look after two," Aleta proposed. "I know just the ranch where you can go for help in finding a horse that needs a home. It can belong to us. Jocelyn can take care of him in exchange for barn privileges."

"She'll like that," her father said.

"You really are broke?" Aleta asked.

Stanley cut in.

"I thought my father went with you."

"He did all the negotiating," Robert laughed at the vision of the negotiations. "Whatever she asked for, he said, 'Done!' Fastest negotiation on record. He gave away every cent I have and put me in debt up to my eyeballs."

Stanley looked confused. "My father's a sharp negotiator. I can't believe he didn't get you what you wanted."

Robert Locke grinned. "Oh, he did that. The only thing. I wanted was custody of Jocelyn. He read Marian right all the way. There is no way a divorce wasn't going to cost me, but I came out with a chance to start over in a place I fondly remember as a child with my two favorite daughters."

"What about Jocelyn's college?" Aleta asked.

"I set up three trust funds before Marian and I met and dissolved our marriage. Jocelyn can draw on hers for college expenses. Paul is the trustee."

"Three?" Aleta asked. "I don't need your money, Dad."

"Well, neither you nor Jayline can touch your trusts for five years. I did that so you wouldn't turn around and give it right back. It's your inheritance."

"In five years, Aleta may need it," Stanley quipped. "I can't believe how fast one person can accumulate animals."

"You have fish!"

"Fish are cheap. Horses are not."

"One horse is all we're getting," Aleta stated flatly.

"I gather you took a buy-out on your partnership," Stanley said, moving back to what happened in the negotiations.

"Marian gets half for the next ten years," Robert said. "She needs some security during the transition."

"Are you going to practice law here?" Stanley asked.

"I don't know," Robert said.

"How about an interim job?" Stanley asked. "Aleta has been bugging me to hire a law clerk. The job's yours if you want it. And if you decide you'd like to practice again, we already have a multi-faceted law conglomerate, and we're just two people. You understand what I'm saying because one of those two people is Aleta and she has eclectic tastes."

"Um... that could pay for my flying lessons. They're pretty expensive. Does it come with health insurance? Working for you could be hazardous to my health."

"I've got a backlog of cases so if next week isn't too soon, I could use you starting Monday."

"That means my retirement lasted less than a week. That's got to be a record."

"Dad, what if Rosalie Hoskinson doesn't drop her bomb, will you regret what you just did?"

"Not for a minute. The time was right."

Lauren came in with lunch at noon, and Lyle carried in a suit, shirt and shoes. "Your father said you wouldn't go to court, even an informal hearing in a hospital gown."

"He has a robe," Aleta observed. "Besides I'm going in hospital garb."

"My father is correct," Stanley said.

"He told me I was to help you dress."

"I can dress myself."

"I'll call the nurse," Lyle said drawing the curtain.

"Honestly!" Aleta exclaimed. "Stanley, stop fussing over nothing."

"Okay, Lyle, let's get on with it."

Harriet showed up thirty minutes before the scheduled hearing. "Stanley, are you my lawyer or Aleta's?"

"I see no conflict of interest here," Stanley said. "Just tell me what you want."

"I want to make my recommendations to the court before Rosalie gets to speak."

"Anything else?"

"That's it."

"No problem," Stanley assured her.

But he was wrong.

Chapter 28

When Aleta was wheeled into Mr. Hoskinson's room, the gasps told her that none of the Hoskinson family members were aware how seriously she'd been injured.

Rosalie Hoskinson was already seated in a chair to the left of the judge's chair. She was dressed in an orange prison jumpsuit with her hands and legs chained. Neil, in identical attire was seated beside her. Behind Rosalie stood Lyle West. Alan Peets, almost a head taller stood behind Neil. Seated on the other side of the prisoners were Cliff, his wife Wanda and Lars Hoskinson's fat-bellied attorney Oscar Johanson.

The court recorder settled herself to the right of the judge's chair facing Lars Hoskinson. Ed Ornstein and Harriet Locke were seated on the far right. Aleta's wheelchair was set next to the court recorder. Stanley was rolled in between his wife and her grandmother. Standing awkwardly opposite Stanley were the opposing lawyers.

West called for four more chairs for the Hoskinson attorneys and then cleared the room of hospital personnel and told the prison guards to wait outside. The bailiff came in and stood with his back to the door and called for all to rise.

Before Judge Davis entered, Aleta leaned over and whispered in Stanley's ear. "One of those men is a reporter."

"Don't worry," he whispered. "Mother will take care of it."

After everyone settled in their seats, Judge Davis asked each person to identify himself for the court reporter. When everyone was finished Judge Davis said, "May I see the bar cards of the gentleman representing the prisoners."

"What about his," Rosalie spit out pointing at Stanley.

"Counsel will tell the prisoner not to speak unless addressed by the court."

Rosalie's lawyer leaned over and whispered in Rosalie's ear.

"I won't be quiet," she declared. "I will damn well talk when I want to. And no damn judge can stop me."

"Chief West, gag her," Judge Davis ordered.

"You bitch...," Rosalie screeched, but the prepared gag went into her mouth with a deft swift motion that surprised the onlookers.

Rosalie shook her head to try to prevent its being tied, but to no avail. She tried to lift her hands but found that the series of chains was fastened to the chair and that she couldn't reach her mouth.

She glared at the judge and stamped her feet in anger. Her lawyer leaned over and told her to quit.

"The judge can throw you out of here," he told her.

Rosalie lifted her eyebrows and saw the seriousness in her lawyer's eyes.

"This isn't a bar card," Judge Davis said to the man standing in front of the table. "It's a driver's license."

"It's identification," he argued.

"Please leave the room."

"But Mrs. Hoskinson requested I be here," he said looking at Rosalie who nodded vigorously.

"This is a closed hearing," Judge Davis said. "I decide who may be present. Bailiff, show the gentleman out."

"The matter before the court is the list of recommendations of the court appointed financial overseer of Lars Hoskinson's assets. Mrs. Locke, are you ready to proceed?"

"I object!" Rosalie's attorney Niles Bissell said.

"To what?"

"To Mrs. Locke making any recommendations. Mrs. Rosalie Hoskinson questions her integrity and therefore her position as overseer."

Harriet leaned over and touched Stanley's arm. He put his hand on hers. For some reason this comforted her.

Bissell continued, "I would ask the court to allow Rosalie Hoskinson to be heard."

"Does Mrs. Hoskinson plan to show evidence of malfeasance?"

"Of planned malfeasance," Bissell said.

"The court will hear what Mrs. Hoskinson has to say. Counsel should warn his client that if she uses foul language in this court she will be held in contempt and stopped from addressing the court further."

Bissell leaned over and spoke earnestly with Rosalie. It was obvious she didn't want to take direction.

Aleta leaned over and whispered to Stanley, "Whatever you do, don't let Lyle leave this courtroom."

Harriet touched Stanley on the arm and he turned toward her.

"Whatever you do, don't let Lyle or Rosalie leave this courtroom," she whispered.

"Stanley," Aleta hissed.

He leaned toward her. "I don't want to, but keep Rosalie here no matter what she says."

Stanley turned back to Harriet, "Rosalie will vilify you. Are you sure you want her to stay no matter what?"

"Absolutely," Harriet said.

He turned to Aleta. "She will malign your grandmother. Are you sure you want me to save Rosalie?"

"No, I'm not sure," Aleta said, "but please do it. Listen to my words. I don't want my hatred to outweigh my conscious choice to do what is right."

"Your Honor," Stanley said politely addressing the Court. "It appears that counsel is having a difficult time persuading his client not to use the word uppermost in her mind. It is a word that my client doesn't wish to hear, but she has instructed me to inform the court that she is willing to have the word spoken since the woman lacks the vocabulary to express herself using alternatives."

Chief West looked at his black counterpart and raised a brow. Peets winked in response.

Judge Davis was taken aback by her son's preemptive plea. She had seen him listening to both Harriet and Aleta with a worried frown as he alternated between the two women. Stanley had been persuaded by them to do something out of character. He had not attempted to manipulate her into kicking Rosalie out of the room although she was certain he had the argument to do it. He had instead capitulated and was allowing the one thing to happen she knew nobody wanted.

"Mrs. Locke," Judge Davis said, "do you wish to resign as financial advisor at this time."

"No," Harriet replied. "Let the woman speak."

Judge Davis turned to Bissell. "I will tolerate a few mistakes as Mrs. Hoskinson tries to find the correct words, but I will not accept any abusive language directed toward the court."

Bissell leaned over and everyone heard him whisper, "You can't call the judge a bitch or she'll throw you in jail."

"Remove the gag, Chief West," Judge Davis ordered. "Mrs. Hoskinson, I suggest you make your point at once."

"Oh, I can do that Your Judgeship," Rosalie spat out. "It's Mr. Hoskinson who's been fooled. He thinks he's got a smart white woman working for him when what he's got is a sneaky Nig... ra woman working him. Nobody told him she was a Nig... ra. Nobody let him know. That's because that little gal that understands him so good is a Neg... ra too."

Stanley sat in his wheelchair and felt the waves of hate begin to wash over him. They were directed at the women on either side of him, but he felt them. It surprised him. The woman had toned down her words but the venom inside those words was as deadly as the words themselves.

He'd known taunting as a child. He'd been bullied and belittled, but this venom was more lethal. It reached down into his very soul.

And I'm not even black, he thought. It's washing over me, soaking into me, affecting me and I'm not even black. He felt his temples begin to throb.

How had Harriet survived? No wonder she hugged her secret tight against her chest. The hatred was as strong, if not stronger, for her because she was a black woman respected as if she were white.

There were African Americans in positions of wealth and power, but he couldn't imagine anyone of them had escaped the experience. While Harriet never said it, he knew that she had every right to do so. He had no idea what being black in this country meant.

He looked at his mother. She was cringing, he could tell. He wondered if the wave of animosity was reaching her as well.

"Mrs. Hoskinson, race is not relative to the charge leveled," Judge Davis ordered sternly. "Address the charge."

Stanley had believed that, if his mother spoke, her words would somehow stop the malignant emotion filling the room. He sensed that, while they didn't speak, Rosalie's views reflected the feelings of many others in the room.

Their very stillness, under the guise of politeness, allowed the evil to grow.

Stanley looked at Alan Peets. The black chief of Oakwood police remained stoic in his expression and posture. He had been through this many times but Stanley guessed that it got no easier.

Then, Stanley glanced at his friend, Lyle West. He too managed to hide his true feelings; however, Stanley could tell he was being affected by the woman. He must dearly wish the judge would tell him to gag the woman again. He smiled inwardly at the fantasy. He knew his mother wouldn't order it again. Harriet had allowed the Pandora's box to be opened.

His mother was going to let her speak. Stanley hoped his biting sarcasm would tone down her words. His ploy had, in fact, worked; however, the despicable attitude that gave rise to the words had not been contained.

He understood why the word "nigger" was such an anathema to the African American ear. It carried pure hatred as no other word in the English language did. So the black populace rose up against the word, hoping that would be enough.

He had just discovered that hatred can ride in on any word. It rides the bull of evil like a rodeo cowboy—proud, defiant and daring. During the ride bystanders are enthralled. That the rider is thrown is immaterial because a new rider emerges from the chute, and the onlookers again watch the match. Those who last the longest are those who become one with the bull.

"It is relevant, your judgeship," Rosalie said her dark eyes blazing. "Those people shouldn't be allowed to mess in a white man's business. They are stupid, ignorant, lazy and evil. That woman over there is the daughter of a bastard son of a plantation owner. Her grandmother was a whore. That's her roots. They ain't pretty roots. They is the kind that spawns evil. She can hide behind her white face, but inside she ain't white. All the pretending in the world won't make her white..."

The judge brought down her gavel.

"Mrs. Hoskinson, either you get to the point or I will excuse you from testifying further."

Both Aleta and Harriet whispered in Stanley's ear. "Not yet!"

"Your Honor," Stanley said. "My clients wish her to continue."

Judge Lydia Davis's jaw dropped. Stanley saw Alan Peets react. It was a slight reaction, but obvious. He was also shocked.

Stanley saw Lyle put the hand holding the gag behind his back. He appreciated the thought.

"Oh, they do, do they?" Rosalie snarled. "As if they got anything to say. They know what I'm saying is the truth and there ain't nobody got the right to shut up the truth. However,

I ain't just making noise, I got real proof she is going to screw my father-in-law."

"Present this proof to the court," Judge Davis demanded.

"It's right there in that list you got under your nose. They want us to pay the hospital bill of a man who tried to burn down the lumberyard. The reason that Nig... ra whore—and yes, your judgeship, I know what I'm saying—is trying to get money out of my father-in-law for her own nephew who was fired for disloyalty and took revenge."

Judge Davis turned to Harriet. "Mrs. Locke, is the man to whom Mrs. Hoskinson refers your nephew?"

"Edward Winslowe is my great nephew. He is the son of my niece. And he is of African American descent as I am."

Harriet felt Stanley's light touch on her arm and stopped talking.

"Why do you feel Neil Hoskinson should pay his hospital bill?"

Stanley's touch told her to keep it short.

"Because he caused him to be injured."

"How did he do this?"

"He set a shed on fire after he locked him in."

"You have proof of this?"

Harriet looked at Stanley, and he answered for her. "She believes this is true. She saw Mr. Neil Hoskinson depart the premises with the shed on fire. She helped rescue Edward Winslowe. To do so an axe was used to break down the door."

"It's a lie!" Rosalie shouted. "The door weren't locked..."

The gavel banged. Rosalie jumped and Judge Davis eyed her sternly. Chief West took one step closer, the gag in his right hand. Rosalie looked back and shook her head.

"Go on, Mr. Praetzel," the judge ordered.

Stanley picked up exactly where he'd stopped when interrupted by the outburst. "Mrs. Locke attempted to open the door. She burned her hand in the attempt. Afterward Mr. Ornstein wielded the axe. They pulled Edward from the building. He was unconscious. Later he told police Mr. Hoskinson had tricked him into entering the shed. The Elyria police investigated his claim and a warrant for Mr. Neil Hoskinson's arrest has been issued. He is charged with arson and attempted murder."

"When that matter has been settled in criminal court, if Mr. Neil Hoskinson is found guilty, then Mr. Edward Winslowe may petition Lars Hoskinson as owner of Hoskinson Lumber in Elyria, Ohio for reimbursement for his medical bills," Judge Davis ruled. "This court is not prepared to order payment at this time. The amount in question, will be set aside and held in trust until the matter is decided."

"Thank you, Your Honor," Stanley said.

"The court finds no malfeasance in Harriet Locke's handling of Lars Hoskinson's financial affairs. She presumed guilt on the part of Neil Hoskinson, the manager, forgetting that despite her witnessing the near death of her great-nephew, a man is presumed innocent until proven guilty. It is a legal technicality, of which she is not expected to be aware. The fact that she did not pay the bill with Lars Hoskinson's funds to which she had free access testifies to her integrity in this matter. Mrs. Locke is expected to act without personal gain. She has done so. The charge of malfeasance is dismissed as without merit."

"Your Honor," Rosalie piped up. Her use of the correct form told Stanley she had been deliberately misaddressing the judge.

She won't get away with the slight, Stanley thought.

"Yes, Mrs. Hoskinson?" Judge Davis responded.

"My father-in-law was forced to put his money in the hands of a Nig-ra whore. There ain't no merit in that at all. You can whitewash it all you want with your fancy words but it's not right. He should have had a say. He should've been told. You should've been told. Don't you agree?"

"I was told," Judge Davis said coldly. "It was irrelevant. I chose the best person for the task. That matter is settled. Let's move on."

"You knew?!" Rosalie exploded. "You set a damned nigger whore over my fa..."

West caught the nod and the gag cut off the remainder of Rosalie's sentence. West smiled as he did it.

"It is apparent to the court, Mrs. Hoskinson, that you have been well aware of the words you choose. You have treated the court with contempt."

Her glance at Stanley and his shake told her not to send her to jail.

"I won't send you to jail as that would be redundant; however, that gag stays put until you decide to apologize to this court and Mrs. Locke."

Judge Davis saw her son's approval in his eyes. She continued, "Mrs. Locke, present your recommendations."

The old man in the bed mumbled, and Aleta listened and replied with a yes.

Judge Davis ordered her to repeat what he had asked exactly.

"With apologies to the court," Aleta said, "I refused to say the word he used aloud."

"You may substitute a more acceptable term," Judge Davis said.

"Thank you, your honor," Aleta responded. "He asked, "Are you a Negro?""

The bearded old man mumbled again.

"You will repeat his words," the judge ordered. "However, I will allow a substitution for that one word only."

"Yes, Your Honor," Aleta said. "Except for the last word, Mr. Hoskinson's exact words were, "Your grandmother is one smart Negro.""

Mr. Hoskinson mumbled more words. This time Aleta repeated them without preamble.

"I think I been wrong all my life. And Cliff, you should be glad she's in charge because now you get everything you deserve. And Neil gets what he deserves."

When Aleta finished, Mr. Hoskinson began muttering again.

"The will is exactly what I want. Mrs. Locke's recommendation about paying the people my son gypped are okay too. And, can I pay Edward Winslowe's hospital bill anyway or is that illegal?"

"I can set aside my ruling," Judge Davis said. The old man nodded.

Rosalie sat gagged while the changes in the will were read and Mr. Hoskinson nodded his approval. Both Police Chiefs and Mr. Ornstein were called up to witness the new will. Both Peets and West found this act particularly satisfying because Rosalie was struggling the whole time trying to remove her gag.

The recommendation for compensation to all those whose claims were verified was ordered paid. In addition, Harriet Locke was empowered to pay out the remaining claims up to the estimated total she had submitted.

As the paperwork was being completed, Stanley rose and walked over to Lyle West and Alan Peets.

"There was an altercation at the Arborville station," Stanley said quietly. "But no one died."

Lyle looked at his belt and then remembered he'd turned off his pager. He was on duty in the courtroom. He knew he was unavailable for an emergency.

Peets had turned off his as well. He looked confused.

"How do you know?" Peets questioned.

"Aleta and Harriet told me that if Lyle left with Rosalie that both would be killed during the failed attempt of Buddy's friends to break him out of jail."

"Saving Rosalie must've been hard for them to do," Lyle commented.

"You'll never know how hard," Stanley said.

He turned to Peets. "I know you know how hard it was. Aleta's never heard that word directed at her before. I'm certain her grandmother was crushed as well."

Lyle suddenly thought of how careful Stanley was with words. "You said no one died. Was anyone injured?"

"I don't know," Stanley said. "However, if any were, they'd be downstairs in emergency right about now."

"Peets, can you handle both of these vermin?"

"Go," Peets said. "There are men outside to help with the transport."

Stanley made his way back across the room as Lyle West approached the judge and was excused.

Judge Davis announced, "There is one more piece of business before the court."

She turned toward Rosalie who, sensing that she was again the center of attention, stopped squirming.

"Mrs. Hoskinson, are you ready to apologize to this court and Mrs. Locke?"

The angry muffled screeches told the judge she was not.

"Chief Peets, Mrs. Hoskinson remains gagged until she is ready to apologize."

Rosalie shook her head violently.

"Your apology to Mrs. Locke will be taken as an apology to this court as well."

The old man in the bed mumbled some angry words.

The judge looked at Aleta.

She translated his words exactly. "I want this crazy bitch out of my sight."

"That's reasonable," Judge Davis said. "Chief Peets, make proper arrangements. If Mrs. Hoskinson refuses to capitulate by nightfall, put her under restraints and have her fed intravenously."

Peets kept a straight face, but Stanley knew he was enjoying this. He had to admit his mother had her own way of reestablishing her authority. One didn't cross her without consequences.

Chapter 29

Back in the room, Stanley allowed a nurse to help him redress. He did it without a murmur. What the two women had endured humbled him.

He would never have been able to withstand such a venomous outpouring with such fortitude. Aleta surprised him most of all. She'd never been on the receiving end of such hatred and still she stayed calm. The two had been united in the common goal of saving Lyle West and Rosalie Hoskinson.

That the price had been a violent assault on their dignity as honorable women was a price they were willing to pay. He knew they could have warned Lyle and he would have listened. Stanley wasn't sure he would have paid such a price to save a woman such as Rosalie. He could hear the soft murmurs of Aleta and her grandmother on the other side of the drawn curtain.

When the nurse finished helping him, she went to draw back the curtain, but Stanley told her not to.

"They need some privacy," he said.

"How can he ever look at me the same?" Aleta murmured. "He was so shaken by it. I could tell."

"He's a sensitive man."

"We were so equal before," she said her voice reflected by her deep sadness.

"You were never equal," Harriet replied, "but you were in love. That hasn't changed."

"How could it not have changed?"

"You notice he kept the curtain in place," Harriet said.

"He can't bear to look at me," Aleta muttered.

"Don't be ridiculous!" Harriet spat out. "He knows you're suffering and he doesn't know how to help."

From the other side of the curtain, they heard Stanley exclaim, "Hello Alan. Am I glad you came."

"That's quite a woman, your mother," Chief Peets observed. "A woman to be admired."

"So is Rosalie ready to apologize?"

"Oh, she won't cave until the IV feedings begin. I think I'm going to misunderstand her until morning."

"You are enjoying this, aren't you?

"I don't think old Rosalie has ever been on the receiving end of prejudice before."

"You're prejudiced?"

"Same as you," Peets said. "So what's with the curtain?"

"I thought they would want to be alone."

"Sometimes white people can be so stupid!" Peets said as he took the curtain and pushed it back. "Hello, ladies. Wasn't the gagging great!"

Harriet grinned at the dark black man resplendent in his chief's uniform. "I hope you had someone below your rank move her."

"I had two prison guards carry her chair and all to an empty room down the hall from here. She's facing the corner. It seemed appropriate."

"That's delicious," Aleta said. "Although I'll bet the irony is lost on her."

"She's going to hate Lydia," Harriet said.

"So how are you holding up, Aleta?" Chief Peets asked.

"I'm okay," Aleta said.

"Like hell you are!" Peets said. "You've got too much heart to be okay, but just so you know, you were a credit to your forefathers today. Your great grandfather would have been so proud."

Aleta flushed lightly.

"So are you throwing another party when you get out of here? We certainly enjoyed the last one, except for my being surprised. I want a party with no surprises."

"Depends on Lauren. She's the one with the arms."

"I'll put the bug in Lyle's ear."

Dr. Cook arrived at six which was when the Praetzel's arrived with Jocelyn and supper. Lydia assured the doctor that Bertha had counted on at least ten.

"But I've only given permission for two visitors," Dr. Cook said. "Even if Aleta decided that that meant two apiece, ten's too many."

"She counted you," Lydia said.

"Well I'm not a visitor."

"Neither are we," Lyle said reappearing with Peets in tow. "Police chiefs have privileges. I'm introducing Peets here to one of the perks."

"So who else did she figure on?" Dr. Cook asked.

"Dad!" Jocelyn cried as Robert entered the room, "Bertha told me my supper was here," Robert explained.

"How did the hearing go?"

"Can't discuss it, Dad," Stanley and Aleta said simultaneously.

"Who do you want to help you, Aleta?" Lydia asked graciously.

"You've got the rhythm down, Mom. You do it."

Jocelyn wrinkled her brow, but said nothing.

"Tell them about their new horse, Jocelyn," her father prompted.

"Who has a new horse?" Lyle asked.

"Stanley does," Aleta said impishly.

"He doesn't ride," his mother said.

"Oh he can't ride him," Jocelyn said.

"What kind of horse can't you ride?"

"One with a broken foot," Jocelyn said. "He has the kindest eyes and he talks back when you talk to him. Anyway, the vet said it would cost a lot to fix him up, but I told the man in charge that Stanley was rich and he had an almost new barn and lots of pasture and that my horse would be there too, so Sterling would have company. He wanted to know if you expected to ride Sterling and I said you didn't know how, but that you'd hired me to take care of him. Then Dad paid the man a thousand dollars and he gave us the horse."

"You bought me a thousand dollar horse that needs vet care and can't be ridden so your horse could have a companion?" Stanley asked visibly upset. "There weren't any cheaper, healthier ones around?"

"We didn't buy Sterling," Jocelyn said a bit stiffly. "You don't buy a broken-down horse. We donated the thousand dollars to rescue other horses. Dad says you can deduct it from your taxes so it's like getting the horse for free, isn't it?"

Stanley groaned. Jocelyn needed a primer in tax law as well as general money management.

Lyle grinned broadly. Stanley had gone from one difficult to manage female to two. There was no way Jocelyn wasn't going to disrupt his quiet family life.

"So where's the horse?" Stanley asked, trying to keep his tone even and reasonable.

"At the vet's. He's got some stuff to do to get him in shape to be moved," Jocelyn said. "They were glad to send you the bill."

Stanley threw a questioning glance at his father-in-law.

Robert shrugged. "Aleta told me to let Jocelyn chose the horse."

"Aleta, sending your mother out to shop for clothes was one thing, but don't send Jocelyn out to buy another horse. Please?"

The entire roomful of people chuckled.

Jocelyn wasn't dismayed. "You'll like Sterling. He's a beautiful Morgan. He's only twenty years old too."

Stanley almost choked on his coffee. "Twenty? I bought an old horse?"

"Old doesn't mean he's no good!" Jocelyn said, her voice trembling for the first time.

Aleta quickly assured her sister that Stanley would love him. "After all, Jocelyn, he loves fish, and they are just swimming eyes that eat. They don't neigh."

"And you can't pet a fish," Jocelyn said brightly.

"Don't say that. He pets his."

"If you want one to ride, there was a nice ten year old Appaloosa at the shelter."

"Really?" Aleta said, interested.

"We could go riding together," Jocelyn said getting excited again.

"Aleta, please tell me you don't ride," Stanley pleaded.

"I do."

"Why didn't you say anything before?"

"You didn't tell me you knew how to fly a plane," Aleta countered.

"He does?" Jocelyn said enthusiastically. "He can give me lessons then. Dad's still learning."

"No, he can't. That's Dad's job," Aleta said.

Shortly afterward Lyle West asked Harriet if she was up to receiving an apology from Rosalie before they put her into bed just in case the idea of an IV had scared her enough to make one.

"I thought Peets was in charge of that detail," Harriet said.

"He's pretty sure she isn't going to apologize," West said. "But he's sure his presence would set her off even if she was."

"Let's give her a shot at it," Harriet said. "It's only fair."

"Lemme go with you, Grams," Jocelyn begged. "Please."

"Not a good idea," Peets cautioned.

"I agree," Harriet said. "This might be a bit too strong for you."

"Grams, I'm grownup!" Jocelyn declared.

"You aren't coming. This isn't a game," her grandmother said.

Vexed, Jocelyn stormed toward the door.

"Just where do you think you're going?" her grandmother asked sternly.

"To the vending machine to get a candy bar, or don't you think I'm old enough to put the quarters in the slot," Jocelyn bit back petulantly.

Before she could be reprimanded, she whirled out the door.

"Let her be," Harriet told her son. "Give her a chance to cool down."

But Jocelyn wasn't about to cool down. Somehow she was going to find out what had happened that afternoon. Nobody was talking. And she didn't like it.

I deserve to be in the inner circle, she determined.

She went straight toward the vending machine in the waiting area and put in a couple quarters. She unwrapped her candy bar as she looked around.

She saw her father duck back inside the room as if he was ashamed to be checking on her. She spotted the guard outside a room at the far end of the hall. Now she knew her target.

She walked calmly down the hall. She had one shot at getting into the room. Still munching on her chocolate bar, she paused in front of the guard.

"This is where they put that woman that insulted my grandmother, isn't it?"

"Move on, Miss," the guard responded firmly.

"I'm on my way to the cafeteria. You want me to bring you anything?"

"No thank you, Miss."

"Chief West and Grams are coming down here in a few minutes," Jocelyn said. "I hope that woman is secure."

Having said that Jocelyn walked to the elevator and pushed the down button. When the doors opened, she got in and pushed several buttons. The door closed.

Just before it was completely shut, Jocelyn pushed the open button. The doors reopened.

The guard was gone. Held taken the bait. She slipped out and hurried to the room and slipped inside. The bathroom was immediately on her right. One step put her inside and out of sight. A second step and she was in the shower. She pulled the door closed.

If she was discovered, she'd be scolded and sent back to Aleta's room. It was worth the risk.

She didn't have long to wait.

She heard Chief West speak first.

"Rosalie, Judge Davis ordered your gag removed at regular intervals to allow you to offer an apology to Mrs. Locke. This is your last chance before you are confined to a bed for the night. Do you want to apologize?"

To the surprise of both Harriet Locke and Chief West, Rosalie nodded. Lyle stepped behind her and removed her gag. Wrathful vituperation exploded from Rosalie Hoskinson's mouth liberally sprinkled with racial slurs and the hateful 'N' word.

Why didn't West shut her up? Jocelyn wondered from inside the shower. She had no idea her grandmother had signaled him not to.

It wasn't long before the shock wave wore off and rage infused Jocelyn's whole being. Suddenly, she could stand it no longer. She burst from the shower and began to yell at the woman sitting in a chair in the orange jumpsuit.

Jocelyn's anger incited Rosalie to further insults only this time she spat them out at the young girl, and Jocelyn was bathed in a volcanic outpouring of hate aimed at her.

The shouting match could be heard in the halls and the nearby rooms.

Judge Davis looked at Aleta who said quietly, "Grams is teaching Jocelyn a lesson."

"How'd Jocelyn get into the room," Lydia asked.

"Snuck in, I imagine," Aleta said.

"Past the guard?"

"Evidently," Aleta replied.

"Should I interrupt?"

"Your order was clear," Aleta said. "Mrs. Hoskinson was to be given a chance to apologize."

"She's not apologizing," Lydia declared.

"I imagine Grams will figure that out shortly," Aleta rejoined. "I must apologize for what happened in court today."

"You?"

"Grams and I are protective of our prophetic abilities. It was either reveal them or let the truth about our heritage emerge."

"So that's what that was all about," Lydia said. "Exactly whose life did we save?"

"Rosalie Hoskinson's," Aleta said.

Stanley smiled wryly at the shock on his mother's face.

"Tell her who else, Aleta," he ordered firmly.

"Lyle West," Aleta said. "But his was a no-brainer."

Meanwhile back in the room at the end of the hall, Jocelyn discovered she'd met her match. Rosalie, who had been sitting bound and gagged for hours with nothing to think about but what more she wanted to say, had built up a reservoir of insults and they gushed forth from her mouth like vomit. The sheer force of the hate which permeated every syllable made Jocelyn retreat and run from the room crying.

Lyle West immediately replaced Rosalie's gag. "I guess Mrs. Hoskinson doesn't intend to apologize."

"What's next?" Harriet asked.

"We need to restrain her," Lyle said. "Then we'll start an IV so she won't get dehydrated."

Rosalie shook her head vigorously.

"I'm not sure what to do about the gag. Dr. Cook is worried she could choke to death."

Rosalie nodded vigorously.

"I have an idea," Harriet said. "It's a little elaborate, but I believe if Mrs. Hoskinson was monitored electronically, that would alleviate the danger of her choking to death."

"Let me fetch Dr. Cook," Lyle said.

In less than ten minutes, Dr. Cook entered the room.

"Hello, Harriet," he said then turned to the woman squirming in the chair, hands and feet in chains. "I understand you angered Judge Davis. That was not wise. Judges have a lot of power. Well, we'll try to make your confinement as painless as possible. I understand you're to be restrained in bed overnight."

Rosalie stamped her feet in protest.

"Maybe longer," Dr. Cook said. "I guess we'll plan for longer. Harriet, let's us step outside and talk."

The two guards were ordered to secure the woman in the bed. Rosalie fought every movement; however, she was overpowered and eventually lay legs stretched out and fastened at both corners at the bottom of the bed. Her wrists were secured by Velcro straps one on each side of her body.

Rosalie thrashed around on the bed, testing her straps and finding them secure. Her screams of protest were reduced to whines by the gag.

Harriet returned with a nurse. Harriet could see the apprehension in Rosalie's eyes.

"Let me tell you what we're going to do," she said calmly.

Harriet could tell from the expression on Rosalie's face that she didn't want her to stay, let alone participate.

Several monitors were rolled into the room and Rosalie winced while the nurse inserted a needle for the IV. Harriet explained each procedure as the nurse instituted them. The fluid dripping from the IV would keep her hydrated, the catheter would keep her dry. The leads attached to her chest would monitor her heart. The tube being inserted down her nose would guarantee enough oxygen to her lungs. The blood pressure cuff would take readings automatically on a regular basis.

What Rosalie didn't know was that the nurses were not to speak to her.

"One more thing," Harriet said and saw Rosalie's eyes traveled to her gown still merely draped on top of her.

"Not that," she replied. "Can't release your arms to dress you."

Rosalie's eyes held her question. What more could there be? She soon found out.

Harriet left the room while Rosalie was given an enema.

Outside Harriet found the two chiefs and confided her worry to them. When the nurse finished, the three entered the room. Each man took out his handcuffs and cuffed Rosalie's hands to the steel bed frame.

"What about eating?" Harriet asked.

West looked at Peets. "The gag's not supposed to come out."

"That's a problem."

"Let's worry about that tomorrow."

The next morning Rosalie woke before it was light. The hours began to drag by. The IV bag was replaced by a nurse. She made the exchange silently in a matter of seconds. Rosalie tried to catch her eye but the nurse ignored her.

Shortly before noon, Harriet Locke walked into the room. Rosalie's fury soared.

Harriet came over to the bed and quietly said, "Your lawyer is going to come this afternoon. Be careful what you agree to."

Having said that, she left.

Who gave her permission to come in any time she felt like it? And who was she to give her advice? Her father-in-law may have been suckering into listening to her, but not her. She was her own woman. And Harriet Locke would rot in hell before she'd apologize.

At noon Chief West entered with a nurse.

"The judge has agreed that someone may feed you but you are not to speak. Is that clear?"

Rosalie nodded. The nurse fetched the tray and West removed the gag. Rosalie opened her mouth and the nurse spooned in some apple sauce. It was instantly spit out.

Rosalie's aim was excellent. The nurse's face was sprayed with the sauce mingled with spittle.

Caught by surprise, West was slow enough replacing the gag, so Rosalie managed to spit out words after the food.

"Tell the bitch judge, she don't feed me like some baby. And you gotta feed me, or I'll sue you and her and the goddamn hospital! And keep that old nigger whore out of my room."

The gag was reinserted and Rosalie leaned back in bed content. They'd see it her way. Her lawyer would see to that. She'd sue the whole bunch. And she'd win. And she'd be rich.

And rich people can get away with murder.

That afternoon her lawyer arrived. Entering the room with him was Chief Lyle West.

"I want this stuff removed!" Bissell said bluntly.

Rosalie smiled inside.

"No problem," Chief West said. "I have the disclaimer forms right here."

"What disclaimer forms?"

"Tell me what you want to remove?"

"The thing in her nose."

West sorted through the papers in his hand. "Here's that form. If we remove the breathing tube and she chokes to death on the gag, you take responsibility for her death."

The young lawyer read the document.

"The court ordered her gagged," Lyle said. "She only has to apologize and it will be removed."

"What is this for?" Bissell asked pointing to a bag suspended from the bed.

"Collects urine, so she doesn't lay in it."

"How does she eat?"

"We tried to spoon feed her but she spit the food out," West said. "She said she wasn't going to be fed like a baby."

"Take off the restraints," Bissell said.

"Restrains are also part of the court order."

"She has to eat," Bissell stated.

"I'll take care of it, if you'll sign the consent form," West said, handing him the form on a clipboard. Bissell scarcely glanced at the form before affixing his signature.

"Please explain it to your client and have her sign as well," West said and then withdrew.

He handed her the form. "Sign it."

He put the pen in her hand and held the clipboard under her right hand. She scrawled her signature.

"Your husband's trial date had been set. Because you are being held incommunicado for contempt of court, yours has been postponed."

Rosalie cocked her head in silent query.

"This is good for us. We'll see their whole case and hear all their arguments before we go to trial. This is a big advantage. I know it's not comfortable, but can you hang in there?"

Rosalie nodded.

"I'll check back in a couple of days. I think you'll win this one."

Rosalie smiled inwardly. This wasn't so bad. She'd show them. She could handle whatever was thrown at her. She wasn't taking back a single word.

Dr. Cook entered the room with Chief West.

"I understand you intend not to apologize."

Rosalie nodded her head.

"Your lawyer signed this form for us to feed you artificially. Did he discuss it with you?"

All Rosalie remembered was that her lawyer had said that she was going to win. She wasn't going to let these sonsofbitches talk her out of victory so she nodded.

"Do you understand the procedure?" Dr. Cook asked. "It's not painful, but it's not one most people would choose."

Rosalie, while confused, decided to trust her lawyer. She nodded.

"Okay, then. Well do it," Dr. Cook said. "The nurse will get you ready."

The nurse gave her a shot, the restraints and monitoring devices were removed and she was transferred to a gurney. She tried to move her arm but found she couldn't.

Bewildered, Rosalie was rolled into an elevator, the IV bag temporarily lying on her chest. She stared at the ceiling as her stomach began to knot up. When rolled into the operating room she took one look at the masked surgical team and her fear ballooned up inside her. She tried to move but none of her limbs responded.

"This won't be painful," Dr. Cook assured her. "I don't think I would have made this choice, but we all have convictions. So just relax."

He nodded at the anesthegologist and the gag was replaced by a mask. Rosalie was suddenly breathing an odd smelling gas. She took a deep breath in order to protest, but that caused her to lose consciousness within seconds.

When she woke up she was back in her room, again restrained and monitored. She glanced at the IV bag and saw a second bag hooked up with brownish liquid inside.

A nurse entered and smiled at her. "Oh, you're awake. Are you hungry?"

Rosalie nodded. She felt a bit dizzy and nauseated. A bit of food would make her feel better she knew.

Without another word the nurse then attached the plastic tubing leading from the brown bag to a holder that snaked out from her stomach. The thick liquid flowed slowly down the tube and she felt the fullness as it entered her stomach. She was being tube fed.

Chapter 30

That evening Judge Davis and Harriet Locke entered Rosalie's room. Her eyes blazed in fury.

Both women looked into her eyes.

"Another twenty-four, I think," Harriet said.

"I didn't think she'd ask for tube feeding. I have to agree with you. Mrs. Hoskinson appears to be in this for the long haul," Judge Davis said. "I think forty-eight is more reasonable."

Rosalie shook her head.

It was noted by both women.

"She says no," Harriet said, "but I think we should check back in forty-eight hours anyway. Longer than that is unreasonable."

When they were back in the hall, Lydia asked, "Is this helping at all?"

"Oh this helped a lot," Harriet said, "but not in a way I would have predicted."

"Tell me how," Lydia requested.

"We couldn't get it through Jocelyn's head this wasn't something neat to share with her friends. Rosalie did in a few minutes what we'd been trying to do for days."

As the two walked on to Aleta and Stanley's room, Lyle West took Harriet aside.

"This morning Rosalie told me to tell you not to come into her room. Is there something I should know?"

"I went in there this morning and warned her about the tube feeding."

"The guard didn't see you," Lyle said. "So you can pretty much go where you want?"

"I can only go where I'm told to go," Harriet said. "Otherwise I'm stopped just like anyone else."

"The judge ordered that no one could talk with her."

"I have higher orders," Harriet said simply. "You can tell the judge what I did, and I won't deny it, but Lyle there's a purpose to all this. I just have no idea what it is.

West pondered what she'd said and finally said, "You saved her life and mine. I can't believe you intend to harm her. And I owe you. But officially you are banned from the room."

"Thank you, Lyle," Harriet said. "I do think that was a singular event."

"You've got Stanley worried, you know," Lyle said, smiling.

"Worried? Why?"

"He's sure you can enter his house anytime you want."

"I can't. I wouldn't. Oh, my does he think I... I haven't... poor guy," Harriet stammered. "You straightened him out didn't you? I'm not Harry Potter with his cloak of invisibility after all... tell me you told him that... Darn you, Lyle, you didn't."

The next morning Harriet walked into Rosalie's room, brought over a chair and set it near the bed and sat down.

Rosalie writhed under the sheet.

"You're wondering what I'm doing here," Harriet said softly. "I'm not sure why I'm here either. I was told to come. And as far as I know I'm here to keep you company."

The writhing increased.

"You don't want my company, is that it?" Harriet guessed. Rosalie nodded angrily.

"Well, I don't want to be here either," Harriet said. "So here we are, two unhappy people and the only one who can talk has nothing to say while the one who can't talk has lots to say. And no I can't remove your gag. So what do we do...? Well, until I can think of something, I guess we just keep each other company..."

The jostling of the bed told Harriet that her companion didn't like that idea.

After an hour of silence, Harriet put back the chair and left the room.

The hours dragged on. Much as she hated the presence of Harriet Locke, Rosalie hated being alone in the quiet room more. The blinds had been slanted so the sun's rays wouldn't hit her eyes but the tilt didn't allow her to see the sky at all.

Rosalie hated the quiet. She wasn't a woman who found pleasure in the stillness of a lake at dawn, so she resented being forced to endure this misery without so much as a radio to help her pass the time. She periodically fought her restraints on the off-chance that one would give and she'd have one limb free.

Those cops were smart to handcuff her wrists, she thought.

An hour before the last meal of the day was served, Harriet Locke again walked into her room.

"Surprised to see me?" she asked. "No more so than I am to be here. This time I brought the Tri City Register to read to you only I won't read it if you'd rather I didn't."

Rosalie nodded.

"You'd rather I didn't?" Harriet asked.

A head shake told Harriet what to do. She sat down and began to read.

An hour later Harriet folded up the paper, tossed it into the wastebasket and left the room. She saw Stanley coming down the hall. Harriet put her forefinger to her lips until she reached him.

"Did I just see what I just saw?" he asked in astonishment. He hadn't moved an inch since he saw her breeze past the guard outside the room. The man never even twitched as she exited.

Harriet took his arm, "Yes, you did. You are still my lawyer, correct?"

She turned him around and walked with him back to his room.

"Not if you killed her," he said.

Harriet giggled, and Stanley knew what that meant. Aleta did that when he said something preposterous.

"And I didn't spy on you either," she added. "I can only enter where God directs me."

"And He wants you to visit Rosalie Hoskinson?"

"Apparently He does," Harriet said. "But I don't know why."

"To answer your question, yes, I'm your lawyer," Stanley said.

Harriet smiled, "I'm surprised you ventured out of your room without your pants on."

"Aleta wanted a candy bar" Stanley said. "And yes, I know it's nearly dinner time, but she's not being particularly reasonable. I was praying they'd have one with nuts. It's supposed to have nuts… Why are we going back? I didn't get her the candy bar."

"You were heading the wrong direction. For some reason you were supposed to see me."

"God wants to complicate my life even more."

"The candy bars are that way," she said pointing past the door to his room. He trotted toward the vending machine.

Harriet entered the room and found Aleta in her wheelchair.

"Hurry," Aleta said.

"Where?" Harriet asked.

"To Rosalie's room."

"We won't get past the guard," Harriet warned.

"You push," Aleta ordered.

Harriet pushed her granddaughter down the hall and straight past the guard. The door opened as the two approached it and they entered.

Rosalie mouthed a string of expletives.

"That's a waste of time," Aleta said. "My grandmother doesn't understand a word you're saying."

A short muffled sound came out.

"Yes, I understand," Aleta said. "Now what did you want to say?"

A long barrage of sounds so dulled they weren't recognizable as words emerged from the woman lying flat on the bed.

"Well…," Aleta replied slowly. "It's up to you; but my guess is they'd just clean you up, change your sheet and put a diaper on you."

More gagging sounds emerged.

"Yes, I can make that request," Aleta said. "And no I can't hear you from my room."

Again Rosalie made a series of tiny noises.

"Yes, I will tell them both tonight," Aleta said. "Okay, I'll tell her right now."

"Tell me what?" Harriet asked.

"That hell will need to freeze over before she apologizes to either you or the judge."

"You left out some words, didn't you?"

"Quite a few," Aleta said. "You've heard them before."

Rosalie, her visage dark, spewed out more choked back utterings.

"We can go now, Grams, she's done."

Silently, Harriet pushed her granddaughter through the open door.

As they were moving down the hall, Harriet commented softly. "I can't understand why Rosalie can receive so many of God's miracles and not recognize them."

"Remember how God hardened Pharaoh's heart as soon as each catastrophe passed?"

"So what did she say at the end?"

"That she was damned if she'd be grateful for my help. An animal was born to serve and that's all I was to her—-me and all my people—and when my children were born she'd be sure everyone knew they were little…oh, Grams, why?"

"We made it back before Stanley," Harriet said. "How did that happen?"

"Help me back into bed," Aleta said. "Quick!"

"Aleta, you stay where you are."

"But then I'd have to explain."

"Exactly

"Grams, I disobeyed him."

"You obeyed someone else, didn't you?"

Stanley walked in. "I wondered why the machine kept giving me my quarters back and just when I was about to give up, it'd throw a candy bar down the slot and return my quarter as well. I've got five kinds of candy for you to choose from."

Harriet slipped out the door.

"I'm so sorry, Stanley."

"You told me you decided to put God first, so why should bother me that you actually did?"

"Rosalie wants the enemas stopped," Aleta said.

"All this disobedience because a woman none of us likes doesn't like enemas?" Stanley quipped. "I take back all the thoughts I ever had about God not having a sense of humor."

"She says she'll use the bedpan every morning on schedule."

"And you're telling me this, why?"

"So you can tell Lyle or Wayne or whoever is in charge."

"And you can't do this, why?"

"Just because…," Aleta said.

"You've been talking to my mother too much. You're beginning to sound like her."

"Good, then our children will turn out to be as wonderful as you!"

Stanley came over and put his arm around her waist, "Come on. No sense letting everyone think you're well."

When she was on her feet, she leaned over and kissed him. He gathered her close and kissed her full on the lips. His hands slid under the hospital gown and moved down her lower back and pressed her into him.

"Don't you two ever stop," came a voice from the doorway. Both turned and blushed simultaneously.

Dr. Chesney entered smiling.

"I came to bring you more chocolates, and I can see from the stash on the bed you were completely out."

"Bernard, why do you have my patient out of bed?" came a second male voice from the doorway.

"Oh shit!" Stanley exclaimed, "Do you doctors have a special radar or something?"

"If they do, I want their equipment," Lyle quipped from behind the two doctors.

Despite his embarrassment, Stanley finished helping Aleta into bed.

After supper, after everyone was gone, and Aleta and Stanley were alone, he asked her if Rosalie had said anything else.

"Only that she wasn't going to apologize."

"Not ever?"

"Her lawyer told her to hold fast until her husband's case went to trial."

"So she's going to hang tough."

Aleta didn't respond. Plans didn't always work out and her stomach told her this was one of those times.

"Stanley, I need you to distract me," Aleta said.

Stanley sat up and looked at his wife.

"TV? A movie?"

"You know how," she said demurely.

"Dr. Cook will pop in. Or Dr. Chesney. Or Lyle. Or my mother. Or somebody," he protested. "My psyche still hasn't recovered from before."

"Everybody's gone," Aleta said.

"You're sure?"

"Absolutely. Besides a little bit of fear adds a bit of spice."

"I like my food bland."

"I'm bland?"

"That came out wrong. I just don't like it extra spicy."

"You can't be hungry already," Dr. Cook said from the doorway.

"I told you!" Stanley gloated.

"Dr. Cook," Aleta said. "Tell him he can kiss me goodnight."

"You can kiss your wife all you want; but that's it!" Dr. Cook said. "And, Aleta, you stay in bed…my stars, I can't believe I'm giving these kinds of orders."

"Goodnight, Dr. Cook," the two patients chorused.

When he'd gone, Stanley rose from his bed, travelled to his wife's bed and kissed her gently.

"Goodnight," he whispered.

"That's it?"

"Yep," he said, returning to his bed. "You shouldn't be… er… jostled. And I know you can't stay still."

"If I promise I will, I will," she returned hopefully.

"Goodnight," he said and turned away.

"Harrump," she grumped.

Exhaustion soon took over and Aleta fell asleep.

Shortly after midnight she was awakened by a kiss. More followed.

"Remember your promise," he whispered.

"I didn't..." she began, then switched to, "Yes, I remember."

The next morning, Aleta awoke refreshed. She looked over at the other bed just as Stanley woke up.

"Thank you for last night," she said, "but why did you wait?"

"So you'd believe I truly still love you."

"I would have known...you're right. I might still have wondered."

"Relax, Aleta, all danger is past. There's nothing but good times ahead," Stanley said glancing toward his wife as he rose.

Suddenly, his bubble burst.

"Tell me that's true. Please, tell me... Aleta, what's going to happen?"

"Something."

"Where? To whom?"

"Here."

"And?"

"That's all I know."

Chapter 31

"You always said you couldn't foresee your own future," Stanley said, buzzing the nurse.

She arrived several minutes later.

"Call Chief Lyle West for me," Stanley said.

"Is something wrong?" the nurse asked politely.

"Nothing you can fix," Stanley grumped. "If we had a phone in here, we could call him ourselves."

"I'll ask," she said and left.

"What does that mean?" Stanley asked Aleta.

"It means she won't," Aleta said. "Relax. Dad will be here with breakfast soon."

"Do you know when this... this thing is suppose to happen?"

Aleta shook her head.

Stanley swung his legs out of bed, put on his robe and stomped out of the room.

"Be nice," Aleta called after him.

Shortly after he left, a nurse appeared. She drew the curtain. She helped Aleta to the bathroom.

"Did you see my husband?" Aleta asked.

"Oh, we saw him."

"He's quite angry about not having a phone in here."

"So we gathered," the nurse said. "Perhaps you don't have a phone to keep you from bothering important people."

"May I have my bath early?" Aleta asked deciding not to argue. One grumpy Praetzel on the floor was enough.

"I can fit a bath in now," the nurse said and helped Aleta back into bed and went into the bathroom to fill the basin and fetch the towels.

"Why is the curtain drawn?" Stanley asked irritably.

"I'm having my bath," Aleta replied. "Did you make your phone call?"

"No."

"So you're going to wait?"

"I've got a phone card," Stanley said, digging in the pocket of his clothes hanging in the closet.

"Drat!"

"No phone card?" she tittered.

"It's not funny," he stormed as he left the room.

Twenty minutes later Lyle West walked into the room.

"I understand you two think you need a phone," he said. "I told you before that was Dr. Cook's call."

"Do you know what I had to go through to get through to you?

Lyle looked at Aleta.

"He told me."

"Stanley, behave," she ordered. "Stanley called you because he's panicking."

"I don't panic!" Stanley denied emphatically.

"Tell me what was so important I had to change into my uniform and come down here," Lyle asked calmly.

"I need a phone in here," Stanley reiterated.

"You need to tell me why you're so upset," Lyle said. "I can leave word at the desk to call me anytime you ask."

"Thank you," Aleta said. "Now, Stanley, get to the point."

Stanley took a deep breath and told himself to relax. Lyle was here.

"Aleta senses something bad is going to happen here in this hospital but she doesn't know when or how or who," Stanley explained. "She always knows who unless it's her."

"Is that true, Aleta?"

"Yes, except for the who part. There are no rules about that."

"So it could be you?"

"Yes, but I think it's someone else."

Lyle took off his hat and sat down. "I hope your father is bringing enough breakfast for three."

"That's it?" Stanley charged.

"I'm here, aren't I?"

"Shouldn't you have men checking the hospital entrances?"

"For whom?" Lyle asked. "The perpetrator might already be inside."

"This floor then?" Stanley said vexed that Lyle seemed to be taking this so casually.

Lyle answered a call on his radio. "Let him through. He's got my breakfast."

Stanley brightened. "You didn't come alone"

"As you said, Stanley, you never panic," he grinned. "I figure you were worried about Aleta."

"Why did it take you so long to get here?"

"I had to position my men," Lyle said. "I thought I did it in record time."

Aleta laughed. "You won this one, Lyle."

"You'll let me know when the danger is imminent?"

"I may not know," Aleta said. "The warning was so vague."

"Don't worry," Lyle said. "We're closer than we would have been otherwise and, if nothing happens, I'll figure the presence of police had the desired effect which is the prevention of crime."

"You're putting a lot of trust in me," Aleta remarked.

Lyle smiled. "You've got a great track record."

Several hours later, during which time West had passed on a number of people, Aleta wished aloud that her grandmother were present.

"She's here," West informed her.

"You mean she's coming up?"

"She's been in the hospital over an hour," West told Aleta.

"Never mind," Aleta said. "I know where she is."

Lyle looked at his friend. "Stanley, does your mother know?"

"No," came the answer.

"Do you know why Harriet is doing this?"

Stanley shook his head and Aleta popped up with a comment that somehow it was important to help Rosalie from going crazy.

"I thought that was the idea," Lyle observed without censure.

"Evidently, there's another plan in the works," Aleta said. "And I'm only guessing, mind you. While Grams and I are furious with her on many counts, and we see her as an enemy of the highest magnitude, one not worthy of our time and concern, nevertheless Grams has elected to give succor to this particular enemy. I don't understand it; but I can assure you it was not of her own volition. I would never do it."

Lyle raised an eyebrow and Stanley hastened to explain. "Rosalie threatened our child."

"Is that why I'm here?"

Stanley shook his head. "Rosalie's threat was a future one. She told Aleta she would see that the families of our children's friends knew that they had African-American blood."

"Whoa!" Lyle exclaimed. "Well, he better have your nose for sure."

Aleta's eyebrows went up.

"His nose?"

"Then nobody will believe it."

Aleta grinned, "I know there was a good reason why I liked it besides just liking it."

Stanley stayed sober. "It's a nasty threat."

Lyle picked up his friend's somber mood. "It is indeed. And children can be cruel as you well know."

"I don't know what to do," Stanley confessed. "This is uncharted territory for me."

"Lauren handled Camay's problem creatively. You might try talking with her."

"Deafness isn't the same," Stanley said.

"Some of the problems are different," Lyle said. "But some of Lauren's solutions might work for you. The main one was to foster strong friendships before Camay went to school."

"I was always reticent as a child," Stanley said.

"That's not a big character flaw," Lyle said. "You made friends"

"Yeah, of the other outcasts," Stanley said sadly. "I wanted better for my children."

"Get rid of you fantasies. They're going to be your children after all. Half of them will take after you, unless you have only one in which case, he'll definitely take after you which means he'll be independent as hell and as unpopular as you were."

"You're not making me feel better," Stanley commented.

"Oh, come on, Stanley, it's not the end of the world."

Stanley was about to complain that Lyle didn't understand when he caught a glimpse of Aleta's pained expression. He realized he wasn't of mixed blood. She was.

"It's just the threat hit me hard," Stanley said, knowing that was the page Aleta was on.

"Your kids will be fine," Lyle said. "They'll have a foot in several worlds just as my kids do. It makes for an eclectic home life."

Shortly before lunch arrived, Harriet left Rosalie Hoskinson and joined the group in her granddaughter's room. She was surprised to see Lyle. He explained his presence.

Aleta asked her grandmother if she had any idea what the danger was and was slightly disappointed that she didn't.

Just as the group gathered around Aleta's bed were beginning to eat, the service elevator door opened and two lab techs wheeled a cart down the hall to Rosalie Hoskinson's room. The guard glanced at their ID badges, opened the door and asked them how long they would be.

"Ten minutes," the woman said.

"I'm going to get me a sandwich," he said rushing toward the elevator, "Hey, hold the door."

Rosalie's eyes widened in apprehension. She wasn't scheduled for any lab work and she hated needles. The nurse had just been in and hooked up her noon feeding. The IV bag was still full.

Her heart began beating wildly, but lunch was being served so no one was watching the monitors. This wasn't the ICU and she wasn't even ill, so their monitoring consisted of glancing over to see if her heart was still beating.

The man stood by the door while the older woman approached the bed. There was something familiar about him, but she couldn't put her finger of what. What she did know is that they weren't acting like the nursing staff she was used to.

The woman donned a pair of plastic gloves slowly as if enjoying Rosalie's mounting apprehension. When the woman laid back the sheet while the man was staring at her she knew she was in trouble.

Her wrists jerked on the handcuffs and rattled them against the steel frame of the bed.

The woman smirked, "Your guard went to get lunch."

The old woman took a wrapped packet out of her pocket and Rosalie fought her restraints even harder.

"Hey, Mom, unwrap her, the man growled.

Rosalie trembled, her eyes were wide in terror.

The old woman's eyes danced with glee. This was gonna be better than she'd planned.

"Give you five minutes," she said as she tore off the hospital gown. The man undid his pants and leaped on the helpless woman. The old lady laughed raucously as she watched Rosalie fight against each harsh thrust.

"Harder!" she cackled.

He pumped viciously spurred on by her encouragement. Rosalie tried to twist away but to no avail.

"He loves it when women fight," the old hen said timing her words with the cadence of the pounding being inflicted.

Suddenly his head was rooting around near her breasts and his mouth closed on one as he heaved himself in and out.

She felt his teeth close and screeched in agony. While almost no sound came out, the old woman got nervous.

"Don't bite," she said, and he let go of the breast.

Rosalie stopped screeching and Aleta, who'd alerted to the muffled agony she couldn't really hear, looked around.

"What is it?" Lyle asked.

The sound stopped.

"Nothing," Aleta said quickly.

Back in Rosalie's room, the five minutes stretched to six, but the old woman didn't notice. This was the best revenge ever.

And suddenly the huge man was done. He flopped on top of Rosalie, and she could barely breathe.

"Get off," the old woman said. "We've wasted enough time."

He crawled off her and zipped up his pants.

"Got one more job for you, son," she said. "Hold her legs apart for me."

Immediately, Rosalie, electrified by the horrors of her own imagination, yanked on one of her ankle restraints and it gave way. The big man; however, already had his hands on her thighs. He pressed down hard as the old woman took the unwrapped thing that looked like a fat greasy thumb and with a practiced hand, stuffed it deep into her rectum, past the sphincter muscles that could have expelled it.

The wrinkled old crow withdrew her hand and ordered her son to refasten the restraint on her free leg.

Rosalie struggled fiercely, spurred on by having successfully freed one leg. She squirmed around, trying to push the suppository out.

This time all four restraints held.

The rough old hand was placed on Rosalie's bare chest and Rosalie twisted away.

The gown was picked up off the floor by the man, who shook it briefly and then laid it on top of Rosalie. His hand stayed beneath it and played with her breasts. He was rough. Rosalie was so distracted by her loathing, she only half heard what the woman was saying.

"It's poison," the gray haired witch affirmed with a snicker. "Phenergan. Works in ten minutes. The beauty of using a suppository is no one will think to look before it's too late to find it."

She lightly slapped the man's hands, both of which were now under the gown, and they were withdrawn.

"The symptoms will confuse the doctors. They'll check everything while you slowly die."

Rosalie jerked her body around hoping to dislodge the dreaded insert.

"Won't do no good," the woman told her. "It's in there tight."

Rosalie ignored her and continued to wriggle.

"I should warn you if you act up, and they give you something to relax you, the symptoms get worse faster."

Rosalie stopped struggling.

"You're still going to die," the woman predicted, "but no one will know. They will come in and take away your food bag and you will look drowsy. They won't even note the symptom on the chart."

"Ma, we gotta go," the man said.

"By the time they hook up your supper, the ringing in your ears will be driving you wild. If not them, then the headaches and dizziness will, but no one will know because you can't speak. You won't be able to see too good, but that don't matter cause you don't have much to look at. Come night you won't be able to sleep and when you do, you'll have nightmares. You'll drool like a dog. Maybe someone will notice, maybe they won't."

"Ma, hurry!"

"It's only been five minutes," the old woman snapped. "That guard will take more than ten. They always do."

"You said ten minutes."

"You had your five. Now it's my turn."

"Tell her why so we can get the hell outta here!"

"Okay. Okay," the old woman said. "Did you think you could blow up my son and I wouldn't come after you?"

And having said that the woman pushed the lab cart out of the room.

Rosalie, her mind and body assaulted and insulted, screamed her agony. It didn't matter that she couldn't be heard. Her soul needed to scream and scream she did.

Aleta heard her scream. She knew no one else did. She was tempted for a brief second to ignore it.

"Rosalie!" she yelled. "She's dying."

Dr. Cook and Lyle West jumped up and ran from the room, Dr. Cook calling for nurses as he ran and West ordering all exits sealed.

When the door to her room opened, Rosalie couldn't lie calmly. She was dying.

West whipped off the gag and Cook stopped the IV drip and the tube feeding.

Rosalie coughed, "Poison"

"How?"

"In my ass."

"A suppository?" Cook asked. He sent a nurse for an enema kit.

"Not a pill? An injection? A gas?"

Rosalie shook her head at every alternative.

When the nurse returned, Dr. Cook said, "You're not going to like this, but if we get even a piece we'll know what we're dealing with."

"She said it would take ten minutes."

"Suppositories usually work fast," the doctor remarked matter-of-factly.

"Who?" Lyle West asked as the doctor and nurse administered the enema.

"Dean Arnetti's mother and brother. He raped me too."

"I need a rape kit, Doc," Lyle said.

"Noted," Dr. Cook responded. "Now, Rosalie, I'm putting in extra fluid hoping to wash away some of the poison before it gets into the system, so it's going to hurt a bit."

"Okay, Doc," Rosalie said. "Don't give me nothing to calm me down. She said it would make me die sooner."

"Did she say how long it would take?"

"She said I was gonna have nightmares all night."

Dr. Cook breathed a sign of relief. "Good, that means it's slow-acting. We have time on our side."

He patted her hand. "Can you stay calm?"

"Yeah, I can do that," Rosalie said. "How come you both came barreling in here?"

"Aleta sent us," Lyle said. "She heard you. None of the rest of us did."

Rosalie covered her shock with an angry retort.

"Don't think that I'm going to apologize to anybody, including her because it ain't gonna happen. It's her fault all this happened in the first place. If she and that n... negro grandmother of hers kept their noses out of my business, none of this would've happened. So they both owe me big time."

"Is their debt paid now?" West asked.

"It ain't never gonna be paid after this. Them and that damned judge. They're gonna be sorry."

Chapter 32

"Got it!" Dr. Cook exclaimed. "Not much left, but enough."

He held up a sliver of the suppository. The nurse pulled a wash basin from the night stand and he dropped it in.

"Tell the lab, I need the answer now. I think it could be Promothiazine Hydrochloride or same drug like that and get another nurse in here."

The interruption had a calming effect on Lyle. "Mrs. Hoskinson, give me the best description you can of each of the two people who attacked you."

Dr. Cook looked up and noticed that Lyle was standing with his back to the medical procedure, so he let him stay. He ordered the nurse to complete the lavage and he began to check Rosalie's vitals.

From Aleta's room, the group could hear the scurrying at the far end of the hail.

"I guess she's still alive," Aleta said sorrowfully.

"Is that regret I hear?" Harriet chided.

"I can't believe how much I hate that woman," Aleta said. "And yet I helped her."

"Maybe it'll turn her around," Lauren hoped aloud.

"You think?" Aleta responded hopefully. "I'd like some good to come out of what I did."

"God never promotes evil," Harriet added.

Aleta relaxed a bit.

"Let's talk about good stuff," Lauren said. "Mr. Locke, have you made any plans. I hear you're moving into the area."

"No plans yet."

"Who's the woman you've fallen for?" Lauren asked.

"Woman?" Harriet and Aleta gasped in unison, their eyes focusing immediately upon his reddening face.

"You're in love?" Aleta asked. "Dad, that's great!"

"You'll need a house," his mother said. "The Tontine has some nice property by the lake. Take your pick. I'll build the house."

"Mom, I have no job!"

"Details! Your mother's rich," Harriet said. "Enjoy your retirement. You and Paul have enriched my life beyond measure."

"We haven't been in your life much," Robert confessed. "I've been busy working and…"

"And so have I," Harriet interposed. "But you shared Aleta with me and through her a wonderful retirement is mine."

"Oh, Dad," Aleta gushed. "Jocelyn will be so thrilled. Living with Grams is okay, but she'll love looking forward to a house to call home."

Lauren laughed. "You've already got his future planned, and you don't even know whether his wife will want to settle down and be a homebody. She may want to travel."

"So who is it?" Harriet finally asked.

"Two prophets in the family, two lawyers in the room and one police chief coming into the room, and none of you can guess?"

"Guess what?" Lyle said. "From the looks on everyone's face, someone is either having a baby or getting married—not necessarily in that order."

"Lauren guessed," Aleta burst forth. "Dad's in love."

"Didn't you guys know?" he asked.

"You know?" Aleta asked, surprised. "If you do, tell us!"

"And ruin his fun? No way."

Harriet switched to the main reason Lyle had returned.

"What about Rosalie? Are we in any danger?"

"The last part's the good news," Lyle said. "No danger to anyone here. This was a personal vendetta. Dean Arnetti's mother and brother didn't take her blowing him up too kindly."

"Is she alright?" Aleta asked.

"The poison was well into her system by the time we got there."

"I sent you as soon as I knew," Aleta said defensively.

"I know you did," Lyle returned. "I was watching you."

"Why was I late?" Aleta fretted. "I'm not usually late."

"I thought you said there were no rules," Lyle reminded her.

"Was she grateful?" Lauren asked. "You did tell her it was Aleta who sent the help?"

"Yes, I did," Lyle said. "But she's angrier than ever. She plans on suing everyone."

"She needs a friend," Aleta said suddenly. It was an absurd comment and shook them all.

Lyle protested, "She absolutely doesn't want your friendship."

Stanley spoke up. "It would be pearls before the swine."

Aleta glared at Stanley, "You're always quoting scripture at me and I don't like it."

"The Bible's got same sensible sayings."

Aleta was ticked off.

"How would you know?" she challenged.

"I read it."

"How much have you read?"

"All of it."

Aleta eyed him skeptically.

"I wanted to be able to put the quotes in context," Stanley explained. "People thought I was gay and were forever attacking me with scripture. And I'm sorry if you think I'm attacking you with scripture. I won't do it anymore."

"It's not that I hate scripture," Aleta said. "It's like having you and God ganging up on me."

"And telling you you're wrong, is that it?" Stanley offered.

"I hate being wrong."

"Maybe in this you're not. Maybe It's me that's wrong and I used the Bible to beat you into not making a choice I don't want you to make."

"You're afraid I'll be hurt?"

"Yes."

"Everyone can use a secret friend, someone to wish them well."

"It's hardly a secret," Stanley said, "because we all know."

"So, we can all be secret friends," Aleta posed.

"She's a despicable person. No one deserves our attention less," Lyle grumbled still angry over the ingratitude he'd witnessed.

"We don't have to love her," Aleta said. "Stanley will tell you I'm right. All we have to do is not act on our hate. And what does hate tell us to do?"

No one spoke. They all knew what they wanted to do. And no one thought this woman worthy of their thought or action. They rebelled against the idea of being kind to such a woman.

Finally, Stanley spoke, "You realize you can't start something like this and ever stop. You're talking about a lifetime of caring."

"So what are we going to do with our hate? Let it eat us up? I've never hated anyone so much. The first time I felt relief was when this idea came to me," Aleta confessed. "So maybe I'm doing it for me. As for a lifetime of caring, do you think I'm ever going to forget the things she said to me? They are buried so deep I don't think I'll ever be able to dig them out and dispose of them. The only chance I've got is to give myself a project every time my hatred tries to overwhelm me."

No one spoke far a long time.

It all made sense.

Then Lyle rose, "Considering how I feel, I wonder if the florist has a big enough vase for the flowers I'll need to send her."

Two days later Dr. Cook walked into Rosalie's room and said, "I have good news and bad news. The good news is that almost all of the poison is out of your body."

"I'm gonna live?"

"Looks that way," Dr. Cook said. "And from the number of bouquets in this room, I'd guess that'll make a lot of people happy.

"Yeah, I got friends," Rosalie smiled.

Dr. Cook read one of the cards. "Thinking of you. A friend."

"And I got candy too. I offer the nurses some and they feed me some," Rosalie said.

"Well, now for the bad news. The judge ordered the gag restored," Dr. Cook said. "Unless you're ready to apologize. Mrs. Locke is in the hospital because her granddaughter's going home, so I could have her here in a minute."

"I ain't apologizing about nothing!" Rosalie declared emphatically. "Those people was meant to be slaves, There's smart ones and there's dumb ones, but none of them is worth shit. And no amount of gagging is gonna make me change my mind. And them that pretends they're white is the worst kind of all. It just ain't the way it's supposed to be."

Chief West walked into the room.

"Have you told her?"

"Yes, and she isn't going to apologize."

"Damn you, doctor. You don't gotta speak for me. There ain't no way in hell I'm ever gonna apologize to one of them black shitheads. That bitch judge'll back down before I do. You wait and see"

West pulled out the gag and put it in Rosalie's mouth. She didn't even fight the procedure. She was determined to be stoic.

Shortly after they left Harriet Locke walked in.

"Wondering where I've been?" she asked. "Sure you do. The answer is you didn't need me."

She went over to the flowers.

"This one needs water," she said taking the glass on the nightstand filling it with water from the sink and pouring the water in the vase.

"Of course, you don't really need me," Harriet said, sitting back down. "But I was ordered to be here… And no I don't take my orders from the devil… Do you want me to put away your chocolates?"

Rosalie nodded and Harriet opened the drawer in the night stand and placed the box inside.

"You know, I've been thinking about our silent mornings and it occurred to me that while I like them, you might not, so I brought a book to read to you. It was written by a southern gentleman, Samuel Clemens, who used the pen name Mark Twain. And no they aren't children's books. I picked one I thought you might enjoy, Huckleberry Finn. Ever read it?"

Rosalie shook her head and Harriet opened to the first page and began reading. An hour later, Harriet's watch beeped and she put a bookmark inside the book and put the book next to the chocolates in the drawer and left.

Rosalie had enjoyed the story and was upset when Harriet stopped so abruptly. The nurse came in and attached her food bag without speaking.

So the judge ordered no talking again, Rosalie concluded. She wondered what the judge would do if she knew about her visitor. Would she throw her in jail?

How come she didn't know? Didn't the guards report her visits? Was it some sort of conspiracy? She decided it was probably a conspiracy. But whatever it was, she wasn't falling for it. She was smarter than that.

Chapter 33

The morning after Aleta had arrived home, Harriet knocked and then entered the house calling, "Aleta, where are you?"

"Getting my bath," Aleta called.

"Where's Bertha?"

'Giving it to me," Aleta called. "Come on in. I'm starting a nudist colony. Of course, I'll be the only one in it because Stanley doesn't like the idea at all."

Harriet entered the bedroom and walked through to the bathroom where she found Aleta in a tub of sudsy water. "I thought the visiting nurse was supposed to do this although I also thought she'd do it with you in bed."

"So did she, so I fired her."

"Aleta, shame on you!" Harriet scolded. "Bertha has enough to do."

"It's no trouble, Ma'am. And I have the time. It's a small house with two very clean people living in it."

"She's talking about Stanley. He folds the clothes that need washing."

"Am I too late for breakfast?"

"No, Ma'am," Bertha replied. "Mrs. Praetzel hasn't had hers yet."

"Then let me make it while you finish up," Harriet offered.

"French toast, right?" Aleta said smiling. "That's the only breakfast Gram's makes."

"Do you know yet who the woman is?" Aleta called as Harriet walked out of the bathroom.

"No idea. Why don't you ask Bertha?"

"Ask me what, Ma'am?" Bertha said as she washed Aleta's back.

"My dad's fallen in love with someone he met out here; but he won't tell us who the lady is."

"Perhaps he has his reasons Ma'am."

"So, he hasn't brought anyone here?"

"No, Ma'am. He wouldn't do that," Bertha said. "He a proper gentleman."

"He is that," Aleta agreed. "He said he wouldn't say anything until after the divorce, papers ware signed. He'll do that after the wedding."

"Will they be back in time for Thanksgiving, Ma'am?"

"Yes, they will," Aleta replied. "You know what I hope, Bertha?"

"No, Ma'am."

"I hope he finds a kind woman. He deserves that."

"Yes, Ma'am, he does."

"I'm really worried about this," Aleta said. "I wish Grams knew who it was so she could find out whether the woman would be upset over his being… never mind."

"Part Negro, Ma'am?"

"You know?"

"Mrs. Locke told me before I was hired. She wanted to be sure I wouldn't have a problem working for you."

"You never said anything," Aleta said as she stepped out of the tub to be dried.

Harriet came to the bedroom door. "If you're almost done, I'll put on the toast."

"Five minutes," Aleta said.

"Why did you schedule a bath before breakfast?" Harriet asked.

"Lauren is coming over to help me plan my get well party and Julie's coming over to cut off what's left of my hair. I want one of those short brush cuts," Aleta said as Bertha began dressing her. "Actually, I don't want one, but I hate my hair as it is and with a short cut Bertha can wash it as easily as my face."

"You are using the wheelchair, aren't you?" Harriet asked.

"Bertha won't let me leave the bedroom otherwise."

"Good for her," Harriet said.

"And Stanley's just as bad."

"What are you doing for walks now that your dad is working at the office with Stanley?

"He's going to take long lunch breaks," Aleta said.

"What about his flying lessons?" Harriet asked.

"He said his instructor moved his lesson earlier so he can take just one long break," Aleta replied. "He goes in way before Stanley so he works a full day."

"Robert would do that," Harriet said. "He doesn't understand the term part-time."

"I'm glad he didn't give up his flying lessons," Aleta said.

"He hasn't said much about his instructor. Has he talked about him to you, Bertha."

"It's a woman, Ma' am.

"A woman?" Aleta reiterated. "I didn't know that."

"Neither did I," Harriet said.

"He said the woman he'd fallen for had a challenging job," Aleta noted.

"I think we've found our mystery woman," Harriet said.

"Let's have breakfast."

Chapter 34

The party was a huge success and no one got shot or sick for which all the guests were grateful. Half the guests-- those without family plans-- accepted Aleta's invitation to celebrate Thanksgiving with her just ten days away. Jayline's wedding was only a week away.

Her father and Hubert Praetzel planned to fly back after finishing up the divorce details. Harriet planned to help Jocelyn pack while waiting for the men. Things went as planned. They all arrived home the night before Thanksgiving.

The Thanksgiving dinner was a happy celebration and much of the talk was about the wedding.

When the group broke before dessert and coffee, Aleta asked her father to walk her to the barn. She wanted to get out and stretch her legs.

Jocelyn and the Cook's twin boys took King out for a short run and as they raced past her one of them brushed against her and Aleta realized how close she came to being hurt. Her father kept her from falling and she was grateful for his strong grip around her waist as they walked.

"I'm surprised you didn't want Stanley to do this," he said. "He's had more practice."

"I wanted to talk to you about how you are," Aleta said.

"Me? I'm fine. You're the one with all the injuries."

"You left everything behind in this divorce. You've got to be hurting."

Robert squeezed his daughter's waist a bit tighter. "Aleta, I left nothing behind. I have you and Jocelyn and her horse. What more could I want?"

"What about that woman you fancy? Are you going to propose now that you're free?"

"I don't know."

"When are you going to tell us who she is?"

"You and Stanley?"

"And Grams."

"You mean two ladies with so much psychic power haven't figured it out yet?"

"Does the woman you're attracted to even know?"

"Not yet."

"Suppose someone else grabs her?"

"That's not going to happen."

"Hey, an attractive, younger woman doesn't just…"

Aleta began, then stopped. "Which part of that is wrong?"

"Both. She's my age. And she has a soft natural attractiveness that comes from a compassionate heart."

"A nurse?" Aleta questioned. "We thought it was your flying instructor."

"She's married."

"So it's no one I know?"

"Ah, Aleta, how wrong you are."

Aleta began reviewing all the nurses that had cared for her at the hospital, but couldn't think of one her father had spent any time with.

Finally the question popped out, "What's stopping you?"

"I just got back. There hasn't been time."

"Dad, you know I'm not letting this go. I'm going to find out who she is."

"There are two problems," her father said soberly. "She has a personal matter that needs to be resolved before she's free and…"

"And what?" Aleta pressed.

"I don't know if she likes me."

"What's not to like?" Aleta asked.

"The race thing."

"Bertha told me that wouldn't matter."

"You talked about me to Bertha?"

"Dad, she bathes me and… well, I asked her if you'd brought a woman to the house. I'm sorry, Dad, I was so curious."

"It's okay, Aleta. I half expected you'd pump Bertha. That's why I've been discreet."

"I hope you haven't been too discreet."

"Meaning what?"

"Well, you've dated her and kissed her, haven't you?"

"No, I haven't. It wasn't appropriate."

"Oh, Dad," Aleta moaned. "Do me a favor. Sweep her off her feet. She'll love it. Make it something she'll never forget."

"I can't do that," Robert said.

"Sure you can," Aleta said. "First dates are never easy so make it special."

"Oh, that."

"What did you think I was suggesting, that you propose when you haven't even kissed her?" Aleta exclaimed. "Dad, that's too spectacular.

"You think so?"

"You've got to get to know her. She's got to get to know you. You've got to spend time together first. I'm sorry to say it, but you have to date first."

"I always hated dating. I'm not sure I can go through that part again."

"There's no way around it."

"Yeah, I guess you're right."

When the two reentered the house, Stanley hung up the phone and turned to the group in the house as Aleta's dad helped her back into her wheelchair and hung up her cape.

"That was Lyle. There's been a new break in an old case. He knew Bertha would love to hear it. It seems Dean's mother once worked in a mental hospital which is why she knew about the drug and how to use it. It seems a co-worker remembered her bragging about how her son had offed a man for five grand. She had the details. Lyle said he confronted Dean Arnetti's mother with her co-workers statement and she confirmed it. It turns out that's why she was so incensed. Rosalie had killed him after he'd killed for her. Lyle called in the insurance man and he was convinced so the insurance company is going to pay. It means, Bertha, that you're exonerated. Isn't that great news?"

Robert Locke saw Bertha pale and rushed to her side. He put his arm around the chunky housekeeper's waist and led her to the couch and helped her sit down.

"Some water," Robert said and Stanley rushed to get it.

"They found out who did it?" Bertha inquired even though she had heard every word of the announcement.

"The case is solved," Robert reiterated. "We all knew you didn't do it. What we didn't know was how much weight you were carrying."

"The suspicion was hard to bear," Bertha said simply.

Stanley offered her the water and Bertha sipped it.

"It's such wonderful news," Robert went on. "So now that you can work anywhere you want, will you leave us?"

Bertha's eyebrows rose. "Leave here? I love it here! And King likes coming here. He loves to run in the fields. Besides now that there's a second bathroom which is practically mine, why would I go anywhere I couldn't have that."

Everyone laughed and murmured that they appreciated the new bathroom too.

"What about after you're married?" Martha asked with a twinkle in her eye.

"I plan on working then too," Bertha replied.

"Who's she going to marry?" Robert asked aghast. He glared at the only other single man in the room. Dr. Chesney grinned.

"Why you, of course," Martha said smiling slyly.

"It's Bertha you're falling in love with?" Aleta asked, her shock obvious. "Why didn't I see it?"

"Because, my dear, you were too busy with other more serious matters," Martha said. "Besides Bertha told me she was worried because she was falling in love with someone in her employer's house. I figured it wasn't Stanley."

Aleta was about to ask Martha why she revealed a confidence when she saw that everyone was watching her father who had taken the glass from Bertha's hand and set it down. He lifted her chin gently.

When her eyes met his, he said softly, "I love you, Bertha. Marry me."

The room was so still that her whispered yes was clearly heard.

Robert kissed her gently. Her hands left her lap and circled his neck. His arms pulled her to him and the kiss lasted for several minutes.

When their lips parted, Bertha suddenly flushed and before she could rise and make same excuse about needing to return to work, Robert rose and announced, "Bertha and I are going to take King for a walk."

Once outside Bertha giggled like a young girl.

Robert smiled and hugged her. "I knew you had a lot of laughter inside of you."

"I always thought if I was ever proposed to again, it would include candlelight and dinner."

"Did your first husband do it that way?"

"He was very provincial."

"Well, I don't want to be a repeat."

Bertha laughed. "Believe me. You're not a repeat. I know why I like you, but I can't figure out why you like me."

"I think the word I used was 'love'," Robert said. "What first attracted me was your compassion and gentleness with Aleta. And your cooking. But I'm marrying you because I love being with you and I want to grow old with you." He stopped and embraced her and kissed her.

"You realize we're being watched," she murmured.

"I know," he said kissing her again. "I've waited so long to do this."

"We hardly know each other." Bertha worried.

"What don't you know?" Robert inquired.

"You were worried about whether I knew the family secret."

"I knew Aleta would confide that to you."

"So when did you stop worrying?"

"The minute you said yes."

"That was a good time."

"What will we do about our jobs? It will be awkward working for your daughter with you coming and going."

"When you enter their house, you're at work. When I take you home at night, you'll be off work. I'll be working for them too, so we'll be in the same boat. I love the juxtaposition in this."

"What about after?" Bertha asked. "Relatives aren't paid."

"Well, I will be, so why not you?"

"I never thought of that," Bertha said. "What about Jocelyn?

"She wants me happy. In her eyes I gave up everything for her. If I'm happy, she doesn't need to feel guilty."

"We could use some of my insurance money to send her to college." Bertha planned aloud. "It can't be an expensive one though."

"You're even more giving than I imagined, but no need to worry. When Hubert Praetzel and I flew home the first time, I set up sizeable trust funds for all three girls. I knew my wife would wind up with everything, and I wanted Jocelyn to be able to go to any college she chose. So we can concentrate on building our life together."

"It's nice to have a future again," Bertha said.

"I'm thinking of taking the bar exam in February when Aleta does and join their firm as a partner. I won't work as hard as I did before. I have a house to build for you and me. My mother gave me a beautiful piece of land near her. I do want to be near her. She's very precious to me."

"I would love to live near her. She had faith in me when most others didn't. I will be forever grateful for that."

"Tomorrow we'll pick out an engagement ring."

"I don't have to have one. In my line of work, a ring isn't practical."

"Then we'll pick out our wedding bands and wear them around our necks until the day we're married."

"That's a beautiful idea," Bertha said. "I love the way you think."

Robert pulled her to him and before he kissed her, he whispered, "Welcome to the family."

Late that night when Stanley and Aleta were alone in their bedroom, Aleta said, "We have the whole day tomorrow to ourselves. Isn't that wonderful?"

"We never have the whole day alone. How'd that happen?"

"Grams is taking Jocelyn Christmas shopping. Dad is taking Bertha shopping for wedding bands and everyone else was just here."

"I can't believe it. Something will happen. I know it." Stanley returned.

"Bertha told me that if I keep my fingers taped I can take the slings off at night after I'm lying down, so I thought tonight as a special treat…"

"For whom?" Stanley asked.

"For me."

"You know Dr. Cook said no sex."

"You can keep your pants on."

"And lie next to you naked?"

"It'll test your will power."

"When did I develop this magical will power?"

"The shower has a cold water tap, you know."

"You have a mean streak. Did I ever mention that?"

"No, I don't," Aleta said. "Now let's take off my shoes, please."

Stanley helped her sit on the edge of the bed, knelt down and gently removed her shoes. "You may sleep any way you like. I'll handle it."

She looked down at him. "It's hard not to feel like a queen right now."

Stanley looked up at her but didn't rise. "I could stay here."

"And you would too, wouldn't you?"

"To make you feel better, yes."

"You know Grams and I talked about Rosalie, don't you?"

"I asked your grandmother to tell my mother what she was doing," he said rising and beginning to undress.

"She said she visited Rosalie for the last time today," Aleta said.

"She told me she had already told my mother," Stanley put in.

"Grams found out that Rosalie had promised her lawyer she'd not apologize in order to push her court date back. By the way Bissell hadn't been back to see her since he signed for her to be tube fed," Aleta reported. "Grams told me your mother made a call and put Bissell on notice that if Rosalie spent one more day in restraints, he'd join her, tube-feeding and all."

"Mother can't do that," Stanley said.

"Bissell got the message. He'd played around with the wrong judge. He high-tailed it down to the hospital and released Rosalie from her promise and talked Rosalie into apologizing.

"She actually apologized?" Stanley asked.

It didn't seem possible that the standstill had ended.

"She said the judge wasn't a bitch and Grams wasn't a whore." Aleta went on, "Grams accepted it on behalf of both."

"So it's over?"

"Yes," Aleta said, but her tone of voice denied the word.

"But not for you?" Stanley guessed.

"Not for me. I'd like it to be, but it's not," Aleta admitted a bit sadly. "Grams says she still vividly remembers the first time someone called her that... that name. You know it doesn't matter how many people say it doesn't matter to them, her calling me that is struck in my psyche. It's like she redefined me."

Stanley began to undress her. "You can't know how much I would like to erase that memory."

"I know," she said stepping out of her skirt.

"If it will help any, I like your black heritage, as problematic as it will be for us in raising our children. And I agree more than one child is a good idea. Now ask me why."

"Because our child will need a sibling who understands?"

"No, because when our daughter wants to know if I ever regretted her conception, I can honestly say that I was so proud to be married to her mother that I not only didn't regret her birth, I rejoiced in it as the best gift God could give me and so I asked for another."

When he finished, Stanley laid Aleta gently back on the bed and carefully removed both slings and taped her hands together. Then he settled down beside her, his body close to hers.

"You've still got your pajama bottoms on," she said.

"Much as you want it, we are not starting a nudist colony of two."

"If you want me to, I'll wear a nightgown."

"Oh, Aleta," he murmured softly. "Don't you know anything about men?"

"What should I know?"

"They love to sleep with naked women."

"Women, not wives."

"If it's a wife, it's even better."

"You are a clever man," Aleta tittered. "Now let's sleep. We've had a full day."

"You're tired?"

"Yes."

"How long do you want to sleep before I wake you?"

"Ten."

"Hours?"

"Seconds."

"I can't count that high."

"How high can you count?"

"One."

"That's good enough," she said as he leaned over and kissed her. And she knew they'd work around Dr. Cook's orders again. It was wonderful to be married to a lawyer.

Lawyers could always find loopholes.

The Prophet Series

The Reluctant Prophet

The Apprehensive Prophet

The Bewildered Prophet

The Overwhelmed Prophet*

The Beleaguered Prophet*

The Dreaming Prophet*

The Tested Prophet*

The Recuperating Prophet*

The Humiliated Prophet*

• • •

* to be released